I0679310

The
Lights
of
Two Pan

Book 2
In the Two Pan Series

B.K. Froman

Morning West Publishing

Oregon

Morning West Publishing
Copyright 2015 Barb Froman

ALL RIGHTS RESERVED.

This is a work of fiction. Names, characters, places and incidents either are the product of the author's imagination or are used fictitiously, and any resemblance to actual persons, living or dead, business establishments, or events is entirely coincidental.

Product names, brands, and other trademarks referred to within this book are the property of their respective trademark holders. Unless otherwise specified, no association between the author and any trademark holder is expressed or implied. Use of a term in this book should not be regarded as affecting the validity of any trademark, registered trademark, or service mark.

Scripture taken from the Holy Bible, NIV. Copyright 1973, 1978, 1984 International Bible Society. Used by permission of Zondervan Bible Publishers.

ISBN: 978-1-938531-18-7

Other Books by B.K. Froman

Book 1
Mornings in Two Pan

To Mom

Sorry it took so long.

1

You're Not Alone

SOMEONE IN TWO PAN is awake tonight, just like you. Maybe you're standing at the grocery store reading this rather than some rag on how to lose twenty pounds in two weeks. Hopefully, you're lazing in a hammock while the moon rests on long rollers of a warm water ocean. Perhaps you're sitting in a donicker in the Rockies as a single star blazes to its end. God forbid you're trying to rest in some uncomfortable chair or airport, waiting—afraid to hope.

Wherever you are, it doesn't matter. Day or night. Or a continent away. Someone in Two Pan is awake with you right now.

It's not a city like New York that never sleeps. It's just that someone in Two Pan isn't sleeping.

A bare bulb hangs from a tree limb over an open truck hood. The lamp of a bedside vigil outlines a window. A lantern casts half-shadows across faces in an open field.

In cities, neon bulbs buzz and hum without human company. In Two Pan, a lone point of light means a citizen is making a community improvement, working on her dream, or trying to keep the pieces of his life from crumbling.

These are forthright folks. You want an honest opinion, you'll get one. They'll tell you if a casserole needs more seasoning, if you shouldn't have tipped for your last haircut, or if your nephew is truly dumb and ugly. If you're gullible, they may embellish their advice a bit, but that comes from living in this unyielding land for so long. Sandwiched between granite mountains and tall sky, they've had to create their own diversions.

To find this hidden place, follow Highway 82 in eastern Oregon until it narrows into gray patchy asphalt. A gut-jostling track continues into the Eagle Cap Mountains. This little-known path winds through the gold camps of yesteryear. Little remains of the gold, in case you were thinking of quitting your job and taking up prospecting.

Local stories are not about the miners, but repeated about the folks who stayed to prod and work the land. There must be something in that beggarly soil, because fifth-generation settlers still own many of the ranches. And therein lies the great mystery of Two Pan: why do these folks resist the shift and shuffle of change?

It's what makes them stubborn, eccentric, and sometimes— a little sleepless.

2

Disappointing the Dead

JIGGS WOOLSEY COULDN'T get the coffin into the hole. He'd made three attempts while the two other men watched through the darkness. No matter how he maneuvered the front-end loader, a corner of the outer vault hung up.

"Hold on! I'll knock off the edges," the man in a light red jacket yelled as he climbed onto a nearby backhoe.

Jiggs motored his farm tractor out of the way, backing between headstones. The steel arms of his front end loader were raised high, harnessed to the concrete box with double straps. The vault slowly swayed in front of him, blocking one of the tractor's headlights, then the other.

Parked between the tombstones of Charlie Spitz and Opal Spinrad, Jiggs listened to the engine rattling the night air and mused how folks who hated each other in life had to sleep beside one another for eternity.

The backhoe clattered forward and cut four bites from the earth. Clumps of dirt plopped from the scoop onto a blue plastic tarp. The scent of fresh-cut soil mingled with diesel fumes. Jiggs wondered if Basil Hinton, working the levers of the backhoe, was the point man for urban invaders. Even though Bazz had been here ten years, he was still a Californian. The sixty-year-old was a decent-enough guy—even elected mayor because nobody else wanted to do the paperwork. Still ... he was an addition to the community, not part of its bones.

Not like the Spinrads who'd been rumored to have staked their claim to land shortly after God pushed the Eagle Caps through the earth's crust. Jiggs glanced at the weeds crowding Opal's stone. No children left to care for her grave. It was her own fault. She'd been a cussing-mean spinster. The kind who sicced her dogs on Halloween pranksters.

The stories of the folks buried in God's Hollow, Two Pan's little cemetery, came easily to him. He'd grown up hearing the sins and glories of each name. Five generations of Woolsey men had been here, wresting a living out of a land that didn't want to be a host. Unfortunately, he'd quietly discovered his family history was only half true. His great-granddad was one of the first to stumble into the territory, but left either idiots or bitter men to populate the family gene pool. That would stop. There'd be stories of respect following his name.

"You want it deeper?" Bazz called to the third man. "If so, we'll need to take the top off some of these stones so I can get a better angle."

Morris Archer, the smallish funeral director, stood next to a pile of dirt, shifting from one foot to the other. His breath fogged in the beam of his flashlight as he yelled, "OSHA says no deeper than four foot ten inches unless there's side support." He turned to stare at headlights traveling up the lane from the main road.

It was just the kind of answer Jiggs expected from the mortician. The Archer family lived twenty-three miles away, but they'd been burying folks throughout the valley for a hundred years. There were tales about great-grandpa Archer crawling into a collapsed mine to haul bodies out so he could bury them again—properly. And even though the Gedding's kid was a

4

hardship case, they'd buried him in an oak coffin, not a pine box. That's the kind of tales that followed Archer's Mortuary.

Jiggs had heard the Jugenmeier family had chosen burial over cremation because Archer had explained that George was too big for the oven. They could get him in, but he'd probably start a fire. Folks could count on Archer's to guide them in the right way to escort a loved one out of life.

In the half-shadows, the Sheriff's seal dimly reflected on the cruiser that had pulled up. Jiggs grimaced and turned to watch the backhoe chug from the open pit, moving in angles between headstones.

"Think you can hit that hole now?" Bazz shouted, swinging out of the seat. "It's deeper than four foot ten, but God and the sheriff won't tell." He waved at the lanky man walking toward them.

Jiggs threw him a look, shifting the tractor into gear without answering. Bazz may have the humor of a local, but not the citizenship. Nobody knew the stock he came from.

When the concrete vault hung directly over the hole, Jiggs jabbed his thumb behind him. Bazz and Archer climbed onto the back of the tractor. Jiggs nudged a lever. With a clank, the bucket jerked. The concrete box inched downward in stuttering jolts.

"Damn. What's that bucket gear have? About four teeth?" Bazz yelled.

Jiggs glanced over his shoulder. "You'll be lucky to have that many teeth when you're as old as—"

The back wheels of the tractor tilted off the ground.

Three men reared back. The sheriff jumped on the back bar. His added weight helped counterbalance the load. The chug of the engine pulsed as they hovered in limbo. They balanced on the front wheels a long moment. Then in a smooth dive, the tractor tipped forward. The vault crashed into the hole.

"If George were here, he would've yelled, 'Timber!'" Bazz said, jumping off the back of the tractor.

"That ol' logger would've dynamited this hole open instead of digging it," Jiggs called back. He frowned at Sheriff Sol Meyers as he climbed off the tractor. "If you're looking for me, you'll have to wait." He took notice that Sol didn't answer him.

Jiggs cut the straps free from the front-end loader. The tractor tilted backward, crashing onto the ground. Bazz jumped. "Damn. Give some warning!"

Ignoring him, Archer directed, "Throw the straps into the hole. We'll never get them from under 1500 pounds of concrete."

Bazz made short work of pushing the dirt pile into the grave. When he switched off the backhoe, it took a moment for the racket of the engine to fade into the silence. The yellow headlights bisected the darkness. With the back of a shovel, Archer began patting the soil into a uniform rectangle.

"You don't have to do that. I doubt if Ol' George's kids will ever come out here to pay respect." Jiggs knew the mortician would tidy a grave even if he were lost in the desert. Archer didn't pause.

The Sheriff looked at Jiggs. "I got a call about God's Hollow. The caller said there were lights in the cemetery. Since I was looking for you, I figured you'd be where there wasn't supposed to be activity."

"Oh. I requested his help." Archer stopped sliding the shovel to work the ground smooth. "I didn't have the equipment to handle Mr. Jugenmeir. And since this was a first-time procedure," he cast a sideways glance at the tractor, "I thought it best to wait until evening and not work in public viewing."

"Hey, what'd George weigh anyway?" Bazz pulled a beer from the cooler on the backhoe and held it up. The others declined.

"Well, I can get a three hundred and fifty-pound man in a regular casket." The mortician went back to his landscaping. "He'd be somewhat squeezed, but the lid would close. So Mr. Jugenmeir must have weighed about four hundred. I had to order an oversize casket and vault, and his children had to purchase two burial plots." He studied the domed pile of dirt as though judging if it were centered on the property.

"It didn't hurt 'em. They have enough money now." Disgust underlined Jiggs' voice.

"Nevertheless, if you hadn't helped, Mr. Woolsey, I would've had to use a field crane from Charlie the Slaughter King."

"Ol' George deserved more than a sendoff by a mobile butcher. I've shared fence lines with his family for as long as I can remember, and then some." Jiggs scowled at the sheriff, adding darkly, "Until now."

"Yeah, about that." The sheriff looked away, rubbing his eyebrow. "I need to arrest you."

Archer cleared his throat, excused himself, walked to his hearse, and began removing flowers from the back.

Jiggs watched him go, then winged a flat-voiced reply toward the sheriff. "I suppose this is about that snaky little funeral crasher with the weird hair." He fanned his fingers above his head. "It was poofed up like some TV preacher." The thirty-something man had been short, moving with squirrelly starts and stops like he didn't know whether to stay or go. He'd stuck his hand right into the middle of the conversation Jiggs was having about the tasty "death ham" Cleova Klegg made for all Two Pan funerals.

"Good afternoon, Mr. Woolsey." The guy had been cheery. Each time he moved, his hair swayed. Jiggs shook his hand, squinting at the top of the fella's head.

"I'm Max Buddy, a realtor over in La Grande. I wondered if you'd had a chance to meet your new neighbors."

Jiggs gave him a condescending nod. "I've known Ol' George's kids all their lives."

Mr. Buddy shook his head rapidly, his hair wafting back and forth. "No. Mr. Jugenmeir's children sold to my client, and on his behalf—"

"Wait." Jiggs palmed a whoa-signal. "What are you saying?"

"My client bought the Jugenmeir property, so I'd—"

"Hold on, Slick. I had an agreement with Ol' George for his two thousand acres. When he was ready to move in with his kids, I'd buy the place. We shook on it."

"That *is* unfortunate. I did not know that. And you had witnesses to this transaction?" Mr. Buddy looked around at the faces of the men, ending with a questioning stare at Jiggs.

"My dad was there, but he passed away last spring. Listen," Jiggs leaned closer, "it was the man's word. We didn't need notaries and news releases."

Mr. Buddy nodded with a concern that didn't reach his eyes. "It's too bad Mr. Jugenmeir had a heart attack before you could make good on your deal."

"What'd you do? Have George sign the deed of sale as the rural fire department was cutting him out of his truck?"

"No." The realtor gave Jiggs a distasteful scowl. "Mr. Jugenmeir hung on a few days in the hospital before he passed. His children made the sale when they got here. Perhaps you should've gone to see him?"

Jiggs carefully set his plate of ham and potato salad on a counter. He swallowed before he looked up, his stare burning into the realtor. "Who wangles property out of a man on his deathbed?"

"His children were grieving, overwhelmed, and had no plans to ever come back here. They were very relieved to sell to someone who wanted the land. It's a shame they didn't know about your interest in the property."

"Listen, I don't know what you've flim-flammed here, but that's not the way we do business in this part of the country. That land is next to mine, and George and I had a gentlemen's agreement. I intend to make sure it's kept."

"Then it'll be a very expensive legal battle, and you'll lose. But really, it can be a win-win situation for everyone, Mr. Woolsey, especially for you." The realtor had one of those grins young men wear when they feel they have a ring in the world's nose, and they're in charge of yanking it.

"Just how do you figure?"

"My client, a doctor in Portland, would like to buy your 1,897 acres and the mineral rights." Max Buddy leaned forward, his face serious. He gave a sideways nod toward the hearse outside the glass doors, and spoke in a low voice. "You know how hard life is here. A couple of bad years ... and folks can lose everything. Why not sell now and enjoy what you've got? You never know when things will surprise you—and end suddenly."

The tractor engine creaked and popped as it cooled, rousing Jiggs from the memory. He squinted at the sheriff. "What were you saying?"

"I *said*," Sol shifted his weight, "at any time, did you feel Mr. Buddy was trying to threaten you?"

"Heck if I know. He was talking about endings, so I showed him one." Jiggs' eyes narrowed. "I concluded our conversation with my forty-six-year-old foot helping his thirty-something ass hurry through the church doors, out to the curb, and into his car. The whole time, his puffy hair jerked side to side like he had a ball of cotton candy on his head. The man should look in a mirror sometime."

Bazz unscrewed the lid on another Pale Ale. "Why's this doctor want your land?"

"Didn't ask." Sparks seemed to flint from Jiggs' words as he stomped a roll of mud into the rut the backhoe had ripped in the grass. "That little fitz-glimmer realtor shouldn't even gawk at my weeds, much less look up my records at the courthouse." He stared without seeing, refiguring something in his mind, then nodded as if he gotten the same answer again.

The mortician straightened from arranging flowers. Colored daisies wreathed the borders of the grave. Purple potted mums sat around the mound with one tired lily at the crest, its bloom bowed as if in reverence.

Bazz rubbed the two-day-old beard he usually wore. "So disturbing a funeral is a jailable offense around here? Good to know."

Jiggs and the sheriff locked eyes. They stood at the same height. Back in the day, they'd traded starting positions as the high school's quarterback. Together, they'd booby trapped Opal Spinrad's front door every Halloween. They'd dumped horse manure in teachers' yards. They'd kissed the same woman.

Jiggs felt, more than saw, a change in Sol's face. A blink, an undetectable tightening of the jaw. Sol's memory seemed to be tipping toward the black hole of Jiggs' hotheaded antics. In high school Sol had pulled him off a fight with four guys who'd stuffed confetti into his car vents. Sol had seen him push a loudmouth out of a moving boxcar. It was Sol who'd heard the family argument at the chili feed the night Ox had declared, "Jiggs is the one who'll lose everything." But what did it matter? Everybody had been there.

Archer stared at his feet as though noticing his shoelaces for the first time. Bazz busied himself, hooking the cooler's lid into place with bungee cords.

"When did a well-deserved ass-kicking become an offense?" Jiggs shot the sheriff a tell-the-truth look. "You used to hand out plenty of them."

"I said I *need* to arrest you. Not that I *had* to or I'm *going* to. Mr. Buddy complained, but he didn't file assault charges. You've got something he wants."

"And he won't get."

"I'm thinking some jail time might've cooled you off. You're becoming like your father. Maybe it would've helped you wake up to the fact there are new people in this county. You need to learn there're other ways to protect what's yours. And as far as the old ways go ... time has moved on." Sol held Jiggs' stare. "But between you and me, Ol' George would've enjoyed a butt-kicking at his funeral."

Jiggs gave him the slightest fraction of a nod. "I'll take that as a warning."

"Well, it was a most interesting service," Archer said, getting into his hearse. With a quick word of thanks, he left. Bazz followed, silently raising his beer as he drove by on the backhoe.

"Lock 'er when you leave," was all Sol said to Jiggs. He got in his cruiser and closely followed the backhoe down the lane.

Silence settled around the tractor. In the distance, two coyotes yipped messages to one another. Jiggs threaded through grave markers, his feet sure of the path to the family plot. He passed his brother's gravestone and stopped in front of his wife's marker. "Well, Katie, you've got George at the feast with you now. I lost my temper at his funeral. I also lost the chance to grow the ranch."

Jiggs stared into the blackness, unable to see her headstone. He wasn't sure what he was waiting for. An epiphany? In his thoughts, his brother's face swam forward instead of his wife's. Pax grinned. Always, that laughing face.

He was frozen that way, forever grinning behind a window smeared with blood. Jiggs slammed the door on the memory, but not before the compulsory tonnage of guilt slipped through, dogging him as he walked through the darkness.

Back at the burial site, two does chewed on the fresh flowers. Jiggs climbed onto the tractor and cranked the starter. The deer bounded a few leaps to the shadowy edge of the head-lights. They returned by the time he'd driven to the gate.

He snapped the padlock in place. The final click assured him the cemetery's residents were secured from the living.

If only it were that easy to lock out the accusations of the dead.

3

Alligator Nights

IT PROBABLY WON'T surprise you that most people blow right through Two Pan on their way to somewhere else. On this September afternoon, the Bilyeaus—headed for Idaho—are lost when they drive into town. Years of experience have taught Tom Bilyeau that his wife can't read a map, and Joan has endured equal years of fuming because her husband won't stop and ask for directions. This wide-spot-in-the-road is a welcome escape from their Buick's close quarters and their verbal lightning bolts.

———

Arms in the air, stretching next to his car, Tom wondered about the open spaces between the businesses along Main Street. He wasn't the type to offer questions—if he were, they wouldn't be lost—but if he *had* worked up the gumption to ask someone, he would've been told that years ago, fires had roared through the town, twice, leaving nothing but ashes. "And each time it was resurrected worse than before," according to Old Man Tower.

The couple glanced at the present day post office, a tiny cement-block building. It wasn't as interesting as the old log cabin that had burned down a century ago when mail came by stagecoach, and the postmaster drew a chalk circle on the floor before he dumped the bag, making folks stay outside the lines so he could sort it.

Tom and Joan walked on by, thinking all the history in town was contained in the impressive building ahead of them. It anchored the corner with solid, rough-hewn granite blocks quarried out of the Eagle Caps. The sign for the Opera House Museum leaned against its steps.

Joan walked stiff-legged to the entrance. "Hello?" she called. Even though there was no answer, she stepped inside, and then peeked back out, waving to her husband. "Come see this."

In the foyer, wood and glass cases displayed yellowed programs, lace fans, and delicate relics of a bygone era. Photographs of Two Pan in its heyday hung from long wires against the twenty-foot high walls. Only pictures remained of the fifty upholstered seats and elaborately carved oak stage.

The hall was mostly an empty cavern, lit by dim sconces. Their footsteps echoed as they peered at the curiosities in the well-maintained structure. The Daughters of Two Pan had coerced their husbands into making repairs after each customary fundraiser. Whitman County men would seriously forewarn any male newcomer regarding the loss of time he'd suffer during elk season, the trout run, and regular rest should he marry a woman with Two Pan blood.

"They must have meetings here," Joan said, sneaking into a side room filled with a massive table made from the oak doors of the former opera house.

"I don't think we're supposed to be here." Tom stared at the antique file cabinets huddling against the walls.

They had entered the heart of Two Pan's government. The city council met in the backstage area. Ancient records and secrets were safe in these archives. Warped with age, the drawers couldn't be prised open, not even by Muley Baker and several of the area's most strapping citizens. The mayor kept the current city records at his repair shop.

Leaving and walking south on Main Street, the couple passed the scattering of houses clustered on Hop Hopkins' property. They glanced at a run-down building, not realizing it had been a thriving saloon. Outlying structures served as a brewery, a smoke shack for curing meats, and a "slop house" that had served miners the famous Two Pan stew.

The couple strolled by the open field next door. "For Sale" signs on cattle feeders, watering tanks, and livestock equipment hid its shady past. Not even a small piece of foundation remained of the ten-room whorehouse. No picture of Opal's Palace was preserved in the museum either—which most men declared was due to the intolerant nature of the original Daughters of Two Pan.

"Good grief!" Joan eyed the canoe and partial Harley frame sticking out of the Latte Da espresso shop that marked the east end of Main. The corner had been a junk pile until nine years ago when hippies had moved in and built a coffee shack out of whatever discards they could find. When they left, Lottie Lubach took over, using it to sell baked goods and escape her recently retired husband.

"Let's give it a try," Tom said.

"I don't think so." Joan kept walking as she stared at a donkey standing at the side entrance. A woman was unhooking neon-colored bags from the animal's harness and chattering away as though catching up with her best friend. She glanced up and waved. Joan crossed the street.

The couple overlooked the true gold mine of the town, Old Man Tower's Salvage. Under forested acres, hundreds of rusting tractors, ore carts, and ox wagons littered the property. Forgotten by time and chaos, old cars sprouted trees through their engine cavities. Moss blanketed the ore crushers and rivet-studded steam tanks. Three Ford Galaxies stood upright, on their rear bumpers, because the salvage yard was out of room. Trails, dotted with hidey-holes, snaked around gutted Model A's and wagon wheels.

They missed the junkyard because Tom, in his hurry to eat and get back on the road, had stepped into a barn-red store with inviting benches on either side of its screen-door entrance. Andrew Grubb claimed that his great-granddaddy had set a plank across a barrel and began selling sugar, salt, and mule shoes to miners at that very spot a hundred and thirty years ago. The shelves of the present mercantile held some of the original merchandise, lost under more recent purchases made during WWII and last week.

The only ghost in the county occupied the office above the store. Residents claimed they sometimes saw the territorial dentist late at night, and stock boys swore they found boxes mysteriously moved into the aisles in the mornings.

"Got any grab 'n' go food?" Tom asked the checker while staring at the tin-plated ceiling.

"I'm not sitting in the car, dripping microwaved burrito juice on my lap." Joan skewered him with a glare. "I'm eating off of a table."

Cleova, the cashier, offered a sympathy smile. "The Bar and Grill's down the street. Good atmosphere."

"Come on!" Joan tapped her husband's chest, dotting the exclamation point in her voice, then turned and left. Tom leaned sideways, staring down an aisle toward the people sitting around a potbellied stove.

Having stretched the kinks out of her legs, Joan took quick strides in the direction Cleova had pointed.

"I would've liked to look around that store a bit," Tom gasped, a little out of breath as he caught up to her. "Did you ever see such a collection of trappings?"

"I thought you were in a hurry," she said, which opened Round 12 regarding pleasure trips. Their sniping caused them to pass the only place that Joan would have liked: the antique shop. If the owner, Dooley Monroe, had been sitting in his usual porch chair, he would've answered their questions and made sure they left with some of Two Pan's junk. But they tramped right by while the narrow-faced man was in the backyard, walking a metal detector over the old site of the blacksmith's stand.

Basil Hinton, Sr. scratched his two-day growth of whiskers and tossed a set of Vernier calipers onto the workbench. He hated the itch of facial hair, but refused to shave *every day*. He'd quit being a corporate-guy to become a bearded-freethinker. Forty-eight hours of stubble was about all he could stand.

The repair shop was supposed to be a place to enjoy his retirement hobby, working on vintage cars. But when the locals found out he was a mechanical wizard, they brought him their broken gizmos, ignoring the handwritten sign taped to his door: I DON'T WORK ON APPLIANCES or JAPANESE ELECTRONIC CRAP. He yawned as he went out the door, heading toward his former restaurant.

Every morning Bazz ate breakfast with the town's liars and shakers at Table 2 in the Bar and Grill. Back in Two Pan's heyday, the building had been one of the area's lesser saloons and included the brothel next door. Its lack of notoriety was probably the reason it had never been torn down.

Bazz said the B-rated cathouse and bar was the height of his social ladder. He'd bought it when he'd moved from California ten years ago. For an out-of-towner, he'd made a success of the Bar and Grill. But actually, he figured his popularity and position as mayor rested on his ability to keep every engine in the county running.

After ten summers of fixing the roof, the plumbing, and the electricity, the gray-haired transplant had convinced his forty-year-old son, Junior, to "get out of that Los Angeles smog-hole" and buy the restaurant.

The change to rural life frustrated his son.

This morning, with a kitchen towel slung over his shoulder, Junior slid a platter of waffles in front of a diner, then pointed to a pile of junk on the bar. "Take your pick when you go."

"What is it?"

"Old license plates I took down. They're free. Just one of the things we do for customers." When the tourist left the café, Junior cornered his father. "You've got more debris than Old Man Tower's yard. Start hauling your scrap next door to the brothel. I've got plans for that wall."

Jiggs Woolsey intervened, giving Junior a challenging stare. "There was a pike and peavey on that wall. You take it down?" He didn't wait for an answer. "It was George Jugenmeir's. He was rollin' trees off the mountain and floating 'em down river before you were even born."

A leather-skinned woman at another table groused, "George probably drank enough beers here to buy that wall."

Jiggs shook his buttered toast at the new tavern owner. "This place is as much about history as it is food." He pushed his plate away. "Maybe more so."

Bazz shot his son an I-told-you-so smile.

Outside the bar, Tom and Joan stared at the narrow architecture of the building. "Now that's old." The wife took off her sunglasses and scanned the windowless façade.

"Look at this arched doorway." Her husband ran his hand over the notches and dents in the door. "They must've hauled this timber a long way by wagon. Oak doesn't grow around here."

Joan pointed toward the opera house. "Do you think it's older than that?"

"Of course! They'd build a bar first." Tom bent closer, fingering a deep divot. "I think this is a bullet hole!"

The door swung open, hitting him in the head.

"Oh! Sorry. I didn't know anyone would be squatting out here." Jiggs' eyes smiled, even though his voice was apologetic. He carried a strip of bacon in one hand and a long wooden pike in the other. Bazz followed him, a piece of truck tire over his shoulder.

"We're admiring the place," the woman said. "Do you know if this building is older than the opera house?" Jiggs stooped and waggled the bacon in front of a hole in the building. A broken-tailed kitten squeezed through the opening, hissing before it nabbed the meat.

"I thought you hated cats," Bazz said with a smirk.

"Maybe the cholesterol will kill him," Jiggs said.

"Excuse me, but is this a bullet hole?" The man stepped farther behind the half-open door, picking at the divot.

"Yep." Jiggs wiped his fingers on his jeans. "Some outlaw went High Noon last week. Tried to kill the mayor here." He nodded toward Bazz.

"Good heavens, what happened?" the man asked.

"I missed." Jiggs shrugged. "Now if you'll pardon me, I gotta practice my aim." He touched the brim of his hat as he walked away, thumping the pike on the ground with every other step.

"He was kidding, right?" The woman watched Jiggs get in his truck.

Bazz smiled, stepped aside, and waved them toward the dark interior with a flourish. "Welcome to Two Pan Bar and Grill. The man behind the bar doesn't have all of his cornflakes in one box, but he can answer some of your questions." He leaned forward, whispering in a confidential tone, "Be sure and ask to see the alligator. It's quite a treat." Hefting the tire tread over his shoulder, he strolled down the street.

A much-abused oak bar with a brass foot rail and spotty mirrors ran the length of one wall. Piles of boxes, license plates, a chrome car bumper, and assorted clutter rendered the counter unusable. Tom and Joan had their choice of round or square tables, each with a tiny plastic billboard displaying a number. Brass fixtures and cobwebs hung from long chains anchored to the ceiling. Their golden light threw shadows on hunting gear and mining tools hanging on the walls. Men in cowboy hats and ball caps eyed the couple as they entered.

Another arched doorway enticed them into a dark room dominated by a walnut billiard table. "Let's eat in here." Tom scanned the plaster for more bullet holes.

"Wait a minute." Joan pushed through velvet curtains. The glare of modern fluorescent lights shocked her eyes. Twenty numbered tables sat in a bare-walled room. A sign designated one corner as the LIBRARY. Ragged paperbacks lay in piles on cinderblock shelves next to an orange, overstuffed chair.

"I believe we should eat in the main area." Joan backed out after a single glance.

As soon as they settled, a skinny blonde dropped plastic menus in front of them. "Drinks?" Misty asked with an attitude that implied words cost money.

"How old is this building? Older than the opera house?" Joan asked.

Pocketing her order book, Misty shrugged. "I'll be back." She was experienced for a twenty-three-year-old. Get the order or stand there narrating like the History Channel. Punishment usually sped up a diner's decision process.

When Misty returned, she wangled food and drink requests out of the couple, avoiding their questions.

The tight-lipped waitress soon scooted plates of steak-stuffed omelets and cheesy tater-tots across their table and tried to make a getaway.

"Wait. I want to know about the Opera House," the wife said.

"Why does it matter, Joan?" Her husband gave the waitress a what-can-you-do shrug. "Do you know if there were any gunfights in this room?"

"Why does *that* matter?" Joan smirked, starting Round 13.

After they'd finished their meal, Junior delivered the couple's bill because he was tired of listening to Misty carp around the kitchen about gawking tourists. "I don't have answers for your questions," he said, pushing his rimless glasses back into place. "There're only old timers' stories. I've heard that the brothel upstairs was pretty rowdy. They finally moved it next door."

"Can we have a look?" Tom asked.

An amused smile crept over Junior's face. "Well ... my dad lives there. Although knowing him, he'd enjoy coming home to visitors touring his bedroom. He loves to tell colorful lies. You just missed him."

"Oh!" The woman seemed truly disappointed. "I think we saw him on the way out. He said we should ask to see the alligator."

Junior sighed and shook his head. He pulled out a chair and sat down. "Yeah, that'd be Dad all right." He waved at the walls. "You see all this crap in here? I'm buying the place from him. He filled it with every useless piece of junk in this county. I've been cleaning it out and incurring the community's wrath ever since. Would you like a coal shuttle? Horse harness? Buggy seat? They're authentic and free."

"Did you get rid of the alligator?" Disappointment rang through the man's voice.

Junior sighed, scrubbing his palm over his face as though trying to wipe away the memory. "A few years ago, Dad and his buddy, who runs a guide service, went fishing in the Florida Keys. Jack Daniels must have been biting a lot harder than the fish were, because late one night, driving back to the hotel, they ran over something—big. It was dark and all they could see was this alligator's tail sticking out from under their car. Drunk and bleary-eyed, they tried to pull it out. It put up such a fight they figured it wasn't hurt too badly.

"They thought it would be funny to bring it home and throw it in Muley Baker's pond—he's kind of a scrapper and they owed him one. To hear them tell it, it was the wrestling match of the century to get that gator into the trunk and slam the lid. They tore out for Oregon right then and there."

"How did they think they were going to get it out of the car?" the woman asked, eyes wide.

"Ma'am, their cheese had already slid off their crackers." He stared at her blank look. "They weren't thinking, ma'am. Dad rarely does. They drove for hours and probably three states before they got the nerve to check on the gator. It had gotten awfully quiet back there, and they thought maybe it had died.

"Armed with tree branches, they opened the hatch and ran. Nothing happened. They crouched low and snuck up on the car. All that was in the trunk was a big piece of tire tread that had blown off a semi-truck."

"Oh, we saw him carrying that!" The woman sounded excited, like she'd placed the last piece in a puzzle.

"Well, I took it down. It's going to live at his place, now." Junior shook his head, staring at a two-horned rabbit skull still gracing the wall.

At two in the morning, Tom and Joan had arrived in Idaho. They were sitting at their friends' table, drinking beer and telling stories about a quirky hamlet they'd passed through. They talked about going back to check it out. Joan doubted if Tom could find it again because he didn't know where he was in the first place.

Round 32 began.

In Two Pan, no telltale light glowed from the windowless Bar and Grill. But inside, Bazz stood on a ladder, balancing a hammer in his grip, the same hammer he'd used to nail hubcaps, cracked work boots, and rusty hay hooks onto walls. When he'd first come to town, people had been polite, but when he'd bought the bar and nailed up mementos of the folks who lived here, they'd adopted him into their community. It was the relics along with a mile of wire and a bucket of bolts and screws that held the place together.

Jiggs sorted through a coffee can of nails, grumbling, "People have been eating at the same tables for years. Junior can't just waltz in and morph this into a California bistro."

"When I told him that, he yanked off his apron and threw it, yelling, 'Is it a sin to clean up this dump? Put spices instead of cheese in the food? Why didn't you make this place a co-op? Let the customers decorate and do their own cooking?'"

"He'll learn." Jiggs shook the coffee can, tweezing his fingers inside. "You make changes by not making any changes."

"At least for a while. I'll help make sure he doesn't run off the customers." Bazz coughed out a laugh. "I believe I've lived here too long already. Doing this proves what a hypocrite I am."

"You're a politician. You needed proof?"

"I thought it'd be okay for Junior to give this place a make-over. Now that he's doing it, I don't want him to. I've put too much into it. I just realized, I don't like change either."

"Well ... welcome home." Jiggs handed up a couple of 10 penny nails.

Perching on top of the ladder, Bazz pounded the dangling piece of tire tread to the ceiling—long after Junior had closed the Bar and Grill for the night.

4

A Town Without Stoplights

A WEEK LATER, Jiggs limped into the Bar and Grill. Earlier that afternoon, a heifer had planted a hoof in the rancher's thigh as he tried to hip lever her into the stock trailer. He tossed his cowboy hat atop a life-sized toy German shepherd sitting on the bar.

The stuffed animal had been Junior's prize at the Whitman County Fair. Jiggs and Bazz had egged the new tavern owner to hurl misshapen baseballs at kewpie dolls in the Daughters of Two Pan fair booth. Junior's grimace became deeper each time he pulled out his wallet, seesawing between wanting to quit and getting something for the money he'd already wasted. "Aren't you going to support the ladies?" he asked his dad forty-five dollars later, when he finally tucked the big dog under his arm.

Bazz arched an eyebrow. "What would we do with two of those?"

Jiggs pitched until he won a small cross-stitched pillow that one of the Daughters had made.

"And what'll you do with that?" Bazz eyed the ruffled edges.

"Don't worry about it." Jiggs walked toward the stalls of the 4-H and FFA youth who'd bought his cattle. He liked to watch them show their heifers and check if they'd won any ribbons. He gave the little pillow to Taylor Kruger since her heifer didn't place high in its class.

Bazz grinned at him. "You know you'll be buying back that fifth-place cow at the Livestock Exchange and paying above-market prices."

Jiggs shrugged. "Somebody did it for my kid. Why don't you buy some expensive hamburger for the bar?" Bazz made himself busy inspecting FFA welding projects.

The German shepherd had taken its place as a mascot and hat rack, nestling amid the bar clutter.

As Jiggs joined Bazz at Table 2, Misty set a mug of beer in front of him, foam sliding down the side. Nodding his thanks, he took a long draw, then rubbed his brow with the heel of his hand. "Why do people think that driving three feet off your bumper will make you move along faster?"

Bazz didn't look up from his newspaper. "Makes me slow down even more. Sometimes I learn new words that way."

"Some guy was breeding me with his car as I drove here tonight. When I didn't speed up, he passed me going uphill with oncoming traffic. Darn near had a 'George-pile-up.'"

"George had a heart attack while he was driving," Bazz corrected.

Jiggs didn't let facts weaken his point. "It's usually a teenager or under-thirty boob in a SUV. You never see a white-haired guy grinding your bumper, trying to get you to speed up."

"Except Old Man Tower. He'll run over you if you don't get out of his way. 'Course, his eyes are about as good as a potato's, so I guess he may not really be trying to push you down the road." Bazz waved at Josie Blevins, the new eighth-grade teacher, scouting a seat from the doorway.

He pulled out the chair next to his as she threaded between tables. "We're talking about Ol' Man Tower. How old is that fossil?" He spoke loud enough to invite public discussion, and diners at other tables threw out comments: "Walked to school with Jesus," "Used to date the Morton salt girl."

Misty set a beer in front of the teacher. The forty-year-old brunette lifted the mug in a silent toast to her tablemates. "Well, he was ancient when I was here."

"I've got news for you, darlin'," Bazz patted her hand. "You're still here."

"I meant, as a girl." Josie gave him a flat stare. "Before I moved away."

"Most folks don't come back," Jiggs said.

"I have good memories of being with my grandparents. It's a great place to grow up. Lots of freedom."

"Now realtors are trying to get everybody here." Jiggs snorted. "All of 'em in a hurry. The only one who should be rushing around is Old Man Tower. He doesn't have a lot of time left."

"The way he drives, he'll have even less," Bazz said.

"See," Jiggs pointed, "that's what I'm saying. These young kids have the rest of their lives to get where they're going. It's old people who should scurry around, cramming experiences into the few coherent days they have left."

"It has nothing to do with age." Josie shook her head. "Your new neighbor came wheeling through town and almost clipped me the other day."

"The important Dr. Jarmin?" Jiggs' eyes feigned surprise. "He's hikin' up property values and building new barns. I see contractors at ol' George's place, working like ants on a Popsicle, and I hear he's only living there part of the year. Thank the Lord for that!"

Jiggs scowled at Bazz, who was now beneath the table, jamming a beer coaster under a steel leg to level it. "These transplants and tourists gallop through, slam on their brakes, slide to the curb, dash in to pick up a soda, then suck the curtains out the window getting back to the highway. You're the mayor. Do something about it."

"Doesn't work that way." Bazz pushed off the floor with a grunt. "You don't get to sit around, expecting nothing to change. If you want a small, close-knit community, what're you doing to help it?"

Jiggs looked at the floor, shaking his head. "There was a time when dogs could sleep in the middle of Main Street."

Josie gave a humorless laugh. "Main Street is so short, you'd only need one mutt."

Jiggs and Bazz passed the rest of the evening dreaming up municipal improvements and tasting beers—blindfolded. Misty swore that she brought them Budweiser every time, even though they'd identified eight different hoppy and nutty flavors, including two brands the bar didn't carry.

When Junior pushed them out the door at 1:00 in the morning, they were primed to begin construction on the town's first speed bump. Boozy reasoning made concrete forms unnecessary. Instead, they mixed batches of cement in wheelbarrows, dumped them in a single row, and smoothed the sides with a chunk of 2X4.

Like many of their strategic action plans, it was more work than they'd imagined, but hours later, a wavy mound lay across the road on the south end of Main Street.

"We're outta mix. We'll have to make a cement run if we do this on the north end." Bazz slapped his gloves together, knocking off concrete grit.

"And pick up some of that yellow highway paint so we can stripe 'em. This is pretty hard to see."

"I think the county uses white chevrons. It needs to look like an official project."

"Nobody's gonna mistake this for county work," Jiggs said with a chuckle that set both of them into tired-stupid laughter.

Bazz went into the bar and brought out a thermos of coffee. They sat in plastic lawn chairs, waiting for any morning commuters. Jiggs rubbed his leg where the heifer had kicked him, and Bazz noted who'd awakened and flicked on their lights in the surrounding houses.

At about six, Jiggs straightened, staring down the street, one side of his mouth ticking up with a smile. "Here comes my idiot neighbor."

Dr. Richard Jarmin's Chevy Avalanche sped toward town. It hit the bump at full tilt. The truck jumped a foot in the air. The tires slammed the pavement, bouncing twice before the rig continued weaving down the street.

"Damn! I think he broke his neck." Bazz watched Jarmin crank his head side to side, working the cricks out of his spine. The sound of the engine faded as the Chevy headed north, traveling considerably slower.

"He'll be concussed for a week. But since he's a doctor, it won't cost him a dime to see himself." Jiggs laughed, then lifted and resettled his Stetson. "The blockhead drives like he owns the road." He stared after the truck as though it were a gut wagon. "Goes right down the middle. If you meet him, you'd better head for the ditch—or he'll put you there. Doesn't even have the neighborly decency to wave."

"He can't afford to go slow. He's thinking of all those billable minutes he'd be losing to Medicare," Bazz said.

"Dr. Dick is a plastic surgeon, for pete's sake. He's as useless as teats on my bull."

"He's been in the bar a couple of times. Says he'd like to put new life into this town. Seems a friendly sort. Why're you so hell-bent against him?"

"Besides letting trees from his home improvement projects fall across my fence? Didn't bother to tell me? Let my livestock wander from Mexico to Canada?"

"I thought he had the fence fixed." Bazz held up the thermos.

The rancher offered his cup for a refill. "Here's the thing. I shouldn't have had to call his office and tell him to do it. His secretary didn't even let me talk to him, just took a message."

"At least it was easy." Bazz poured, then screwed the lid on.

"The man's apology should have come with it. And he replaced my fence with something your dog could knock down. He could've used locals who needed the work, but he hired some professional yahoos from the valley. And the real twister—they moved the fence half a foot onto my side. I had it rechecked. The survey equipment showed the old property line was off, but the dirty slinker should've called or said something beforehand. First he took George's land out from under me, now this."

"Probably didn't read his manual on how things work out here," Bazz said. "Then again, you could've hired the fence built your way and sent him the bill. You let him get the jump on you."

"Obviously you haven't read the code book either." Jiggs scowled. "You don't mess with a man's boundaries. We should put his picture in the Bonehead Hall of Fame because if a fella's gonna glom onto six inches of his neighbor's pasture for a half mile, then he oughtta have the spine to do it face to face. That's just basic decency. My family's had that property for the last hundred years. I don't plan on some amenity rancher nibbling away all the land around here."

"Then you'd better do something. I heard, since you wouldn't sell, he's trying to buy another spread—Hop's ranch."

Jiggs' nostrils white rimmed. He spoke through clenched teeth. "Son. Of. A. Monkey! What's he going to do with a thousand acres? He doesn't produce a thing and drives land prices up for folks who do. A young couple starting out can't afford property around here anymore. He'll put up another flashy bronze gate hinting how much money he has, and that's the most he'll do for this place besides talk good intentions."

"If it bothers you so much, do something about it."

"I've got cattle to raise and a ranch to grow. I don't have time to dink with Dr. Dick."

Bazz stared at him. "In the past, your antennae only picked up three channels: water, weather, and livestock, but now you've got another subject to add to your complaints. Urban growth."

The speed bump dominated discussion groups throughout town. The morning Bar and Grill commentators—who tended to be Democrats—wanted bumps installed in front of the school and the football stadium. The bull session at Grubb's Mercantile was full of Republicans who were opposed to it. What would be next? Traffic tickets for speeding?

Lottie Lubach's business at the Latte Da picked up because people had time to read the daily specials on the sandwich board as they slowed for the bump. She sent a box of peanut butter filled doughnuts to Bazz and Jiggs. When her husband, Zimm, painted a skull and crossbones on the hump, sales improved even more.

It was a week before Jiggs and Bazz had time to work on the north end of the street. "Seems we opened a can of worms," Jiggs said one evening at the bar. "You'd think people would appreciate their children and animals not getting run over."

"How many people does it take to change a light bulb in Two Pan?" Bazz stared at the cluttered bar. "Nobody knows because we're not willing to change anything."

Jiggs nodded, eyes afire with inspiration. "I have a new old-fashioned idea to slow down the world."

At five the next morning the men sat in their lawn chairs again, observing whose lights were on and why they were up so early. They had a thermos of coffee and Lottie's newest menu item—popovers—which she'd nicknamed "The Bump."

A few hours earlier, they'd hammered a spike almost flush with the asphalt and tethered the stuffed German shepherd to it. "If somebody hits the dog, it'll rebound and reset itself," Jiggs reasoned.

The few morning commuters heading to work from the backcountry hit the bump on the south end of town. The gray shape of the dog was visible in the dim light at the north end. Most drivers braked, and slowed. One even stopped and tried to coax the mutt off the street until Jiggs yelled, "Leave my dog alone! He's got rabies!"

At about six, Dr. Richard Jarmin entered town. The windows of his Chevy were splashed with dried red mud, the remnants of off-roading in the Eagle Cap boonies. As soon as he eased over the bump, he hit the gas. In seconds, his tires screeched, but he still clipped the hound. Pulling over, he leaped out, and sprinted to his victim. The dog's head hung by a raggedy strip of fake fur. One yellow plastic eye had a dead stare, cotton batting bulged from the other socket. A snaggy slash across the belly leaked sawdust guts onto the pavement. Jiggs and Bazz tried to look like bystanders at an al fresco cafe, but their snorts and choked laughter made coffee bubble out their noses.

Dr. Jarmin's face was a thunderstorm. He jabbed his hand in a "halt" signal toward the set of oncoming headlights and tramped to the sidewalk. "You think this is funny? It's an outrage that—" The crash cut him off.

When Old Man Tower had bucked over the speed bump, his head connected with the steering wheel. Free of the old coot's control, the vehicle careened down the road, sideswiping Jarmin's truck. A golden rooster tail of sparks sprayed behind the Chevy's door as it skateboarded down the street.

Mr. Tower panicked again when his Buick plowed over the dog, The tether ripped out of the pavement and wrapped around the bumper. Like a wide-eyed man who *knows* his driving days are numbered, he sped away, the semi-headless German shepherd jinking right and left, bouncing off the pavement until the strap jerked loose from the Buick's bumper.

For a long while Jarmin stood motionless, staring after the tail lights. The sound of Jiggs tossing the skinned door into the truck bed roused him.

"That'll be easy to hammer out," Jiggs said. "Barely noticeable."

The doctor eyed him up and down with a scowl. "Your names?"

"I'm your neighbor and owner of the livestock you encourage to roam the country. This is the mayor. And that," Jiggs pointed, "used to be the Bar and Grill's mascot. And just so you know, I'm not selling you my land, but I'll gladly buy yours, which is what George intended in the first place. Because, to you this place may be an eye blink in the road, but it's where *we live*. You need to slow down. You hit the town donkey, and there'll be a lynch mob after you."

"Obviously, you've been drinking," the doctor said. "We'll see how funny you think this is later." Without another word, he walked to his vehicle and buckled himself in. He turned and gave a dark grin and a single wave through the mud-splashed back window as he drove away, wind whipping through the gaping opening where the door should have been.

In the gray dawn, Jiggs stared after him, remembering another grinning face behind a red-spattered window. It had started with the same kind of taunting. Pax had been smiling as he'd ironed a blue-plaid, pearl-button shirt. "Finish the chores tonight, little brother. I've got some man-plans."

"This is your third weekend celebrating your twentieth birthday. I'm not doing crap for you." He should've left it there. But no. He'd continued mouthing off, trying again and again to grab that freshly pressed shirt until Pax had slapped the toe-end of the hot iron on his arm.

He'd walked away, scowling a go-to-hell stare. In a moment he'd shot back into the room, taking it to the next level as he usually did when he ran out of words. He swung a baseball bat directly at his brother's ribs. Pax jumped aside, knocking the blow askew with the iron.

He moved forward, taking full cuts.

Pax backed away, circling the furniture, fending off the bashing, and trying to get in a few licks with the iron. When the steam plate fell off, Pax hurled the appliance at his head and ran out the door.

He threw himself in an arcing defensive-end dive. Both of them rolled in the dirt beyond the front porch.

"Stop it, you stupid little prick! Don't make me hurt you." Three years heavier and taller, Pax crouched on top of him, a knee pushing deep into his guts.

He lashed out. Pax's reach was longer. The crunch of cartilage sounded inside his skull. His vision went white for a moment. His mind blanked. In all the years of their free-for-alls, they had never punched each other in the face—until now.

A few feet away, the pickup engine started. He stumbled his way to vertical, his eyes watering, blood dripping from his nose, which now sat crooked on his face. "Get out, you shithead." He smacked the window with bloody hands, glancing around for his baseball bat.

The truck motored forward. He lumbered alongside, beating the window. "You shit! I'll kill you when you come back. I'll be waiting up for you."

Laughing, Pax shot him the finger and hit the gas.

"Hey!" Bazz slapped him on the shoulder and Jiggs blinked, squinting through the gray light. "Don't worry about Jarmin. I'm guessing he's learned his lesson. I'd better get some warning cones out of the shop."

Jiggs continued to stare down the road, though the truck was gone. Guilt shackled a millstone onto his shoulders. Maybe it was because of the prank. Maybe it was about Pax. Either way—the less to do with Jarmin, the better.

Sheriff Sol Meyers conducted an investigation in the following weeks. No tickets were written. He informed Dr. Jarmin that because he'd left an unattended vehicle in the middle of the street, with the door open, he'd best repair his own pickup. Besides, Mr. Tower didn't have insurance. He didn't even have a driver's license. The sheriff confiscated the old man's keys as an official gesture.

A month later, a big-shot from the State Highway Department drove all the way from Salem in response to a formal complaint.

"That little pimple?" Jiggs pointed to the snaky hump. "Without it, Main Street would be a drag strip. It's nothing. We've got potholes and road ripples so big we use 'em for landmarks. Why don't you fix the washboard roads to my house instead of harassing us taxpayers who are improving our community?"

The state man gave the rancher an impatient stare. "That sounds like a county problem to me." He ripped a pink sheet from his clipboard and thrust it at Jiggs and Bazz. "You'll be receiving a bill for removing the bump and patching the hole you made when you pulled the stake."

*

"Hey!" Bazz called when the rancher wandered into the Bar and Grill a week later. He had the bowels of a small electric motor scattered across the table. Eighty-some-year-old Cliva Spinrad sat across from him, beaming and watching him resurrect her black, antique fan.

Junior shot eye-darts as he carried clean mugs from the kitchen. "You've got a shop down the street, Dad. People eat at that table, you know."

Everyone ignored him, including Jiggs, who took off his hat. "Evening, Miz Cliva. May I join you?"

"If you take some zucchini."

"Sure. Finding homes for your vegetables seems to be your constant mission." She shrugged as he sat down. "You think you've got your money's worth outta that fan yet?"

"It was my mother's." She nodded. "It's still good, but it makes a noise."

"Speaking of noise ..." Bazz glanced up as he seated a bushing. "Your friend, Dr. Dick, came by yesterday. He left something. Wanted folks to know he could take a joke." Bazz nodded toward the bar.

The German shepherd, missing after the wreck, now sat among the liquor bottles on a shelf. Its body tilted like a drunk about to hit the counter. Adhesive Batman bandages formed an "X" over the empty eye socket. The head was duct-taped onto the neck, crooked, as though the dog had been badly exorcised. Grotesque black stitches jagged across its concave belly where sawdust stuffing should have been. The heart-shaped sticker on his saggy chest proclaimed, I GAVE BLOOD TODAY.

Jiggs flared a nostril. "I can't stand that guy. Somebody needs to get him out of this town."

5

The History You Don't Know Yet

GROW UP. THEN LEAVE.

It's the main ambition of a kid. Especially a Two Pan kid. After all, it's difficult to mine rich dreams from a hard-scrabble town.

As adults, they'll fondly remember the summers of their youth and endless trails in the Eagle Caps. They'll wow their friends, bragging of formative opportunities like panning for gold, stealing moonshine, rolling tokes, and driving at the age of twelve.

Without a thought for their abandoned kingdom, they'll take their hard-earned experience—from hijinks that would've put them in juvie anywhere else—and they'll move somewhere else.

Anyplace with decent cell phone service. And jobs. Malls. Movie theaters. A city where they can start over. A place where neighbors can't recite the history of their crazy uncle who sold bears. Or being chased out of a privy by wasps. Or their great idea that set a house on fire.

Staying in Two Pan after graduation is not for the fragile. So when someone like Nap Woolsey or Josie Blevins returns, the community treats them special. They fawn over them like new, young members who've joined a dying church.

It is indeed the return of the native.

———

"University almos' ruined that Woolsey kid." Guntis Kral sat on the bench outside Grubb's Mercantile, talking with ranch woman, Belle Chere. The old German's wife stood next to him, shifting her grocery sack from her left arm to her right as they watched Jiggs' son walk toward the store. Nap Woolsey had topped out at six foot, a bit taller than his father, but he had the same ambling gait. "You should hear him talk. Buncha computer ideas about cows. Surprised he isn't in some dairy state."

Seventy-year-old Belle, in her cowboy hat with the coon tail trailing down the back, squinted at the boy. "Wonder if he's for hire? I need some 'bob-wire' strung. Hard work ties 'em to the land."

"*Oh bruder.*" Mrs. Kral rolled her eyes and jerked her bag of groceries to wedge them higher on her hip. "Getting kicked, squeezed, stomped, and stepped on, doctorin' cows for screw worms isn't any kid's idea of paradise."

Guntis stuck out his hand as Nap drew near. "Son, when you comin' for dinner?"

"Whenever you get the table loaded, Mr. Kral." He shook hands, then extended a palm to Belle Chere but had to maneuver around Mrs. Kral, who'd slipped an arm around him, giving him a sideways hug.

"I'll make you one of my famous peach cobblers," Mrs. Kral said, pushing him back to look at his grown-up height.

"Lemme get those groceries for you, ma'am." Nap took the sack. She grabbed his elbow and ushered him toward the truck, jabbering non-stop.

"Young pup has more patience than Jiggs did at that age." Guntis Kral rose slowly, unkinking his frame. "But then, he didn't grow up with an S.O.B like Ox Woolsey for a dad."

The welcome wagon was less obvious for Josie Blevins. She was forty when she returned. She'd only spent summers in Two Pan, but folks knew the hard truth of her history and the stock she came from. Her grandparents, the Roggs, were infected with bone-weary poverty.

She'd moved away and was working in a Portland high school when her grandmother and grandfather died shortly after Easter last year—as though they were in a hurry to get to heaven and see if Jesus really had risen from the dead.

Months later a white legal envelope arrived at Josie's apartment along with bills and the annoying perfume samples falling from the Macy's ad. It contained a deed and a letter from Stilson, Beltos, and Riley. In formal legalese, the attorneys indicated her mother, who lived in Florida and had inherited the estate, no longer wanted the old house and land. It was now Josie's. Within twenty-four hours she'd secured a teaching job in a community that struggled to maintain its census numbers.

"There are huge rats up here," Nap shouted.

"You want a shotgun?" Jiggs yelled at the opening in the kitchen ceiling.

"I don't think that's a good idea." Josie frowned.

"He'll use a four ten." Jiggs winked. "Less damage that way."

Josie studied him. "I'm not sure when folks are joking around here." A furry carcass dropped out of the hole, landing between them.

"Your sense of humor will grow back." Jiggs stooped, then held up the stiff, dry corpse, its tail pinched between his fingers.

Josie dug through one of her moving boxes, her nose wrinkled. "They must've moved in when the old place sat empty. When I got here, it sounded like they were having bowling tournaments in the attic." She held open a black garbage bag. "I bought poison by the case and lobbed boxes up there like grenades. If any still survive, they've learned to be quiet."

"Check out this one," Nap yelled from above them. Another carcass flew out of the ceiling, a charred stump where the head should have been.

Jiggs yelled into blackness, "Did you find where he chewed through the wires?" He jumped back, dodging another stiff rodent falling to the floor.

"They're bare in several spots. Might as well replace it all," Nap called. "These wires must've been strung about the same time Two Pan got telegraph service." His head stuck out of the ceiling opening, a hiker's headlamp banded around brown hair bleached golden by too many days in the sun without a hat. "And you should see these walls. Looks like a patchwork of scrap lumber."

"Just keep the rats comin', and figure how much wire we'll need," Jiggs said.

"I've got some gloves and a mask." Josie pawed through another cardboard box.

"Gotta baseball bat?" Nap asked.

"Here." Jiggs pitched a broom in the air. Nap caught it and disappeared. A dusty, cracked, bent-toed boot dropped from the hole.

Josie watched it bounce down the ladder rungs. "Granddad pieced this house together with whatever free lumber he could find. He had more time than money. Mom hated it here. That's why she's in Florida."

Jiggs had moved a few feet away to the entry to the dining room. He studied it a moment, then hefted a newly-purchased door into the opening. "That why she gutted this place?" With a sideways nod, he signaled Josie to balance the door in place so he could tap the pins into the hinges.

"We don't talk much. I'm guessing it was about money. There were titanic fights about spending anything in this family." She added a sad laugh. "Grandma patched socks' heels and toes until the only original fabric was in the arch. Even when they became too threadbare to hold stitches, she didn't throw them away. They went into her clamp-mop with the other rags. One time Grandpa noticed and roared, 'What the hell are my good socks doing in there?'

"He tried to jack open the jaws of the catch saying, 'Listen, Lady Astor, don't go throwin' somethin' away 'cause it gets a little used.' When he yanked on those nasty socks, cloth strips flew out like a fabric fireworks show. Grandma stormed off. It was their routine about money. The culmination of being together five decades and having said everything that needed saying."

"Your granddad's ability to squeeze a nickel was well known." Jiggs tested the door, swinging it open. A couple of mouse carcasses dropped through the opening, smacking the garbage bag below.

"All my life, Mom told me how my grandparents had consigned her to social damnation. She wore feed sack dresses, and her donated clothes were recognized at school by the previous owners. I think she turned antique vultures on this house so she could get back at her folks. I couldn't believe it when I saw this place. Anything old was gone—even the door moldings."

Jiggs fit a knob onto the door. "Funny how some people want to keep memories. Others wanna wipe it clean and make something new. I couldn't talk to my dad about touchy subjects, unless I wanted a few loose teeth." He tightened the screws and tested the knob. "Parents have a way of gouging deep ruts through lives."

Nap yelled. Banging and cursing echoed above them accompanied by footsteps pounding through the back of the house.

"He's found a live one," Jiggs said.

The silence seemed loud after the stomping and swearing stopped. "Is he okay?" Josie whispered, staring upward.

Jiggs cocked one eyebrow. "If he was taken down by a rat, he needs to reevaluate his life."

After a minute, Nap appeared at the opening. "I think I got 'em all." He tilted his broom and a smashed carcass dropped into the garbage sack. "And there's a tiny room back there. A board covers the crawl hole. That's where I found the rat—and this stuff."

He handed a white metal cake tin down to Josie. "You'll have to help me carry the suitcase. The handle's been gnawed off," he said to his dad.

"You like your sink?" Nap worked up a white soapy lather, holding his palms under the old hand pump that stood beside two dinged graniteware sinks.

"I remember it was a big deal when they replumbed for an indoor toilet. Grandma insisted on keeping the pump." Josie ran her fingers down the handle, stopping where a patch of paint was rubbed off. Polished iron the width of a woman's hand showed through. "I don't know why it's still here. You'd think if people bought rusty bird houses and glass doorknobs, this would've been gone."

Nap grinned at his dad.

Jiggs jabbed an elbow in his son's ribs, warning him with a hawk-eye glance as he moved him aside. He gave the handle several pumps. The metal rods moved down and up in whispers. Clear water gushed from the curved spigot.

Josie gave them a puzzled look, but both men were silent. She wrapped her fingers around the worn spot. "I like hanging onto a simpler time. I can keep their memories alive." She looked up. Nap and Jiggs were drying their hands and watching her.

"You say you need roof work, too?" Jiggs quickly tossed his wadded towel on the counter.

"I hired someone. I don't want to ask for favors."

"Folks don't know you yet. When they do, you won't have to ask. They'll offer. Nap and I can look at it."

"No. You've done more than enough."

"We don't mind, but if your roof man is here in the daylight, see if he can find that outer rat hole." Jiggs moved toward the door. "No use laying wire till it's plugged."

"Now, I'm going to pay you for this job."

"No. You're not," Jiggs said.

"Nap? I know every young man needs spending money."

His blond hair fell into his eyes as he shook his head. "That's just The Way, ma'am."

"What way?"

"The way things are done here," Jiggs said. "Always leave a gate how you found it. Never ask a man the size of his herd. A handshake seals a deal."

Nap picked up the litany. "Never criticize a man's horse, dog, or wife."

"And always help a neighbor in need." Jiggs pointed at Josie.

"Is that written down anywhere?"

"It's only country courtesy." Jiggs smiled. "It'll all come back to you."

"Then how about I cook you dinner on Sunday? Do you like fried chicken?"

"Never complain, no matter how hungry, hurt, or thirsty you are," Nap quoted, then added, "And I really like cheesy mashed potatoes."

Jiggs pushed him through the door. "Don't invite yourself or try to make things over."

"Don't ride out in front of the boss," Nap yelled from the yard.

"Wait." Josie fanned her hands. "Help me check ..." She pointed to the black metal suitcase and cake tin on the table.

"Sorry ..." Jiggs stared at them, giving a small headshake. "I believe that should be between you and your grandparents. Never pester someone for personal details." With a nod, he stepped through the door.

Josie sat in her dark kitchen. On the table in front of her, a gooseneck lamp puddled a lone spot of light on the old cake tin. With caution, she pried off the lid. A handmade wooden box nested inside. A whiff of cedar arose when she opened it, revealing a bundle of letters bound with red ribbon. Beneath them, black and white photos littered the bottom of the box.

Now in the late night hours, her grandparents seemed to rise from the pictures and live again. Buforl Roggs was seventeen, strutting in front of a camera in his cowboy hat. His loose scrawl read, "Miss you," on the back of the picture postcard with one cent postage. Zinnia Spinrad looked nervous in her long, dark dress with a big bow in her hair.

Josie stared. Who *were* these people? Younger, fuller in face, with their arms around each other? She'd never seen her grandparents touch each other or say an endearing word in all her life, yet here they stood, arm in arm, smiling into the camera.

Short notes told her that Granddad had gone to Washington state to work on the railroad. Grandma wrote there was a dance the weekend he planned to come home.

They danced? They hardly spoke cordially to each other. Josie flipped back through the papers. It *was* her grandparents. They'd once cared for each other.

Her mother appeared in pictures as a toddler, sitting on the wooden porch, hugging a black and white dog. In another, a traveling photographer must have come by during haying season. Her grandfather held the reins of two Belgian draft horses. Her mother—who looked six years old—and grandmother stood on top of the tall, loose hay, their rakes at attention. Exhaustion and grimaces creased their faces. Now this was the family she knew. Tired. Unhappy. Poor.

A smile touched Josie's face and a warmth welled inside of her as she looked at her grandmother's crimped-up handwriting. She had once held this stationary. Her granddad had gazed at the postcard of a blushing Zinnia Spinrad and read it over and over. At one time, they'd been in love.

How had they grown into two old people hurling insults at each other? The cards and the notes didn't document that part of their lives. Did hard work and a child drive the civility out of their marriage until they were two worn shoes, paired together because it was too tiring to break in new ones?

They once had nicknames for each other. Josie would have said it was a lie if she weren't looking at "Sweet Girl" and "My Boy" in their own handwriting.

Bewildered, she laid the photos aside, staring at the pocked metal suitcase. The two thumb latches made a loud *thwunk* as she sprang them.

In a slow, cautious motion, she lifted the lid. Crumpled sheets of yellowed newspaper, dated 1933, lay on top. Beneath them, canning jars sat swaddled in newsprint. She pulled out one of the blue-glass containers and peeled its newspaper wrapping away.

Green bills, rolled tight like cigarettes, stood crammed in tiers in the jar. Coins sardined between them. Seven quart jars were full. One had a few inches of empty headspace.

"I saw it coming." Her granddad had bragged to her about the Great Depression. Nobody'd listen to me, so I withdrew ever'thing but five dollars. The next week, they shut down the banks."

"What'd you do with your money?" she'd asked as a little girl.

"Stuck it under my mattress. Never trust a bank," he'd warned her with a wink.

He hadn't put it under his blue-and-white-striped ticking. She'd looked. Obviously, he'd never put it in the bank either.

She let go of the breath she hadn't realized she was holding. Her fingers touched the top of each jar, checking if they were real. How much was in here? How long had her grandparents been misering their dollars?

Who would've ever dreamed that the Roggs even had money? She glanced at their pictures. Why did they turn out as they did? The answers had died with them. Their quirky little habits—Grandma ate tomatoes with sugar on them, and Granddad poured his coffee into a saucer to cool it, then back into his cup—nested only in her thoughts. The death of memories was like rubbing words off a whiteboard. When Josie was gone, her grandparents would vanish forever.

———

In Two Pan, the dark hours of the night birthed the moments residents could see most clearly. Shocked and confused, Josie sat at her kitchen table and stared outside. There were no lights, no evidence of anything beyond her windows. She speculated that if time were a color, it would be black. A relentless eraser, mopping out secrets and lives. Without evidence to prove a person, a love, an endeavor once existed—it all faded away.

She sighed.

She had left these simple-thinking people to follow modern dreams. All that formal education and training—only to discover that Granddad and Harry Truman had been right: "The only thing new in this world is the history you don't know yet."

Josie pulled a blanket around her shoulders. What was left of the night ticked by as she came to know her grandparents—again.

An heir of Two Pan had returned.

6

Watching for Coyotes

EVERY TOWN HAS a "good kid" or a "real sweetheart." It's a local honor, although there are no epitaphs on Two Pan gravestones to prove this. Like most children, a candidate has been scolded, joshed, and nudged into adulthood by everyone in the county, but the exalted moniker is bestowed only on the rare youngster who shows saintly restraint and forgiveness with idiots, bullies, and blowhards.

This youth laughs when the high school football team sets his Toyota on cinderblocks while he's at his first prom, or when pranksters tie a dead coyote to her bumper so Sheriff Meyer will pull her over. They are the butt-end of most of the jokes around town, and have learned how to prank back—which magnetizes them for even more gags.

In Two Pan, the "good kid" is Chicken Thief Bob. His hoe-handle body is easy to poor-mouth. He's all bones wired together with muscle fiber. His brown, hound dog eyes take in everything, though he rarely passes the information along. He exudes a looseness in his posture, his smile, even his gawky walk—swinging one elongated foot forward, then the next, swaying like a sailor.

Most evenings, he arrives at the Two Pan Bar and Grill covered in white dust from his gravel-hauling job. Misty slides his Budweiser in front of him by the time he drops into a chair. She tries to do this for all the regulars, but she especially takes care of Chicken Thief Bob since he towed her car from Minam at two in the morning when she couldn't think of anyone else to call. He's a good kid, you see.

————

"Thanks." Chicken Thief grabbed his beer. "I see Junior is jerking with the Specials."

"He says it's too hot to stand in front of a vat of boiling oil, so the July special is chef's salad," Misty said.

Chicken Thief pointed to Bazz sitting across the table from him. "Then how'd *he* get chicken?"

"'Cause he fried it himself, and he doesn't give a damn what his son says." Misty threw a warning look at the mayor.

"I'll have the fried chicken, too. Make mine mashed potatoes instead of cheesy tater tots. And add extra white gravy. Please?"

She blew through pursed lips, lifting her bangs from her forehead and muttering as she left.

Without looking up, Bazz swaggled a cheese-tot in a puddle of ketchup. "You happen to know anyone who has cattle for sale?"

"No. No, I don't." Chicken Thief paused in mid-heft of his beer. "Oh, wait a minute; I did hear of somebody who wanted to sell his herd." He lifted a chin at Jiggs, who was tossing his hat on the duct-taped dog.

"Hey, Bazz." Jiggs reached down and scratched the head of Curious, the small, black and white pooch lounging under the mayor's chair. "How's the cattle market these days?"

Misty stared at the mayor as she set a frosty mug in front of Jiggs. "You're investing in beef now?" Several people at other tables snorted suppressed laughs.

"I'll have the fried chicken special. Thanks, Misty." Jiggs held up his beer and gave a nod.

The slender blonde shifted her weight to one foot and slapped her hand on her hip. "Tonight's special is chef's salad. *Chef's salad*. Got it?"

Jiggs' forehead wrinkled into furrows. "Tuesdays are fried chicken night. Always." Several people at other tables murmured in agreement.

"Would you like to speak to the owner?" She leaned forward, her voice heavy with threat.

"No. No. I don't want to start a ruckus. Lemme see a menu."

Bazz stopped eating, aiming a surprised stare at the rancher.

"And you." She tapped the mayor on the arm as she handed Jiggs a plastic menu. "What's up? Why're you being so quiet tonight?"

"Because I'm tired. I've been up since—"

"I'll have the fried chicken with a side salad." Jiggs smiled into the young server's best glare. "I ordered salad. I really don't even want the darn thing."

"I'll take it," Chicken Thief said.

"Fine. Then put some mashed potatoes on the plate for me." He held up the menu for Misty to take.

"I'll have that, too," yelled a woman at another table.

"Me, too," Zimm called out as he pushed his salad away.

In less than a minute, Misty trudged away with orders for six plates of fried chicken.

"Aw shit!" roared a voice in the kitchen. Junior, wearing a long black apron, burst through the swinging door and stood in the middle of the restaurant. "I know nothing changes around here." He glared at diners. "However, the special tonight is chef's salad. I repeat, chef's salad—not fried chicken."

"Oh. I didn't take the special, I ordered off the menu." Jiggs smiled. "Me, too" chorused from several tables.

"It's over a hundred degrees today. That fryer—"

"Yeah, that's why we came here," Tracy, the feed store lady said. "It's too hot to cook at home. We can take our business somewhere else if you want."

Junior's body sagged. He scanned the staring faces, then sighed and footslogged toward the kitchen. As he passed his dad, he growled, "You started this."

"And ... it's been that kind of day." Bazz tossed a chunk of chicken skin to his dog, who had moved a few feet away to a floor mirror.

"Well, it just got worse." Jiggs nodded toward the smooth-faced man in a blue shirt and gold-patterned tie, coming through the door.

Bazz waved Dr. Richard Jarmin toward their table, but the doctor shook his head. "That's all right. Just picking up my order." He strolled to the cash register at the bar.

"Suit yourself." Bazz nodded, then cranked his voice up loud so the whole bar could hear him. "It seems that *someone* put an ad in the paper with my phone number." He gave Chicken Thief a deadpan stare.

"You know ... I happened to see that and cut it out." Chicken Thief shifted to one cheek, snagging his wallet from his back pocket. A couple of chuckles slipped from surrounding tables. "Cattle for sale," he read. "One shy bull. Three heifers. Never bred."

Guffaws squawked around the room. Diners hollered across tables. "I called him before chores," "Me, too," "He's downright unsociable in the mornings," "Hung up on me."

"Call earlier tomorrow." Bazz waved away the insults. "I'm forwarding everything to Chicken Thief's number."

The young man shrugged. "I'm up that early anyway."

"Why's he called Chicken Thief?" Jarmin asked Misty as she set a glass of ice water in front of him.

"Because they're all idiots. You want anything else?" She stared him down.

"Good grief, Misty," Bazz called across the room. He went to the bar and unpinned a clipping from a cork bulletin board. "At least tell him about our famous citizens." She rolled her eyes and walked away.

Bazz filled a mug and carried it and the laminated newspaper clipping to his table. "It's ale. Real beer." He set the brew in front of the gravel hauler. "It'll make hair sprout from your ears." Chicken Thief took a sip and grimaced.

The mayor put on his half-lens reading glasses. "Chicken Thief Bob is a gold-member of the Bonehead Hall of Fame. According to the *Minam Monitor* ..."

"At 9 p.m. last Saturday, Highway Patrolman Steve Smith received an unusual call. Arriving at the intersection of Highways 82 and 3, he found an overturned poultry trailer and the wreckage of cars blocking the roadways.
Police reports indicate that the semi-trailer, owned by Oakburg Corporation, was hauling 4,000 chickens to slaughter."

Bazz looked up as Jarmin gave Misty a twenty and turned to leave. "Wait a minute, Doc. This reading is for you ..."

"It is unclear whether the semi or one of the cars was trying to change lanes. The ensuing collision tipped the chicken trailer as it slid through the intersection and into the cars waiting to cross.
No human injuries were sustained, but live and dead chickens were scattered across the highways, in ditches, and on cars. Various authorities rounded up the remaining 3,600

*live chickens stunned by the cold night air as they stood,
looking at the incident. Two Pan resident Bob Koosh—"*

Bazz swept his palm toward Chicken Thief, who was shaking his head.

*"—was stopped at the scene when police noticed his bulging
jacket. They discovered three chickens under it."*

Bazz took off his glasses and encouraged the diners. "Let's give it up for our own local kleptomaniac—Chicken Thief Bob."

Hoots and applause followed. Chair legs banged against the floor. Jarmin gave a nod and a busy-man's smile as he headed for the door, carrying two white bags.

Chicken Thief stood, holding his hands up to quiet the crowd as Junior slid his dinner onto the table. "Let me explain—" He had to start over several times to out-shout the jeers. "All I can say is, I was trying to calm those hens by covering their eyes, so they'd go to sleep. Those of you who know me know that I would never hurt an animal. I like chickens."

"What's that on your plate?" Jiggs asked.

A sheepish grin crossed Chicken Thief's face as he stared at the golden pile of breasts and thighs. "But I didn't hurt 'em," he said as he sat down.

Josie took the empty seat next to him. "I passed Jarmin at the door. Why'd he say, 'Welcome to the circus'? Did I miss something?"

"Nope," Misty grumbled and plunked a ceramic plate piled with chicken and mashed potatoes in front of Jiggs. "It's salad night. You *do* want chef's salad, *don't you*?"

The teacher threw a quizzical look around the table.

Chicken Thief whined to her, "I'm crimeless. They never brought charges." Beer slopped onto the table as he grabbed his brew. "It's all a buncha battlegab."

"So, is it fried chicken or salad?" Misty gave her an impatient stare.

Like a kid looking for help on a test, Josie scanned faces again. Several patrons were giving her a suspenseful look. Jiggs focused on his mashed potatoes. Bazz stared at the piece of tire nailed to the ceiling.

She frowned. "I'll have … uh … the … salad?"

Groans erupted from several tables. Misty shook her head and turned away. Before Josie could say anything, Chicken Thief banged his mug on the table. "You need to find something else for your public readings. I don't want people thinking I'm a thief."

"Nobody believes you'd steal anything." Jiggs' eyes riveted the young man. "Jarmin doesn't give a rat's tail. He couldn't wait to run out of here. And if we believed you were a thief, we'd take you behind the bar and beat the monkeys out of you."

"Hell!" Junior stuck his head through the doorway. "Who ordered the chef's salad?"

The bar fell silent. Chicken Thief pointed to the teacher. Josie's eyes popped wide. Her head hunched into her shoulders. "I didn't know … no one would tell me …" she apologized as Junior strode toward her. He grabbed her and planted a kiss on her lips. "You ordered tonight's special. So it's free." He pivoted and hurried back to the kitchen.

"Good Lord, your honor's been marred. Now you'll have to marry him." Bazz shook his head.

"Now I'll have to kill him." Jiggs had an easy smile in response to her wide eyes.

Chicken Thief stared at the kitchen doorway. "No wonder Jarmin wants to add class to this place."

"What—" Josie asked as Misty scooted a salad in front of her.

"We make our own entertainment here." Chicken Thief waved at the tables around him. "You notice nobody is on the phone? We didn't have much technology when you were a little girl visiting your grandparents. And we still don't. I'm sure you've discovered 'no service' is common in the shadow of the mountains. No movies. Very little TV." He filled her in about the fake ad, and the fried chicken rebellion. "We come up with our own dramas."

"You mean like that weird photo gallery in the vacant store?" she said.

"No, woman. That's art." He stared at her with a condescending frown. "Spooner Hunter, our local artist, got a grant to take a picture of every citizen of Two Pan. You're supposed to show up 'as you are.' He puts a copy in the window. He'll take pictures again in ten years. I had my photo snapped in my gravel-hauling clothes. I hope I'm not still wearing them by the next picture."

"Why aren't there more photos?"

"Folks are a little slow to catch on to art."

"Well, I think it's monkey-stupid. We all know what each other looks like," Jiggs said.

"Where do you get these words? Monkeys?" Bazz tossed another piece of chicken skin to Curious, who sat splay-legged in front of the mirror. "I can't wait for the day I see you mad enough to cuss."

"My mom said foul talk was for ignorant people who couldn't think of fitting words. The day my brother died, I swore off cussing." Jiggs wiped his mouth and laid his fork across his plate.

Unspoken questions floated in the pause that followed. Chicken Thief finally filled the gap. "Why didn't you teach all that to your son? I've heard Nap swear a snake out of a hole."

"That's what a liberal arts education will get you. That, and the opinion that I don't know how to grow calf-crops. It's all been modernized. Nap says he can run a ranch from a computer. *Pfft!* Kids." Jiggs grimaced and pushed his chair back.

Bazz pointed toward the kitchen. "I told him not to change fried-chicken Tuesdays, but what do I know? He's going to detonate when I tell him I booked a catering job for him."

"Who's having a party?" Chicken Thief asked.

"Dr. Richard Jarmin."

"Hey!" Chicken Thief leaned forward, dropping his chair onto all four legs. "I didn't want to say anything while he was here, but his realtor came sniffing around, trying to buy Hop Hopkins' place."

"Did he talk to Hop or his son?" Bazz asked.

"Hop wasn't tracking too good, so he tried to convince Frank." Chicken Thief wiped his fingers on a napkin. "Said that Jarmin wanted to bring in more elk and put cabins out there. In the fall, it'll be for hunters, and in the summer, he'll rent to tourists."

"He should call it Dickville," Jiggs grunted.

Bazz raised his hand like a publicist quietening an irate press. "Is Hop going to sell?"

"He's not even dead," Jiggs snarled. "What kind of sorry so-n-so tries to glom onto a deed as he pushes a man into a grave?"

Chicken Thief leaned forward and said in a conspiratorial whisper, "Hop wouldn't talk while the realtor was there. Frank was really pissed. He doesn't want the ranch. He'd like to have it all over and done with. It's a shame."

"Jeep 'n' eagles ..." Jiggs grumbled.

"You want to keep this town the way it is?" Bazz asked Jiggs. "Here's your chance. Go talk to Hop and other ranchers. Don't let an outsider buy up everything in the county."

"I'm not banging on doors. You're the politician. That's your job. I only want to live quiet and peaceful—in a town where I know my neighbors."

"Well, the twenty-first century does business a little faster than you did on the Chisholm Trail," Bazz said. "Some day after Hop passes, you local ranchers will meet for coffee and decide how to divide up the property and who's going to buy what. Why should Dr. Dick wait on you cow-relics?"

"Because it's the decent thing to do. That guy must've been raised by badgers."

Chicken Thief hefted his beer to concur. They sat in silence and stared at the other patrons.

Misty had served the last plates of fried chicken, and several tables were paying their tabs when Jiggs snapped off a question. "Why's Jarmin having a catered party?"

Looking at the tire-tread hanging from the ceiling, Bazz sighed. "If you'd ever come to a town council meeting you'd know."

Josie met the rancher's eyes. She shook her head. "I haven't had a clue since I walked in here."

"Your amigo, Dr. Dick, came to the Council the other night." Bazz tongued a tooth, choosing his next words before he spoke. "He wanted approval for a resort project. A small one. He says it would bring people to the area to spend money and create jobs. He'd like to infuse 'new blood, new ideas, and new enthusiasm into our structure.'"

Jiggs' hand mimed a puppet's mouth, his fingers tweezing open and closed. "Bull. Bull. And more bull." He added a disgusted look. "So what's this catered dinner about?"

"Well, we're studying his proposal for impact," Bazz said. "In the meantime, he's wining and dining a few folks. What bothers me is he's trying to buy land before we've approved anything."

"Sounds like a Trojan horse to me. He keeps sinking lower in the dung pile. He's about as sincere as the offers you got on your shy bull that doesn't exist."

"Some folks like his project. We need the jobs."

"Craphouse crickets. You can't be serious."

"Jarmin is out talking to people, trying to make this the place he thinks it can be. What're you doing to make this a 'quiet, peaceful' town?"

"I'm raising cattle."

Bazz slid his plate onto the dirty stack on the table. "Well, hating a guy isn't enough reason to vote against the project."

"*It is* in my book." Jiggs threw up his hands. The conversation stalled, everyone staring in different directions.

After a moment, Chicken Thief shook his head, studying the bubbles rising in his beer. "It's weird that Jarmin is trying to create a business doing what folks around here do for free— hunt. Any of us could take his customers and show 'em more game and a better time. I'm gonna enjoy watching him waste his money, trying to change this place. It's been here since God invented granite."

Jiggs gave an approving nod. "You know, Bob ... you're a good kid."

Awake at two in the morning, Jiggs waited for the phone call that wouldn't come. He wrestled with his pillow and kicked his sheets for a while. Defeated, he got up, slipped through the patio doors, and dropped into one of the yard chairs. From habit, he scanned the dark horizon. His neighbor's pole lights, miles away, were off and would snap on at five. Farther west, the sky lightened slightly with a faint glow coming from beyond the hill—the small town of Minam. According to the lights, all was as it should be. Resting his head back, he rocked in the lawn chair and gazed at the stars.

A coyote's howl repeated twice. Each time it started low, swooped to a higher pitch, and dropped again. A sirening call announcing change.

The coyotes had a different bark the night he'd ridden out to check on Elsie, his first show cow. He'd worked with her for months, washing and combing her, painting her hooves, teaching her to lead. At eleven years old, he'd won ribbons, but his pride bloomed in the future she represented. She was his starter herd. She was heavy and round with her first calf.

He'd heard the snarls before he'd seen anything. They'd attacked as Elsie had given birth. Hunks of flesh were missing along the calf's neck and spine. He was still warm, lying in his afterbirth, blood saturating the ground around him. The coyotes had ripped flesh from Elsie's legs and hindquarters, too. She lay panting, the tip of her tongue sticking out of her mouth, her eyes showing mostly white with fright, as though wondering what had happened.

Jiggs' stomach crawled up to his throat. He put his small hand on her neck and whispered, "Hey, girl." Grunting with pain, she flailed her feet, trying to rise. Her wounds pulsed blood.

He didn't remember getting on the horse, tearing across the pasture, but events seemed to slow and crystallize upon seeing the light in an outbuilding. He shouted between sobs and thwacked the loop of the reins against his horse. The shadowy figure of his dad was outlined on the roof, hammer upraised, pounding the corrugated tin. Pax, his fourteen-year-old brother, stood on the ground, handing up nails.

Ox Woolsey had climbed down the ladder by the time Jiggs slid off the still-moving horse and stumbled forward crying, "Dad! Coyotes chewed up Elsie and her calf. She's hurt bad."

The back of his father's hand caught him across the face. His bottom lip split. His tongue touched the raw line where his teeth had gouged pink flesh inside his mouth. A coppery taste seeped down the back of his throat. Elsie's bloody legs flashed behind his eyes as though he tasted her wounds too.

"You left her to suffer?" Ox Woolsey yelled, inches from his face.

"I came to get help," Jiggs cried, stepping back.

His father moved forward, towering over him. "Those coyotes went right back at her and the calf the second you left. Why didn't you stay? At least put her out of her pain before you came squealin' back here like you were the one hurt!"

Jiggs stared at the ground. "I didn't have a gun."

"A gun? A man can't take three steps without falling over granite. If you don't have that much of a brain to throw rocks at coyotes or to bang her between the eyes with one stone, then you can't be trusted with a gun. Here's a tool for you." He rammed the hammer he was still carrying against Jiggs' chest. "You left her to be mauled alive. Now go take care of what's left of your animals. You understand?"

"Yes, sir." Jiggs swallowed his sobs. With the back of his hand he wiped the snot from his nose.

"This isn't about you, so you can stop that blubbering right now. And this isn't the only cow in the world. It's an animal, and it's on your shoulders to keep her from sufferin'. Now get your ass back there, and do what you hav'ta do. Got it?"

Jiggs turned away. Years later, he would learn his dad had pointed at his older brother, drawing an invisible line to Jiggs and giving a nod.

But that night, he only knew that his brother caught up to him before he made it back to Elsie. It was Pax who brought a gun and put the cow and calf out of their misery. It was Pax who sat in the pasture with him the rest of the night. His brother helped keep vigil, making sure the coyotes didn't return to devour the remains of his dreams.

The sound of the patio door sliding open behind him roused him from his thoughts.

"Whatcha doin', Dad?" Nap padded across the concrete and offered him a glass of milk.

"Just sitting." Jiggs took the tumbler, remembering the times in years past his son had rescued him with a glass of milk. "Why're you up?"

Nap plopped in a chair, his leg hanging over the side, "'Yotes," he said, even though there wasn't a howl throughout the countryside.

"Yep. Me too." Jiggs took a swig of milk.

The night dew cooled the air. Rose petals dropped onto the patio as a wandering breeze carried the scent of dry grass. Miles to the east, a dog barked, then fell silent. Three small shadowy forms waddled across the dead lawn.

"She only had two this year," Jiggs said softly as the skunks stopped and sniffed a spot in the grass.

"Yeah. I think she had 'em in the old barn since we tore down the shed."

"That should make it interesting when we start stacking hay."

"Yep."

They watched the three bushy tails work a circle around the maple tree. Snuffles accompanied the sound of long claws scratching dirt as they looked for grubs.

"Everything okay, Pop?"

"I believe ..." Jiggs expelled a deep breath like a man who'd been holding it for a long time, "we need to buy the Hopkins place right away."

———

Sometimes you won't see lights in Two Pan, but someone is awake. Father and son talk in the starlight. Skunks sniff and paw until they make a complete circuit around the tree. They head toward the smell of watered soil under the rose bushes. The mother stops. Her kits freeze behind her. The man-voice is too near. Her head dips up and down examining the air. She can smell wet dirt. And worms. She stares at the humans. So close. So dangerous.

She turns and patter-foots away, her brood right behind her. At the tree, she stops to look and smell again. The man-noise is a hushed drone, their human-stink carried away by the breeze. Another night will be safer. The trio waddles across the yard, leaving the sounds of the executive board of the Rocking W Ranch fading behind them.

7

Purple Sage

THERE'S ALWAYS SOMEONE who was there before all the others. Even before Old Man Tower moved to Two Pan, Hop Hopkins' family had anchored into the bedrock and watched dirt roads turn into asphalt. If you're fortunate enough to intersect Hop's life, you'll hear stories about chasing wolves, running errands for miners, and breaking horses for Teddy Roosevelt's cavalry.

He's quick to tell you that he wasn't the first one here. "Those early settlers were wild cob-rollers," Hop exclaims. "Icel Poley used to catch bears for a living." The old gent will guffaw, and you know you're missing a lifetime of myth and adventure that happened before you'd even heard of eastern Oregon.

In order to take in one of Hop's yarns, you have to get him to open up, and that means you're either working or hunting with him. If you're a strapping high school football player, the coach will tell you to take an underpaid, muscle-shaking summer job with Hop Hopkins. "Best conditioning program in the county," he swears. "A two hundred-pound linebacker is nothing after dead lifting hay bales, wrestling calves for branding, digging post holes in granite, and chasing stray stock through puckerbrush."

Everyone works, including Hop, until there's nothing left in a body to sweat out. Then he calls for a break. He'll gesture around him with a gloved hand. "I remember my pap and grandpap digging out the stumps and rocks to clear this land." He'll take a drink of the cool water he's dipped from the meadow spring. "It was back-breaking work, something you boys wouldn't know fart about."

The young hired hands are usually too tired to make any smart comebacks.

"Grandpap wanted to pull the stumps with the horses, but my dad insisted on blowin' em. It takes a good black powder man to blast a stump straight up. That wasn't Dad. I was just a little cub and Ma kept me in the cabin so I wouldn't get skewered. One day there was a *BOOM,* and a stump as big as a washtub crashed through the roof. That was the end of the blastin'." He'll give a nostalgic chortle then start working again. "Okay boys, let's break a sweat."

Dooley Monroe was one of those boys. He knows all the stories. The forty-five-year-old has hunted with Hop every season. He was with him the day Hop pointed to a distant road tracking up a mountain. "I remember when the mud was so deep mules couldn't light a wagon through that pass." The old cowboy's arm dropped with a jerk, then he fell from his saddle and lay paralyzed on the ground while his heart fibrillated. That was the last time Hop Hopkins sat a horse.

Widowed for years, he recovered alone in a nursing home for three months—that's all Medicare would allow. He wasn't the best of patients.

Because Dooley's antique business wasn't demanding, he offered to be the daytime caregiver in exchange for a small stipend. Hop's son, Frank, quit his engineering job in Seattle and took the evening watch.

Now, the former cowboy lays in a hospital bed installed in his living room and stares at his world view of the Two Pan Bar and Grill.

It is the closing of an era. Roles shift. The son takes care of the father. And the summer ranch hand tells stories to the man who was here before all the others.

———

Dooley and Jiggs talked quietly while the weathered patient made rasping noises in his sleep. The caregiver arose, tossed a few bundles of sagebrush into the wood stove, and stirred last night's coals. "Hop's always cold," he explained, "even in the middle of summer. Frank and I keep a few embers stoked to take the chill out of the room." He failed to mention that the tiny flames seemed to ward off an unexpressed rawness between the men.

Dooley glanced at the eighty-year-old skeleton harnessed with an oxygen hose in his nostrils. He rubbed the bony shoulder that poked a hill in the sheets; he liked to wake the old man gently. Dooley couldn't imagine being shaken out of dreams and having pills stuck in your gullet like they did at the hospital. They were always in a hurry because they had more pellets to push down the next patient. Then they'd leave the room while the patient was wondering where he was, or if it was just another dream.

The old man's rattling voice coughed and caught. "Dooley? I'm afraid I fell asleep on you there."

"S'allright, Hop. You got company."

"I enjoy sittin' by the fire. Smellin' the outdoors," the old cowboy said, his eyes still closed, working his mouth to wet his tongue.

"Here, Hop." Dooley stood next to the bed, holding a box of juice. He bent the straw to touch his patient's cracked lips. "Take a drink of this to get you goin'."

With the first sip, the faded blue eyes flashed open. "Say, ain't we fancy. Orange juice in camp." Fluid spilled from the corners of his mouth. Hop feebly wiped his chin with the edge of the sheet while Dooley pulled a towel from the bed table.

"Yep. Open up, Hop. Swaller one of these pills with the next mouthful." He slid a white tablet into the old man's partially open jaw. "Now take a drink."

"What's the pill for?" He gulped it down.

"Takes the piss and vinegar out of old coots."

"Damn. That's what keeps me goin'," Hop gasped.

"Well, they'll never get it all out of you." Dooley held up a small can of protein drink, shaking it in front of his friend. The clouded eyes stared past Dooley's shoulder.

"Who's there? Who're you?"

"It's Jiggs Woolsey, sir." He took a couple of steps toward the bed. "Remember, we hunted together, and you used to work me to death each summer when I wasn't sweating for my dad?"

Hop stared as though straining to make a connection between Jiggs' face and pictures stored in his brain.

"Ox Woolsey's son," Jiggs prompted. "You and dad always made me be your blood trailer when you wounded an animal."

A spark lit in the old cowboy's eyes. "You're gonna bury me."

Jiggs blinked, then collected himself. "You still want to be carried out to the old home place?"

Hop faded into reverie, staring at the camera-eye in his mind. Jiggs turned to Dooley. "He's slipped since the last time I was here. Has he started talking about dying now?"

Dooley nodded. "He comes and goes."

"Remember how we helped him tear down the rotted buildings on his grandpa's homestead to make it easier to hay? It's been at least twenty-some years. We cleared everything except a lilac bush his great-grandma brought to Oregon. Last summer he told me, 'If I die before you do, bury me next to this bush.' I can't believe he thought of that now."

"He seems to remember those times better than yesterday."

Jiggs held his straw hat with both hands, shifting from one foot to the other. "This is wrong. I've bothered him enough. He should be able to rest without doing business."

"No. Wait. It might give him relief. And he could get worse tomorrow. You never know." Dooley bent and rubbed the old man's shoulder. "Hop? Hop? Jiggs needs to talk to you."

The old man's eyes opened and focused past Jiggs, out the window. His jaw hinged and unhinged as though he were chewing his thoughts before spitting them out. "Damn donkey's here again. Get my gun," he rasped. Coughing spasms took over.

"I'll take care of this." Dooley already had his hand on the door. "Keep talking to him. Hermes always clears his mind."

Jiggs patted the old gent. "You don't believe those stories, do you, sir?" The old man hawk-eyed the refugee donkey that patrolled the town.

Its home base was the feed store, but the neddy freed himself from his corral to escort kids to school and deliver donuts for the Latte Da. Summer lawnmowing jobs required he be chained in the person's yard because he'd Houdini out of straps and ropes. Despite his former starvation by busthead owners and torment by a pack of mongrels, he was a gentle soul, except he'd kick a dog over a shed if it happened to cross his path.

Shortly after he came to Two Pan, an ailing citizen passed away. Folks recalled the donkey hanging around the front door. Then another person died while the neddy was grazing in her back yard. It sealed his reputation. He became the donkey of death. A four-legged grim reaper wearing a bell. He was dubbed Hermes, the conveyor of souls to the afterlife. He scared Hop into the present.

Through the window they watched Dooley grab Hermes's halter. The old man glared after them until the white-scarred legs of the donkey were out of sight.

"He's just an eating machine like your horse," Jiggs said.

"Maybe," Hop wheezed. "I'm not takin' chances."

"Hop," Jiggs didn't look up as Dooley came back in the door, "I'm sure sorry to bother you with this, but I'd like you to know whenever you're finished with your ranch, I'd like to take care of it. I'd consider it an honor if I could buy Shiny Creek."

The old man studied his face with the probing eye of a prospector.

"I ... I mean ..." Jiggs stuttered under the critical stare, "if nobody in your family ... if you don't have plans for it already."

The old man's jaw worked as he studied Jiggs. Finally, he gestured toward his caretaker. "Dooley would get to hunt on it whenever he wants?"

"Yes, sir."

"And Ennis ... he's ... a friend."

Jiggs arched an inquiring eyebrow at Dooley, who shrugged.

"He's a good man," Hop whispered. "He's kept an eye on the ranch for a long time. He'd need a place to stay when he's here. I couldn't kick him out."

"It'd be open to your friends." Jiggs nodded.

The old man held out a frail hand. "Your father was a man of his word. I know you are too." He swallowed and stiffened with pain. "You take care of my ranch." Years of calluses hung on the loose skin of his hand. Jiggs clasped the trembling fingers and remembered when he'd seen these fists lift eighty-pound bales of alfalfa overhead and throw them on a hay wagon.

Looking at Dooley, Jiggs added, "And if you want to split off a piece for this guy here or for your son to keep in the family—" Dooley was shaking his head with a mad-eyed stare.

"Frank doesn't want it," Hop said with surprising force. "Doesn't want to work that hard. Never had to ..." His words slowed and telegraphed his journey back into his mind.

"Hop?" Dooley squeezed the slack, bowed shoulder. "Hop? You okay?"

He gave a start, "Say, why're we sitting here rachet-jawin' instead of huntin'?" The broken-down cowboy's head bobbed as he replayed a scene in his mind. "The deer will be layin' down."

"Nope. You already got yours. Now it's time for your breakfast. Miz Lottie's chocolate-banana muffins—your favorite."

Hop opened his mouth like a baby bird. Dooley dropped a tiny, mushed piece onto the coated tongue and watched him try to swallow. "Here, wash it down."

The old man pulled his cheeks to his nose, "I hate that protein stuff."

"It'll give you energy to skin out that deer." He waggled the can. Over his shoulder, he whispered to Jiggs, "Sometimes eating something helps." Dooley slipped tiny spoonfuls of vitamin-loaded applesauce and sips of protein drink into Hop. "You need a little lip balm. You're getting pretty dry."

"I can do it! I'm not helpless!" Hop said, as Dooley suffered the shrunken man to fumble the tube from his fingers. The cylinder rolled off the sheets and under the bed. "Get me a big tin of udder salve instead. The ladies love that cow smell." Hop gave a chuckle that lapsed into coughs.

Dooley straightened sheets and moved half-full cups of food to a tray. "One more," he nodded at the pill he held between two fingers.

"Damn! I'm pretty sure I already took that one!" The morning's effort left him wheezing. Dooley stood by the bed, patting the old gent's shoulder, encouraging every gasp.

"Will he remember—?" Jiggs stopped, his forehead furrowed. When people had visited Katie in her final days and talked about her instead of *to* her, it made his heart constrict. He shouldn't be here, hurrying along Hop's death.

Slowly Hop's breathing came in regular pulls. Except for strained rasps, the room lay silent. Stepping close to the bed, Jiggs cupped a soft shoulder that was formerly muscle. "I'll talk to your son. No need to bother you more." Watery eyes studied him with a faraway strangeness.

"I know you." Hop nodded, then laid his head back on his pillow. From his closed eyes, a tear traced the line of wrinkles.

When the pattern of breathing slowed to regular breaths, Dooley rose with the tray. He pointed a finger and nodded toward the kitchen.

"Give the fire a poke," Hop mumbled as they left. "I love to smell the sage."

A dry rasp etched its way through the channel of the old man's throat. His son, Frank, taking over the night vigil, glanced up from his book and reached into a plastic bucket. He plucked one of the ice chips he'd made by beating a tray of cubes with a meat mallet, and dropped the frozen piece onto his father's tongue. The wrinkled lips closed and the sliver began its futile roll. The old man never awakened through his unconscious request for moisture. For relief.

Frank wished his father were dead. Guilt stabbed him for the notion. It must be two o'clock. During the night's thinnest hours, uncensored thoughts crashed through his mind like a home invasion. Silent what-if's. The nasally counsel of his cousin buzzed in his head, providing little comfort: "You're a chickenshit if you wish they were dead, and you're a chickenshit if you keep them alive to suffer. Seems you're just a chickenshit no matter what you do."

He studied his father's tight-skinned face. The nit-picking eyes and carping mouth were at rest, but he could still see the martinet in him. Maybe it was justice that he had a chickenshit for a son. The old man would probably agree.

In the last half hour, Frank hadn't turned a page in his book, *Geometric Dimensioning & Tolerancing*. It didn't matter that he could design bridges or dams. He didn't rodeo or football and for that, he would always be the weak link in his father's genetic chain. His most odious sin was that he didn't want the family ranch. "The land our family worked years to own and improve. It's a hellish shame." His father's condemnation chewed through the guilt, leaving his self-worth in shards.

The old man rasped as though they were both having the same dream. Frank slid another ice chip into the mouth that had screamed into his face as he left for university, "... backbreaking work. For what? You certainly don't appreciate what it took!"

Frank whispered to the sleeping form, "You didn't do it for Mom or me. This was all about you. I roped, branded, and bucked hay so I could earn enough to get out of the sticks and go to college." He groaned, resting his head back on top of the padded chair. Now he took on-line classes for his master's degree by day, studied and watched his father at night. Here he was—back in the sticks.

Frank put the heels of his hands in his eye sockets and rubbed. Two in the morning. Were good and evil waging war in people's dreams everywhere in the dark half of the world right now?

He crumpled a greasy hamburger wrapper and winged it toward the trash. It caromed off the wall and onto the floor. "Ah, well, I wasn't good in basketball either." Frank stood and stretched. "Not that you ever came to any of my games." He retrieved the garbage wad and dropped it into the thirty-gallon trashcan next to the door.

At the front windows, he paused, staring across the street. The signage lights were off at the Two Pan Bar and Grill. Misty had brought him the hamburger a couple of hours ago, just before they shut down. She or Lottie Lubach was always leaving food behind the screen door, tapping the window if it was something that needed to be eaten right away.

Tonight, Misty had brought Hop a milkshake. "I know he's not supposed to eat a lot of fatty food, but I thought a sip might not hurt. He loves them so." She handed over a bag. "There's a hamburger for you in there." She wouldn't come in. Just stood on the uneven stone steps, waiting for something else. He said "thanks," but that didn't seem to be what she wanted. She'd turned and left without a word.

The language of math and computer code he could comprehend, but women were illogical design functions. Why couldn't they say what they wanted instead of making everything a cryptic experience? And why did people bring Hop anything? The only gift his father had given him was a ready slam and a tongue scorching. How could so many people adore the man?

A rap sounded next to him on the window frame. Frank jumped and swore. Two black eyes stared through the screen, inches from him. A frizzy red beard covered the bottom half of a shadowed face. The short, stocky figure wore an old fedora pulled down to his eyebrows. He looked like a cloning accident between Indiana Jones and Gimli the dwarf.

An earthy chuckle drifted through the window and Frank, still wide-eyed, opened the door.

"A mite jumpy tonight?" Ennis O'Day offered a meaty hand as he strode inside.

"I didn't notice you coming up the steps." The young engineer made sure he gave a firm grip to the handshake.

"Sorry to frighten you, laddy. I stowed some bundles of sage by the garage." Ennis ducked his shaggy head toward the bed. "How's he doing?"

Frank closed the door and jammed his hands into his back pockets. "Good days and bad. He seems to spend more time inside his mind than here."

"Don't we all, son?" The squat man grabbed the chair Frank had been sitting in and pulled it to face the bedside. He leaned close, studying Hop's sunken eyes. "He's wasting away. I once saw your father beat a cougar with a tree limb when it jumped his dog. That cat was snarling and leaping just to get away, and he didn't even like that dog. Hard to believe this is the same man. What's the doc say?"

"That he's making a slow, steady slide into congestive heart failure. He'll need to have his lungs drained again, soon I think. But he won't stay at the hospital."

"I don't blame him. They just stall death in the most painful ways."

Hop's eyes fluttered open. He cleared a tickling cough from his throat. "I must be in hell," he mumbled.

"And it's good to see you, too, old friend."

Hop nodded toward his son. "Banty, start locking the door."

Frank was fourteen the last time his dad had referred to him as a puny rooster. He'd responded with a red-faced scream, saying the nickname needed to come to a "screechin' halt." For several weeks afterward, the old man only addressed him as, "Hey" and "You there." But the damage was already done in front of the summer workers. Frank lived his high school years known as "Banty."

The young engineer leaned against the doorframe and watched the Irishman settle in for a makeshift conversation. He'd watched since he was little, but he'd spied back then. Whenever he'd heard his dad talking softly in the middle of the night, he'd slip out of bed and sneak into the blackness of the kitchen, silently snaking his body between chair legs to hide under the table. From his secret lair, he gaped at Ennis O'Day sitting in the living room, bathed in lamplight.

He'd been petrified of the caveman. His red hair sprang out of his head like the Troll dolls the fourth grade girls brought to school. Bushy eyebrows and a wild beard covered the rest of his face. Only his nose and lips showed he had any non-hairy flesh to his bulk. Truly, this was the face of an axe murderer. It was also the eyes in Frank's nightmares.

Riding fence solo at thirteen years old, Frank had felt like a true mountain man. At twilight, he'd cooked a passable dinner and spread his bedroll to watch the heavens roll westward.

A flicker of movement caused him to look across the flames into an unnaturally hairy face and black eyes staring at him. He gave a yip and scrambled backward on his palms and heels, dragging part of his sleeping bag through the fire.

The way Frank remembered it, he had one short-lived moment of terror, and then the face vanished into the darkness. For the next five nights, he sensed those eyes on him. The deeper he rode into the mountains, the more the hairs on the back of his neck tingled. Whenever he took a leak, he expected the crazy vagrant to step from behind the tree he was wetting down and laugh like an avalanche rolling down the hillside. Though those eyes didn't reappear, Frank never stopped looking over his shoulder.

His father had said the burly man was just a friend who drifted. However, when he added, "No need to tell anyone he's here," Frank guessed the guy was avoiding the law and accused his dad of harboring a murderer. Hop hit him so hard, he saw stars. So Frank reasoned the human hairball was a deadbeat wanted by collection agencies, if not the courts.

When his father fell ill, the black-eyed man often corporealized and faded at their door. Always late at night with never a sound coming or going. He still made Frank jump.

On one visit after Hop had drifted to sleep, the room hushed into silence. Frank felt those eyes watching him again as he tugged a lock of his hair and wrestled with a vector calculus problem. Without moving his head, his eyes slid sideways to peer at Ennis.

"You've used a tree's worth of paper there, son. You got the problem licked?"

Frank closed his eyes and scrubbed his face. "No."

"What is it?"

"Materials bending." Too tired to explain shear strength and plastic strain, Frank pushed the text of mathematical hieroglyphs toward the shaggy bum.

Ennis put on a pair of metal-rimmed glasses. He stroked his beard as he read, and then with a sigh, he slid the book back. "I don't know what they're trying to teach you here."

Frank nodded, staring at the pink eraser rubbings that had collected in the spine of the text. Maybe the hairy coot would leave now so he could get back to studying.

"Here's how I'd solve the blasted problem."

Frank stared at the calloused, stubby fingers, uplifted and waiting to receive the pencil.

The scratch of graphite, sliding furiously over the paper, played counterpoint to Hop's wheezing. Then he handed over the paper, those piercing eyes watching the response.

The man was brilliant. He had devised a solution in less space than most mathematicians used to address an envelope.

"That's ... Who are you?" Frank asked.

The stout man shrugged. "A lost soul. Just trying to find my way back."

"Back to what?"

"Ah, now, see ... solving construction problems is easy compared to milling those questions."

After that, each time Ennis had appeared, Frank studied the hermit, logging facts that belied his camouflage. As a child, he'd been so wary of the vagabond's explosion of hair, he hadn't noticed that his clothes had a durable quality. Well-oiled hunting boots, thick canvas coat, lined flannel shirts. His bulky hands showed the rawness of constant abuse.

At one time in his life, he had to have been a scientist or a civil engineer; he knew too much about kinematics and materials bending. Frank never asked. He understood privacy. He would not jeopardize their fragile amity by asking personal questions. Whatever made the short man leave civilization was his business, but what kept him in the Eagle Caps, Frank suspected, was gold in one of the canyons.

The room had quieted. Hop's breathing had fallen into the murmur of restless sleep. "I've got some news for you," Frank announced. The stout Irishman simply raised his eyebrows in a question. "I was told Dad sold the ranch today."

The dark eyes blinked as he scratched his forehead, "I didn't even know he wanted to sell."

"Some doctor made me an offer a couple of weeks ago," Frank said. "Then Jiggs Woolsey, one of the local ranchers, dropped by today and proposed to buy the land and take care of it."

The thick-bodied man sat still. "What sort of fellow is he?"

"He's all right. Raised old school, but I don't think it all took. He's got a reputation for going off half-cocked. Knockin' heads together, then getting the facts. He said it was okay for you to stay whenever you like. If he'd refused, that would've been a deal breaker for Dad."

Ennis O'Day shook his head and fed the coughing patient an ice chip. "Is it a done deal?"

"I haven't seen any money or signed any papers."

"Good." The Irishman pegged Frank with a measured look. "You still don't want the home place?"

Frank shook his head. "This isn't the kind of work I want. This ranch made Dad a hard man and left Mom and me struggling for ourselves. I'm sick of it."

"Laddy, I can tell you for a fact that he was as much in love with your mom as any man could be." Ennis' quiet voice matched the silence of the house.

Frank shrugged. "All I can remember is *her* waiting on *him*. She'd sit on those front steps treading time for what seemed like all day when I was little. When I started helping Dad, he'd joke that we'd better get home or Mom would be so mosquito bit from sitting out that we wouldn't get supper."

Ennis leaned forward, fixing Frank with his eyes. "You were too young to know, but your dad moved off the ranch and bought this house in Two Pan because he felt bad about her being stuck miles from town with no friends and unable to drive. It liked to have killed him, but he moved off the land for her."

"Well, he was never *here*. Always at the ranch, so he couldn't have missed it too much." Frank stared at the papery skin of his father's face.

Ennis shrugged, resting his elbows on his knees, letting his brick-like hands hang limp. "But she had friends that could stop by and take her places. She could see you and all your school activities. Believe me, boy, I'm not saying your dad was perfect, but Hop loved your mother and you."

"He slept here. That was about the extent of his family involvement."

"Let me tell you something you'll learn if you ever have a kid. They don't come with technical manuals. You have a blubbering whelp you have to turn into a man, so you think back to when you were a tyke, and use that as a blueprint. Unfortunately, my dad was a mouthy little man who liked to use his fists when he was sober. Lucky for my brothers and me he was drunk most of the time. I knew I could never raise a kid. But your dad, he raised you like his dad raised him—to be the extension of his dream."

"I had other plans."

"So it seemed. I'm sure you can understand it was just like bending steel or breaking a horse. Your dad put a little compression here, tension there, so you'd mold to the place you were supposed to fit."

"I'm not a piece of metal."

"That's a woman's argument—" He held up a rough hand to stave off debate. "But you're right: you're not a tool. However, women will send their men out to dig ditches or punch a clock all day, but their children ... they swaddle in bubble wrap. They'll squawk and shelter their babies from being scared, hungry, bleeding, or anything that pushes a boy to become a man. It just won't happen if you leave a lad with his mother all the time. Hop pushed you."

"That's like planting a seedling then screaming at it every day to turn it into timber. A kid will grow into a man. You can't stop the biological process."

"So a father cheers when his son grows up, then he watches the young jack kick dirt all over his dreams."

"Having a big ranch is the ambition of people like my dad or Jiggs Woolsey." Frank's raised voice made Hop twitch in bed. "I design hydroelectric turbines. Isn't everyone entitled to his own dream?"

"Sure, son, sure." Ennis's voice was even quieter than before. "But you can't fault your designer for trying to mold you into the form he originally conceived for you."

"He could have paid attention to the resistance factor and altered his methods."

"You know, things don't always function according to the schematic. Kids have their own ideas. Life has an unkind way of hacking one's program. My old mom always said it was God's sense of humor."

"Dad didn't find it funny. He was critical of everything. He could have at least supported me in something I wanted to do."

"Sure, but it's not about you anymore, Frank. Let me explain this so you'll understand. You know that the strength of a component is based on the maximum load it can bear before it yields or falls apart. Hop is like iron. You have to apply a lot of stress before he reaches rupture. And when force is applied to metal, the layers of atoms move in relation to the other layers and you get ..."

"Slip." Frank finished the sentence, staring at the frail body Ennis pointed at.

The bearded man nodded. "Your father has slipped. He is past elastic strain. He will not return to his original dimensions. The stresses associated with the cyclic loading of life have finally caught up to him. He is experiencing material failure. He knows the ranch isn't your dream. Seems to me he's trying to make it right by closing it up and giving you what he could. You'll have money and won't have to worry about the land. He'll rest easier knowing someone will take care of it. Sounds like today, he sold his family's dreams—for you."

Frank blinked, his eyes turning glassy. "That'd be a first. Why would he do anything for me?"

"Regret. Love. We all do the best we can, and sometimes when we don't know what else to do, we push harder or go haywire ... or even ... give up—"

"Dad never let up." Frank shook his head.

Ennis talked over the young man's words as if he hadn't spoken. "Then there's the guilt. When we finally get a little distance from our situation, we can see that maybe we expected too much. Maybe we gave up too soon. Maybe a kid isn't a lost cause. But what's the right way? Only God knows, and He's tight-lipped, wanting you to find out for yourself."

The rhythmic hiss of the oxygen machine and Hop's wheezing accentuated the sudden silence. Frank sensed that Ennis had trod dangerously close to opening a door long shut. They stared at the feeble patient, each waiting for the other to cross the boundary with a word.

After a long minute Frank shifted, leaning his shoulder heavily against the wall as he blew a long breath between tight lips. The confessional moment passed. The doorway would remain closed. He waited until the air felt neutral again then said, "He never showed any regret or love."

"I've had a bit more time to wrestle a problem like this." Ennis stood to leave. "I've come to the conclusion that love takes many forms." He crossed to the door, pulled it open, and stepped into the darkness. "It makes a person sit on a step and wait for hours. She's probably sitting in heaven, waiting for him right now."

"That kind of love goes beyond forgiveness," Frank said.

Still using his steady, quiet voice, Ennis turned back. "I know an angry son who's sitting all night next to his dying father. Is that love or forgiveness?" He walked into the night, adding, "I'd give everything to have either."

"Why do you care?"

The voice trailed away as it moved into the shadows. "I'm trying to find peace before I hand in my Two Pan membership card."

The young engineer stepped through the doorway. The mysterious figure had melted into the night. Years ago, he'd tried to track Ennis after several of his late visits. Darting through backyards. Strangling himself on clotheslines. Cursing dogs that gave away his presence. Sometimes, he'd catch a glimpse of the man getting into his truck. It was parked in front of a different house each time.

Frank stood on the steps and breathed the foretelling scent of fall. He scanned the town to see who else was awake. His light was the only one on.

Lamp-glow spilled through his doorway. It caught the neon eyes of a cat out mousing. She slunk, belly low, behind thistle weeds, and lay flat, her tail twitching.

A cool breeze rustled the maple next to the house. Several leaves corkscrewed to the ground in front of the cat. She whipped her head at their soft landing.

Blocks away, an ignition cranked. A motor came to life. A smile crossed Frank's face with the familiarity of it all. The whiskered man had ghosted his family for twenty-odd years.

If men like his dad and Jiggs Woolsey were part of the settlers who had never left, and *he* was the son who had returned, then Ennis O'Day was the resident who had never existed.

Frank cast a final glance around town, then went back to his duty inside, leaving the cat to continue her hunt in darkness.

8

Geese Don't Change

JIGGS, ARMS CROSSED over his chest, leaned against his truck. In the dusky evening light he studied the vee of geese flying over Main Street. Centuries of instinct and the earth's mysterious magnet conspired to draw the birds to warmer climes, but at the moment, they honked complaints about finding a pond and settling for the night.

Swaths of red drowned in the darkening western sky. To Jiggs, fall arrived like a surprise visit from messy relatives. One day it was pleasant and the next, the breeze had a bite and yellow leaves matted the ground.

He checked his watch for the third time, his father's voice awakening in his head. *You'll learn, Tool.* As a kid, he'd spent hours checking his watch, waiting for Ox to unprop his leg from the bumper and quit talking to a neighbor. He bet he'd logged enough seat time to equal a year of his life.

Ox had answered his impatient complaints with, "Someday this might actually leak into the cracks in your skull: Most business is conducted in the parking lot. I just sold four heifers," or "I traded for a new pump."

He'd give his dad a teenage smirk. What could you expect from an old grouser who insisted on driving to each store to pay his bills with cash instead of writing a check and slapping a stamp on an envelope? The only time his dad used a phone was to talk to relatives or call in a fire. Progress was lost on these coots.

Now the world had moved on. At forty-six, he was one of the relics—paying bills with checks instead of online and *still* doing business in the parking lot.

The flock of birds diminished into the evening sky. He watched, feeling like one of the geese, bound to rituals he didn't understand while everything around him had changed.

"You waitin' for an invitation to come inside?" Chicken Thief sauntered toward him.

"Hey, Bob. I'm hanging around to talk to a man about a dog."

The gangly man stopped. He knew what Jiggs meant. There was no privacy at the Bar and Grill. He gave a single chin nod. "Well, it's steak night. Everybody will show up eventually." Chicken Thief ambled back toward the restaurant, pausing in front of a showroom-shiny, black Cadillac Escalade. "Hey ... I heard about this. Get a load of Dr. Dick's new pavement princess. I saw a website that had the perfect gifts for the man who has everything. I got him a couple of welcoming presents."

"You're more charitable than me," Jiggs said as he watched Chicken Thief retrieve something from his Toyota and affix it to the bumper of Dr. Dick's SUV.

A pickup honked as it sped by. Chicken Thief straightened quickly. Jiggs waved at the passing neighbor with a single cock of his hand.

The street was empty of people when a Ford F250 drove up. A stocky man with fleshy jowls and avocado-shaped ear lobes got out. Creech W. Walters ran a guide service over in Enterprise. It was supposed to be a front to let him write off the cost of hunting and fishing around the country, but his choice of the few goods he offered was so astute, he sold more than he intended. He was booked as a guide most weekends because his stories of trekking the wilds were more entertaining than the fishing or hunting.

In college he told people the "W" in his name stood for "Wildass," but now he said it stood for "Wilderness," and like Abe Lincoln, he had a different tale for each person who asked how he got it.

"Thanks for driving over," Jiggs spoke hurriedly as though he had a train to catch right after shaking hands.

Creech leaned against Jiggs' truck, measuring the rancher's face in the lone streetlight. "I recalled it was steak night when you phoned. Good excuse to talk face to face about your deal."

"Remember last spring, before Dad passed, you told me a doctor you'd guided elk hunting wanted to buy property?"

"I heard he bought the Jugenmeir place before you could get to it."

Jiggs' words slowed, weighted by thoughts of his missed opportunity. "Seems I'm playing by an outdated set of rules."

"Word is, he's after more land to set up a hunting resort."

"And I'm trying to keep him from getting it."

"How's that going?"

"Man oh man." Jiggs stared at the ground as though he'd find a starting place there. "Well ... I had a meeting with my banker."

"You need a drink? Like a Saint Bernard, I keep a few on hand."

Jiggs nodded. "What do you know about business plans?"

"They're mostly fabrications that look good on paper. Few of them work the way they're supposed to."

"You know how to make one?"

"Probably not one they'd accept, but I could lie and cobble something together. Why?" Creech pulled two Olys out of the cooler in the back of his truck. "This okay? I don't keep anything stronger." Jiggs nodded. Creech pointed to the vacant lot scattered with farm equipment for sale across the street. "Kinda private over there. I like the dirt and weeds better than the pavement."

Jiggs twisted off the cap as they sat down on a cultivator. "My dad banked at Minam National when Big McGinty owned it. I grew up with his son and dealt with him. I explained what I needed, signed a paper, and closed the deal with a handshake. That's how we've been doing business for the last twenty years. But now ... you'd think I was trying to buy the Sears Tower."

"Commerce has changed since you sold horses to the Union."

Jiggs stared at a star framed by dark clouds. Creech let the silence spin itself out before he spoke. "What're they asking for?"

The rancher shook his head, still studying the sky. "Little McGinty said this was a real estate loan. Completely different animal. They need a budget and a time line—when I'm buying and selling cattle and the cash flow for the next five years. I've gotta explain how I'm running a ranch *and* buying this land in addition to getting equipment and making improvements on the whole shebang. He called it, 'all my cash needs and assumptions—*on paper.*'"

"I suppose how nosy they are depends on how much money you're willing to put in up front and the actual value of the land. It's the Hopkins place, right? I hunted there with Hop years ago." Creech took a swig of his beer.

"Everybody's been to Shiny Creek Ranch. McGinty knows the property." Anger edged Jiggs' words. "Still, I have to pay some yahoo to determine water and feed supply and natural resources. He says I've gotta have a professional assessment and demonstrate I can repay the loan."

"That's what bankers are supposed to do—protect their money. Seems like some of them have named each dollar bill and want to board them in good homes."

"Little McGinty knows the place is valuable." Jiggs' voice rumbled in a deep-throated growl. "The little money changer eyeballed me and asked, 'Do you plan to run it differently from your present ranching operation?'"

Jiggs jumped off the cultivator like it had gone red hot. Beer sloshed out of his still full bottle. "It took me a minute of staring at him to get myself settled down. I thought if I punched him like I used to in high school, I'd never get the loan. He probably remembered Dad ranting how I was so brain-poor that I couldn't find myself in a mirror."

He gave a snort. "I told him I'd run it same as any other spread. I'm buying Shiny Creek to keep it from being developed into postage stamps. It was like talking to a cow. Nothing registered. The little bean counter kept going on about my business plan."

Creech leaned forward, resting his elbows on his knees. "Jiggs, there's one thing I understand about the financial system: banks rent money. It's that simple. That's all they're in business to do. Oh, they may give you sympathetic grins and advertise they want to create a better community, help po'folks own a home or give some schmuck a start, but in reality, they only care that you can repay their money. The bank doesn't care if it's a lifelong dream, an invention to save mankind, or running guns. All they're concerned about is whether you can pay them rent."

"You don't know the half of it. They want two sources of repayment: a primary cash flow from the operation and a secondary source if the first one doesn't pony up. That's when they repossess and sell it." Jiggs pushed his cowboy hat to one side with his thumb so he could scratch over his ear. "I don't get it. I've always paid them back on time—usually early. Yet

Little McGinty says a big real estate deal has to go through the loan committees of several other participating banks. All they know is what they see on paper."

Creech watched a truck with a drooping muffler rumble down the street. "Well, with so many banks in trouble, there're more regulations in place now. Paper reports are everything."

"See, that's the problem. These suits and ties sitting in offices have no connection to the land. If they'd spent hours pulling up hawkweed or lugging stones uphill to make rockjacks, they'd know the difference between a successful rancher and a gimcrack." Jiggs emphasized each point, stabbing the air with his beer bottle. "The land is as much a part of you as—"

"Jiggs, they don't care." Creech interrupted. "Their responsibility is to ensure the bank meets a set profit margin. They're supposed to be responsible to their shareholders, not you."

"All right. I'm a stockholder in that bank. I went to the annual meeting, a fancy catered affair at the Minam VFW. I don't remember saying how much money we had to make on every loan. Nobody promises me how much I net off every head of beef. I have to feed and sell them for what the market will bear. There're no guarantees, but they want me to assure them that they'll make a set profit?"

"Business has changed."

"Everything's changed. I never imagined this would be a gut buster. I thought I'd simply get a loan and save the land from being turned into a strip mall for elk hunters. This is too much aggravation. Let somebody else fight Jarmin."

"There are other lenders out there besides Minam National."

"You think they'd want any less assurance?"

"You know who I bet could help you?"

"Donald Trump?"

"Your son. Didn't you once tell me that Nap had to take some agri-business classes for his Animal Science degree?"

The silence was loud.

They watched several people come out of the bar, get in their cars, and drive away. Jiggs finally took a swig of his beer. "I'm 'shamed to say, I never even thought of that. Nap's got the whole herd set up with microchips. He scans a heifer's ear and can tell you her birth date, lineage, shots, and when she last had her nails done. 'Course, I store the same information up here." He tapped his temple.

"With this new property, I think you've outgrown your old records system. Besides, the next time you're kicked in the head, you'll get a 'File Not Found' message when you try to retrieve that data. It's time to change."

"Craphouse crickets," Jiggs sighed.

Down the street the black Escalade's engine started, though there was no driver. Lottie Lubach, who'd just gotten out of her car, cupped one hand beside her eyes and peered through the Cadillac's window. Her husband, Zimm, latched onto her arm and tugged her toward the restaurant. She batted his hand away.

Creech coughed a short laugh. "You hear that Lottie took down some no-good who was stealing the old Harley frame from the front of her coffee shop?"

"How? She doesn't weigh as much as a wet stick."

"Blinded him with a can of bug spray."

"What will it be next?" Jiggs was still shaking his head when Dr. Richard Jarmin exited the Bar and Grill with takeout containers. He glanced at the men as he got into his SUV. Creech lifted a hand. Jiggs glared. "There's a white-collar thug for you. It's not freezing or baking out here, so why would he auto-start his vehicle, unless he's robbing the place?"

"Because he can." Creech looked at the weeds growing around the cultivator. "He sent me a form letter about development in Two Pan. Talks a good game. He's got people thinking about it." As the Escalade drove away, Jiggs could see

Chicken Thief had slapped a sticker on his bumper: *Support your local lawyer. Make your son a doctor.*

"This was a better town when nobody knew we were here. You gotta stop guiding bozos into the backcountry," Jiggs said.

"They'll just keep coming. That's why you need to buy Hop's ranch."

"It all comes back to that, doesn't it?"

The men sat in silence. Dusk blanketing any further questions. Finally, Jiggs jerked his head toward the bar. "Buy you a steak? I can't stay real late. I guess Nap and I will be burning the midnight oil. Maybe all that money I spent on his education can net me a business plan."

"Sure." Creech arose, pulling in a lungful of cool air tinged with the scent of wood smoke. "Summer is turning. Smells like hunting season's coming."

"Yeah," Jiggs said, "everything's changing."

9

A Kink In the Community Rope

NAP WOOLSEY HAD created one business plan in his life. It was for an economics class, and he considered it a pencil exercise for people who wanted to open dog-washing parlors. He'd done just enough to get a "C" on his work.

With the same fervor as the class assignment, Nap devoted himself to the loan project. It took five days to dream up information for a semi-credible plan. Jiggs contributed by frequently warning, "Hurry up. Hop might die any minute. The probate could hold us up for months."

They bought a fancy folder—Nap swore you could improve any document by using laser printing and putting a serious-looking cover on it—and drove it to the Minam National Bank.

Little McGinty, short, round, and looking more like a walking sack of quarters each day, took their completed documents with a handshake, a vacant smile, and the well-oiled promise that he'd get back to them if he needed more information. As the squatty banker escorted them to the door, he casually dropped a smoking pile of manure onto their hopes.

"I had no idea that Shiny Creek was such a popular piece of property." Little McGinty's eyes were buggy as though he'd been zapped with a cattle prod. "Dr. Jarmin came in. He has a lot of financing ideas about it."

Jiggs' nostrils flared and white-rimmed. His breath caught. A fever-burning craze flashed in his eyes like a wild horse in a chute.

Nap may not have been good at business plans, but he was an excellent agri-manager. He herded his dad out the door before he went over the top rail.

"My father taught me a cheater can't argue if your fist is in his mouth." Jiggs massaged his knuckles. "Long ago I swore I wouldn't be like Dad, but I haven't had this much of an urge to belt someone in twenty-five years." He stared at a scene in his mind as Misty set celebratory beers on the table.

Bazz squinted in disbelief. "What're you talking about? You kicked a realtor's butt a couple of months ago. I'd say your Gitmo relaxation techniques aren't working."

"I didn't say I was successful," Jiggs snapped back, "but folks watch out for each other here. That changes when you get the likes of Dr. Dick, who won't put down roots and invest in the people."

Josie frowned at him. "He set Blake Anderson's nose after the last football game. I hear he didn't charge the family a cent."

"What's the matter with a crooked beak?" Jiggs tapped the bump on his nose. "It's a rite of passage." He fanned a dismissive wave. "To Jarmin, we're simply the folks who keep the gas station and restaurant open between his visits. Maybe a good drumming would change his mind about being here."

Bazz flicked the rim of his wine glass making it *ting*. "You touch him, and you'll get your ass handed to you by a lawyer and your ranch added to his collection. Be smart. Thoughts can't roll off your tongue like a gumball machine. You've got to be a rebel without getting caught. I learned it in grade school."

"Criminy! Now there's a skill to be proud of," Josie said.

Bazz leaned forward, his face in a serious stare. "In L.A., it was called staying alive. My fifth grade warden, Mrs. Gardner, didn't care whether you learned or not. She wanted you to sit up, regurgitate words, then shut up. It was all about obedience."

"We call that parochial catechism." Josie didn't look up from her menu.

Bazz shrugged. "I used to write captions for the pictures in my books. If Dick and Jane were looking at an injured bird, I'd write, 'Jane, you're so ugly that bird dropped dead just looking at you.' Penciling in cartoon bubbles kept me busy while the rest of the eraser lickers were sounding out two-syllable words."

"Sounds like you weren't challenged in class," Josie said.

"Oh, there were challenges. Epic battles with the teacher. Everything I know about corporate survival I learned from that old harridan. Either you became cleverer or she broke you. She liked to announce that my mom couldn't volunteer because she *had* to work. She didn't mind pointing out how the color of someone's skin held them back. Hell, she even hated westerns on TV because they drank whiskey."

Josie cast a skeptical eye at the mayor. "I think that's your passive-aggressive memory kicking in. Kids remember only the bad parts and forget that anything good ever happened during a school year."

Misty delivered another merlot to the mayor. Without interrupting the conversation, she took their dinner orders, pointing a pencil around the table. Each diner underlined a menu item with their finger.

"I'm not joking." Bazz wagged his head at the teacher. "The kids who got hot lunches got to line up first. The rest of us waifs had to root through the shelves of the coat closet for our sack lunches. One day, someone shut the door on me. I got left in there. Kids weren't allowed to stay in the classroom during lunch, but I thought, *What the heck? Why not?* I sat in the closet and ate my sandwich in the dark. It was only going to be an hour. Unfortunately, after thirty minutes, I needed the bathroom. Mrs. Gardner had us trained to go only at noon recess. If a kid asked to go any other time, the old battle-ax announced it to the class. She'd hold a discussion about rules and planning while the poor sap shifted from foot to foot. Scotty Wyskup was always peeing his pants."

"I can't believe—" Nap started.

"Hey. We couldn't wander all over school like kids do now. We didn't even get out of our seats to sharpen a pencil without asking permission. It would've been a near-death experience to leave the safety of that closet and get caught by a hall monitor. But I was desperate. So ... I did my business. Left a little pile in the corner of the closet."

Everyone stared at him. Then they groaned. Jiggs waved him away as he scooted back from the table.

Bazz held up both hands. "I'm telling you, at eleven years old, the terror of the old witch's wrath called for do-or-die actions." He nodded toward Nap—who was the only one still looking at him. "I covered it with old lunch sacks that were lying around. When the class returned, I made an inconspicuous exit. For the rest of the day I lived in a cold sweat."

"Who discovered it?" Nap asked.

"Strangely, it took a while." Bazz smiled. "Each day I breathed a little easier and worked on my innocence. Finally, some girl complained that the coat closet stunk. Mrs. Gardner dispatched all the poor kids saying, 'You brown-baggers go in there and clean up your spoiled, half-eaten sandwiches.' In a few minutes, two girls started shrieking. My face was a rock."

Bazz scooted his wineglass aside, and Misty set a hot platter of spaghetti in front of him.

"The teacher should've knocked you on the head as a general suspect. What did she do?" Josie asked.

Bazz rubbed a chunk of parmesan over a grater, dusting his noodles. "Went nuts. She kept howling that in all her years of teaching—which was probably about a hundred and twenty—nothing like that had ever happened. She interrogated every girl in that class, hoping to find a snitch."

"You ever get caught?" Nap asked through a mouth full of burger.

"No." Bazz glowed with the smile men reserve for the completion of a Herculean project. "Proof that God watches over babes and fools. She retired after that year."

"Like I said, passive-aggressive behavior," Josie said flatly.

"Bunch of hornswoggle is what I'd call it," Jiggs said.

"For those of you untrained in corporate survival," Bazz stopped winding noodles on his fork, "it's called passive resistance. Instead of reacting, you choose the time and place you'll *act*. Mrs. Gardener was as predictable as a knee jerk. She couldn't crack me because I wouldn't respond to her. And that's what you do with bosses, battle-axes, and the Richard Jarmins of this world." He stared at Jiggs. "They think they know how to push your buttons. You don't let them."

"You should have your own radio show." Jiggs threw him a sideways smirk. "People could call in and learn how to lie, cheat, and other crap from the master."

Tearing a hunk from his Texas toast, Bazz swabbed the spaghetti sauce on his plate. "I'm saying that in my day, kids were more creative about pulling stunts. They didn't spray paint their names on road signs." He raised an eyebrow at Nap. The young man shrugged and waggled his head with an I-was-young-and-stupid expression.

"I can't believe any teacher could get away with her attitude." Josie jabbed her fork into her potato salad.

"This was the fifties, darlin'. It was an old school for blue-collar kids and teachers ready to retire. The protocol was to cauterize bad behavior with public abasement, and if that didn't work, then the principal got to wallop students with a big board drilled with holes."

"Hey, yeah." Jiggs smiled. "We kept a running tally of our licks on the wall in the boys' locker room. Sol Meyers and I were tied until our big fight on the last day of school."

"Sheriff Meyers?" Nap asked. "You fought Sheriff Meyers? He's a head taller and has fifty pounds on you."

Jiggs nodded. "I'd given your mom a promise ring. Sol tried to convince her she was making a mistake."

"He was sweet on Mom?" Nap's eyes widened.

"Now there's an example of no reaction, like you say." Jiggs pointed his fork at the mayor. "I let him win the contest for most licks. I figured it was consolation for his heartbreak. We knocked each other down, then helped each other up a few times. He got five licks for starting the ruckus. I got four for going along with it, but I should've thumped him a couple more times. I didn't mean to let him set the school record."

Nap fell back in his chair. "In high school, he was always rousting us for ... well, things you didn't know about. I thought the guy was a Boy Scout."

Jiggs gave his son a measured look. "You think we were born this old? Believe it or not, we sowed wild oats. Still do. And by the way ..." he pointed, "I knew about your antics. Sol told me."

"I hate this town." Nap's face twisted with disgust. "Everybody finds out everything." He pushed his plate aside and started in on his dad's fries. "What about you, Miss Blevins? Got any closet skeletons you can talk about?"

She shook her head. "I'm the outsider. You all tell me things about my life that I didn't know. I had no idea I'd been driving Granddad's truck around with his pistol under the seat." The men nodded as though she'd said she had a battery under the hood. "And I wasn't aware that I had a post office box. The postmistress gave me my grandparents' box. She said she has a sorting routine and didn't want to change it."

"And Miz Cliva saved your grandmother's sink for you," Nap said. Jiggs dropped his fork and rolled his eyes as he looked away. "She didn't know yet? Somebody actually kept a secret in this town?"

"Not anymore," Bazz said.

"Miz Cliva wanted it to be an anonymous gift—she's the town's secret keeper." Jiggs shot his son a quick glare, then turned to Josie. "She was your grandmother's closest friend. It made her fitful to see strangers carrying off your grandparents' things at the auction. She bought the sink and pump. Chicken Thief stayed all night until we could get padlocks on the doors."

"I wondered how it had survived ..." Her voice faded.

"We twist you into the community rope—whether you like it or not. But sometimes ... a piece of the rope is kinked and needs to be cut out." Jiggs' gaze focused on the door.

Dr. Richard Jarmin stood at the entrance. His magazine-handsomeness caused a few stares. Thirty-eight years old, he'd enhanced the good looks he was born with through surgery and chemical peels.

His father had encouraged him to join the family practice of reconstructive medicine. "We can clean up on these baby boomers," he'd said. When Oregon offered stipends to physicians who located in sparsely populated areas, it was a watershed opportunity to open a satellite office, next to a new regional hospital. It also allowed him to write off the expense of a vacation home in the next valley.

"Mr. Mayor." Dr. Jarmin strolled toward the group. "Could I talk to you sometime about a problem I'm having here in town?" Nap and Josie exchanged glances.

"Now's as good a time as any," Jiggs answered for Bazz as he pushed the chair beside him out a few inches with his foot. "Then when you're done, you and I can talk."

"Dad ..." Nap laid a hand on his father's arm.

Jiggs gave his son a flat stare. "The doctor's welcome to join the discussion." He turned an amused look toward the plastic surgeon. "This is my son, Nap. And this is Two Pan's newest educator, Josie Blevins. We were conferring about problems that won't go away."

"Sounds perfect." Dr. Jarmin relocated the chair a couple of feet farther from Jiggs' personal space and sat down. He flashed a smile toward Josie and introduced himself, and then he extended a hand to Nap. The young man gave him a meaty handshake and a warning look.

Jarmin stretched his legs in front of him, crossing them at the ankle. He kept his hands in his lap as he threw a question into the air. "Is there a wine list?"

Misty pushed a laminated sheet under his straight nose and triangular chin. "Your order's almost ready."

"Seems we're seeing a lot of you lately." Jiggs wiped his mouth and tossed the napkin on his plate.

The doctor gave the waitress a brilliant smile. "I'll have a glass of pinot gris. My wife has a number of functions that she's chairing in Portland right now. I'm baching it for a bit and eating out." He turned his attention toward Bazz. "And each time I stop in Two Pan, I gain another bumper sticker."

"You braggin' or complainin'?" Jiggs asked.

"Well, because my bumper is covered, and they've started sticking them on the back, I'm lodging a complaint."

"That just shows you're being welcomed into the community," Bazz said.

"Really?" Jarmin said flatly. "The last one said, 'Too many folks are itching for something they don't want to scratch for.' Miss Blevins, you're new here, too. Are you getting stickers on your vehicle?"

"I ... uh ..." She glanced around. Folks gave her suspenseful looks. "You know ... one time I ordered a salad and got kissed. I don't have a clue how anything works around here."

Laughter came from surrounding tables. Dr. Jarmin sipped his wine, waiting for it to recede. "Is there a way to stop it? I don't notice a similar problem on other vehicles. I'll be glad to donate to any good cause which might keep stickers off my vehicle."

"We do things different around here," Jiggs' voice cut across the table. The chatter in the bar dropped to a few mumbles. "For instance," he turned his chair so he sat square-shouldered, facing the doctor. "Whenever you have an old dead snag and it falls on your neighbor's fence, you fix the fence like he had it—or better. And you help him round up the animals that got loose."

Jarmin cocked his head. He returned Jiggs' stare with a laconic smile. "I work in our Portland office part of the time and part here. I apologize I wasn't aware there was a problem until you left a message. You shouldn't have any more concerns. My fence man assures me I now have the best barrier that money can buy between our properties. A four wire, high tensile, New Zealand, electric fence."

"For horses." Jiggs gave him a dark stare. "I've got cattle."

"Those mares are my wife's pride and joy. I'd think you of all people understand why I can't have them rubbing against barbed wire."

Jiggs leaned toward the doctor, his eyes smoldering. "You realize—"

"Hey, Nap, did I tell you—" Bazz's raised voice cut through Jiggs' words, "—how my fifth-grade teacher was *predictable*?"

"Yeah," Nap said. "With some people, you know what they're gonna do before *they* even know." Faces turned, staring at the two.

"Sorry," the mayor shrugged, "just continuing our earlier conversation since we're not a part of yours."

Jiggs gave them a tight-lipped smile, then turned back to the doctor. "Dick, did—"

"It's Richard. I don't go by Dick."

Jiggs tapped the table with a moment's thought. "All right. Did the clodpoll who built your fence mention my bull could walk right through those wires? And when your power shuts down, my herd will be scattered over the next county and back."

"Won't happen." Jarmin took a drink of his wine. "The fence will always be electrified." Snorts of laughter erupted from surrounding tables. The physician looked around. Diners grinned at him; some shook their heads. "I've been assured the power is reliable. There's even a backup system."

"Yeah," a man rasped in a false-hushed voice, "when the car battery goes dead, maybe the copper-top bunny will help out."

"Sorry, but your man didn't tell you much about electric fences." Jiggs picked up his beer. "No matter. I've already taken care of the problem."

"Yes, I was told you were constructing a barbwire fence on your side."

"You were *told*?" Jiggs moved to the edge of his seat, squinting at the man. "Don't you ever walk your own property?"

"Fifth grade sucked for me, too," Nap spoke overly loud, staring at Bazz. "I knew exactly what the teacher was going to say. It made me want to leave school, you know?"

"I know." Bazz nodded solemnly. Jiggs' eyebrows knotted together. The doctor wore a quiet smile.

Tension bobbed around the table for a few moments until Jiggs took a swig of his beer and shifted in his chair. "You know, Doc, before moving the fence over a foot, I would've appreciated it if we could've talked about it." There were grumbles from the surrounding tables.

The doctor turned and stared as though they were disruptive medical students. When they'd quieted, he turned back. "I suppose that should have been done. I simply instructed the company to survey the property and set the fence." He drained his wineglass. "I apologize. When I was informed, I didn't think a few inches of prairie grass would be that important to a successful rancher such as yourself."

Nap pushed his chair back, making signs to leave, but Jiggs stilled him with a look. "Well, Doc, you'd probably consult with a client if you were resetting his nose and it came out a little bit to the left, or if one eye was going to end up higher than the other. Folks like to know when you're changing the things that are a part of them."

The physician cleared his throat. "Personal appearance is a bit different, but I see the point you're trying to make. I agree that change can be difficult. So how do we change the situation so your barbed wire doesn't cut my horses?"

"No problem." Jiggs dismissed the idea with a single head-shake. "As long as your electric fence works, those ponies will never reach a prong."

"I see." The doctor arose, throwing a dark-eyed glance at the chuckles coming from the next table. "Excuse me," he called to Misty, who was behind the bar. "Is my order ready yet?"

"Whenever you are." She slung dishwater from her hands and held up a white sack.

He walked toward her, pulling a couple of bills from his money clip. As he looked up, his expression changed to dumbstruck. "You *kept* it?"

"Yep." Misty lifted the stuffed German shepherd—wearing Jiggs' hat—from the bottles behind the bar and thudded it in front of her. Sawdust sifted onto the counter.

The dog was exactly the way he'd returned it to them: listing sideways, its head attached with duct tape, and long, black crosshatch sutures stretching across the chest and belly. Someone had taped his business card on top of the grotesque Frankenstein stitches: *Dr. Richard Jarmin, M.D., P.C., Reconstructive Surgery.*

Jarmin laughed soundlessly as he reached for the mangled carnival prize. "It was supposed to be a joke."

"Oh, no." Misty pulled it away. "He's in the Bonehead Hall of Fame. We used to keep him on the bar, but he kept falling over. We have souvenirs of all the important antics that take place here." She flourished her hand toward the walls like a game show hostess, then snapped the money from his fingers.

The doctor wore a tight-lipped smile as he walked away with his food. "Well, it's good to finally be a part of Two Pan."

At the door he hesitated, tucking his money clip back into his pocket. "Since I'm part of the community, I suppose the neighborly thing is to let you know, Mr. Woolsey ..."

Grinning, Jiggs turned to give the doctor his attention.

"It seems that we're in a bidding war for the same piece of property—Mr. Hopkins' Shiny Creek Ranch."

Jiggs stiffened, his knuckles whitening as he gripped his mug. "No. Sorry to break it to you, but I've already got a commitment for that land."

"Oh?" A slanted smile split the doctor's face. "I see." His single nod was more of a man making a point than someone agreeing.

The bar was silent as the door shushed closed behind him.

10

Support Your Local Everything

YOU'LL WONDER AT the short stride of autumn in Two Pan. By the first of November, the peaks of the Eagle Caps wear white capes from several dustings of snow. Cold air bites bare necks and ungloved fingers. Low in the valley, crimson leaves flash white undersides as they spiral to the ground. Gray plumes twist upward from chimneys, scenting evenings with wood smoke.

Football schedules for the Minam Warriors hang in store windows. Being the smaller school, Two Pan High was absorbed into Minam when rural districts consolidated in the '90s. Having the better field, the football team chooses to play at Two Pan.

A plaque next to the arena gates proudly states, *Not a cent of state or federal money was used to construct this stadium.* The community built their own venue with donated rock, steel, and many late nights. It doesn't have artificial turf, but the grass rivals prestigious country clubs. The Daughters of Two Pan run the concession stand. Elk chili, fry bread, and homemade apple pie outsell popcorn and hotdogs. The home-grown pep band of donated instruments and volunteer musicians pound out the national anthem and rally tunes. Sometimes they even play to the same beat.

———————

Bundled against the night air, two youths stood outside the door of the Bar and Grill, waving booklets. "Twenty-five coupons good at stores here and in Minam. It's a good deal, Mr. Woolsey," a blonde said as she fed Hermes a carrot. Red and gold pom poms stuck out of the donkey's harness and fluttered in the waft of every car that drove by. 'SUPPORT THE TEAM' sparkled in glittery letters from the sign around the neddy's neck.

Jiggs scratched Hermes between the ears and fished his wallet from his hip pocket. "Does it have that buy-one-get-one shrimp dinner like last year?"

"Yes, sir." A round, red-headed kid splattered with freckles nodded. "Mr. Hinton—the young one, not the mayor—didn't wanna put it in. He said they lost money on it last year, but it sure helped us sell Booster Books."

"Here, sell me two, so he can lose more money." Jiggs handed the kid two twenties.

The teenage girl began playing her flute, walking back and forth along the street. Hermes followed, bumping her with his nose. Folks who'd parked in front of Grubb's veered from the mercantile and hiked toward the music.

Jiggs entered the eatery and shucked out of his coat. He waved his Booster booklets at Bazz, who clenched a pair of wire strippers in his mouth, his hands twisting the copper ends of wires sprouting from a hole in the bar. Through his teeth, he mumbled, "Dey made twelf hunned dollars las' year. We los' money."

"Well, prepare to lose some more." Jiggs held up two fingers as he eased into a chair.

"You can eat two dinners?" Misty asked, pulling a spigot handle to fill a mug.

"Nap's joining me. We're celebrating."

"Good news?" Bazz glanced up.

"Kind of. The appraisal finished today, so we might be one step closer to getting the loan. Of course, with my crap for luck, it came in lower than what I agreed to pay Hop."

"Can you appeal?" Bazz asked.

"Doubtful ..." Jiggs nodded thanks to Misty as she unloaded a beer from her tray. "Little McGinty said the bank would only give me a percentage of what it appraised at. Now I have to put in more upfront money."

Bazz watched the needle on his amp meter as he tested two wires. "You'll have to renegotiate the selling price."

"Nope. That's what Jarmin is hoping for. Hop's waiting for me to get the money scraped together. I don't want to backtrack on the deal. Tell him his property isn't worth what he thinks it is. Besides, Dr. Dick's dandelion-haired realtor is sneaking around behind me, waving fistfuls of money and telling Hop he can wrap the transaction up immediately. I shook on the deal. I'll keep my word and pay the difference outta pocket."

Bazz disappeared under the bar. More wires snaked through the hole. Jiggs tapped a rhythm to think by and nodded to several people who entered. "I hate to drain my cash reserves going into winter. It's not a good time."

"There's never a good time to spend all your money." Bazz reappeared, frowning. "You up late last night? You look as bad as Roofus." The mayor hooked his thumb toward the stuffed German shepherd.

Jiggs studied the tie and Halloween goggley eye someone had added. The floating pupil stared upward. "Actually, the mutt looks better than me."

"Well, since you probably don't even own a tie, I agree," Bazz said. "What happened? You finally did a day's worth of work, and it about killed you?"

"Hop's hay was stacked in an open field. We moved what we could into sheds. It was half-past dark by the time we got the flatbed loaded. Nap drove it on ahead. The dozen bales that were left I threw on my truck. Before I got out of the field, I had a blowout."

"And I bet you bought one used tire to replace it." Bazz flicked a switch. Over the bar, a Walking Man beer sign glowed neon yellow. "You're so cheap, you'd save chewin' tobacco."

"I haven't bought anything yet." He flipped through his Booster Booklet. "I'm using an old tire that was lyin' on the barn roof to keep the tin from blowin' away. Nap had unloaded the truck, eaten, and showered before he noticed I wasn't home yet. Seems like I waited half the night for him to come back. Then we had to unload the hay in order to jack up the truck."

Several folks at other tables laughed. Bazz drew a beer for himself and sat down. "If you'd part with a few dollars that haven't seen the light of day since you put 'em in your wallet, you could get a cell phone. Call for help. Move into this century."

"A phone wouldn't help. Service is spotty. For what they charge you to use those things I could make a long distance call to hell."

"That's just a local call in California." Bazz nodded.

"A phone woulda ruined it. It was getting dusky. Just a few stars overhead. I stretched out on the hood to wait. The air was so thick with the smell of summer grass, I coulda scooped it into jars." Jiggs stared at the bubbles rising in the beer.

"Imagine that," Bazz said. "A hayfield that smelled like grass."

"That's what I mean. I'd been there most of the afternoon. I was covered in hay and dust and that was the first time I'd even noticed how it smelled. I lay on that ol' truck, letting my bones sink to the bottom of my body, breathing in the last of summer."

The feed store lady, sitting at Table 4, bobbed her nose in the air for her tablemates' entertainment.

Jiggs paid her no attention. "That's when I spotted shadows tumbling right over my head. Bats. I don't know how long it's been since I've seen bats. Then I realized I haven't looked up lately."

"I've always said that about you." Bazz arched an eyebrow. "Half the time you don't know where you are."

Jiggs slouched back in his chair, stretching his feet in front of him as though he were lounging on his truck hood again. "Over at the edge of the field, elk materialized out of the dark. There was more snorting in the woods behind them. It struck me that Hop, his granddaddy, and before that ... maybe even the Indians, had been right there and watched the same thing. Season to season, time spins the same events over and over. I'm like that spider who only sees what's shakin' his own web. I never considered it could change."

"What change is that?" Bazz asked.

A few quiet conversations were taking place at tables along the wall, but most of the bar was hushed. The sound of an electric mixer hummed from the kitchen. In the side room, billiard balls clacked.

Jiggs stared at the wall of mementos. "When I was a boy, I'd yank bales onto the flatbed and have time to look around before the loader spit out the next one. Once a hawk swooped next to me. Wings wide, talons bared, right into the mow-over. It struggled to take off again. When it did, a rabbit dangled from its feet, kicking the air. I could've reached out and touched them. Bull snakes slithered through the stubble, looking for mice. Every hay season, after sunset, there are elk. All that'll change when newcomers move in and build houses."

He didn't tell them how he stared at the night and wished he could stop time. Or that he wanted great-grandkids to stand in that spot and watch the same things. He didn't mention that as night dropped around him, he sensed he was part of a greater design: earth, air, stars, and galaxies. The land was the only thing around him he could count on to continue after he'd left this life. He kept his thoughts to himself, mostly because he didn't know how to express the logic he felt in his soul: If he could keep Two Pan the way it was, his dad, mother, and all the Woolseys before him could live on. Especially his brother. Maybe it would lighten his burden.

Jiggs swallowed and leaned his head back, staring at the "alligator" hanging from the ceiling. "It got so dark I couldn't see my hands. Overhead, one of the stars was moving. I figured it was the International Space Station. It was just them, up there with all their technology, and me, in the middle of a field with a broken truck. Staring through the sky at each other. I decided ... I'd put up with the banking hassle of buying this land. I'm not gonna let change bulldoze our lives here."

The bar was silent. The muted notes of the flute outside could be heard. No one spoke. Starry summer nights bloomed in the diners' imaginations. Some stilled their tongues, knowing that holding onto the past couldn't control the future. But they chose not to say so. Secretly—it was their hope, too.

With a slow exhaled breath, Jiggs came back from the moment. "It was the best time I've ever wasted."

Bazz nodded thoughtfully. "You know, you're pretty clever. You'll do anything to get out of stacking hay in a barn."

Their stare-off only lasted a few seconds before Nap came through the door waving a Booster Booklet. "Pop. I got a shrimp dinner for us." Jiggs held up his coupons. "Oh, great!" Nap wagged his head. "Why didn't that freckled little jelly bean tell me you'd already bought some?"

"Why would he ruin a sale?" Bazz asked as he left for the kitchen.

Chicken Thief Bob and Josie were right behind Nap, laying red papers on tables.

"Kevin asked us to spread them around," Chicken Thief said as he plopped into a chair. Misty set beers in front of them.

No More Pet Problems
Kevin Salaras, Pet Behaviorist, will reveal the secrets of well-behaved animals.

*No More Chewed Shoes/Scratched Furniture
*Stop "Accidents" on the Carpet
*No More Yapping
*Bring Your Animals

FREE PRESENTATION: Two Pan Bar and Grill
Wednesday, November 28th
7:00 PM

Jiggs glanced at the flyer and rolled his eyes. "For pete's sake. I can tell you how to keep a dog from eating your boots and peeing on rugs."

"What's the trick?" Misty asked.

"Don't let 'em in the house! That's just common sense. They're animals. They were created to be outside."

"Well, I have a cat that gets mad as hell if I leave her alone too long." The petite barmaid frowned. "She shreds toilet paper and scatters kitty litter."

"Now see ... you probably believe some horse hockey about your kitty exhibiting an alienation response. It's your basic line of thinking that's all whopper-jawed."

"And why's that?"

"First of all," Jiggs tapped the table to emphasize each word, "all cats are from hell. That's just a basic truth." Misty threw her bar towel at him. He ducked. "And secondly, if you'd keep the cat outside, your feline could hunt, make love, and sharpen its claws; you wouldn't need a scratchin' post or a box of gravel for it to do what any animal does naturally." Jiggs gave a hard nod as though that closed the subject.

"She'd run away, or the coyotes would eat her."

"There you go. Problem solved!" He threw up his hands. "And the advice was free."

"I'll go hear what Kevin has to say." Misty walked away. "It's free, too."

"Hey!" Jiggs called after her. "Nap's dog can count cattle, and my horse could use the internet if he could get his hooves on the keyboard. I know what I'm talking about."

"Well, that'd be a first," Bazz muttered as he dropped into a chair.

Jiggs pushed the flyer toward the mayor. "Look what Kevin is up to now. That guy's antenna doesn't pick up all the channels. Once, he got the brilliant idea of training coyotes to be seeing-eye companions. Someone in Baker actually bought one. Right away, neighborhood cats vanished and every change in the moon was an aria."

Chicken Thief didn't laugh with the others. "He can't rodeo clown anymore since he got hurt. But I suspect by dodging horns, he probably learned to read animals pretty well."

"If he understood bull signals, he wouldn't have gotten run over so many times." Nap slung the flyer across the table.

Bazz caught it as it flew over the edge. "Well, his lug nuts may be rattling in his hubcaps, but at least he's trying to do something for the community." He gave Jiggs a look.

"Hey! I'm waiting on a loan so I can keep memories like these alive."

Bazz waggled the flyer at Junior as he came out of the kitchen. "Why're you letting Kevin put on his dog-and-pony-show here?"

The forty-year-old gave Bazz a malevolent stare, pulled a bottle from the wine cooler, and approached Table 2, violently twisting the corkscrew. "Did you sell me the bar or not, Dad? Can I run it or not?"

Bazz shrugged, looking at the Formica tabletop as though it were artwork that demanded study.

Junior dropped his voice to an accusing whisper, "You know … you started it. You let every Tupperware party, bridal shower, and cow council meet in the back room. *Good for business,* you said. *They'll buy something,* you said."

Bazz scowled. "I never let anyone who forgot to pay their brain bill have an animal exhibit here. You're probably breaking a five-inch stack of health codes."

"Don't even talk to me about animals." Junior leaned closer. "I've got a donkey and mangy mutt who crap out front. In here, I've got *that.*" He waved toward the small dog sitting splay-legged in front of a floor mirror, admiring his studly parts. "Take Curious to that meeting. He needs help."

"What's the matter with him?" Bazz nodded approvingly at his black and white mutt.

"Shit," his son whisper-yelled. "You don't think that's weird?"

Bazz gave Jiggs a serious stare. "You're an animal expert. In your professional opinion, is that aberrant behavior?"

The rancher rose out of his chair a few inches to make a studied look at the dog. He sat back down, and steepled his fingers. "Heavens no! That's natural enough. Man or beast." Josie and Junior groaned. "Listen. I'm gonna tell you something I learned from an old, old Indian." Misty paused next to the table. Jiggs continued, "I use this secret technique with

Curly Dogs. He's the only horse I know that can do long division and tiptoe across a cattle guard."

"C'mon, what is it? I've got tables to serve." The waitress juggled baskets into one hand and snagged their empty mugs with the other.

He dropped his voice, forcing his tablemates to lean closer. "Keep your dog outdoors ... then it won't have a mirror to expose itself to." He leaned back, speaking loudly, "They're animals. That's what they do. They were created to be outside!"

"Life has made you hard, Jiggs." Chicken Thief shook his head, "You've been cuttin' and brandin' too long."

"Hey, Junior!" Jiggs called as the proprietor headed back to the kitchen with the wine. "I've got three coupons, so I'll have six shrimp dinners. We're celebrating the possibility of becoming big-time, *outside*-animal owners."

Junior paused and counted, "You've only got five people."

"I'm taking one to Curly Dogs. He likes a little treat after finishing The New York Times crossword puzzle."

Rays of acid burned from the restaurateur's eyes as spoke in a sing-song voice, "'Leave the shrimp dinner in the Booster Book. It'll help the kids. It'll be good for business. They'll buy beers and desserts.'" He squinted at his father. "And so it begins." He trudged toward the kitchen, leaving a feeling of burned airspace behind him.

Josie cocked her head, watching him tromp away. "He loves his work, doesn't he?"

"Someday, he'll poison all of you, and I won't arrest him." Sheriff Meyers' six-foot-five body filled the doorway of the Bar and Grill as he stuffed his wallet and Booster Booklet into a back pocket. He wore his off-duty uniform of plaid shirt, leather vest, and jeans.

"Hey, Sol." Jiggs waved. "Do your John Wayne walk over here and join us. You can have Curly Dogs' shrimp." The big man removed his hat as he ambled toward the table. "He's been working on that walk since high school." Jiggs grinned. "Irks him when I point it out."

"I wanted to talk to you." Sol looked at his school rival, then nodded acknowledgments around the table as he sat down. His slow, bass voice carried through the bar. "You still trying to buy Shiny Creek?" Jiggs nodded. "Word at the Minam Cafe is that Jarmin told your banker he plans to put cabins and a hunting club on that property. He even promised he'd move all of his business deposits to the Minam First National if he got to do the project."

"That's an interesting bribe," Bazz said.

"That son of a bitch!" Nap dropped his chair to all four legs.

Misty set a Dr. Pepper in front of the sheriff. His big hands covered the entire glass as his fingers wrapped around it. "Course it's all hearsay, you understand."

"I heard it, too." Chicken Thief nodded.

"Why didn't you mention it?" Nap stared at the lanky face.

"'Cause I figured Jiggs would go out and do something stupid."

"Damn straight! One big bucket of kick ass is coming down on that twisted tub of guts." The young man punched his fist in his palm.

"Nap." Jiggs' voice sharpened. "There's a lady in your presence."

"Your past is what he's counting on," the sheriff said. "If he can get you or Nap in an assault lawsuit, he'll squeeze till you're broke or backed away. Actually, it's supposed to be the realtor who'll bait you and take the hit. Supposedly Jarmin is offering him free plastic surgery. At the Minam Café, odds are three to one you'll punch him in the face."

"I hadn't heard about the betting." Chicken Thief slapped Jiggs on the back. "Lend me a five, and I'll put money on you."

"He means to have that land." The sheriff aimed a serious look at Jiggs. "No matter what it costs. Watch yourself."

Misty circled the table, setting platters heaped with shrimp and coleslaw in front of each person. "You don't seem worried, Jiggs."

"Let the odds get higher before you place bets." Jiggs gave the sheriff a quick eyebrow raise, like one jock signaling another that it was time to steal a rival's mascot. "Thanks, Sol. I'll talk to Little McGinty about the bribe. We'll discuss this as one Two Pan graduate to another."

"I saw Jarmin at the courthouse this morning. He told me this was a *privileged* place to live." One corner of the sheriff's mouth turned in a slow grin. "I believe he isn't too happy. He feels we're a *'close-knit bunch.'* Said it's hard for someone to make changes that benefit the community."

"Well, that's sad that he feels left out. I'll have to give him another bumper sticker," Chicken Thief said. "You'd think fifteen would be enough."

"I had to agree with him." Sol nodded. "Told him it started when the settlers took the first wagons apart and helped each other carry them piece by piece over the pass into this valley. That's the only way folks in this place have survived."

Jiggs picked up the announcements to make room for hot cornbread and dipping sauces. He stared at the red flyers. "I think I'll go to this shindig. Kevin, the pet whisperer, could use some support."

"While you're at it, have your picture taken for the Our Town Art Project," Bazz said. "Only four people have had photos taken so far."

"You'd better slap your photo everywhere and go to that pet meeting, too." Sol gave Bazz a that's-for-certain nod. "You need to start gathering your constituents. Jarmin asked me how he could become the mayor of Two Pan."

11

Run-Ins with Winter Spirits

FOLKS WHO LIVE in Two Pan year 'round find that winter blows in early and clings to the mountains until long past spring. Tourists and amenity ranchers quickly vacate the area. The daylight hours have little time to melt the worries that pile up in the dark. Days of colorless repetition are haunted by three winter spirits: isolation, wind, and one-digit temperatures. The young battle these spirits with ease, but eventually each soul, regardless of age, finds a way to fight back.

It's what makes Two Pan residents stubborn, creative, and sometimes—a little sleepless.

———

Two sixteen-year-olds hunkered in the dark alley next to the doorway. One brushed his shoulder-length hair from his face as he glanced behind him. His man-child attempt to grow a beard culminated in a sparse goatee under his beak nose. "C'mon. C'mon," he growled.

The shorter, pimply-faced blond swirled the dial of a padlock, "Shut up."

"I thought you knew the combination."

"I can't see a damn thing."

"Cheap bastards oughta put a light on the side of the building."

"Shut up. The owner'll hear you." The short teen hunched over, his face inches from the lock, his fingers twisting the dial in increments. "Did you put the tin can in front of his door?"

"Yeah, yeah." Gil Gedding glanced at the back door of the house forty feet away.

"You didn't put it on the hinge side, did you? It needs to clatter down the steps if Grubb comes out."

"It's a sucky idea. Just open the damn door."

"Got it." The blond kid unthreaded the lock from the hasp and pushed. The old door remained stuck in its frame. He put his shoulder against it, braced his feet, and heaved. It screeched a wood-on-cement groan, opening a foot. The boys froze, watching the house.

"Move, Shorty. Move. Someone's coming." Gil shoved through the gap into the black interior, pushing both of them inside. He turned and threw his body against the door.

"My hand!" the blond kid yelled, raking his fingers free. He crammed his fist into his armpit, muffling pain-filled grunts as they leaned against the door, listening.

The sharp-nosed kid looked around, his eyes acclimating to the diffused light from the Pepsi cooler. "HA!"

"Be quiet." Shorty flexed his bloody hand.

"Awww, shut up. No one's coming. I just wanted to see how fast you could move."

"You're an asshole." The short teen glared at him. He bent double and sneaked to the self-serve area to daub the bloody seepage and wrap his knuckles with napkins. After a quick look toward the plate-glass storefront, he dropped to his hands and knees and crawled across the abused oak floors fragrant with oil and dust.

Gil Gedding ignored his friend and strolled to the beverage cooler. "Why're there cartons of cottage cheese and containers of worms with the beer and pop?"

"What in the hell are you doing?" Shorty squeaked in mid-crawl.

"Getting somethin' to drink."

"Get down. We only came for cigarettes."

"I'm thirsty." The old building creaked. Both teens froze in their positions, listening. The cooler that held locally grown hamburger and steak hummed. Gil coughed a cautious chuckle.

"Yeah, okay," Shorty whispered. "Get me one, too." He took off, knee-shuffling down the aisles. Several fat tubes of hand cream clattered to the floor as he passed. "That was me," he whispered and paused to put them back on the shelf.

"Your mother help you figure that out?" said his friend.

To the short young man, the scuffle of his crawl seemed thunderous. He did a forward roll and landed behind the oak and glass counters running the length of the room. Heaps of junk lay on the glass shelves inside: mule shoes, tie studs, pill boxes, and cigarette holders along with fishing lures and carbon paper. He'd heard that most of the merchandise had been there since Oregon had achieved statehood. It was all for sale if a person could find something needed in the mess.

The cigarettes were shelved about five feet off the floor. He'd have to stand and take a chance at being seen through the storefront. His heart pounded in his chest. This was like the movies where the hero flung himself behind a desk and reloaded his gun while the bad guys fired a million rounds at him.

Inching his head up, he peeked through the glass counter. He halfway expected to see the owner looking in the window, his hands cupped around his face. The dim streetlight showed only a gray, frozen Main Street.

Like a gopher out of a hole, he popped up and snatched a pack of cigarettes. Back on the floor, he checked the window before crawling toward the back of the store. In the next aisle, Gil Gedding walked slightly stooped so he was five feet tall instead of six.

"Are you friggin' nuts? Get down," Shorty hissed.

"Nobody can see us back here," he laughed. "Why're you whispering?"

" 'Cause I don't wanna get caught."

"Nobody'll find out." Gil held up a package of teriyaki meat strips. "Jerky?"

"What the hell are you doing? This isn't a shopping spree."

"Why not? Don't start getting girlie."

"Look ..." Shorty's his eyes flogged his accomplice. "When I told you I knew the combination, I said we'd get some smokes."

"So what'd you get?"

The short kid ignored him, kneeling in front of the potbelly stove and stirring the embers with a poker. When he'd finished, he rolled back, sitting cross-legged, and held up cigarettes.

"Camels? One pack?" Orange light and shadows chiseled the long-haired kid's features making his nose more beaklike. He plopped down heavily. "I thought we was gonna party."

The short blond tamped the package. "This is not the place."

"It's got everything we need, including ... beer."

"Gimme mine."

Gil rolled the Oly across the floor. "Hey, you're bleeding."

"Yeah, asshole, you tried to take my fingers off in the door. Hurts like hell." Shorty held the cold can against the back of his hand.

Gil froze. "Somebody's here," he whispered.

A compressor hummed background sounds. In the listening stillness, the pungent scent of treated floorboards seemed stronger. The shadows in the aisles appeared darker, but there were no unidentified noises. "Stop with the scare tactics. It's not funny," Shorty said.

"I swear. I heard someone." Gil took a quick drag on his cigarette. "Walking around." He stared at the ceiling and jerked the smoke to his mouth again. "Overhead."

"Could be the dentist." Shorty removed the napkins and dabbed at the raw skin over his knuckles. The boys caught each other's eyes when a creaking rafter sounded like a voice. "That was almost human," he murmured.

"Don't try to scare me." Gil sneered and sat taller.

"I'm not. Weird shit happens at this store."

"Like what?"

"Things get moved, and nobody's touched them. People swear they hear the dentist wandering around on the second floor. His office is right above us. Mr. Grubb let me see it once. It's like he went to lunch a hundred years ago and will be back any minute. Everything's layin' out, exactly like he left it: old instruments, a leather appointment book..." Shorty made claw hands, "his next victim."

"Bullshit. I heard nobody knows what happened to him." The long-haired boy drained his beer.

"He disappeared and left everything behind, even his clothes."

"Like my old man does."

"He still peddlin' meth?"

Gil stared into the fire a moment before flicking his cigarette butt into the embers. "I'm goin' up to see the dentist."

"Shit no."

"Why not? C'mon."

Shorty leaned forward, his eyes wide. "You hear that?"

"What?"

"Shhhh ... listen." The compressor had turned off. Silence rolled through the aisles.

"What?"

"Footsteps," Shorty mouthed.

The tall boy shook his head. The smaller one tossed his bloody napkins onto the coals and pushed the iron door shut. It scritched closed with a metal *EEERK*. The teens sat in the dark without moving, their eyes flitting side to side, listening, waiting.

"There," whispered Shorty. "Hear them?"

"No."

The short boy shrugged, then carefully placed the beer cans in the trash. A soft *thunk, thunk, thunk,* echoed through the room.

The sharp-nosed kid tapped his friend on the shoulder, nodding and pointing overhead, eyes wide.

"Ha! That was me." Shorty thumped the plastic trashcan, replicating the footsteps. "You should see your face."

Overhead, a slamming *THUD* reverberated through the floorboards and across the store. Elbowing Shorty to get to the door, Gil reached it first and wrenched it open. Shorty slammed into him, knocking both of them onto the ground outside. Twenty feet away Hermes screeched. *AW-EEE.*

"Shit!" screamed Gil, his legs trying to gain traction on the frozen grass.

The donkey brayed faster and louder. *AW-EEE, AW-EEE.*

Shorty yanked the door closed. Gil had already disappeared around the front of the building. The young man's hands shook. On the third attempt, the lock slid through the hasp. A light came on inside the Grubb house. The donkey still sounded off like a siren.

The lock clicked into place. Shorty stumbled through his first few steps, his knees trembling. He pulled his hoodie over his head. Neural messages from his brain finally reached his feet. *RUN!*

As soon as he rounded the corner of the store and dashed onto Main Street, the braying stopped. A heartbeat later, the clatter of a tin can echoed down the alley.

The short boy didn't feel the wind or one-digit temperatures as he ran into the night.

Early each morning—before chores—the dark winter spirits visited the ranches. The cattlemen studied the sky, looked at the thermometer, and then assessed their haystacks. Sometimes they even watched a forecast, wishing that they, too, could get paid for guessing the weather.

Using these three variables, they performed complicated algebraic equations—without calculators—predicting if they would be able to feed their herds through the winter. If the answer was no, they ordered grain or searched for more hay and refigured their diminishing profits—again, without calculators.

This morning, Jiggs, bundled in layers of long underwear, jeans, down jacket, and a farmer hat with earflaps, stood at the edge of a frozen pond. He tugged on his lariat with the end-loop attached to a calf; its front hooves had punched through a slush spot close to the middle. He gave a cautious heave, afraid of strangling the little maverick, but the animal didn't budge.

Taking tentative steps, he edged farther onto the ice. It crackled and groaned, but held. "C'mon. Fight." The calf looked at him goggle-eyed. "C'mon, Stupid. Get out of this mess." Snapping the rope, he took a couple steps toward the animal. It scrambled its hind legs, trying to run.

The CRACK split the chilled air. In slow motion, he saw the calf drop into the ice hole at the same time he felt himself falling. A fiery chill poured into his boots. Relief surged through him when his feet hit bottom before the water reached mid-thigh. His body teetered for a moment. Then he fell backward, clipping his head on the ragged edge of ice before he went under.

Everything went white for an instant.

He willed himself to stand. Water streamed out of his gloves and poured off his elbows as he rose. His hands still pulled at the rope, but the calf had given up. The lasso was the only reason its head hadn't slipped through the hole.

Stiff-legged with the weight and chill of his clothing, he staggered to the truck, water pouring from his coat like a soaked mattress. An icy breeze blowing from the south petrified his muscles as he fumbled a half hitch around the bumper. It probably wouldn't hold, but it was the best his deadened hands could do.

Like tongs, his fingers fumbled with the key to start the engine. His feet were beginning to numb. He used his hands to pick up a leg and stomp it onto the accelerator. The truck jerked in reverse, popping the calf out of the hole, dragging it across the ice and up the bank before he could get stopped.

He jumped out and waddle-dragged the animal into a nearby shed, shouldering his way between the barreled bodies of cattle. When he let go, the calf tottered for a moment, then collapsed to the ground.

Freezing water squelched in his boots as he trotted back to the truck. His hands slipped as he groped a bale from the back. They slipped again and again as he hefted it to the shed. Twice, he stuck his hands in a cow's leg pit to warm his fingers enough to cut the twine. Using hay as a squeegee, he rubbed the calf. Jiggs' body was shaking so hard the hay joggled out of his fingers.

He staggered to the truck, got in, and sat, watching his bare hand quiver on the steering wheel. Only one glove. *When did I take the other one off?* When his fingers warmed enough to throb, he emptied the water from his boots onto the floorboard. No way would he open the door and let any heat escape. He'd seen the survivor shows where wind and wet clothes were a ticket for hypothermia.

With hands as dexterous as hooves, he shucked off his coat and everything he wore, then sat naked, shivering, with his fingers stuck in the heating vents. It was a relief that no one was around for miles even though the wilderness guy never seemed embarrassed to be buck-naked, squatting next to a fire, chatting about survival. Jiggs grimaced. The guy also toasted rats like marshmallows and ate them with their fur on, so maybe he wasn't so smart.

The only dry clothing he found was a greasy cotton shirt under the seat. He slipped it on. His head hurt like a nail was sticking out of the back of his skull. With his fingertips, he gently explored the egg-size lump while his eyes watched the shed—the calf still hadn't gotten up. *Bound to happen.* Giving a long groan, he pulled wet boots over the biting nerves in his toes.

The wind flapped the long-sleeved, plaid shirt against his body as he got out of the truck and limped to the shelter. Several times he wrestled the calf to its feet only to have it totter and drop. "C'mon, Stupid. Get off the ground. It's colder than a well digger's willy out here."

In the lee of the shed and surrounded by warm bodies, he rubbed the calf again, propping it against a cow. It wouldn't last the night. He'd have to get the trailer, haul it home, and revive it in his bathtub. On his way back to his truck, he paused long enough to pull the free end of the half hitch from the bumper and let it drop. There was a time he would've whipped Nap for leaving a good throwing rope wet and freezing on the ground.

If only he'd gotten gas before he'd started chores, he could have sat until his fingers had blood in them again, rubbed the calf every now and then, and coiled up the rope. But he hadn't. It would've added ten miles of backtracking this morning. The needle on the gas gauge pegged empty. It often lied. He put the truck in gear. It was fifteen miles to the house or twenty to Slat's Gas station.

Jiggs had great faith in his bad luck, so he wasn't surprised when a mile from home, the engine stuttered and died. He rapped the gauge. *Idiot!* He checked his watch. The bezel was fogged. It had stopped. The wind bent the tall grass and whistled in the cracks of the truck. Nap might come along soon. He'd wait.

As usual, you never listened. Ox Woolsey's voice rang loud in his head. *Shoulda filled it up when it was half empty, Tool.*

Jiggs sighed. Usually he did, but he'd been burning more fuel, checking cattle twice a day. If he weren't buying more land, he could afford a new truck with a working gas gauge.

How'd you even survive this long, Tool? Ever hear of a spare can?

He and Ox had rarely talked when they rode together. Now the old man's voice stalked him. Jiggs stared at the flayed heads of tall grass bowing to the wind. "C'mon, Nap."

By the time his legs had begun to shake uncontrollably, his dad's voice had gone silent. Probably because the old jackass was about to see his predictions of stupidity come true.

The day after Pax's funeral, Ox had insisted they do chores as usual. It had been a scorcher of a day. Jiggs had slouched, unnoticed in the shade of the feed store, watching a spider ambush a box elder bug. He stayed close enough to hear when Ox and Guntis Kral stopped yammering, and it was time to go.

"Hayin' season's coming up. We all miss your oldest boy." The German's gravelly voice carried sympathy. "He'd work all night and still be goin' the next day."

"You could count on him." A draining silence filled the space after his dad spoke, as though both men were waiting for a breeze to carry the grief off the words.

"Well, you still got Jiggs. He's a good kid," Guntis said quietly.

"He's a bone idler. He'll lose everything as soon as he gets it. I'm glad I won't be 'round to see it."

"He ain't settled yet. He's still got growin' to do."

Ox's voice took on a growl. "He's got a brain the size of a duck's. All his life he hasn't thought beyond the next meal. Everything he does is with one foot outta the stirrup."

"You were stubborn, too, Ox—and wild. I remember when you—"

"But I worked damn hard. The ranch came first. I made plans, and I made 'em happen. Jiggs rolls out of bed every day, stumbling into whatever's goin' on. He doesn't think. Or plan. The wrong son died."

Jiggs was in a lead bubble, dropping through deep water. He couldn't pull a breath. His dad's words replayed again and again. Surely they'd change with the fourth ... fifth examination. They didn't.

When it was finally time to go, he helped load feed sacks and got in the truck. Halfway home, he quietly said, "You think I should be dead instead of Pax?"

Ox Woolsey's eyes widened then stared down the road. "I don't want either of you gone, but he was the responsible one. You spend more time figurin' how to get outta work, if you even think at all."

"What the hell do you mean, telling people I'll lose the ranch?"

"The way you're goin', you prob'ly will."

"Pax wasn't perfect. You don't know the times I had to do his work. You don't have a clue what he was really like."

"I know what you're like." Ox turned an iron stare toward him.

"I didn't sneak off and drink." The shame and venom in Jiggs' voice was palpable. "I didn't call and cuss—" He stopped. He'd vowed never to talk of that phone call. Pax's voice—sloppy drunk—cussing at him.

A gut-cold shiver shook him out of the memory. The wind, pressing the grass to the ground, made the fields as vacant as he felt. He'd spent his life trying to fill in for his brother and to prove his father wrong. He'd accomplished neither.

He slammed the steering wheel with his hand. How did he get into these crap-pit situations? If people marked time by death, "before Pax's accident," "after Katie's passing," then Nap would be saying, "After Dad froze to death—naked."

"No way." Jiggs picked up his wadded jeans and stuck a fist in one leg. Like a wet snake, it clung to his arm. Icy water dripped onto the seat and puddled in a seam. He dumped them back on the floorboard and stared at the pasture. Cross country, it would be over a half mile. Maybe more. He could walk it in twenty minutes, less if he jogged. Hummocks and cowbellies rolled across the land to his house. He probably couldn't run the whole thing, but he'd work up a sweat—or lay in the field with a heart attack. But naked? It must be sixteen degrees out there ... and with wind chill? He eyed his soggy pile of clothes again.

Jiggs peeled off his cotton shirt, wriggled it under him, and tied the ends, forming a flimsy diaper. He checked the rearview mirror. Now, he hoped nobody would drive by and spot him. He wrung water from his coat then slipped it on, sucking air between clenched teeth. At least it came to his hips.

When he stepped outside, he felt every part of his body, even his eyeballs, shrink in the polar breeze. His old man would've died with icicles hangin' off him rather than risk getting caught naked. As he squeezed through the barbwire fence he realized his father would've never been in this fix. *I planned better,* Ox Woolsey's voice belittled him.

Jiggs yanked the ends of the knot, tightening his diaper invention. "I'm building the Rockin' W bigger than you made it, Dad. Better than Pax would've done."

The wind blew his voice away.

With one hand clamping his hat on his head and the other holding the knot on his loincloth, he took off running against the winter spirits.

The distance felt like it had stretched to four miles by the time he reached the house. For a few minutes he thought Nap was going to find his frozen body propped against the porch because he couldn't make his dead fingers open the screen door. What a stupid way to meet his Maker.

Using elbows and arms to pinch and pull the latch, he finally he got inside. He ran cold water over his hands until a thousand stinging needles let him know his blood was thawing.

In twenty minutes he'd gotten back to the truck and dumped a can of gas into the tank. Shivers still shook his body and his feet were half-numb, but he figured it was a scabby way for the calf to die, too. He'd haul it back and give it a warm shower. He could save a calf. He could save land from being developed. He could change the future.

Gravel sprayed behind the trailer as he drove off in a desperate attempt to defeat his father's criticism and the winter spirits.

Junior sat at the Two Pan Bar and Grill, looking at gourmet magazines. Los Angeles sucked, but at least they had decent food. He stared at mostly empty chairs where live, paying customers, instead of winter spirits, should be sitting. This wind forced him to serve Two Pan Stew as his special—everyday—because folks wanted comfort food. The below-zero nights forced him to close early because few people came in after 8:30, but the spirits didn't leave. They sat and watched him figure out how he was going to pay bills.

The ex-Californian had adopted the credo of wilderness survival: keep improving your situation. He and his dad had spent their extra time upgrading the lighting and the brew taps.

Now he was reviewing recipes. Not that he'd ever get to serve Wasabi Salmon to these yokels. Maybe he could sneak this Drunk Steak onto the menu since it was marinated in two kinds of vermouth.

He stared at the "Today's Special" sign: STEW. It had been that way for two weeks. The only word that changed was the meat content. Sometimes it was rabbit. Sometimes buffalo. Often it was steak—which some joker changed to *snake* one day. Whenever the stew pot got low, a different meat was added and cooked again. The famous Two Pan Stew came from a miner's recipe and was a savory olio of vegetables, herbs, and various meats blending into a stomach pleaser.

"Where's the little cornbreads?" the lone diner at Table 4 asked.

"I baked it in a pan and cut slices today," Junior said without looking up from his magazine.

"I like the little muffins."

"Same batter, different pan; that's all."

"No. They taste better. They're sweeter," the man said.

"Beef, potatoes, and sugar, that's all folks want around here."

"I'm partial to macaroni if it's got a lot of cheese on it."

"Oh yeah, how could I forget? Cheese. Cheese in the tater tots. Cheese on the burgers. Chili and cheese on the fries. This county is a regular hothouse for bad taste and cardiac emergencies. I should install a defibrillator next to the door."

With a squint, the diner eyed Junior. "You ever consider taking a trip?"

"Would that improve everyone's dining requests?"

"No, but I reckon it improves a newcomer's attitude. As I remember, your dad used to get drunk and take off to Florida—in that order—when winter started in on him."

"You're right ..." Junior's voice drifted away. Dad could babysit the restaurant. The old man loved this place.

Like a prisoner who's found a gap in the concertina wires, Junior began making plans to escape. Somehow, by tomorrow, he'd be drinking an Appletini on a beach, being caressed by warm ocean breezes.

Each afternoon, the citizens at Grubb's Mercantile openly plotted against the blue funk the spirits brought. The grocery-hardware-automotive-clothing store had become a fortress in time of winter siege. Residents of Two Pan enhanced their survival strategies by pushing miniature carts through narrow aisles and stockpiling magazines, batteries, and big cans of honey roasted peanuts. The main brain trust sat in well-worn armchairs around the potbelly stove at the back of the store.

"I can't believe they had an electric guitar in the band at last Friday's basketball game." Millie's arthritic fingers pulled her stocking cap down to her eyebrows. "In my day, we had brass horns and big snare drums."

"In your day, the horns were from rams and the drums were hollowed logs." Whit winked. His stocking cap matched his wife's, except he wore it piled up over his big ears.

Curly-haired Maxine grunted as she thudded her groceries on the floor and joined the group. "Well, at least we've got a band. Most schools play recorded music nowadays."

"I can't believe we've had two band teachers quit in three years," Andy Grubb said.

"I can't believe they've got an electric guitar." Millie made a face. "I don't know what they're playing. It's all shrieking noise to me."

"Anyone who plays an instrument can be in the band, even you." Willa glanced at the old woman and moved away from the stove, fanning herself. "I think it's great that eighth-grade teacher stepped up and put out a call to the community."

"Sounds like pianos and silverware being tossed down a gully," Millie muttered.

"Isn't that new teacher Buforl Roggs' granddaughter?" Whit asked.

"Who woulda thought she'd come back to her grandparents' old place?" Maxine raised her eyebrows. "Obviously she's not like her mother. Not everybody leaves because we're at the edge of the world and have rotten weather."

"This weather's nothing." Whit gummed his mouth, working up the saliva so he wouldn't go dry in the middle of his story. "Back in thirty-three, when I was only a little mutt, there was eight foot snowdrifts in—"

"Okay, I've heard this one." Maxine rocked forward, trying to free herself from the low chair.

"Well, we need a good three or four feet of snow." Whit tugged at his cap. "Those mountain tops are patchy with brown spots. If we don't get moisture pretty soon, we'll be buyin' water like we buy gas. There won't be much pasture grass this year. I don't know what these ranchers are gonna do for hay. I already heard of several buying feed."

"Prices at the mill are up twenty percent over last year," a man said.

Whit shook his head with a depression-era stare. "I'm glad I'm not in the beef business."

"I'm glad I'm not in the band." His wife's face twisted.

Whit ignored her. "It's our president. All the big corporations have a hand in his back pocket. The little businesses—"

"Okay, now I *am* leaving," Maxine said. "I heard all this yesterday."

"Go on." Whit shooed her away as though he were herding a cow. "I keep telling ya that the Republicans meet over at the Bar and Grill."

"The coffee's better here," she said. "There's a warm fire. It's supposed to cheer people up."

Cowbells clanged against the outer door, announcing another customer. Millie's eyes brightened. "That's what that band needs instead of that screechin' guitar. Hey, Andy, lend us your bells for next Friday's basketball game."

The owner shook his head as he cleaned the coffee table and dumped the old grounds. "The Doc's ghost was stirring last night."

"Ooooooo! What happened?" Maxine asked.

"It was about two this morning. Hermes started braying. You know, you can tell his emergency squeals from his get-out-of-here bawls."

"Sounds like that band at the basketball game." Millie scrunched up her face.

"Hush!" Maxine waved her quiet. "What happened?"

"Hermes cut loose right under our bedroom window. About gave me a heart attack. I scrambled up, knocking Dorothy's cat off the bed, then tripped over it, trying to get to the door. Dorothy's yelling, 'Don't hurt Kitty.'

"I got outside and there's that jackass—in my garbage. Cans and sacks everywhere. He was gazing down the alley, and then he looked at me with one of his, 'Oh-hi-there-howya-doin' stares. Papers hanging out of his mouth."

"He wouldn't bray unless there was trouble," Willa said. "When that fellow tried to steal Lottie's motorcycle—"

"Quiet!" Maxine scowled at her. "We want to hear about Doc." Willa shot eye daggers back.

Andy slid a tray of new grounds into place. "Willa's right. Hermes is usually accurate about trouble, so I checked the store. All the doors were locked, but inside ..." he paused, looking to see if he'd pushed the brew button.

"What? What?" Maxine coaxed with a roll of her hand.

Andy nudged the toggle switch, and a red light came on. "Inside, there was a package of marshmallows in the middle of an aisle."

Disappointed groans erupted along with a fair amount of eye rolling.

"And ..." the proprietor held up a chubby finger. "Upstairs, in the dentist's office, a medical book was lying open on the floor. A big thick book." Andy spread his fingers four inches apart. "There's a vacant spot where it sat on the shelf, and the books on either side of it are undisturbed."

"Aw ... somebody looked something up and forgot to put it back," Whit said.

"Nope. I have the key. Doc's ghost was moving things around last night."

Maxine rubbed her arms. "Ooooh. That gives me the willies." She switched to a seat nearer the stove.

"I believe it," Willa said. "I've seen lights. Late at night in the upstairs windows." She pointed and nodded. "Kind of a glowy vapor."

Maxine waved at her to be quiet. "What page was the medical book open to?"

"Disorders of the lung."

"Uh-huh. Maybe Doc's ghost is trying to tell us something. Maybe someone in town has a lung disease," she said.

"Hop Hopkins' lungs don't work so good anymore." Millie shrugged.

"Well then, it only took Doc about a year and a half to figure out what everybody already knows," Whit said in a dry voice. "I guess that's why the quack had to leave town so quick."

Andy Grubb squinted and scratched his head. "I checked everything again this morning. There was a little dried blood on the alley door, but it was padlocked. And I don't know how that donkey got in my yard."

"Oh, he can find an unguarded garbage can as soon as it's put out," Maxine said.

"But I closed the gate last night." Andy frowned.

"That poor donkey." Willa fanned herself. "He's such a people person. He stands outside the gym while we're at the game. Then he guards the town all night. We should do something for him."

"Give him a bell and put him in the band," Millie called out.

"Stay home by yourself, if you don't wanna hear the music." Whit poked her arm with his knobby finger.

"You should get you a dog, Andy," a portly man said as he parked his shopping cart next to the group. "Hermes hates dogs. I got a litter of pups that's ready to be weaned."

Whit smacked his lips, shaking his head. "This town was overrun with dogs before our Hermes came. Packs of 'em. Raidin' garbage cans. Fightin' over who peed where. All of 'em hikin' a leg on what didn't move. Then our Donkey of Death got loose. Those dogs circled, barked, and snapped like they was gonna eat 'im alive."

"Everybody knows this story, Whit. Let's go home." Millie pulled her cap farther down on her head. Tufts of white hair duck-tailed out the back.

"Ol' Hermes stood, head down," her husband went on, "ears sagging, and eyes half-closed like he was asleep. He waited, lullin' 'em closer. Them dogs were lungin' and barin' their teeth. They was gonna tear him up." Whit exposed his dentures and growled. "They didn't know that donkey could kick forwards, backwards, and sideways without even cockin' his leg. They kept circling closer 'n' closer, and when they got within ju-u-u-st the right range ... Hermes looked like one of them kung fu fighters. Dogs were yelpin' and flyin' all over the place. That burro kicked and started bitin' chunks outta them hounds. Blood and screamin' dogs—"

"Okay, I really am leaving this time. I dropped by to get cheered up," Maxine said, heading toward the door. "I'd heard this story, but it wasn't the R-rated version."

"Took care of the dog problem." Whit followed her, pulling on his coat. "Only that old stray, Potty, is loose now, and he steers clear of Hermes. I'm not scooping dog logs out of my yard anymore."

"Now you've got donkey crap." Maxine paused at the jangling door.

"Don't hate him because he's Democrat," Whit jeered, then dropped his jaw at the customer coming through the entry.

"Good Lord. You look three days dead," Maxine blurted. "What happened to you?"

Jiggs wasn't wearing his hat, exposing a face that was red and puffy with patches of yellow rimming his ears and nose. "I went polar swimming with a calf this morning. Got a little frostnip. I think I could freeze the sun just by sneezing on it."

"You need to get to a doctor." Maxine leaned close, inspecting his eyes.

"Forget him. How's the calf?" Whit pushed the door shut behind Jiggs.

"Half dead. I put him in the shower and thawed him. He's under a blanket now. I'm joining him as soon as I get gas and groceries."

"Jason," Andy Grubb yelled. "Get Mr. Woolsey's grocery order out of the back and haul it out to his truck."

The short, blond stock boy hopped up from where he knelt, putting cans of chili on a shelf. "Sure thing. Lemme get my coat."

"Ya need to take better care if you plan on clobberin' that doctor fella about Hop's spread," Whit said. "I'm rootin' for ya."

"Hush, you old fool," Maxine said, examining Jiggs' skin as he tried to pull away from her. "That doctor isn't here for the winter, and Jiggs isn't going to punch anyone."

Glad to see the teenager reappear with a grocery sack in each arm, Jiggs stepped aside. He pointed to the missing skin across the boy's knuckles and fingers, hoping to transfer Maxine onto anybody else's wounds. "What'd you do there?"

Jason took a half step back. He glanced at his boss; his eyes darted away. "I tripped."

Several seconds of silence hung between them. The young man shifted to one foot and assumed a blank stare. The proprietor's voice was soft, "When you come back, get some salve and bandage it."

"It's okay." His head gave a micro-shake as he tried unsuccessfully to twist his hand so it wasn't displayed on the outside of the grocery bag.

"I'd prefer you take care of yourself," Andy continued softly. "I count on you to help with this store. We all do." He waved toward Cleova, the checker, and the customers milling about.

Jason briefly checked the owner's searching eyes. "I'll run this out to Mr. Woolsey's truck, then be right back for Mr. and Mrs. Barrick." He nodded toward an elderly couple deciding between cream corn and whole kernels.

Cowbells jangled as he closed the door behind him.

"Now that noise will chase away the dark spirits," Millie said as she joined the group.

"I wish it were that easy," Jiggs mumbled. He glanced up at Andy Grubb. The proprietor had a punched-in look. Jiggs followed Andy's gaze. Both of them watched the teen duck his head, running through one digit temperatures, as the winter spirits howled through metal-gray skies.

12

Hanging Loose

THE HONEYED NOTES of a slack key guitar filtered through
the speakers, the drifting harmony filling the bar with South
Sea music and imaginary sunshine.

Jiggs looked at the electric tiki lights crisscrossing the ceiling. Fabric-flowered leis dangled from the wall mementos,
including the jackalope and the ceiling alligator. "I don't come
in for a couple of weeks and this happens?" He eyed a paper
menu decorated with palm trees and redundantly named
entrees.

"How's that calf?" Amusement spanned Chicken Thief
Bob's face as he watched Jiggs.

"Dead." The rancher's mouth flatlined. "Four others are
weak and croupy." He sat down, still looking side to side with a
squint. "I heard Junior gave up and ran away. Did he sell the
place?"

"Naw. He came back and declared nothing was comin' out
of the kitchen with cheese on it."

"What about the tater tots?" Jiggs twisted right and left,
checking out plates of food on other tables.

Josie smiled as she took a seat. "You eat pineapple, or you go to the Minam Café for your burgers. The Huli Huli chicken is really good."

"How long's this gonna last?" Jiggs asked Misty as she set a beer in front of him.

"Probably till the new wears off." She pointed around the room. Every table was full. "You ready to order? Lomi Lomi salmon is the special tonight."

"Why aren't you wearing a grass skirt?" Jiggs leaned back, looking up at her. The server turned and walked away.

"He doesn't know any better, Misty," Chicken Thief called after her. "He's been talking to cows for a couple of weeks." He gave Jiggs a look that asked if, indeed, he'd been born in a barn. "She won't be back. She poured a beer in Muley Baker's lap for suggesting a coconut bra. I'll hafta take our orders to the kitchen. What d'you want?"

"Teriyaki beef with mango bread," Josie said.

"Sorry. When did everybody get so thin-skinned?" Jiggs grimaced. "Just soup and salad for me. I recently discovered I'm a little out of shape." He rubbed his belly expecting the feel of concrete abs he'd had since high school. Somehow they'd become covered with a layer of sponginess.

"Then don't come on Friday. Junior is baking a *Kalua* pig. The ground's too frozen to dig a hole, so he's doing it in the oven. Big luau." Chicken Thief shook his hips as he left for the kitchen.

"I need to ask you something." Josie said it so quietly, Jiggs had to lean close and ask her to repeat herself.

He swallowed. His breath caught in his chest with the realization it had been a while since he'd been around a woman his age that he'd liked enough to ask out. Now he was alone at a table with her, and because of the Hawaiian music this wasn't a communal conversation with the entire bar participating.

"Most people know about my grandparents' poverty. But are there other family secrets I haven't found out yet?"

Quicksand. Women loved to ask questions that caused regrets, and he was a master at digging deeper sinkholes. He studied the table. Should he tell her that her soft-spoken grandma had helped bury a man? Or that she and he were distant cousins. Or that he was privy to any of this because Miz Cliva had conscripted him as a secret keeper when Ox had died. He cleared his throat. "What brought this on?"

"I visited Miz Cliva to thank her for saving the pump and sink. I had other questions, too. It seems I'm the only one who didn't know about my mother."

Jiggs shrugged. "There's only one way to keep a secret around here." He looked into her anxious face. "Do what you need to do with no one around. Then never tell anyone about it." She opened her mouth, but he cut her off. "I know what I'm talking about. Never breathe a word of it. Only then ... you've got a middlin' chance of it not rolling through the tongue waggers." After a couple of seconds, he dropped his gaze to the table.

"I can trust you. I found—" She stopped as Chicken Thief approached.

Jiggs closed his eyes. This is how Miz Cliva said it would happen; people would unload their burdens, and by the time he was eighty, he'd be privy to the sins of the whole community. For now, he just wanted to know this lovely lady a little better.

"The soup tonight is something made with coconut milk," Bob said, sliding into his chair. "I figured you wouldn't eat it, so I ordered you a big shrimp salad instead."

"What if I don't like that?" Jiggs asked.

"I'll eat it."

"That's what I figured."

Bazz sashayed by, wearing a flowered shirt, grass skirt, and carrying a tray. "What're you high rollers drinking tonight?"

"I hope you've got shorts on under that get-up," Jiggs said. "My horse's legs aren't that hairy."

"Bring Curly Dogs in. We'll check, and he can wear the skirt."

Jiggs cocked his head, studying Bazz's tropical frock. "Why are you waitin' tables?"

"I'm working an event in the back room." He set his tray down and lowered his voice. "Dr. Dick's entertaining the prominent citizens."

"What a skunkmonkey. Why didn't he take them to a decent restaurant?" Jiggs asked.

Bazz leaned forward with both palms on the table and lowered his voice even more. "It's a sham. He's really angling to be mayor and convince them his projects will help the whole county, cure rabies, and bring peace to mankind."

"And he's having his meeting here?" Josie scowled at the back room. "Right in front of you?"

"Maybe he figures throwing a little money at the restaurant will buy my vote, too." Bazz fanned his hand to show what he was wearing. "Obviously, darlin', I'm not too worried about my reputation." He picked up the tray and left.

"Who has he got back there?" Jiggs called to Bazz, but the question was lost in the notes of a slide guitar twanging "Kuhio Bay."

"I'll scout it out." Chicken Thief jumped up, leaving Jiggs and Josie alone again.

"Have *you* ever successfully kept a secret around here?" she asked.

Quicksand *and* barbwire. Women were like obstacle courses; a man couldn't maneuver through and stay in one piece. His real family history was tales his father had punched people in the mouth for telling. Ox may be dead, but he wasn't going to unearth those stories now. "What're you angling at?" he asked.

"Forget it." She shook her head.

Jiggs heard more annoyance in her words than the situation called for. After all, he was the one dodging her bullets.

"What about your banker?" she said. "Is he a decent guy? I need to visit with someone about investments."

"Little McGinty?" Jiggs noticed his tongue loosened up if they were talking about a subject free of trip wires. "My family has always banked with his family. I went to see him a couple of weeks ago about my loan. He gave a handshake that I'd be treated fairly, but he was a sneaky little fart in school. A couple of times, I had to—"

"You're trying to buy that ranch?" she interrupted. "To save it from development?"

Jiggs eyed her a moment, trying to connect the topics. "Yeah ... Shiny Creek. It's certified as a Century Ranch. A property that's been continuously owned by a family for more than a hundred years. The Hopkins are buried there, all the way back to the great-greats."

"Would you consider a different lender—" she began.

Chicken Thief bumped the table, sloshing the beers as he hurried into his chair. "You can't believe who's in that back room. Everybody with a store along Main Street, and Guntis Kral."

"How'd he get an invite?" Jiggs squinted.

"That tight-fisted ol' Kraut can wheedle a free meal out of a homeless man," Chicken Thief said.

"What kind of hornswoggle is Dr. Dick selling?"

Standing behind Jiggs, Misty thumped his salad onto the table, making the rancher jump. "He's telling them how his resort will improve the tax base. Fund city improvements. Tourism will increase, which will provide jobs. Soon we'll have a Fourbucks Coffee Shop. Whee." She slid plates in front of the others. "He had Lottie until he said that."

"Now that I'm buying Hop's place, where's he think he's going to get enough land for his big-deal project?" Jiggs smiled.

Misty glanced at Chicken Thief, who looked away. She turned to leave.

"Wait a minute." Jiggs put out a hand, blocking her exit. "What gives?" He stared at her.

After a moment of eye dueling, Misty's shoulders sagged. "All right ... but don't get mad. Promise?" Jiggs nodded. "Well, sometimes I run food over to Frank before we shut off the grill, and he tells me things, you know?"

Jiggs' stare sharpened. She continued, "Dr. Dick has visited Hop a few times ... now don't explode." She fanned her hands. "He hasn't got to talk to him. Frank says his father has been asleep whenever Jarmin drops by. But I wish the jerk would quit waving all kinds of opportunities under Frank's nose. Money. Job offers with some engineers he knows in California. Jarmin says it's possible Frank could become a full partner in a firm in a few years."

Jiggs' face hardened. His teeth clenched. He pushed back from the table and stood.

"Whoa, buddy!" Chicken Thief grabbed Jiggs' arm. The rancher jerked free and started for the back room.

"Jiggs!" Josie hurried through the bar. She ducked in front of him, putting her palm on his chest. "I can help. I've got money—"

He pushed her hand aside. "Hop and I have a gentleman's agreement. If Jarmin thinks he can undercut it like he did last time, then he needs a lesson about cat-footin' in other people's business."

Nearby tables had stopped eating to watch and listen. Muley Baker, wearing his usual denim jacket with the arms torn out so his biceps would show, threaded his way between chairs, heading toward them.

Misty linked an arm through Josie's. "You're not getting through."

"Move." Jiggs' voice was low. He gave a hard stare at the schoolteacher. "I don't want your money."

Chicken Thief joined the barricade. "Hold up, bud. You said to wait till the odds got better to place a bet. Don't go jumpin' the gun on me. Now if you go gettin' physical about it, Dr. Dick's the one who'll win."

Muley's voice came from behind Jiggs. "That quack is all frosting and no cake. I'll hold these three if you wanna go in there and beat the guts outta him."

Jiggs blinked at the muscle-bound, twenty-year-old's statement. It was something he would've spouted when he was younger—when he'd let his mouth work before his brain was turned on. He cast an acid stare at Muley, turned, and strode toward the exit.

"The alley door to that room might be unlocked," Misty whispered, watching Jiggs leave.

"I'll stay with him." Bob ran out of the bar.

Ten minutes later, Josie was raking their untouched plates into take-out boxes when Chicken Thief stuck his head in the front door. "Get Bazz!" he hollered over the wavering chords of "Ka Huila Wai."

"He's in that meeting." Josie pointed toward the back room.

"Get him outta there. Try to be quiet about it."

She hurried into the back room, and a minute later Bazz crossed the bar, tossing his grass skirt on a table as he went out the door.

Pool stick in hand, Muley Baker watched from the darkened billiard room. "What's goin' on?" he yelled to Misty.

She shrugged and held up an empty mug. "How about another beer?"

Muley flipped the pool cue, gripping it like a club. He headed out the door. The waitress shot Josie a doomsday look.

In five minutes, Muley returned. "Nobody out there. Thought I could smell a fight." He ambled back to the pool table, scanning for rowdies among the Hawaiian diners.

"What's happening?" Josie asked when Misty handed her a tray.

"Who knows? They're all idiots. Help me, would you? Jarmin said to serve his guests as much booze as they wanted, but Junior's filling them up with food instead. He ordered a truckload of expensive supplies and has been happily cooking for days. Bazz says if we give them too much liquor, they'll believe the hogwash Jarmin's dumping on them. I've got to keep the fancy platters rollin' into that room. Could you watch the tables in here?"

For Josie, it was a half hour of delivering beers and looking up at the door every time it opened. When Jiggs, Bazz, and Chicken Thief finally walked through it, they were smiling and chuckling.

"It's all good." Bob's fingers circled in okay signs. His eyes glittered like a kid who'd stolen the answer sheet to a test.

"All right," Misty chided as she joined them. "You're grinning like a bunch of cartoon squirrels. What'd you do?"

"Man talk and fast thinking." Bazz tapped his temple. "That's all." The men looked at each other grinning, but no one said a thing.

The server rolled her eyes. "Okay. Be that way, but I'm not listening to any whining later. Now help me clear dishes. It's starting to pile up back there."

"No problem, darlin'." Bazz gave her a lazy salute. "I bet Dr. Dick's guests would like to eat more and hear about his great project." He grinned at Jiggs and Chicken Thief.

"Grab your grass skirt," she said flatly.

"They thought I was an idiot for wearing shorts in winter." Bazz hooked a thumb at his friends as they walked away. "Called me a Californian. I've been here ten years."

"I've got cats that've lived here longer than you, and you *are* an idiot," Misty said. "Besides, it looks like you bleach your legs. Don't you ever ..." Her voice faded into the bar noise and Hawaiian music.

Jiggs hadn't spoken to anyone since he'd walked in the door. He sat at Table 2, his eyes shining with excitement, unaware of Josie's glare.

"Hey! Let's celebrate," Chicken Thief said, getting up to rummage liquor and glasses from the bar. "I know where they keep the good stuff."

"So what was the fast thinking?" Josie asked, her voice sharp.

Jiggs glanced at her. "You know how I told you earlier, if you want to keep a secret, tell no one? It applies here." He rubbed his hand across the back of his head as he looked at his boots.

"So, I've offered you help, then spent the last half hour worrying, and you tell me it's a secret? Even though others know?" Jiggs sat mute and wide-eyed. "I see." She stood and left.

"Where's she going?" Chicken Thief set a tray with three beers and three shots of bourbon on the table.

Quicksand, barbwire. *And* thunder. Jiggs nodded to himself. "She wants to know what we did."

"Never pester someone for personal details," Bob quoted the well-known creed of The Way. "Besides, everybody'll find out soon enough." He dropped a shot glass in his mug and slurped the beer as it poured over the side. "You doin' okay?"

"Dad may have been right about me." Jiggs stared at the floor. "I just did the stupidest thing in my life—or the smartest. I'm not sure which."

13

A Donkey Wind

FAR ABOVE THE sixtieth parallel in the Yukon Territory, two winds wrestled and chased each other, rising up the face of a butcher-sliced summit in the Mackenzie Range. Soaring from the tip of the peak, snow spun after them. A cross breeze caught the ice crystals and trailed them like a glittering pennant, streaming from the crag.

The two currents coiled around each other, spiraling upward until they could climb no farther. With delighted shrieks, they fell in a dive, compressing and warming themselves. The old, growling winds that met each morning around the pinnacles cursed the young updrafts as they smashed against the face of the mount.

With the first few passes, the youthful gusts made snow fall from limbs, and coerced trees to clack their branches in forced applause. When the blasts gained enough speed and power, they discovered they could crack the sheet ice from bare cliffs and send rocks bouncing down the wall face.

Baying and howling, they repeatedly rose higher and drafted youthful gusts from the surrounding crests. Soaring downward, they attacked the flagged trees, the survivors of ancient weather battles. The old spruce wore their few branches like medals on one side of their boles. The juvenile winds vandalized them, twisting their limbs until they cracked and moaned. With squeals, the rebel gales and their followers spiked into the atmosphere again.

Diving toward the mountain, they sensed a change. A gateway had opened in the hemisphere. Somewhere a low-pressure zone had been born. With screams of freedom, the winds roared toward it. Their exodus sucked others into their wake with keening and wailing, as they streamed southward. They bullied the clouds away from them. Moisture would make them heavy and slow. Ripping through thin vapors of atmosphere, the howling pack raced faster. They dropped in bursts across eastern Washington, steamrolling plowed wheat fields and shimmying road signs.

The cows heard the wind caterwauling from far away. Its chorus of angry voices bickered and shrieked, claiming to be fastest, most powerful, or most enduring. Their arctic fists plowed into the cattle, making the animals scatter in search of trees, a ravine—anything to protect them.

In Two Pan, the blows hit buildings with an explosive *WHUMP*. Rafters creaked with grunts of fatigue. Screens flew off windows, tumbling end over end. Shingles stood vertical before they were torn away, flipped and juggled by acrobatic gusts. Airy hands slid behind the wooden screen door of Grubb's Mercantile. The spring croaked as gales battered it back and forth, tearing the hinges from the frame. Treetops bent toward the ground. The tempest circled and redoubled its effort until branches thrashed and writhed, splitting and tumbling through the air in company with signs and tarps.

Hermes stood in the street in front of the Bar and Grill, braying at the wind. His bawls were snatched by shrieking surges before anyone heard them. A Chevy pickup stopped. The gust caught the vehicle's door as it opened and flung it toward its hinges. A woman got out, ducked her head into the wind, grabbed the donkey's harness, and tried to lead him to his pen at the Feed 'N' Go. Laughing airflows bombarded them, making her stagger and Hermes kick at his invisible foe.

Above them, a thick, black electrical line ripped from its transformer. It fell to the ground, spraying white sparks and writhing in a wind-tossed dance. The woman's shriek was louder than the donkey's, but both were drowned by the roaring whirlwinds. The donkey and woman ran in different directions. The town fell into darkness.

That was the first night.

"The place looked closed, and then I saw someone coming out the side door." Whit's pale eyes peeked from under the three stocking caps swaddling his head. He stood in front of the checkstand in Grubb's Mercantile, rubbing gloved hands together.

Cleova Klegg, in a down jacket and earmuffs, punched the keys on an antique black register. "I put up a sign to use the other door." She banged a lever as though she were giving Whit's head a thump. A bell dinged and a drawer shot out. "Nobody reads anymore. You'd think they'd figure it out with the screen door ripped off."

"You lose power here in town?" A shopper plunked an arm-load of soup cans into a tiny shopping cart.

"Keeps going off and on. You might wanna pick up some bread." The checker nodded toward a shelf scattered with a few loaves. "They get it fixed and another line snaps. We're keeping the ice cream outside to stay solid, and the milk in the back room so it doesn't freeze."

"I'd hate to be hangin' off a pole workin' in this." Whit pulled the layers of stocking caps off his bald dome, exposing a ring of white, flattened hair. He squeezed several loaves of bread, then tucked one under his arm and shuffled toward the stove.

There were more people than usual sitting around the pot-belly. Whit waved his hats at a tiny woman. "Hey! Republicans meet over at the bar. You're in my chair."

The proprietor, Andy Grubb, stopped stirring the embers and shook the poker at the old codger. "It's first come, first squat, Whit." He tossed a chunk of wood into the firebox and latched the door.

"I've been sitting in my chair, solving the world's problems for the last twenty years. I got the cushions rooted out so they fit."

A woman who weighed no more than a lamb got up. "Didn't do a very good job at world peace, did ya? Take your chair. I'll cart supplies to Miz Cliva. I didn't see a light at her place last night, so I checked on her. She'd run out of lamp oil." The woman pointed at the carping old man. "We all need to be helping each other right now."

"You're a sweetheart." Whit winked as he slipped by and sat down before she was two feet away. "Thanks for warmin' it up. That howling wind kept me awake most of the night," he grumbled as he fussed his rear deeper into the cushions. Comments flew.

"Sounded like coyotes on the roof."

"Wore me out. I slept with a pillow over my head."

"My thermometer was pegged at minus twenty this morning."

While temperature comparisons and damage reports were given, the narrow aisles of Grubb's filled with residents stocking up. A second ring of shoppers, still wearing coats, stood behind the chairs circling the stove. The old store with its twenty-foot-high ceiling was hard to heat. Each time the door opened, a frozen gust pushed inside.

When the lights flickered, *Uh-ohs* jumped from mouths. A few seconds later, the electricity died. Andrew Grubb climbed a ladder and held matches to wicks of the dusty brass lanterns that had hung from the ceiling since the store had opened a hundred and thirty years ago.

Outside, the tempest catapulted corrugated tin from sheds. Bazz, wrapped in a fur-lined parka and insulated overalls, had been up since 4:30 that morning trying to start trucks and cars. He watched a rusty tub bounce across an open field. Hermes trudged toward the Latte Da with a mother and a cluster of children clinging to his harness. The adult waved, but her words were asphyxiated by gusts. Bazz assumed she must have cabin fever if they accompanied Hermes as he made his donut deliveries.

Throughout the day, gales wrangled the town and shrieked without stopping. In pastures, cattle gathered in ravines, heads down, eyes closed. They stood without grazing. The gusts gripped the plywood walls of their range sheds and levered them against the frame, testing the nails. Boards and tin flapped against posts, adding to the cacophony of the storm.

On his night vigil, Frank Hopkins added another log to the stove. Above the roof, the drafts circled the chimney, whipping to the north, then to the south; they stuffed the smoke back down the pipe. Frank coughed and cursed. To him, the rumble of the brawling air sounded like guffaws. When he looked out the window, the streets of Two Pan were dark. Only Bazz's house, running a generator, showed a twinkling of life.

A second night fell on Two Pan.

By the fifth day, the wind had changed from the noise of a locomotive to a keening lament. Residents were now used to the biting cold, but stayed inside, dispirited by the mournful squall. School remained closed. Hermes opted to stay in his shed, even though the winds taunted him, banging his metal gate open and shut.

Josie Blevins praised herself for having insulated her attic, yet the old farmhouse was still so drafty the teacher closed the new doors throughout the house and slept in the kitchen near the stove. Fingers of cold snuck under the thresholds. Wind imps whistled in the corners of her windows. When she held a hand in front of an electrical outlet, she could feel cold air breathing out through the slotted nostrils.

At the Two Pan Bar and Grill, water pipes buried two feet deep froze from the street to the building. Bazz used a flamethrower that he'd modified to burn blackberry bushes and scorched the ground until water ran out of the faucets. He stacked bales of straw over the thawed dirt. Soon, he received phone calls to rescue others.

Each day, Jiggs and his son took hay to their cattle. The herd at Starvation Ridge had taken shelter in the ravines. The men had moved their new bull to the barn because he wasn't range-hardened. Every day, Jiggs expected the bull's big hoof to pound his face when he inspected its scrotum. That five and a half-inch diameter of fertility had cost twenty thousand dollars, and it was the future of the Rocking W. He wasn't taking any chances with frostbite. Jiggs' horse didn't appreciate his new bovine roommate. Curly Dogs turned his rump on the rancher each time he checked on them.

In the fields, the elk and deer had moved down from the ridges. Jiggs and Nap brought feed and waited in their trucks until the cows and heifers finished eating. As soon as the truck drove away, the elk moved out of the forest and into the herd.

At other pastures, the cattle stood with glazed eyes, buckled to the earth inside open sheds or behind trees. Harrowed by the wind, they ate and drank very little, even though Jiggs fed and broke the ice twice a day. At these fields, the rancher dragged bodies of frozen cattle into a pile, usually the youngest. When dusk settled on the fifth day, six had fallen to the pitiless winds.

Each day dawned clear with a pale sun and the ever-moaning gales. Moisture had been freeze-dried out of grasses, leaving them brittle and stiff. By the sixth day, folks eyed their haystacks and woodpiles. They might make it through this blow, but it was only the tail end of February; winter was far from over.

At the Bar and Grill, tropical music played for the breakfast crowd in an attempt to overwhelm the anxious cry of the gusts. For the first few days of the storm, business had been bad, and the bar closed by seven, then people began seeking each other as a remedy to the constant torment. Today, breakfast tables were full of folks trying to drive away the whine of the night.

"I found four dead sparrows," the feed store lady said as she pointed out her order on the menu for Misty. "I've got feeders out, but the poor things froze to death." Stories and worries coursed among the tables.

Junior set a cardboard box of to-go containers in front of Chicken Thief Bob. The gangly man counted the boxes. "Now, tomorrow's Saturday. I'm bringing Miz Cliva and Old Man Tower in for breakfast, so don't make them a take-out." The tavern owner grunted an affirmative and retreated to the kitchen.

Muley teethed a semi-circle bite in his toast, shaking his head. "He won't come with you, Bob. That old salvage man doesn't go anywhere unless he drives."

"I thought they took his keys after he ripped the door offa Dr. Dick's truck," a thin man said.

Chicken Thief shrugged. "He hasn't had a license in fifteen years. But he needs to get things, so he goes. Even *he* has enough sense to stay put this week, so I'm bringin' him here."

"You're a good guy," Muley mumbled, his mouth full.

The lights flickered twice. Diners paused with forks or coffee cups midway to their lips and waited. The lights stayed on.

"Hey, Bob, thank Miz Cliva for Hermes' ear covers," Tracy, the feed store lady, called out. "He hates 'em and shakes 'em off, but don't tell her that."

Bob hefted the box to his hip. "I see Hermes at some of my stops, showing his teeth and bawling at the wind. He looks pretty stylish in that yellow serape and those green legwarmers."

"I bet he's waiting for someone to die during this storm." Muley pulled a knife across his throat, his tongue out, and then continued buttering another piece of toast.

"Stop that," Tracy said. "That's the last thing we need."

The room went dark. A couple of diners flicked on the flashlights sitting at their tables while others lit the lamps on the walls. Junior peeked out of the kitchen to see if everything was okay, then went back to his gas grill. As Chicken Thief Bob opened the door to leave, a chilling gust hurried in, blowing out the lamps.

At Shiny Creek Ranch, a young heifer was edged out of a range shed. Born late, she was small and found herself pushed to the front of the three-sided structure. Through the night, the breeze cupped its icy hands around her head and massaged her ears until they were stiff, and she couldn't feel them any longer.

As pink streaks smudged the gray dawn, the little heifer dropped to her knees. Dry fingers of air swiped the steam from her nose. She closed her eyes and rolled onto her side. Her heart thudded one last beat and became still. Glacial winds wrapped her in their shroud, stealing the last heat from her body, and soon, her black hair lay stiff, smoothed by polar fingers.

When Jiggs arrived, he pried her off the frozen ground so he could get into the shed to spread hay among the cattle. A movement in the trees, twenty feet away, caught his eye. A doe watched him. Her fawn, almost as big as she, stood nearby. They retreated into the forest as the rancher laid a flake of hay next to a tree and anchored it with a fallen branch.

He walked back to the sheds and pushed his way through the cattle, checking them for stiff, scaly patches of frostbite. Cold air seeped inside of his coat as he removed the tin of salve he kept next to his body so it would stay soft. He rubbed it on tails and ears. Even out of the wind and sandwiched between the cows, his bare hand lost circulation. He squinted in disgust as he thought about the meteorologist on this morning's farm report. The man had stood in a warm studio, pointing to a map of the world and blathering about famous winds like the Horse Latitudes, where sailors had dumped bloated horse carcasses overboard because the hot, fickle gusts had stalled. Naming nature didn't change its wrath. Watching animals die didn't make a job less painful, no matter what a scorching sun or a freezing wind was called.

The doe and her fawn had returned, shivering and pulling at the hay. Jiggs' face was stony as he put on his glove, staring at the carcass of his calf. This storm was Cow Killer to him. His dad would have used the old name, Death Winds. It didn't matter, it was all a waste.

The silence awakened them. In the newborn hours of the seventh day, folks were startled out of their sleep by what they did not hear. It was dead-air quiet. They came out of their houses in pajamas and stood wrapped in blankets and over-coats to stare at wracks of clouds floating in a black, soundless sky. Sharp starlight winked at them as they waited, listening as though this were only the eye of a storm.

A coyote gave a yip. Another answered. Hungry animals were coming out to hunt. In hushed voices, folks dared to hope it was over. How could something torment them so, and then disappear without a trace? One by one, they took a last look at the sky and went back to their beds.

Miles above them, another portal had opened. The screaming gales had shot like comets, hurrying toward another land and time zone. The sorrowful tailwinds were the last to follow. They ebbed from Two Pan, carrying the last breath of Hop Hopkins and leaving Hermes standing quietly on the old man's doorstep.

14

Handcuffing the Lights

IN TWO PAN, when the first day of March arrives like a lamb, residents say they can feel Earth turning, just for a day, as the seasons change.

A crystal-blue sky domes the rolling hills of sagebrush. Last week's winds fade to a whisper. Cool air, drawn from the nearest peaks into the valley, carries the scent of pine and cedar.

Today, black-barred shadows stretch beneath the wooden barricades sitting across Highway 82A. The spur road that snakes through Two Pan and crumbles into the Eagle Cap Mountains is closed until 2:00 this afternoon.

———

At the barriers, Curly Dogs sidestepped, his ears twitching. Jiggs patted the Appaloosa's withers, knowing the horse sensed the heartache in the hushed voices and somber looks. He too, felt the press of a dark cloud riding his shoulders, growing, waiting to burst.

In front of Jiggs, vapors of steam curled from the nostrils of the four heavy-footed Belgians harnessed to a Conestoga wagon. Muley Baker sat on the buckboard and pulled a worn leather glove onto each hand. He flexed his fingers, snugging the tips into place. Taking the reins, he arranged the straps between his fingers. Troy Archer, plain-faced and tall, whose most noticeable feature was his bony Adam's apple, climbed up the wheel and sat next to Muley. Without speaking, he zipped a down jacket over his black suit. The lead horses tossed their heads and snorted their impatience.

A quarter mile ahead of them, red and blue lights began flashing on the Oregon Highway Patrol car. Muley gave a gentle snap on the reins. "H-yup." The covered wagon rolled forward.

When Jiggs was very young, his grandfather had taken him to watch a similar procession. "See how the honor troupe hangs back?" His granddad had pointed at a group of horsemen. "Never follow a death wagon too close."

"Why, Grandpa? What'll happen if you do?"

The old man had simply shaken his head. "Don't crowd death, son. Give it wide respect."

Jiggs waited until the Conestoga had moved what he considered a proper shadowing distance, then nudged Curly Dogs. Five riders, wearing oilskin dusters, cowboy hats, and black armbands like his, joined him. They rode two abreast down the highway, staring at the countryside, not speaking. Occasionally, one would glance in front of him at the two drivers framed by the arched opening in the wagon's canvas cover.

In the narrow wagon bed laid the plain brown casket of Hop Hopkins. His familiar black Stetson rested on top instead of a spray of flowers. "Bury me in my hat," the old cowboy had told his son. "It was damn expensive, and I don't think I'm gonna get all the wear out of it."

A white gelding, tethered to the bolster ring, was supposed to follow the Conestoga, but without the weight of his master, Eagle gaited alongside the rig, preferring the view of the open country. A black scarf swayed from one side of his empty saddle. A pair of hand-tooled boots, with the head of a long-horn stitched on the toe bugs, swung from the pommel.

More than forty horses and riders trailed the six pallbearers. Ranchers gave a somber nod when they caught the eye of a friend. They spoke in single word sentences, if at all. The clop of hoofs became their marching conversation.

Cars and pickups followed the riders. The cavalcade stretched over a half mile as cattle—some with their heads over gates—watched. A few people stood by their mailboxes. More cars and trucks waited at graveled intersections along the five-mile trek and joined the honor train as it passed.

People from all over the country had returned to Two Pan. Young men who had spent summers repairing and sleeping along miles of Hop's fence; middle-aged men who had learned a hard day's work, bucking hay in Shiny Creek's pastures; old men who had scars and creaking joints from helping Hop break horses. They brought their families. They came home where their memories and their lives intertwined.

After the service at the football stadium, the Daughters of Two Pan fed everyone at the Opera House. After all, Hop's wife, Dottie, had been a quiet but solid pillar of their organization. Laughter and stories rang from the old auditorium as folks restitched their lives into the fabric of the town.

At seven that evening, Miz Cliva declared that her "eighty-year-old bones" were tired and asked if Jiggs would walk her home. Before they got out the door, he felt a pat on his arm and heard a voice pitched an octave too deep, like young men do when trying to sound older. "I need to talk to you." Jiggs turned to see Max Buddy, Jarmin's realtor.

He turned away, putting a hand under Miz Cliva's elbow, escorting her down the steps.

"Wait a minute, Woolsey." Max dodged down the stairs, his puffy hair wafting back and forth, and placed a hand on Miz Cliva's arm to stop them.

"This isn't the time or place," Jiggs growled. "Take that hand off her unless you want your teeth rearranged."

"Go ahead, but you'd be smarter to hear my offer." The realtor's stance was rigid, his lower jaw hooked out.

The corner of the old woman's square, hard-sided, black handbag banged him in the groin.

Barking a short yelp, he bent double.

"Pssaw! Such an ill-mannered boy." Miz Cliva frowned as she stepped around him.

Jiggs pushed Max out of his way and caught up to her in two strides. "I believe, ma'am, that's a side of you I've never seen."

She looked up at him, her voice slow with reflection. "We all have our secrets. Besides ..." she smiled sweetly, "I bet two dollars on you. We're going to win."

Seeing her to her door, Jiggs tipped his hat. "Thanks ma'am, but I can't let you fight for me." She gave him a chiding smile and went inside.

He walked to the stadium, sorting the day's events into piles he could deal with. The fracas with the realtor made the dark cloud on Jiggs' shoulders heavier. Miz Cliva banging the realtor in the stones for him ranged somewhere between sad and perfect.

Curly Dogs was tied to the first high line. Because the horse could untie himself, a metal carabiner secured his lead to the high rope strung six feet off the ground. He'd been fed, watered, and groomed; now he was busy ignoring Hermes, who was hitched at the next loop in the line, ten feet away. The little donkey had stretched his rope taut so he could stand as near as possible to the big Appaloosa. Jiggs gave the 4-H and FFA kids fifteen dollars for watching his animal and led him away. Hermes let out a snuffle, watching them go.

A Comanche moon was rising, making it easy to find the trailer Nap had pulled to town. Jiggs took his time, enjoying the silence and their soft shadows following them across the pavement. As he bolted the trailer door, he noticed the donkey still watching them. He strolled back to the animal. "You lonely, little guy?" The rancher scratched behind the jack's ears as he untied his lead rope. "Yeah, I know."

He led Hermes to a new spot under the trees and nearer people. Someone had started a fire in an old oil drum, and a group of kids and adults were warming themselves, sitting on hay bales around the blaze. From the shadows, Jiggs watched them, their features half-shadowed in the firelight. Hermes stood patiently next to the rancher as long as he was being patted.

It was their faces that had stopped him. Most of them were kids who had gone to school with Nap. Now they were young men and women. Some of them had kids of their own. When had he become old?

There were people he recognized at the funeral today and names he couldn't recall. When had the edges of his memory begun to fray? Maybe it was because he hadn't seen them since … he couldn't remember the last time he'd seen them. Life had slipped by. Part of him had been on hold after Pax died. Another big hunk erased itself after Katie passed and he had a thirteen-year-old to raise.

When he'd awakened from his grief, he hadn't exactly picked up his old life. There wasn't music in the house. It was Katie who always had the radio going. He never took the energy to drive over to someone's place and visit. It was hard without her—she was the talker. Jiggs rubbed the donkey's muzzle. "You wish you had a buddy to visit with, Hermes?"

Someone sitting around the fire strummed a guitar. There had been music at the funeral, Western songs on an acoustic guitar. Most of the ceremony had been a blur of feelings he'd tried to swallow down, and wetness he'd blinked back. There were so many stories about Hop. How he'd gone on his first cattle drive at fourteen. How government records showed he'd broken over 10,000 wild ponies for the cavalry.

He couldn't remember the words that the Cherokee Lutheran minister had said, but the meaning stuck with him. In a quiet, comforting voice he'd talked about the certainty of change. Jiggs frowned. It'd be a relief to feel that confident and calm as everything and everyone grew up, grew old ... and moved on.

The kids jumped off a stack of bales, then climbed up and did it again. These little guys wouldn't remember this night. They wouldn't know who Hop Hopkins was. They didn't even know who he was. Why was he trying so hard to save this place? No one would be thankful. They wouldn't even remember him.

In that stark moment, he could put a name to the dark cloud squeezing his throat and freighting his steps. Change.

He'd been so clever—or so stupid—the night of Jarmin's meeting. He'd found Hop Hopkins awake and alert and had written out a $5,000 check—every cent in his checking account—as a down payment on Shiny Creek. The mayor was able to supply the quit claim deed and notarize the signatures. Jiggs didn't want them to say anything until it had been recorded at the courthouse.

"Afraid Jarmin will jump your claim?" Bazz had kidded.

For Jiggs, that was part of the reason. Mostly it was because he didn't want anyone shaking their head or laughing at him. He'd bought a ranch during a drought, in a bad market year, unsure if he was going to get financing, or be able to make the payments. Once again, he'd gone off half-cocked.

When Hop Hopkins had finished signing, he'd grasped Jiggs' hand. A single tear had rolled down the sunken cheek, as he rested his head back on the pillows. "Make sure I'm buried. You know where."

"Yes, sir. But let's wait a while on that."

Jiggs understood. Hop wanted Shiny Creek to go on forever like it was, too. Moneyed men like Dr. Dick saw these acres as the dividend of an empire: dollar signs and bragging rights. In a landscape studded and trussed with cell phone towers, satellite dishes, and optical lines for computers, the world was galloping past them. If he could shelter a parcel, maybe change would settle someplace else.

It was a dream—a cracked one, perhaps—but he felt it to the root of his being. It would prove his dad wrong. The Woolsey spread would be bigger than his old man had dreamed. And he'd keep the community from becoming a collection of strangers. He'd hold back change. Maybe it would make up for Pax. It had to work. He was tired of guilt's chokehold and how life would've been different and better if his brother had lived.

The notes of the guitar drifted into his thoughts. Firelight flickered across faces. Laughing. Singing. Weaving memories together. Just yesterday, they were all people he knew. Today— he wasn't so sure. Tomorrow, twenty years would have streamed by, and different eyes and names would be here. He sighed. He was trying to do the impossible: handcuff time.

Hermes butted his shoulder. He'd stopped patting him. "You need a good combing," he said, feeling the grime from the neddy's dust baths coating his fingers.

Watching from the shadows, Jiggs felt like an intruder. Children squealed. Couples sat on doorsteps, leaning against each other, listening to guitar chords drift down the street.

Jiggs led Hermes into the circle of firelight and reacquainted himself with the younger folks watching the horses. Children stood on top of the haystack yelling, "DONG-kkey!

DONG-kkey!" until their parents made them hush and lead the jack through the rope lines, checking the animals again.

Excusing himself, Jiggs went to the Bar and Grill to collect Nap. As father and son walked to the truck, Jiggs extended his palm. Wordlessly, Nap tossed him the keys.

Years ago, he'd had told his son, "If I ever hear of you downing a pitcher then getting behind the wheel, I'll use the cattle prod *and* a whip on you. You call me. Anytime. Anywhere. I'll be there—no questions asked." Nap, having heard the lecture since he was three, often told Jiggs he should practice what he preached.

They were silent as they got in and pulled away. Jiggs stopped before turning onto Main Street. When the truck didn't move, Nap looked at his father, then leaned forward, following his gaze.

"Go another way," Nap said quietly.

For the first time in almost a year, Hop Hopkins' house was dark. In the past, there had always been a light in the windows—no matter the hour. Hop was there, fighting for a breath or dreaming of cattle drives. Frank was there, studying. Sometimes they saw his silhouette looking out, watching the world pass by. In the loneliest hours, someone was keeping vigil in Two Pan. Now, the windows stared, black and vacant. Already the house was losing the feel of the man who'd lived there.

Jiggs pushed the stick into gear and turned toward Hop's old home. As they neared, he saw two people sitting on the doorstep. Between them, a tiny candle cast a wavering golden circle on the cement. Jiggs nodded to himself. A number of people would be awake tonight. There'd be late-night vigils all over Two Pan. Hearts grew deep roots in this backbreaking land. His face hardened with resolution as they drove past. Maybe he couldn't stop change—but he *would* slow it down.

15

Secrets of the Eagle Caps

FRANK'S EYES WIDENED, then blinked. He drew a quick breath for a question. Three heartbeats passed before he let his air slip out as a sigh instead. A masked calmness smoothed over the revulsion in his face. His eyes cut away.

Jiggs knew the thirty-year-old would eventually say yes even though obscenities must be shouting in his thoughts. Jiggs hadn't been long-winded or delicate. He'd simply asked, "Do you want to help me bury your dad tomorrow?"

"Why are you doing this?" Frank squinted, shaking his head a fraction. "The funeral home—"

"Because it needs to be done, and I made your dad a promise." The duty-bound look in Jiggs' eyes cut off further discussion. "We'll be digging with shovels," he added. Frank gave a tight-lipped nod.

The next day, they saddled their horses at Shiny Creek. It was apparent the young engineer hadn't ridden in a while. It was also obvious that Eagle didn't think too much of having anyone other than Hop on his back. Jiggs had to give the younger man credit. He didn't complain. He didn't cuss or whack the animal even when the horse attempted to go under low hanging branches. He got control and made Eagle walk to the old homestead.

Frank took the shovel Jiggs handed him, inspecting it with an engineer's eyes for form and welds rather than a laborer's scrutiny for splinters. "Why're we doing it like this?"

Jiggs stabbed his spade into the sod and pried up a bite of dirt, spider-webbed with frost trails. "You've got other people buried out here, right?"

"Five generations. Well ... not right here. They're scattered around. Seems every time they added another piece of land, they picked a new site to be buried. My forebears didn't believe in density living—or dying."

"They all went to their final resting place by hand," Jiggs said. "Seems wrong to haul machines in here and claw their spots open."

Frank shrugged and thrust the blade into the ground, following Jiggs' rectangular outline. "I don't think we'll need this much excavation. Probably fifty cubic feet will do. I ordered a biodegradable coffin. The one at the funeral was a rental, if you can believe it."

"I'll take your word for it." Jiggs tossed him a pair of leather gloves. "You're the engineer of this project."

Without speaking, they took turns digging. Sometimes one of them used the mattock, hacking through errant runners of the nearby lilac or loosening rocks.

When the cavity was about two feet deep and the dirt pile about knee high, Jiggs straightened and stretched his back, gazing at the big bush. "Looks like this'll get frozen back." It was a pedestrian observation—the kind of statement a person throws out when he takes a break from focusing in front of his nose. It was the key that unearthed a cellar of memories.

"My great-great-grandma planted that lilac," Frank said, cutting and tossing dirt out of the hole. "She brought an all-but-dead root from her 'beautiful Missouri' and buried it here in hopes she'd have a piece of home to look at." Jiggs had heard the same from Hop when they'd worked this field together. Frank paused, knuckling his back. "She hated it here."

Jiggs' eyebrows rose. He gave Frank a look before plunging his shovel back into the ground.

"She left a journal." Frank stepped out of the hole to give him more room. "It's not a particularly happy memoir. What choice did she have? She followed her husband into the wilderness, had a kid every eleven months for five years, then sometimes starved and often froze until she died of old age at thirty-one. She's buried over there." Frank rested a foot on the lip of his shovel and nodded toward the forest. "The trees have grown up around the markers now. All of this was once a big meadow." He waved his gloved hand in a circle.

Jiggs paused, leaning on his shovel. "Years ago, I helped your dad clear away the log buildings. The old homestead had already fallen down. It was a rough day."

Hop Hopkins' face swam in front of him as clearly as it had twenty-five years ago. He'd seen Hop take some mighty blows from every creature that had a hoof, but he'd never seen that kind of pain on a face. The old cowboy had pinched the bridge of his nose and closed his eyes as he waved toward the pile of burning logs. "It rips me up," he'd said. Anger had filled the spaces between his cracked words. "I spent years helping my Pap fudge together these old buildings. Patch and repair, and they kept falling apart. It all rotted and felled to sawdust. Everything a man works for falls to nothing."

Twenty-one years old at the time, Jiggs hadn't known what to do or say. The old cowboy had given him a sorrowing look that still haunted him. Not until today did he understand what Hop had lost. Part of his childhood. Part of his life. Part of the security that comes with belonging to a place, and then discovering that it never really belonged to you. The land may abide you using it for a while, but it will go on long after you've become part of the soil. If only he could go back now. He'd know a word of comfort.

He glanced up to see Frank watching him. The younger man became pointedly busy. Jiggs went back to digging. They worked for a while, each keeping to his own thoughts. Then Frank loosed a memory into the daylight. His voice was over-loud. His words held a skinned, raw timbre. "You may've liked working summers for Dad, but fulltime—it was torture. He was good at tongue lashings for the simplest things. For variety, he'd add full-swing licks with a belt. But his specialty was ridicule. I gathered quite a collection of names because I was a lousy roper. Never mind that I won grand prize at the science fair every year. He never came." The dirt pile grew with each shovelful of childhood.

"Sounds familiar," Jiggs grunted.

Without giving directions, or breaking the flow of the stories, they moved out of each other's way, jumping into the deepening hole, or pulling one another out. After several hours, Jiggs went to his horse and returned with a couple of white paper sacks. "Lunch. Lottie made it for us."

As he ate, Frank continued talking. Impatient memories crowded together, interrupting another story mid-way through. His reservoir of recollections had burst. Abruptly he stopped talking and inspected the cross-section he'd bitten in his Chocolate-Volcano Bar. "What're the depth requirements for burial?"

"Well, you're the engineer, but I believe it's more of a personal matter. It's got to be deep enough that both you and your father will rest in peace," Jiggs said.

Frank nodded slowly, staring at nothing. After a moment, he jumped up, stuffed the brownie in his mouth, walked to the grave, and hopped into the pit. His gloves arced out of the hole and onto the ground.

The sound of digging followed. In rhythmic intervals, yellowish dirt flew upward. It was one of the mental videos that Jiggs would carry away from the day. Each shovelful was accompanied by a muffled grunt, then a thud. Clods rolled down the pile and into the hole, trying to sneak back to their rightful place. Jiggs escaped into the forest. He looked for a dead limb to use as a ladder, relieved to be away from the constant thump of soil, like the beat of a burial dirge.

Frank insisted on being in the hole, leaving Jiggs to haul dirt to the top. The deeper the young man dug, the grittier his recall of childhood: His dad's grinding stare when he finally gave up baseball. Criticism for failing his .driver's test with a white-knuckled grip on the steering wheel and sweat ringing his arm pits. The football boys, summer hired hands, tossing bales at him, knocking him off the hay wagon. His father's eyes—a cold, passionless stare—as he watched. "Grow a pair and be a man about it," he'd said.

Frank swallowed dust and sour bile. His voice quivered as his throat closed. "And Mom ... alone in the dark. Bug bites on her arms ... waiting for him to come home." His breath died to a whisper. The grown man, now an adolescent again, sank to the bottom of the grave, silently sobbing.

Jiggs seesawed between avoidance and obligation. When he'd lost his own dad, he'd been addled, but kept it to himself. He'd hated the man and loved him, unsure which emotion would fight its way to the top. When Katie had passed, he'd felt gutted, walking around without seeing or feeling. The pain that gathered behind Frank's guts and erupted in muffled gasps was too familiar. It made part of his heart bleed. A part he thought had mended.

He jumped into the hole. Birds and sunshine were immediately replaced by choked weeping and crumbling dampness. He laid a hand on Frank's back. "Your dad could be a real hard ass at times."

Frank barked out a laugh, turning his face away as he wiped snot on his sleeve. "He apologized, you know. Said ... he was sorry."

Jiggs' throat hurt from trying to throttle the feelings climbing his windpipe. He sat back against the damp wall and rubbed his forehead. "Well, at least he told you that much."

"For years I'd wanted an apology." Frank swallowed. "And the moment I got it ... it wasn't enough. I was still mad."

"Yep," Jiggs took off his hat and rested his head back against the wall. He stared overhead through the dirt window at blue sky. Both men sat for a time. Jiggs concentrated on loosening his jaw without letting a sound escape. Frank stared at tiny granules hanging from roots and snuffled. When the sound of his breathing quietened, Jiggs said, "Let's get out of here."

They sat at the edge of the pit with their legs dangling into the grave. It was another image Jiggs would take away from the day: their feet hanging into that dark hole. The air smelled like clear ice. The sunlight's warmth was comforting. Birdsong reached them as soon as they climbed out of the cut. After being in the ground, life seemed to wrap around them in the smallest of details.

The rancher studied the circles of dirt on their knees. "TV makes dying seem quick. It'd be something if people uttered words that made everything all right, then closed their eyes and left. But they don't."

"Dad asked me if he was going to make it." Frank poked the blisters on his palm. "What was I supposed to do? Lie and give him hope?" He shrugged. "I told him the truth."

"Seems to me, Hop would want to know what to expect."

"Then he started getting his financial affairs in order, saying goodbye to people, and making peace with God." Frank rubbed the side of his hiking boot against the limb-ladder. A damp roll of dirt fell into the hole.

"Is that where the Cherokee preacher came in?"

"Yeah. That's when he apologized. Dad even got baptized. He seemed at peace after that."

Jiggs nodded, watching their heels tap the dirt wall of the grave.

"I'm not merciful like God." Frank scrubbed his hand over his face then the back of his head. "I don't see how you can live a lifetime, hurting others, then at the last moment say you're sorry. You're forgiven. Rest in peace. What am I supposed to say when my dying father apologizes, and not really an apology? Just a ... feeble, 'I did what I thought was best for you.'

"I wanted to scream in his face, 'You could've *tried* to listen. Stopped judging me and supported something I wanted to do.' But I didn't. Like a coward I said, 'I understand.'"

Jiggs let the silence spin out for a while, then, "You sent your dad out in peace, saving yourself some guilt over yelling at a dying man. Sounds wise to me."

"Now I'm stuck with all the unresolved crap."

Jiggs nodded. "Not that I'm any expert ... I tow a horse trailer of guilt behind me, and many nights I've wished I could turn back the clock. Do things different." He chanced a sidelong look at Frank. "A grief counselor talked to me when Katie was dying." Seeing no surprise in the engineer's face, he continued, "It seems folks try to wrap things up near the end of their lives—their *own* crap, not everybody else's. The counselor said it helped the patient feel life was complete. Helped them find resolution. Katie wrote letters. She wrote some for Nap's birthdays, and one to his future wife, whoever she'll be. Wrote one to grandkids she didn't have yet. She wrote me letters to be opened on each of our wedding anniversaries for the next five years."

"Did it help?"

Jiggs shrugged. "Helped her. I guess that was the point."

The distant whistle of a train floated across the valley. The men stared at their feet. Jiggs said quietly, "I opened 'em all and read 'em."

"At once?"

He nodded.

"Even the ones to Nap and the grandkids?"

He nodded, again. "Like you say ... I was stuck with a lot of unresolved crap. Now my dad's passing ... that was different. He thought I was too stupid to take over the ranch. And ... I guess I was, because I never asked him about wills, papers, or bank accounts; and he never told me anything. 'Course, he was never gonna die. Everything was a mess. It was hard. I finally figured out that forgiving him didn't mean the rough-edged guff he gave me was right. But letting loose of it got me to realize that the past didn't matter. It broke my anger about him."

"How?"

Jiggs gave the younger man a sober look. "I buried him. Just like this."

Frank returned the rancher's gaze. His eyebrows relaxed, and the lines softened at the corners of his mouth. "How long does the peace last?"

"I'll let you tell me. Let me know in a year." Jiggs pushed to his feet. "You think this hole is deep enough?"

Frank pulled out the limb-ladder and heaved it aside. "I believe I've hit the bottom."

The following day, Archer's Mortuary delivered a fibrous, kayak-shaped casket to the empty farmhouse at Shiny Creek. Frank watched Jiggs loop several timber hitches over the coffin to secure it to the hay wagon. "You expecting Dad to jump out of there?"

"He was a bronc rider. He liked to be snug in the saddle." The rancher pulled the running end of the rope and tied it off.

Frank snapped the reins, giving his father his last ride to the original homestead, bouncing up a rutted road overgrown with weeds. Jiggs held Curly Dogs back, giving the death wagon wide respect as they followed.

When they entered the arching trees at the edge of the meadow, they could see ropes, pulleys, and a mule. A short man with a red wooly beard, wearing a fedora, held the reins of the animal and gave a single wave of his hand.

"Ennis!" Frank jumped down as soon as he got the wagon stopped.

The short man gave him a bear hug, pounding him on the back. "I told ya I'd be here. Are ya survivin', Frank?"

Jiggs waited for them to finish their exchange. It was the most cheer he'd seen on Frank's face in a year. So this was the fellow Hop had made special provisions to stay on the land. In the last month, Jiggs had ridden over most of Shiny Creek, but he'd never seen his strange guest. An old pickup was in a shed, and there was evidence that someone had been around. He'd found wires mended where trees had fallen on the fence. And after the storm, patches of shingles on the house had been replaced.

Ennis O'Day introduced himself, extending a meaty hand. The scruffy man came only to the rancher's chest, but his body was thick and muscled. His eyes seemed to know a constant joke as they beamed from under his hat. He reminded Jiggs of a walking brick with a sense of humor.

"If ya don't mind ..." The Irishman used a tone that said he damn well didn't care what anyone's objections were. "I'd like to be payin' my respects and helpin' with the interment. Frank told me of it last night."

"Frank's the man in charge. I'm only a friend of the family." Jiggs nodded, wondering how they'd communicated.

Over the grave, the Irishman had set up a framework of poles and pulleys. Jiggs backed the wagon to the hole. They pulled the casket into a corded sling.

"One last ride, Hop." Ennis smiled. "I'll try to make it smooth." He chuckled as he led the mule away, and the biodegradable coffin lowered silently into the grave.

"I understand you've been around here for a while," Jiggs said as he and Frank shoveled soil into the hole. The dirt no longer echoed on the casket. Now it mounded with a welcoming pat, as though it were glad to return to where it belonged.

"I come and go," Ennis said. "I can't stand crowds or shallow people. There are apartment-loads of them, and they seem to be multiplying like stress fractures on the planet." He and Frank grinned at each other, enjoying a private joke. When the final scoop fell on top, Ennis pulled a bottle from his saddlebag.

"How is it I never see—" Jiggs began.

"He's like Bigfoot." Frank smirked. "Always fading in and out of the trees right next to you. He used to scare me when—"

"Let us pay respects to the departed." Ennis held up a bottle of Jameson.

The men positioned themselves around the mound as the Irishman unscrewed the cap on the whiskey. "Hop, in all my life, you provided the only base I could anchor to. I vow I'll help finish what you started. May you be forty years in heaven before the devil knows you're dead. Goodbye, friend." He tipped the bottle, took a long swig, and then passed it to Jiggs.

"Hop, thanks for stepping in and being there. I'm sure you're riding where the tall grass grows." He glanced around the clearing. "You'll always rest in peace here." He took a drink and passed the bottle on.

Frank stared at the mound. "I said pretty much everything I wanted to say while I was at the bottom of that hole." He shrugged.

"Just speak whatever comes to mind, boy." Ennis waved him on. "Take a last time to address your old father, then get on with your life."

Frank held up the bottle of amber liquid and sloshed a couple of glugs on the mound. "We'll seal your grave with a drink, Dad. Enjoy eternity. And I hope they stuck your hat in your casket because I'm not digging you up if I find it later." He tipped the bottle to his lips. Jiggs and Ennis shot each other amused looks. The young engineer handed the bottle back to Ennis, then walked away and picked up a rope, looping it between his hand and elbow.

"Frank told you we'd be here?" Jiggs passed the folded netting to the Irishman.

Ennis stuffed it next to his pulleys in the mule's saddlebags. "I've been checkin' on him every night. I promised I'd look after him." He gave Jiggs a skeptical look. "I can see how you'd be wonderin' what sort of man is out here on your property. I believe that bein' a man of these hills yourself, you know the unspoken rule." Ennis checked both saddlebags to make sure they were evenly weighted and not rubbing the mule. "It's easier out here. I have an idea. I design it. I build it. I sell it. I do a little prospecting. I roam these hills, in the summers. I take care of what needs to be taken care of—if I won't be botherin' you."

Jiggs held out his hand. "It was okay by Hop; it's fine by me. I'll pay you for the repairs you've done around here."

"Not necessary. Being here, trying to find a little peace, is quite enough."

"Is there a way to get ahold of you if I need to?"

"Winters, I go to Arizona or the Cayman Islands." He gave a wink which Jiggs couldn't decode. "Frank will be finishin' his master's degree. I'll be around more since I'm keepin' an eye on him. You could leave a message with him." His callused fingers tied off leather cords, and he gave the saddlebags two pats.

Ennis circled Frank in another bear hug and said so long. In the short minutes Jiggs spoke to Frank, watched him climb into the wagon, and snap the reins, the Irishman had disappeared. Jiggs stared where the mule had been tied, and figured he'd gone east.

Some things were better left as mysteries. He and Hop had once found a wooden bowl in a nearby rockslide. Hop said it was a burial site. He'd explained how the Indians had made a pocket in the rocks for the body and gifts, then replaced the stones. The grave would be protected from animals, and year after year rocks would roll down and bury it deeper.

Jiggs snorted. They'd be safe—except from humans. He knew the unwritten rule Ennis spoke of. You couldn't tell people about mysteries like discovering a skull or a grave. Someone, sitting in a government agency or a museum, with nothing to do, would string yellow tape around the spot, then excavate half the mountain. They'd do scratch 'n' sniff tests on the bones, then put 'em on display. So much for "the undisturbed sleep of our fathers." He turned away from Ennis' escape route. To protect the secrets of the Eagle Caps it was best to follow the unspoken rule of prospectors: keep your gob shut.

He blew out a breath as he swung a leg over his saddle. Instead of burying grief today, he should've been celebrating. The bank loan had been approved this morning. McGinty said if everything went right, they could sign the papers in a couple of days.

It didn't feel special now. It was like having a birthday after having forty-six of them. It was the same as the day before. Glad to be alive, but it was only going to get harder to stay that way.

He rode under the trees, and turned Curly Dogs for a last look at the grave. The clearing was smaller than he remembered twenty-five years ago. Trees had slowly reclaimed the open space around the homestead, but Hop Hopkins could rest. The old cowboy would no longer be pained by nature as it clawed his buildings apart and threatened his weak grasp of ownership. Now he was part of the land.

Jiggs took a deep breath. A little part of him had died as they'd dug the grave. He'd lost a mentor, a friend who'd been there when his father hadn't. Tiredness rolled over him. Now, he faced years of replacing decayed boards, pounding fence posts squeezed from freezing ground, dredging ponds that filled in, and cutting back forests that threatened hay meadows. He might sleep, but nature wouldn't. Every minute of each day, something would be rusting, eroding, falling down, or filling in. His work would continue until he rested like Hop.

This is only the beginning, Tool. Jiggs ignored his dad. The work had begun long ago, rising to meet it had started when he'd buried Ox. Since then, he'd been able to run the ranch as he'd seen fit. He and Nap had bought a new bull and more land, and settled into a good routine. It was a "beginning." A good one.

The saddle creaked as Curly Dogs took a step. Jiggs pulled his shoulders back, adjusting to the invisible weight. Maybe he couldn't stop nature, but he could chase after it like the men who'd tried before him.

A willow thrush flew in dipping arcs and lit on the mound. It flicked clods with one foot, and then the other, cocking its head to inspect the dirt. The bird didn't seem to mind that death had been planted there. Peace still lived in the meadow.

Jumping to another dirt clod, the thrush watched a man on a horse ride slowly out of the sunlight into the shadows.

It returned to searching the soil.

16

Whopper-Jawed Signs

JIGGS RAN HIS hands over his jawline, checking for cuts and blood. He stared at the mirror, making sure he hadn't caught the mole beside his ear with the razor. Doubts crept back in. Did he always look this tired or had he simply gotten used to the face staring back at him? It had taken two weeks of inner sparring to work up the gumption to ask Josie Blevins out. Maybe to a movie so they wouldn't have to talk much.

Their paths hadn't crossed since the night he'd jumped off a financial cliff to buy Hop's property. He'd intended to ask her out last night, but his bathroom mirror had said otherwise. He had "orphan hair" as his mama used say. It edged over his ears and collar with a "You don't look like you belong to anybody" message. He decided to get to a barber before casting his heart out on a line.

Tonight, he'd raided Nap's bathroom. Tubes, bottles, and cans lay across the counter and in the sink. He wasn't sure if he was spraying on deodorant or cologne, but Nap usually smelled like a rich man's clothing store.

As he drove to town, he refined his plan. Josie usually ate at the Bar and Grill on Tuesdays and Thursdays. He'd wait until everyone was distracted and then ask her out. He needed a big commotion like Muley Baker's rattler incident.

The brawny man had been in the alley, trying to skin a nine-button-tailed rattlesnake. Its afterlife reaction was to coil around his arm. When he walked into the Bar and Grill with a snake for a bracelet, most diners didn't notice the rattler's head was missing—they scattered. "Get the hell out of here you fractious cretin!" Junior had cussed until his eyes bulged.

Muley made amends by asking him to cook the viper and dragging folks out of their vehicles to spend the next hour with snake nuggets, spicy dipping sauces, and beer. That was the kind of distraction Jiggs hoped for tonight.

He parked in front of the Bar and Grill, stalling his mission with the decision to get milk. A high priority item, he reasoned, since he was completely out. A few crickets made noise, hiding in the little moisture there was under the building. Other than that, the night was still, except for voices coming from the alley next to the Mercantile. Jiggs walked by. Stopped. Took one slow step back, listening.

"Give it to me, you little dipshit. Nobody'll know."

"Everybody'll figure out. Who else would know the combination?"

The short stock boy who worked at Grubb's was lodged in a corner, trying to grab the fat end of a baseball bat.

A sharp-nosed kid stabbed the bat into his ribs. "What the hell do you care? They'll never miss a few cigarettes and beer."

"Leave me alone, Gil." The short teen flung his arms over his head as the long-haired kid cocked the wooden bat.

"I once worked a guy over with one of those," Jiggs said. "Worst night of my life."

Gil Gedding spooked. He jumped and swung at whoever was behind him.

Jiggs leaned back, but still got clipped on the arm. "Son of a monkey!" He wrenched the bat from Gil's grip. Blond-haired

Jason peeked one eye from beneath his arms. The rancher rubbed then stretched his arm several times. "All right. I've stood in front of my dad or the principal too many times to ask what this is about. You'll both lie if you say anything at all." He flipped the bat, catching it with one hand on the narrow end. "You boys need to learn to settle your differences with what God gave you. Go ahead. Get this over with—use your fists."

His words seemed to hang in the air a moment as the teens translated the meaning. Gil reacted first, throwing a right into Jason's cheek. His second punch glanced off the shorter kid's shoulder making him fall into the wall.

"Leave him!" Jiggs commanded. "Let him clear his head."

Gil didn't step back. He paused, hovering over the shorter teen.

Jason launched off the wall, his head ramming Gil in the chest, his fists rapidly pounding back and forth without much power.

Gil drove his head between Jason's legs, and stood, toppling him. Then the long-haired teen jumped, landing with one foot on Jason's leg as though he were trying to break a piece of wood.

"Hey! No jumping," Jiggs called.

Gil raised a foot to do it again. The end of the bat rammed him hard in the stomach, driving his air out. He bent double.

"I *said* 'no jumping.'" Jiggs grabbed the hawk-nosed teen by the back of the shirt. Hair and fabric wadded in his fist as he dragged the kid away and shoved him toward the street. "What's your name?"

"Screw you."

"He's Gil Gedding. Boxer Gedding's kid," Jason said.

"That explains a lot," Jiggs muttered. "Did your pa teach you bring a bat to a chicken fight?" The teen stared at him with raptor eyes. "Go on. You got your licks in. Get out of here." Jiggs waved him away.

"That's my bat," Gil yelled.

"I'll drop it off at Sheriff Meyers. Pick it up from him."

The teen pointed as he backed away. "I know where you live."

"Everybody knows where everybody lives around here. Come see me if you've got something else to say. Now get goin'. Go cool down." Jiggs turned and extended a hand to the kid on the ground. "It's Jason, isn't it? Stock boy at Grubb's?"

The blond-haired teen ignored Jiggs' extended hand. He pushed himself to his feet, watching Gil walk off. "What the hell, Mr. Woolsey? You gave him an open invitation to kill me as long as he did it with his hands."

"Doubtful." Jiggs turned and ambled away. "He got in a few face punches. That usually satisfies a need to prove something." Jason didn't move. He stood, glaring. Jiggs turned back to him. "You'll learn—when someone starts fighting dirty, it'll only go sideways from there. You'd best do whatever you can to get away. 'Live to fight another day.'" He nodded toward the front of the alley. "C'mon." Shame and anger radiated off the boy as they walked.

"Why don't you come work for me during hay season?" Jiggs heard the words coming out of his mouth as though this had all happened before. "Best conditioning program in the county."

"I've *got* a job," Jason said as they turned onto Main Street. His tone was short and puckered with grudges.

"Your choice. Work it out with Andy Grubb." Jiggs opened the mercantile door. "Let me know." He went inside. Jason didn't follow.

Things were changing. When did he become the guy who helped young men fill the chinks in their foundation? He wasn't even finished with his own son. He passed through the aisles, wondering why he was volunteering to grow a backbone on other folks' kids?

Because it was something that needed doing. Turning boys into steady men. Why was he stepping into Hop Hopkins' role?

"Are you finished yet?"

Jiggs looked around to discover he was holding open the door of the dairy case, lost in thought. A brown-eyed, twenty-year-old woman waited behind him.

"Whoops. Sorry," he mumbled, hefting a gallon of 1% from the shelf and heading up the aisle. He set the plastic jug next to Cleova's register, still mulling over his new role.

"You look nice tonight." The checker's fingers danced over the keys. "How was your winter? Lose any cattle?"

"Seven." His face pulled into a sober frown.

The twenty-year-old had followed him. No milk in her hand. She stepped closer, skewering his light brown eyes with her dark ones. "Why do you raise animals to be killed?"

Jiggs squinted. "Pardon, miss?"

"So you make defenseless animals stand outside and freeze to death while they're waiting to be slaughtered?"

"No. They have shelter, but when temperatures drop below freezing for weeks, some may … die."

"Why don't you bring them inside? The Europeans do."

Cleova barked out a laugh.

"Yeah," Jiggs said, "they house all ten of 'em. I've got—"

"Why kill them?" Another young woman wearing a yellow bandana and holding a box of matches joined her.

"Because folks like to eat them." Jiggs shrugged.

"So you help people raise their cholesterol and create a nation of heart patients that require long-term health care? Not to mention Mad Cow, E. coli, and risks that come from shoddy processing?" The brown-eyed woman stood with her hands on her hips.

"Nobody's forcing them to eat it," Jiggs said.

"That's like saying you can cook or sell drugs; people don't have to buy them." Bandana-woman rolled her eyes.

"Have I offended you in some way?" Jiggs asked. "Ran over your cat? Spit in your yard? Breathed your air?"

"Your trade is offensive to everyone. Besides the health risks, there's the fuel consumption from hauling cattle which adds to emissions. Their methane alone has added to global warming."

"Those are dairy cattle," Jiggs said with a frown.

"Oh? Your cows don't fart?" Bandana-lady's matches rattled as she gestured. "I suppose they don't create waste, so there's no manure in creeks either?"

"No. My water sources are fenced. I take care of my land."

"You've moved in where there should be open prairie and fenceless valleys. You big operators gobble up the acres and water. Little guys don't have a chance at sustainable farming. This would be a wonderful place if there were more available water."

"So would hell." Jiggs gave the young woman a pointed nod and pushed a five-dollar bill toward Cleova. "I only came in for a gallon of milk."

"Why ..." Ms. Bandana's words were greased with anger, "is man the only animal that drinks the milk of another species?"

Jiggs shook his head. "Lady, I don't know what's got your hair in a knot, but I'm one of the good guys. I take care of my animals. I tend my land. I give back to my community. And I like milk." He shrugged, palms up. Cleova dropped change into his open hand. "My neighbor is the one you want to lecture. He's one of those guys who collects farms to raise three or four horses."

"Do they eat the horses?"

"No." Jiggs squinted at her. "His nags have more papers and titles than the queen."

"So he doesn't leave hundreds of animals in the freezing weather, waiting to be slaughtered, then hauled in belching diesel trucks to filthy processing plants so someone can get their dose of heart attack at a fast food restaurant, and I can spend my taxes supporting farmer subsidies and a deficient health system?"

Jiggs stared at her, opening and closing his fingers next to his pressed jeans.

Ms. Bandana raised her chin, daring him to refute her. "That man sounds like a hero to me."

Jiggs turned on a boot heel and walked out of the store, letting the screen door bang behind him.

What was wrong with the world? When he was a teen, if he'd talked to an adult like that Gedding kid had in the alley, his nose would've been backhanded to the side of his face. And why did that woman think he was terrorizing America because he raised cattle? Had there been some sort of Rapture, and he was left behind with all the bughouse cases?

With clenched jaws, he strode to the Bar and Grill, flung open the door, crossed the room, and dropped heavily into the chair next to Bazz.

"You kill somebody?" the mayor drawled, looking up from his newspaper.

"Fixin' to." Jiggs stared at the door, tapping his finger on the table.

"Dr. Dick?" Bazz asked.

"He'll have to take a number."

Misty set a beer in front of the rancher. "No problem. I heard Jarmin's back. It's his turn to relieve his partner and take the spring shift in the Oregon outback."

Jiggs glared. "Some little ... honey-bunch ... over at Grubb's ... just compared me to that monkey's brother—and he came out better."

"Who did?" Misty asked.

"Somebody who thinks my trade is a meat locker of iniquity. She said I was a big operator and an ugly animal abuser." Jiggs took a long pull from his mug.

"I disagree," Bazz said. "You're not ugly, although Dr. Dick is a lot better looking. Course, that's probably not his real nose and yours has been broken a few times, but it gives you character. I think he owns more land, too. Not that you're competing."

The door swung open and Zimm Lubach hollered, "Hey, Jiggs! You left your milk." He chuckled as he set it in front of the rancher. "And your bat." He held it up to show the nearby diners. "Look what he's started carrying around town. That should make the odds go up. I was in the cereal aisle when this gal ..." He launched into the story. Others bombarded Jiggs with wisecracks, but he didn't hear. He stared at the door.

Josie and Chicken Thief Bob were trying to get around each other in the doorway. The lanky man stood aside, bowed, and let her pass through first.

Chicken Thief plopped into a chair. "Guess whose SUV I saw at the gas station last night?" Jiggs watched Josie sit at another table with Lottie Lubach and listen to Zimm recount the beef skirmish.

Misty set a beer in front of Bob. "Yeah, we know. Dr. Dick's back from his winter hiatus. And Jiggs is gonna butcher some vegans. Now you're caught up with the conversation."

"Wait a minute. Why's—"

"Oh, some Free-The-Cow groupies came through, and Jiggs got caught in their sights." Misty flipped her towel over her shoulder and walked away.

"I could use a MEATatarian bumper sticker. Dr. Dick has removed all of those stickers I gave him last year. It was a nice, intelligent collection."

"I think he's had enough. You're not starting that again?" Bazz asked.

"Mm-huh." Chicken Thief nodded, wiping beer foam from his mouth with the back of his hand.

Bazz looked at the ceiling, "I have to hear about this in Council meetings, and you're gonna spend a few nights in jail for destruction of property."

Chicken Thief pointed a finger at Bazz, giving him the stink-eye before he turned to Jiggs. "Drinking a little heavy tonight, aren't you?" He waved at the gallon of milk and empty mug next to it.

"I'll put that milk in the fridge for you," Misty said. "You want anything else?"

"Thanks. I'm kinda fog-brained right now. I should've bought milk last," Jiggs said. "Could you bring me a bourbon and better company?"

Bazz's eyebrows rose to his hairline. "Drinking better stuff since you and Dr. Dick are members of the Excessive Acres Club?"

Jiggs let out the slow breath of a man who was about to take a long walk into hell. "Shut up." He stood, and moved five feet to the table where Josie sat.

He stood next to the schoolteacher. Zimm was acting out the guerilla vegans shaking matchboxes. "Excuse me, Josie, would you join me at the bar? Zimm hasn't been vaccinated against run-at-the-mouth-disease. I think we can find better company."

"Heads up, Jiggs," Bazz called out. "Your better-looking brother just came in the door."

The chiseled cheekbones of the man in the entryway emphasized his intelligent green eyes and straight Roman nose. His gray suit jacket hung open, revealing a plum shirt, unbuttoned at the collar. Jiggs and Bazz exchanged their dislike of Richard Jarmin with a glance.

The doctor's eyes scanned the room, pausing at the stuffed dog with crow's-feet stitches across its belly. His business card still prominently hung on the collar. He put on a Chiclets smile and turned his attention to Bazz. "It's been a while, Mr.

Mayor." He extended his hand. "Perhaps you'd join me at the bar while I wait for my take out? I'd like to visit with you about a promising, new project." He then nodded a silent greeting to the rest of the room. His gaze floated over Jiggs, landing on Josie. "Would you be able to join us, too, Miss Blevins?" Jiggs watched her rise and follow Bazz across the room.

"Well, there you go, Jiggs." Zimm winked. "You got her to the bar."

"How does your wife tolerate you?" Jiggs asked.

Lottie Lubach looked away like a woman who's afraid too much truth seeped through her eyes. "Why do you think I work?"

Jiggs returned to Table 2. Chicken Thief joined him and hitched his head toward Dr. Dick. "I just slipped outside. You know what that turkey turd has done? He's put powder coating on his bumper and tail gate. It's like the stuff they put on restroom walls at movie theaters so you can't write on them."

"Write on a lot of toilet stalls, do you?" Jiggs asked.

"Just Bazz's number. Nothing sticks to *it*, either."

"What're you gonna do with your bumper sticker collection now?"

"I slapped it on top of his cab. It'll be sun baked by the time he notices it. I'm disappointed people won't be able to read them. I take a lot of effort to pick out the right sentiment."

"What'd this one say?"

"Honk if the twins fall out." Chicken Thief smiled.

Jiggs stared at the trio at the bar. He'd wished for a distraction. Somebody who controls fates must be having a belly laugh right now. "How long is that forty-cent piece gonna talk?" Jiggs said, watching Josie smile and look up at the doctor. Bob stared at him.

"What?" the rancher growled.

"I can give you some advice on how to get a date, but you'll need to apologize to her first."

"I'm wondering what business that skunk-monkey's discussing that he can't tell everyone." Jiggs took a drink.

Misty set another beer in front of Bob. "I couldn't stay close enough to hear."

Jiggs drained his bourbon. "I'm out of sync with everything. I'm nuts for thinking Jarmin's a parasite because he buys land and doesn't produce anything. Those veggie gals think *I'm* a villain because I actually use the land. And, why do I need to apologize to Josie? What'd *I* do? When did the world get so mushy?"

"Aaah. It all depends on your point of view. Nothing's ever black or white." Chicken Thief stroked his chin, one eyebrow higher than the other. "Did you get your hair trimmed, shirt pressed, and slap on some cologne, or am I simply dressed shabbier than usual?"

Misty poked Bob in the shoulder. "Or ... are you vandalizing Dr. Dick's truck or decorating it?"

"Good example but I don't really care." Chicken Thief hoisted his beer in silent salute to Jarmin then took a drink. A grin stretched across his face. "Is the attractive new schoolteacher interested in going out with Jiggs ... or not?" Misty hurried away from the table.

"You've stepped over the line, buddy boy."

"You're staring a hole through her. You're out of practice. You know, there are eight men for every woman out here. If you don't make a move, somebody else will. I can give you advice."

Jiggs rose and pushed his chair in. "I think I can figure it out." As he left, he stopped at the bar, slapping Bazz on the back, not waiting for Jarmin to pause his soliloquy. "I need to talk to you about a welding job as soon as possible."

"Bring it by the shop tonight, I'll be working late." Bazz gave him a nod, then turned his attention back to Jarmin.

The rancher stood for a moment, feeling like a kid not chosen for a sandlot baseball game. He hesitated, then walked away. "Jiggs!" Misty hollered across the room from the kitchen doorway. "You want your milk?"

He caught Josie's bemused look as he turned around. Something about her one-sided grin reminded him of the time Dooley Monroe had hidden his clothes after P.E. class. Jiggs had rummaged the lost-and-found barrel for something to wear. As he traipsed to the office in a pair of stretch-tight gym shorts, guys whistled and girls in the hallways had that same entertained look. No, Josie didn't smile at him the same way she beamed at Dr. Richard Jarmin.

"Keep it." Jiggs made a slashing motion.

"Don't forget this." Zimm tossed him the bat. Jokes followed as he made a conscious Gary Cooper amble, trying to escort his dignity to the door.

Outside, he leaned against his truck, breathing deeply. Could things have gone any more haywire? He'd racheted up his nerve to ask Josie out, and Mr. Plastic threw a monkey wrench into the whole thing. What was happening?

He made a living the way his family had for the last century. Now, it was politically incorrect and ruining the planet. He was trying to keep a wanna-be land baron from moving hardworking people aside, and those gals crucified him for it. When did the world start spinning whopper-jawed?

An arctic blast had taken part of his calf crop. He'd signed bank papers on the same day he'd buried a friend. This spring had been bone dry, forcing him to feed and threatening to keep him from making loan payments.

He glanced at a man getting out of a Toyota RAV4. "Bound to happen," he muttered, confirming his bad luck.

Max Buddy walked toward Jiggs, the pouf of hair on top of his head jerking with each step.

Jiggs held up a hand, giving him a warning look. "Not to-night, puffball. I'm not in the mood." Behind him, the bar door swung open. Zimm and Lottie stepped out. "Craphouse crickets," Jiggs grumbled. "I can't catch a break."

"You listen, Woolsey." The realtor stood close, making as if he were going to tap Jiggs' chest, his hand fluttering away at the last moment.

Lottie tugged her husband's arm. "Zimm, do something before it turns ugly."

"I've got money on the realtor," Zimm said. "No offense, Jiggs, but I know your history."

"Everyone knows about you, Woolsey." Max Buddy's voice deepened and picked up speed. He stuttered a little when Jiggs moved the bat to his other shoulder but continued, "You're ruining this community. Delaying these folks from retiring." He nodded toward Zimm and Lottie. "Keeping others from jobs. That's all they talked about at the development meeting. You're the biggest disappointment this town has produced."

"That's not what anyone said at Jarmin's meeting," Lottie squeezed between the Realtor and Jiggs. "And unfortunately for me, Zimm is already retired." She threw a long-suffering look at her husband, and then an angry scowl at the land broker. "Why're you lying like this, Mr. Buddy?"

Jiggs looked down at the small woman who only came up to the top button of his shirt. Still gripping the bat, he used both hands to move her to the edge of the sidewalk, speaking slowly. "Thank you, Lottie. Really. But I can do my own fighting."

Beyond Lottie's shoulder, sitting in the RAV4, Jiggs recognized the face of the brown-eyed vegan. She watched him from the passenger side of the car. Her bandana-friend stared out from the back seat window. The windows began rolling up.

"That your car?" Jiggs asked the broker, pointing with the bat. Max Buddy stood still—even his hair.

"Let's put everything on the table, puffhead." Jiggs scanned the short, cocksure stance of the Realtor and categorized him as a guy who played football from his armchair. "You want me to punch you, so you can hang me with threats and a law suit until I let go of the Shiny. Right? Lemme ask ... is it worth it, prostituting yourself like this? How much is Jarmin paying you?"

"Not a cent. People are afraid to tell you what they think of you. You're a hot head. And a dinosaur. Your time is over. I'm simply acting as I see best for everyone."

"So that's the measure of you? You brought in a couple of vegans to prime me to punch you?" He pointed at the car. "You'll have to do better than that if you're gonna take a hit for Jarmin." Jiggs gave him an iron stare. He jerked forward, feinting an attack. Max Buddy jumped back. Jiggs walked past him.

"Why don't ya knock his headlights out?" Zimm said as he and Lottie followed. "That'd teach him something and not cost you the bet." Lottie dug her elbow into her husband's ribs.

"You do it." Jiggs strode on. "He lied about what you said, not about me. I *am* a hot head and a dinosaur." He turned, walking backwards, and tossed the wooden bat. "When you're done, leave that with the sheriff."

Zimm, built like a stump, grabbed and missed. The bat clattered on the sidewalk, rolling to the feet of Max Buddy.

Jiggs kept walking, glancing up at the stars, cold and glittering. Silent. Unconcerned with his plight.

Nothing was working. Nobody was calling him a hero for trying to save the town. He didn't even have milk for cereal in the morning.

17

The Stars Have No Ears

LIGHT GLOWED THROUGH the doorway and windows, casting slanted golden rectangles on the ground outside of Two Pan Repair. Inside, the smell of oil and grease drifted through the garage. A dying neon bulb hummed from the ceiling. On one side of the shop Jiggs took apart a carburetor while he waited. "So what'd Jarmin want?"

"Some B.S. strategic planning session. Who knows what he's really after? Toss me the hammer," Bazz said as he held a lawn mower wheel to an axle. He'd waited three weeks for a replacement bushing. It didn't fit. He pulled the piece, examining the steel ring on his palm. Someone had changed the part after production. American manufacturing had become shoddy, run by propeller-headed kids who couldn't even balance a checkbook. He'd have to heat the wheel and seat the bushing with a block and mallet. He sighed as Jiggs handed him the tool. His eyes felt like they were sinking in their sockets.

A quick scent of sulfur rose from the match. He lit a propane torch and adjusted the flame into a blue arrow. Steadily, he waved it across the steel. His eyes wandered to the big clock on the wall: one in the morning.

Snapping off the torch, he grabbed the hammer, tossing it slightly to adjust his grip. As he gave the hot hub a couple of taps, the crunching sound of tires on the gravel driveway filtered through the open doorway.

"Finally!" Jiggs said. "Sorry to make you wait. Nap must've had trouble moving the baler from Greenduck."

"It happens." Bazz shrugged. From haying season through harvest, he spent odd hours keeping tractors running and implements patched for most of the county. The rest of the year he revived whatever dying machine had been dragged to the shop.

He'd spent twenty years as an equipment mechanic at Boeing in California. Owning a small restaurant-bar in a forgotten byway was supposed to be a slow life. It had consumed every weekend and vacation. He'd gladly sold it to his son. Junior was the obsessive one. The one who was wiser than his old man. Let him worry about perishables and the Oregon Liquor Commission.

He frowned at the line of lawnmowers awaiting repair. When had he last worked on his '49 Chevy truck that was supposed to be his retirement vocation?

Bazz walked to the doorway, resting his palms on the lintel. Light from his shop fell across an unfamiliar SUV with kayaks strapped to the roof. "Nope. Not Nap."

Jiggs joined him to peer at two young men walking around their vehicle to trade places. The new driver gave them a single chin-tuck as he got in the car.

Bazz raised a hand in response. "I wonder how much farther those daredevils have to go, and if they'll be too tired to paddle once they get there."

"Probably not," Jiggs said. "They're young and no doubt full of energy drinks."

The men stared at the red tail lights snaking down the road and kept staring long after the sound of the engine had faded.

"Twenty-somethings on a summer adventure." Bazz leaned against the doorframe and blew a long breath through puffed cheeks. "Work and study in my early days robbed me of that time to enjoy life."

"Yep. That's what Nap says. He complains he never has enough time to see his girlfriends anymore."

"How're you getting along, running the ranch together without Ox?"

"I'm old-fashioned. Ignorant. I don't tell him anything and I'm wrong most of the time."

"That stage lasts about forty years. Look at Junior."

"Great. I've got that to look forward to." Jiggs glanced at his watch. "Nap must be broke down somewhere without cell service. I'll find him. When do you think I could get that part welded?"

"I'll be here. If it's not you, it'll be somebody else with an emergency. Call when you find him."

He watched Jiggs' tires spit gravel and his truck speed away. In the distance, an owl hooted for a mate. With a groan he pushed off the doorway. As he trudged back to the workbench, his gaze fell on the hammer lying by the tire. During the years leading to his bachelor's degree, he'd worked as a framing carpenter on a crew supervised by his father. His dad had told him at the start that he'd need gloves and a hammer of his own. He'd found a new one—with a black head and eight-sided, bright yellow handle—in his mother's tool box. Since it was unused, it would be perfect for his summer job.

On the first day of work, his dad pointed at Bazz's tool belt. "Let me see that." Bazz delivered his sturdy, unscarred tool.

His father weighed it in his hand, then handed it back. "Not much of a hammer."

While pounding ten-penny nails into studs, Bazz soon learned what his dad already knew. The hard oak handle was as unyielding as stone. Its eight sides were difficult to grip, even with gloves, and when his hand sweated in the summer heat, the shaft twisted with each strike, bending the nail. He spent nearly as much time straightening or pulling nails as driving them.

On a morning, two weeks into the job, he was yanking hard on a nail when one of the claws broke. He fell backward, landing splay-legged on the particle board floor. Bazz got up, slapping sawdust from his jeans. In amazement he examined the broken head. He'd never given a thought to how it was made. It had never occurred to him that a hammer could break.

That afternoon, he was framing a window opening when he felt eyes watching him. He concentrated on hitting the nail square so he wouldn't have to pull it out in front of an audience.

"Looks like you broke your hammer." His father's voice rolled over his back and settled like a weight on his shoulders. Expecting a lecture, Bazz focused on his aim and pounded his target without speaking. "Cast iron—that's all it's good for," his dad said and walked away.

He kept using it, but had to borrow a pry bar to straighten or pull the bent nails. Wherever he worked, he took the tool along in his belt like a pirate stumbling around with a bulky saber.

Several times his dad suggested, "Why don't you take some of your money and buy a good hammer?"

But he was nineteen and mad at the world, so he just grunted, "It works. Leave me alone." He stuck the broken-claw, slick-handled hammer in his belt loop and carried it to prove a point. To his way of thinking, buying a carpenter's hammer for a summer job was a waste of money and silently bound him to the occupation. He was going to be an engineer. He needed every penny he could save for college. He'd use a rock lashed to a stick if need be.

About three weeks later, he was beating a 16 penny nail through a 2X4 when his father walked up. "Let me see that." Scowling, Bazz slapped the wooden handle into the upraised palm and waited for another evaluation. Instead, his dad gave him the tool he was carrying. It was a new top-of-the-line item. A slim, fiberglass handle with a rubber grip molded into a forged steel head.

"Where'd this come from?" Bazz asked, suspecting something parental—like buying a hammer for him. He resented it.

"Just try it. Tell me if it's any good," his father said as he walked away, taking the yellow hammer with him.

From that first stroke—the sound ... the feel—this hammer was different. The head didn't rebound after striking a nail. The shaft surprised his fingers by staying locked in his grip, without the twist he expected on impact. And it was balanced. The weight lay evenly, almost lightly, in his hand. He bent very few nails that day. Using that hammer felt like an extension of his arm. He hadn't been driving nails before; he'd been bludgeoning them into place.

"How'd that hammer work out?" his dad asked at the end of the day.

"It's all right," Bazz said tonelessly. "Where's my yellow one?"

"I threw that son-of-a-bitch away."

"How much do I owe you?" He stared at his dad with the sullen displeasure perfected by young men carrying chips on their shoulders.

His father never replied—he walked away. Bazz never brought it up again. He understood the act was one of those father-to-son gratuities that would be meaningless if reimbursed.

The sound of the hoot owls interrupted his thoughts. Bazz picked up the hammer, his hand testing the balance. He'd used it four more summers, working his way through college. He was still using it—forty years later.

Stepping outside, he drew a deep breath. The crescent-bladed moon hung low in the west. Overhead, the residents of the Milky Way fanned through a velvet sky.

He wasn't a wildly religious man; he'd kept his faith closeted to keep from burdening others. He did believe that God put a light in the sky to memorialize each human who ever walked the earth. That's why some stars shone brighter than others, but he didn't believe they listened to the conversations of man. He figured when a person finished with the bramble of problems that was life, they weren't interested in watching any more of it unravel. There were better things to do in eternity. No reason to turn their ears toward anything left behind.

He searched the sky for the star that might be his father's. Billions of stars. Billions of lives that had passed. He hefted the hammer to the twinkling lights and gave a nod.

Back at his workbench, he set the wheel hub on an anvil and worked his grip until the hammer felt balanced in his hand. "You were right, Pop," he said. "It took me a while, but you were right."

His voice blended with the *clang* of metal and faded into the symphony of crickets serenading the stars.

18

Some Things We'll Never Know

AT FIVE IN the morning, Chicken Thief Bob walked into the deserted Bar and Grill. He stuck his head through the kitchen doorway. "Junior? You back here?"

"Whaddya need?" The tired-looking owner stuck a butcher knife through a fifty-pound mesh bag of onions, slicing open the top. Yellow bulbs tumbled across the stainless steel work area.

"Too early for breakfast?"

"The door's open, isn't it?" Without looking up, Junior began peeling an onion.

"You feel like making me a Two Pan omelet before I haul gravel?"

"Hell no." He pushed the papery skins into the vegetable sink. "But you're going to want one anyway." He glanced up, raising an eyebrow questioningly.

"I can go to the Latte Da if I'm bothering you." Chicken Thief's voice was flat as he rocked toe to heel.

Junior slapped his knife on the counter and yanked a skillet from the rack. "Anyone else out there?" He fired up a burner and grabbed a bottle of chipotle-flavored olive oil.

"Just me." Chicken Thief returned to the dining room and started the coffee brewing behind the bar. He slid onto a chair at Table 3, the morning discussion table, which filled up early. If he arrived late, he had to throw his comments into the pool from the second row. Sometimes chairs circled three-deep around the area. State of the Union speeches had that effect.

Regulars drifted in. Someone brought Bob coffee as a conversation warred about the knuckleheads in Whitman County using their city money on urban upgrades.

"That's what it'll be like if we start that doctor's development project. Everything'll look like a metal Box-Mart," said a fat rancher in faded overalls who needed two scoots to get his chair close to the table.

"I say that's a good thing," a square-chinned man answered. "Look at Cartwing's Feed Store. Now that they've fixed it up, you don't have to worry it'll collapse if you buy the feed sacks stacked around the support posts."

"That old place would've lasted another fifty years." Bazz slid into a chair and the discussion. Dark circles underlined his eyes, matching a scratchy overnight beard. "They knew how to build 'em in those WPA days, gentlemen." He took a careful sip of his steaming coffee.

A loud thump turned heads. "I'll get it." A turkey-necked rancher was already rising. When he swung the door open, Hermes, wearing a harness adorned with colorful sacks, stepped inside. "Whoa there, donkey." The rancher put a gaunt shoulder against the animal and tried pushing him back.

"Rattle the treat can. He'll turn around," Zimm called. "And Tracy says to only give him half-a-one. He's getting fat."

"I can handle a donkey." The bony man talked low to the neddy, backing his front feet out of the entrance. "Which sack is the Grill's?" he called out.

"Orange!" several voices answered together. The man unclipped a waterproof bag of Almond Joy muffins from Hermes' day-glo harness, then fed him a donkey treat.

"Here." Bazz traded a flat orange bag for the full one. "Hook it good. It's Lottie's payment." The skinny man pinched it into an empty clip and gave the donkey two pats on the rump. Hermes clopped to his next delivery, colored bags flopping against his sides.

"Has anybody ordered?" Bazz held up the muffins. Four diners shook their heads. Chicken Thief Bob stared at coffee vapors twisting in a curlicue above his cup.

"Junior!" Bazz yelled. "What're you doing back there?"

The words coming from the kitchen were garbled, but the tone was similar to an erupting volcano. Bazz winced. He pointed at Zimm. "What'cha want?" Each diner gave an order until he got to Chicken Thief, whose eyes were playing an image that wasn't in the room.

Bazz kicked Bob's boot. "What's the matter? You trying to levitate that jitterjuice with your mind?"

The gravel hauler shook his head, casting off the dream. "Driving here I saw ... I don't know what I saw. It was the darnedest thing ..."

"That was the mayor." The bony man winked. "He looks pretty bad if he hasn't shaved. When was the last time you changed the cardboard in your razor, Mr. Mayor?" The men sniggered.

"I've been up all night welding. Jiggs' baler broke down. You guys go on down to the Ritz for breakfast, while I clean up." Bazz picked up his coffee cup and headed toward the kitchen.

"Well, what'd ya see, Bob?" Zimm asked.

"I think it was a ... I guess they like to be called 'little person.'" Lines creased his forehead, making him look puzzled and worried at the same time.

"You mean a midget?" someone asked.

"He just told you," the turkey-necked man scolded. "They're called little people."

"Where?" Zimm said.

"Out on Highway 3 by Mud Creek." Chicken Thief leaned forward and circled the top of his cup with his fingers. "I guess it's a Greyhound stop. I've noticed the sign, but never seen any one waiting there until now. It was after four thirty—still kinda dark. I'd been up all night tryin' to get my truck running. When I finally finished, I decided to come on in for breakfast."

"What was this alleged little person doing?" Zimm asked.

Bob scrubbed his hand over his face. "I don't think I imagined it because he had a suitcase. And here's the really strange thing. He was dressed in a white business suit. I didn't see him until my headlights flashed on him as I passed. He was standing off to the side of the road, but it was definitely a suit with light-colored shoes and a dark tie. He was about three feet high. Just ... standing there."

"Maybe it was a drug deal," Zimm offered. "I bet that suitcase was full of dope."

"Maybe it was a ghost," said the bony man.

Bob shook his head. "What would a little person be doing all the way out here, waiting for a bus, in a white suit, before sunup? I can't figure it."

"I can tell you about him," Junior interrupted, carrying Bob's breakfast and the coffee pot to the table. "Here's someone who wears a white suit because that way people will treat him with respect. You guys look like gypsies and street bums. He's traveling from the West Coast to the East by bus because he doesn't want to pay outrageous money to be treated like livestock by the airlines. He doesn't sleep well in a strange place, so he gets up and waits by the side of the road for the next bus. He gets his hopes up when he hears a big engine coming down the road. And he watches a beat-up gravel truck rattle right past him. He's saying to himself, 'What's that Neanderthal-throwback doing all the way out here? Dressed in worn-out clothes, hauling rock around before first light?' He's probably staring out the bus window right now thinking, 'Civilization decays when you leave the city.'"

"Thank you, Mr. Barkeeper," Bazz said from the kitchen doorway. "We're all refreshed and challenged by your uniquely ignorant point of view." The group laughed as Junior tromped away.

Bob stared at the steam rising from his coffee. He had the feeling that the little man in the suit had been up all night like him—trying to fix something. "I guess we'll never know," he said.

Each year, before Memorial Day, the Daughters of Two Pan—and their coerced husbands—cleaned up God's Hollow and its 171 residents. The rest of the year it was up to the families, or the kindness of the Boy Scouts, to keep scraggly weeds from climbing the grave markers. Josie Blevins carried out her family responsibility at noon that day with a pair of dull shears.

At first she stayed off the casket area and worked from the edges; but with only eighteen inches between the headstones, her feet intruded on the eternal neighbors, Art and Bee Monroe.

The Monroes' loving grandson, Dooley—Two Pan's antique/junk dealer—had decorated his grandparents' graves with hanging chimes made from old silverware. At the ends of the plot, he'd added heavy brass urns full of red plastic flowers and an ornate iron headboard which Josie had kicked over, twice.

It seemed improper to sit on top of her grandma and grandpa, but she did it anyway, pulling weeds, cutting the few dying tufts of stem-grass, and working wild flower seeds into the broken soil. She pointed her shears at the black letters etched in the headstones. "Grandma, you have some explaining to do."

"You getting any answers?" The quiet voice startled her. A brief glance revealed a man leaning against a pine tree, hat in hand, an earnest question in his eyes.

She turned back to her work, replying in a tone that could chip ice. "Hello, Jiggs."

"I was over there." He waved toward the far side of the cemetery. "Visiting family. Sorry if I'm disturbing anything."

She brushed clippings away with a gloved hand.

"I wanted to say I'm sorry I was rude to you." Nap had made him rehearse an apology. His son had explained that when he'd rejected Josie's offer to help, he'd rejected her. "What I turned down was charity," he had argued. "No Woolsey takes a hand out."

He and Nap had gotten so verbally tangled, debating the hornet's nest of how a woman's mind worked, they'd let the burgers burn on the grill and ended up drinking beer and eating cheese slices and potato chips for dinner.

He'd reluctantly practiced the apology in case he wanted to use it, but it didn't make a lot of sense. Probably because he didn't remember many details about that night, except draining his checking account to put a down payment on Hop's ranch and having desperate hope that the bank would make him a loan—and soon.

"Josie?" She didn't look up. "I know you were trying to help. And I appreciate it." He waited, pulling the brim of his hat around through his fingers.

She pointed her shears at the end of the weedy graves, away from her. "Take a seat."

He hesitated. If he stayed standing, it would be simpler to ease away, but during their father-son discussion, Nap had boomeranged Jiggs' own wisdom at him. "Well, Dad, you're always saying, 'How important is it to you?'" Jiggs put his hat on and settled cross-legged as she continued to work.

"I was wrong," she said. "I now realize I shouldn't have offered you money in public, but turning it down isn't what bothered me."

Jiggs shifted, glad he was out of reach of her scissors and wishing the ground wasn't so hard. He had no script for this. They hadn't rehearsed anything more than an apology. Sure that whatever he said next would be wrong, he said nothing at all.

"You didn't trust me." She looked at him with a narrowing stare. "You guys came back to the bar, all *ha-ha we're so smart* and *you don't need to know*. I had tried to help, and you didn't trust me to keep a simple secret."

"I didn't mean it like that." Jiggs looked down. "I felt like a tight end after the ball's snapped. I was spooked, goosey, and trying to figure out which way to jump to avoid being blocked."

Josie gave him a skeptical frown.

"Remember how I said if you want to keep a secret in this town, don't tell anyone? No one was supposed to breathe a word about my deal. Jarmin might've filed an injunction before the deed was recorded." Jiggs rubbed his forehead, his voice slowing. "There're rumors he's going to contest it anyway, saying Hop wasn't in his right mind. It's the same as you keeping quiet about the money you found in your attic." Josie looked up with a wide-eyed stare. "See ... you understand," he said. "The more people get involved, the messier your situation gets."

"Good grief!" She threw an exasperated look at the sky. "Well, obviously that secret has made it all over town. I should've gone to a coin dealer three counties away." She slung weeds toward her pile. "And it's not the same thing at all." Her shoulders sagged, but her face was like stone. "My grandparents cubby-holed cash for years. They lived hand to mouth when the truth was—they didn't have to. I'm not trying to hide what was done. I'm looking for answers because their close-fisted ways certainly affected my mother's life and ultimately mine."

Jiggs chopped his hand against his palm as though cutting through her words. "That's what I'm saying. Your mother is a prime example. It's hard to keep her secret buried in a community where everybody is scooping through the dirt."

Josie stared at him, her throat mottling with color. Her lips tightened into thin lines, thunder clouds rolled in her eyes. "And *what* do you know about my mother?"

Quicksand. Jiggs gauged the distance to his truck. "Well ... uh ... they say she ... figured out a way to inoculate herself against poverty."

Josie gave him an angry glance. "When I came back here, I figured folks would look at me and say, 'Isn't that Buforl Roggs' granddaughter?' But now I find out they're pointing. 'There goes Laura Jean's daughter. Wonder if she knows about her mama's sugar daddies? Too bad her father didn't have enough spine to do anything about it.'"

"Well, nobody thinks you're sleeping in the next county, too."

Josie's eyes popped.

"I mean ... nobody thought your mom was a hooker. They figured she was looking for a gravy train."

Her eyes widened. Her mouth twisted.

"That didn't come out right. Look, some people may suspect that you only came back to get your grandparents' money, but you're not like your mother."

"Mom doesn't even know about the cache!"

"Exactly. But folks expect money is a motive for any Roggs because of your granddad's history and your mama's conniving ways in the bedroom."

Josie's breath caught. Fire filled her dark eyes.

"Oh ... man oh man. I'm sorry. You're not like that. Look, I'm only trying to assure you that I know you can keep a secret. I'd trust you into the next century and back. I don't know how to say it without screwing it up."

She stabbed the spade into the ground and stood. "You think that's a better explanation? You could've given me a heads up about the rumors. You're always talking about community, yet you don't trust anyone in it." She headed for her car, leaving her tools behind.

Jiggs closed his eyes and let out a long breath. "One night, years ago ... the phone rang. It was 2:03. Since then, I wake up most mornings at 2:00, waiting for the phone to ring again. It never does."

Josie's steps slowed.

He took another deep breath. "It's my brother, Pax. He's taking full advantage of being twenty. He's sloppy drunk. Slurring his words. Cussing me every other sentence. He wants me to come pick him up. Hours earlier, we'd had a knock-down battle. He'd coldcocked me. Broke my nose.

"I'm mad enough to bust boards over his head and *now* he wants a favor? 'Walk home, you so-n-so,' I tell him. I call him a few other things." Jiggs risked a glance at her. She stood, unmoving, her back to him.

" 'Come get me, shithead!' is the last thing I hear out of the receiver before I slam it down. He calls again. I feel pretty powerful, him beggin' and me cuttin' him off. After the third call, I take the phone off the hook. I don't know where he is. Don't care."

Above them the wind blew through the pines, sighing and changing the pattern of shadows on the gravestones. Jiggs stared at the ground and swallowed. "The next thing I know, Dad is shaking me out of sleep. Pax has run off the road and rolled his truck. He's dead."

Josie turned, the corners of her mouth slack.

"I've been sorry and trying to make up for it every minute the rest of my life." He looked at her, his face telegraphing despair. "I trust you can keep *that* secret."

"Good heavens." She walked toward him. "Are you telling me in a town this size, no one knows?"

"No one." He shook his head. "I didn't know what to do when Dad woke me up." He stared at the ground again. "Dad already figured I was worthless, so either I told him and confirmed it, or I kept it to myself, proving I was worthless because I couldn't confess the truth: I killed my brother."

Josie slowly sat down. The sigh of the wind filled the gap in their words. A mourning dove echoed a coo, but stopped abruptly at the high-pitched screech from a circling hawk. Jiggs silently rooted for mice in the area to find cover.

Removing her gloves by pulling on each fingertip, she folded them together and held them in her lap, letting the stillness weight her words before she spoke. "Why do you think *you* killed him?"

"He'd be alive today if I'd picked him up. Sure we fought, but when your brother's in trouble, you back him up. It's the way we were raised. When people ask for help, you give it."

"How old were you?"

"Seventeen."

"And you've been carrying this millstone all these years?"

He shrugged. "Katie was the only one who knew, but she's gone. I wondered if Dad suspected. Sometimes he'd look at me with such disappointment. Pax and I lived in my granddad's old place, next door to the main house. Dad had to come get me because the phone was off the hook. He never asked, and I never said anything. If I could do that one night over ... if I hadn't of been so stupid-mad. Sometimes I look at the 4-H and FFA kids and think ... Pax would have grandkids by now, and they'd—"

"Stop it. Just stop it." Josie's eyes drilled into him. "You have no right to feel sorry for yourself. Your brother made the choice to drink and get behind the wheel. He could've slept in the truck or on the floor wherever he was. Didn't he have any friends? Where were they?"

Jiggs jerked. Hadn't this woman heard him? What was wrong with her?

"And so what if you had picked him up?" she started again. "You don't know he'd be alive today. He might've run off the road on another drunken night. He could've gotten kicked in the head by a bull. His horse might have caught a foot and rolled, punching the pommel through his chest. He—"

"But it didn't! I explained it once. Leave it at that." He glared at her, anger cinching his throat until he could barely swallow.

Josie was silent, returning his stare. After a moment, she cocked her head and quietly said, "I guess we'll never know." She put on her gloves and began working again.

This was a good time to leave, but he couldn't get unrooted. There'd been years of close calls on his life. He'd taken crazy chances because he hadn't cared. There was no accounting for death's randomness. Every year, some idiot mistook someone for a deer. A horse lost its footing and rolled a rider into a canyon. For a moment's breath, he allowed himself to think about all the possibilities he had refused to remember for him *and Pax.*

A high-pitched screech splintered his thoughts. Two crows darted around the red tail hawk, diving and pecking as they circled above the graveyard.

"Secrets," Jiggs said softly.

"Pardon?" She frowned.

"How many of these folks out here had secrets, do you think?"

She followed his gaze around the cemetery. Rays of sunlight came through the trees, spotlighting obelisks, gray-green with algae and tilted with age. Two plots over, a new granite stone gleamed, displaying an oval picture of the deceased. Along the rows of markers, lambs and angels atop headstones kept vigil, their features abused by many winters. "I think …"she focused on the hole she'd gouged in the dirt, "they all took secrets to the grave with them. Everyone has a past."

Jiggs watched the crows go at the hawk. One at a time. They approached from behind, but they gave a loud squawk, announcing each attack. The hawk didn't complain. Jiggs rooted for the red tail.

He watched Josie cut the dried stems partially covering the names on the headstones, then looked across the cemetery. "A lot of these graves are empty."

"What?" She frowned at him.

"They may have monuments here in the family plot, but they're buried on their own land. Dad's is vacant. Hop Hopkins' name is next to his wife, but he's resting on his old homestead. There're others."

Josie's eyes stayed on her hands as she clipped gangly tufts of grass. "Your wife?"

"No." Jiggs' voice softened. "She wanted to be where there were people." A bittersweet smile crossed his face as he pushed the weeds into a clump. "I have to come here to talk to her. But I don't get any answers, either."

Josie looked up. Jiggs' straw hat shaded his face, but his features held no mockery. "I'm sorry if I sounded … harsh."

"You sure don't mince words." Jiggs let out a wide-eyed sigh. "I needed to hear it. Katie used to remind me it wasn't my fault. I haven't heard that in a while."

"Well, it'll be better when you start believing it yourself." Her voice came out like a teacher's. Jiggs' mouth turned down in slow motion as he looked away. "I'm sorry," she said. "That was rude of—"

"No." He pulled a weed twined with tiny black pods. "You're right. I've hung on, thinking I could make things right. I tried to do the work for both my brother and me. But it's never seemed to pay off my guilt. The one thing I wanted to hear, kind of an absolution I guess, was my dad's words, 'Good job, son. Your brother couldn't have done any better.' He took those words with him when he died. I think he'd finally decided I was a decent son ... but ..."

"You'll never know. Not knowing doesn't mean it isn't true."

He shook his head. "Not for nothing, but Dad was right about me. I got in over my head when I bought Shiny Creek."

"Sometimes you don't know how deep the water is until you jump in."

"Sometimes I wonder how long I'll be able to tread." Silence strung out between them. The hawk and crows were gone. The sun angled into other parts of the cemetery. He was suddenly aware that he felt tired. Towing secrets through life was like driving a tractor through muck. It could be done, but it took a lot of juice. "My Dad socked away secret money, too. Not a lot, but I found it buried in a jar under the feed trough in the barn. They lived hard times." Jiggs shrugged. "Lotta folks lost everything. I guess standing in a soup line is something you never forget."

"So when things got better," Josie said, "why didn't my grandparents spend some of it? I need a damn good explanation because I grew up constantly hearing about my mom's feedsack dresses and patchwork shoes. It molded her into a bitter person. She still has the tiniest handwriting I've ever seen because they only bought one package of notepaper for a school year."

"Who can explain why my dad, your grandparents—or your mom—did what they did? They were scraping by." He cocked his head and gave her a meaningful look. "Doing what they thought they had to do to survive. Fear, pride, and the lack of cash will push any of us into strange corners."

Josie gave a mirthless laugh. "I stupidly thought I might find an answer here. My grandparents scrimped for so long, I wondered how they'd want me to handle their nest egg. It feels cursed. It made my whole childhood a lie. I feel like it was hoarded with pain and I have to use it for good to offset the sacrifice." She gave him a sheepish look. "So I offered it to you. Well ... you know how that turned out. You didn't want it. And if Mom found out it existed ..." She made an exploding noise accompanied by fanned fingers.

A frown tilted one side of Jiggs' mouth. *Bound to happen.* This lovely woman had waved cash in his face and he'd insulted her. Maybe he could talk to her about a loan if it didn't rain soon, and grasses didn't start growing. "So your mom doesn't know about it?"

Josie shook her head. "When I thanked Miz Cliva for my sink, I told her about the attic money. She told me about my mother. Said I should keep whatever I found to myself. Thank heavens Mom lives in Florida."

They worked without speaking. The silver spoons over the Monroes' graves chimed a *tink-tink* melody in the breeze.

Jiggs used the scissor points to rake the weeds into a pile. "I'm probably sticking my foot in my mouth again, but I'll tell you what I'd tell any friend. I've wrestled most of my life to show I'm no halfwit and prove my dad wrong. Now, he's gone and I'm the one stuck with the worries and day-to-day problems. I've concluded that I have to do what I think is best. So ... you have to do what you can live with. Your grandparents may have agreed, or disagreed with whatever you do with their money. You'll never know—as you tell me."

Josie turned over the words, and then nodded. She pointed at the tombstones. "They gave me an education that took me away from Two Pan, but I know what Grandma wanted more than anything was to have me near. I took the cash and put it in a foundation for a college loan for Two Pan kids. If any graduate returns and works in the area for five years, the debt is forgiven. It's a way to get an education and come home again. I was worried it wasn't what my grandparents would've wanted, but you're right. It's my responsibility now. We'll never know about the what-ifs of the past."

Jiggs nodded with a thin smile. He'd been trying to dump the past for years. He was going to tell her how moving forward with life was mired with sinkholes. He wanted to let her know those flower seeds she was poking between dirt clods would never sprout. But the words piled up behind his tongue. He also sensed for some strange reason, it was going to get easier to talk to her.

"Would you like half of my lunch?" she asked as she crawled past him toward a paper sack sitting in the shade of a headstone.

"Well ... okay."

She gave him a glance. "You were barely on the first rung of manhood. Your long-ago mistake is safe with me." She unfolded a checkered napkin and placed a peanut butter and jelly sandwich between them.

"A mistake?" He watched her divide apple slices into two piles.

"That's a start." She set out a carton of juice. "It's not a permanent character flaw. Forgive your mistake."

He let out a sigh. A mistake made worse by his brother's drunken errors. If one of them would've made other choices, things might've been different. They'd never know.

They sat in the sunlight, surrounded by markers that covered lives and misjudgments no one remembered. Jiggs felt as though pieces of a hard shell were breaking loose inside of him.

Maybe there was a way to start over. To sleep through the night without staring at the clock as it flipped to 2:03. To stop wishing he could do one night of his life over. To live without guilt.

A faint smile, like the curling tip of a leaf, touched the corner of his mouth.

19

Meteors and Hayfields

SUMMERTIME IS SHORT, but the individual days stretch long and lazy. The sun rides through a sky of robin egg blue, baking pastures and shimmying mountain vistas in heat waves. Sunsets wash the land in red. A white-hot slash hovers at the horizon before the fireball drops over the edge of the earth. Colors deepen to purple and fade to black. In Two Pan, in the belly of the night, ranchers return to their fields and start working again.

———

Kheerhk... hissed the walkie-talkie earlier that evening. "Hey, you ever seen a coon monkey?" Petey asked. The whirr of the loader had accompanied the high schooler's transmission as he circled the field.

When they'd started haying the Bonewash, Nap had handed Jiggs a walkie-talkie. "I know you hate technology, but with two trucks and a baler, we can work smarter if we let each other know what's going on."

Jiggs had squeezed his laugh into a mere flat line and dropped the irritating device into his shirt pocket. Mostly, the boys driving the trucks talked back and forth; they rarely called him as he dragged the baler around the field.

"What's a coon monkey?" asked Jason. He'd arranged to work afternoons at Grubb's and nights for Jiggs.

"Well, I was huntin' with this ol' boy from Oklahoma who trained this monkey to hunt. We weren't out very long before my dog treed a raccoon. This redneck hands the monkey a twenty-two, and it scampers up the branches. So—" *Kheerhk* ... The radio hissed static. "Wait a minute. Nap's bangin' on the cab, sayin' the bales are coming too fast." Petey yelled, "Shut up and work harder, losers!"

Jiggs, listening in, could imagine Petey sticking his head out the window and hollering at the stackers. The boy called them a few more names, then spoke into the microphone, "Now ... we shined our spotlights up the tree, but didn't see any raccoon. Finally, the ape jumps down and shoots my hound. That Okie says, 'Sorry, but my coon monkey can't stand a lyin' dog.'"

"You're not funny," Jason said, a smile tinting his voice. "Okay. Did you hear about the preacher and the bear?"

Jiggs flipped the "off" switch, relieved to hear only the methodic thumping and tying of the baler behind him. He preferred to follow the windrows and his own thoughts rather than be interrupted by the hissing banter between Petey and Jason.

To be sixteen again. No worries. No fear. He reminded himself that he was going to stop dancing around the shadows in his boyhood. He'd forgive himself.

Jiggs fished the radio out to tell Petey to slow down, hesitated, then slipped it back into his pocket. Eventually, Nap would pull the young diphead out of the truck and knock him around for driving too fast. That was the trouble with hiring high school boys, even though his son was barely man-grown himself. Young men preferred to use their fists to discuss driving skills.

What Nap needed to do was put Petey in the back. The kid would learn what it felt like when bales flew off the loader so fast he'd be buried and his arms turn into rubber. The problem was that no one wanted to be with the young idiot while he was swinging a hay hook on the back of a moving flatbed.

Now, at three in the morning, Jiggs stood alone in the field, flexing his hands. His fingers still tingled from gripping the vibrating steering wheel for so long. The silence of the stars seemed loud after hours of the baler's *whump-roar*. The hay trucks were gone, unloading their stacks. He tossed his hat onto the tractor seat and walked around the equipment to look inside the knotter box. It was too dark to see into the black cavity, but the proof was behind him. Starlight showed faint outlines of bales, each with one fluffy, fat end confirming that the knotter had broken. Nap hadn't even picked up the last seven, knowing they'd fall apart as they came off the loader.

"Bound to happen," Jiggs mumbled to the guts of the machine. During haying season, breakdowns were expected, but there wasn't time for it this year. They needed to finish this pasture and beat it over to the Oven Bake. After that, he'd worked a deal for shares on Zimm Lubach's place. None of these fields were producing much. Too dry. He needed every bale he could get his hands on for winter. The more hay he had stacked up, the less grain he'd have to buy. Who'd have thought this drought would last? He should've had more faith in his bad luck before he committed to a huge loan.

From under the tractor seat, he pulled out his orange, beat-up water thermos. He opened the spigot and ran a cool stream over his face. It dripped off his chin, and tickled down the back of his neck. "Don't waste the drinkin' water," he could hear his father say as he shut off the tap. Wouldn't that man shut up after a year of dirt-napping?

Jiggs rubbed his face with both hands, pushing the droplets toward his ears. It made his collar itch worse. Hours of grass, dust, and sweat nested on the back of his neck. He stared at the jug. He could imagine the feel of the cold water and how his shirt would stay damp afterward. He'd have to battle years of his dad's voice to pour it over his head like he really wanted to. Jiggs pulled a wadded kerchief from his back pocket and rubbed the water off his face, then wiped his neck.

A motor whined in the distance, not rumbling enough to be the flatbeds returning. Leaning against the tractor, he breathed in the cool night air and surveyed his land.

His dad had passed 1,897 checkerboard acres in pretty good shape to him. Would he have anything left to pass on to his boy? He'd been late with the loan payments—then missed the last one. In a good year, there'd be no problem, but this wasn't a good year.

Headlights bounced across the field. The dark shape of a '68 Chevy pickup crunched through dry stubble and stopped as the driver killed the engine.

Bracing both hands against the truck's door, Jiggs leaned toward the window. "You're moonlighting awfully early this morning."

"If you'd turn on your radio, you'd know I was coming." Pieces of ice stuck to the brown bottle Bazz passed through the window. "Sorry, it's not that ditchwater with foam you drink."

"It's cold." Jiggs held the Hefeweizen against his forehead for a moment. "That's what counts."

"Nap called." Bazz pulled the handle on the door and waited as the rancher stepped out of way. "Broke your bill hook?"

"Yep, you wouldn't happen to have one for a double knotter in that traveling beer wagon?" Jiggs waved toward the back.

"Well, now it's going to cost you extra." He held up the two-fingered metal part. "You're like those people at the bar who yell at Misty if she forgets to bring them ketchup. You want something, and you think insults will get it for you."

"What's she do? Spit in their beer?"

"No, she's too nice. I do it."

Jiggs looked at his bottle and shrugged. "You always carry knotter parts for a New Holland baler and drive around at ... " He rotated his wrist back and forth in the starlight trying to read his watch.

"You know, they make those with lights now. You'd have to part with about twenty bucks, but at least you'd know what time it is before you bother anybody."

"I figure they'll tell me. If you call somebody right now, they'll say, 'Whaddya want? It's three in the morning.' I don't need your glow-in-the-dark, Batman watch to tell time. Look at the stars."

Bazz studied the pasture blending into blackness in all directions. It would have been impossible to discern where the earth stopped and the sky began if not for the starry pinpricks. "I think you're wrong. If you call folks at this time of night, they don't announce the hour. Their hearts freeze with fear. Only bad new comes after midnight."

"You're right about that," Jiggs said with a quiet seriousness. "But I know from experience that when the phone rings, a person looks at the clock."

"Bull hockey. We'll call Chicken Thief Bob and test your little theory." Bazz flicked his cell phone open and squinted at the signal strength before pushing buttons.

"Hey, Bob. What'cha doin?" Bazz said into the receiver. He looked at the rancher. "He says he's sleeping." The mayor gave a chuckle. "Well, this is Jiggs Woolsey, and I just wanted to know if you looked at the clock before you answered."

Bazz held the phone out so both of them could hear. The device spewed a litany of foul names, then fell silent. Its neon-blue florescence highlighted Bazz's arched eyebrows and surprised frown. "He hung up on you."

Jiggs pointed his bottle at the phone. "Call him back." Bazz punched a button and put the phone on speaker so they both could hear.

"It's almost four in the morning," an enraged voiced rasped across the quiet pasture. "Whaddya want?"

"Sorry, wrong number." Bazz snapped the phone shut. "Okay. You're right." He drained his beer and dropped the bottle as he walked toward the baler. Pulling an elastic-banded light around his head, he surveyed the metal innards.

Jiggs picked up the bottle and chunked it into the back of the Chevy. "I don't even let twine tails stay on the ground."

"I would've gotten it when we were done. While you're over there, get my socket set out of the back," Bazz said, his head and hands inside the machine. "What are twine tails?"

"Those pieces cut off after the knots are tied. Some machines push 'em out into the field or into the bale. They get eaten, then there's another problem your cow's stomach has to deal with."

"For a man who has nothing more to do than watch his cattle convert grass into meat, you sure worry a lot."

The rancher set the toolbox on the ground next to Bazz and opened it. "Yeah, I suppose I do." His voice carried more desperation than he'd meant to let seep through.

Bazz continued, "Now, I'm not saying you're watching reruns of *Dancing with the Stars* during calving and haying season, but it's the cows and that macho bull of yours that do all the work. You sit back and count their money."

When there was no response, Bazz pulled his head out of the knotter box and gave him a look.

"Can you fix it tonight?" He stared back, squinting against the glare of the headlamp in his eyes.

"It'll take about an hour to reset everything."

"Lend me your phone. I'll call the boys and tell 'em to get back out here. The walkie-talkies are out of range."

"Kinda runnin' 'em hard," Bazz said as he handed over his phone and went back to work. He had to stop to educate Jiggs on which buttons to push, and then hurl a few techno-phobe insults.

Jiggs paced to the middle of the field to make the call. He had to step over windrows of hay that lay like giant carpet rolls the length of the pasture. The sound of banging metal punctuated the night. Bloody curses were added whenever Bazz deposited knuckle skin on steel parts. Jiggs gave his orders to Nap. As he snapped the phone closed, he knelt and felt the leaves. A slight dampness from the night air brought out the scent of the alfalfa.

What had he done? Put everything his dad and granddad had worked for at risk? No. He was moving toward the Bonanza-dream he'd had since childhood. It'd be different if Katie were alive. Maybe. She'd grown up on a commercial ranch in Idaho. She'd have understood.

Her half-human appearance flashed in his mind. He'd tried hard to flush it out, but it was the last image he had of her. Like her cancer, that picture had grown fibrous attachments to the mental room he'd kept for his wife. It was always the first to greet him when he opened the door.

She lay in skeletal paleness with tubes running from her body. She wasn't even a familiar shell of the woman who made him bounce along rutted roads at fifty miles per hour to get home and hear her laugh.

He pushed the memory away with a heavy sigh, finding himself squatting in the middle of his pasture, crimping damp stems between his fingers.

Maybe it'd rain in time to get a second cutting. *Maybe.* With each step back toward the baler, his confidence drained into the baked ground. There was a small window of time to put up hay. He checked the eastern horizon. The dampness would vaporize with the sunlight. There wouldn't be enough moisture to make the stems and leaves stick together. They'd have to wait another night. Lose more time.

"Now I know what a calf feels like when I rubber band his nuts," he said, peering over Bazz's shoulder to see how the job was progressing.

"How do you figure?" Bazz pulled twine with one hand while making small turns on an adjusting nut with the other.

"Shiny Creek. It's squeezin' me. I missed a loan payment. Little McGinty says he can't change the payments or fees. He calls every few days, encouraging me to sell some equipment which I'll need later. Or take half-finished cattle to market and get half price. Just get money. Of course, if I sell now, I won't have income later. It doesn't matter to him."

"Dr. Dick will always take it off your hands if you get strapped."

"That mud shark couldn't tend a bag of dirt."

"Sorry. Just trying to help. Try a few bales. Let's see how it's knotting." Bazz waved toward the tractor and watched Jiggs climb up and sit heavily in the seat, his hand rubbing his chest, as though soothing its beat. "Maybe you can find someone who'll lease the land or loan you money," Bazz said. "Why don't you come to the next Council meeting? Folks will support you. Ask around for a tenant."

"I don't need help. I need the planets to align, the heavens to open, and some luck to fall out. I bet the family farm on getting this hay in ... and the next season's and the season after that. I'm holding my breath, hoping every piddlin' cloud will dump moisture on my side of the range. What's left of my calf crop is healthy, but I can always look forward to scours, roundworm, or some thief giving one-way rides in the middle of the night. Not to mention the international tariff might be slapped on beef because of Mad Cow, and the bottom will drop out of the cattle market—*again*.

"If my twenty-thousand-dollar bull pulls a stifle, or twists a foot, he'll have to be put down. I've wagered my family's life work and my kid's future on things I can't control. I'm beginning to have a few more doubts than usual, but I'm *not* going to neighbors and begging them to bail me out."

"Why don't you worry about meteors and nuclear attacks while you're at it?" Bazz slapped the rancher on the back. "Let's go with what you can control. Try the baler."

Bazz paced after the machine for a few hundred feet, checking bales and signaling for Jiggs to stop a couple of times so he could make adjustments. When tight rectangles of hay chugged out the chute, the mayor ran beside the tractor and gave the thumbs up signal. He watched the baler until it faded into the darkness.

Soon two flatbeds rolled into the field. One truck parked; two young men hooked the automatic loader to the other truck, then jumped on and began stacking as the headlights followed the line of new bales.

Like an insect with glowing eyes, the tractor and baler chewed the field in slow spiraling laps. The rhythmic whomping of grass being stomped, folded, squeezed, and tied radiated into the night.

Bazz unscrewed the cap from a bottle of lager beer and leaned against his Chevy, watching the stars watch him until bouncing headlights flashed across his body. He recognized the outline of a light bar on top of the car as it stopped behind his truck.

"You're out late, Sheriff," the mayor called as the car door opened.

"Got a complaint." Sol Meyers unfolded his just-under-seven-foot-frame from the cruiser, arched backward, and Y-ed his arms, inhaling the grass-scented air. "Got a call that machines over here in the Bonewash are running all night. Keepin' folks awake with all this industry."

"Chicken Thief shouldn't have suckered you into coming over here—"

"It was Jiggs' neighbors—the Jarmins. I explained that haying was going on all over Whitman County during these summer nights. It'd be going on for at least another coupla weeks."

"Naw, I think it'll be over sooner. Jiggs is on a mission. He's working those kids so hard, they'll sleep for a month. Besides, we're at least seven miles from their property. If this keeps them awake, I'm surprised they don't call you about barking coyotes and bugling elk."

"Got a second call a few hours later. They said trucks were racing up and down the road. Horns honking, kids yelling. Big trucks, full of hay."

"You figure it's these felons here?"

"There always seems to be what we in law enforcement call 'suspicious activity' wherever you're at."

"You sure it wasn't Chicken Thief Bob yanking your chain?" Bazz offered a beer. The sheriff waved him away. Engines droned in rhythmic chorus as the men watched headlights circle the field. The eastern horizon was beginning to streak with light gray patches. The first truck stopped, dropping the automatic loader behind a line of bales. The truck bed looked as though it carried a thatch house without the roof. A young man ran across the field and jumped onto the running board of the second truck. He slapped the window with a howl, then opened the door and yanked the driver to the ground. The boy lay in the stubble as the youth disappeared, screaming, to the other side of the truck.

"They okay over there?" Bazz leaned forward, squinting.

"Yeah. They shouldn't have fallen asleep. He's rousting them out. You couldn't pay me to be that age again." The sheriff shook his head. "That one on the ground is Jason Markum. Works for Andy. He and the Gedding kid broke into the store this past winter."

"Heard they didn't take anything," said the mayor.

The sheriff shook his head. "Didn't look like it. We keep an eye on 'em. Andy's waiting for Jason to apologize."

Bazz laughed. "He's got a long wait. Most young men figure if they don't talk about a mess, it'll be forgotten. At least that's how I handled it. How about you?"

"I never did anything wrong," the sheriff said, a grin in his voice.

As the first truck trundled across the field, Jason pushed himself from the stubble and gave the other boys a one-fingered salute. Lights flashed and the horn honked as a bare butt stuck through the driver's window. The truck weaved across the field before the gluteus pulled back inside. The hay carrier corrected course and made for the gate.

"Well, I can't top that." Bazz said. "They must not be afraid of you."

"Guess I gotta talk to them. No need to be waking up the citizenry on this quiet early morning." The sheriff made no attempt to get in his cruiser. They watched the second team hook up the loader and rumble down the snaking line of bales. After five minutes, Sol Meyers asked, "What time does the Bar and Grill open for breakfast?"

" 'Bout a half hour." Bazz noticed he could see the face of his watch now.

The sheriff flexed his shoulders. "Maybe I'll see you there," he said and got into his car. His tires crackled through the stubble as he drove toward the gate. When he reached the road, the siren went on. Its yodel gouged a hole in the morning. The noise moved down the road and the cruiser's tail lights became red dots in the dawn's grayness.

Across the countryside, coyotes howled, dogs barked, and roosters squawked their replies to the high-pitched wail. Bazz smiled. The sheriff was miles from the pasture before the cacophony faded away.

20

Lights on Starvation Ridge

"BOUND TO HAPPEN," Jiggs muttered.

After three hard weeks of haying, he'd finally finished—only to be greeted with this. His eyes burned from another sleep-broken night. How, in forty-six years of living, had he come to be a lodestone for bad luck and extra work?

He gripped the steering wheel, fighting to keep the truck and horse trailer hurtling down the road rather than snaking airborne into a ditch. Frustration pinched his face. His jaws ached from clenching down on too much worry. He hoped something would be left by the time he got there.

Papers and plastic ear tags vibrated faster on the dashboard as he sped up, trying to overdrive the path his headlights cut into the darkness. He hunched forward, straining to see through the bug-splatted windshield. The last house lights were eight miles behind him. Ahead, blackness reigned where flatland collided with the forest growing up the side of Starvation Ridge.

The truck passed the first rock cairn, standing tall as a man, and Jiggs felt a heartbeat of relief. He thought of them as sentries. He and his father had each worn out a pair of boots lugging stones to build the three miles of fence anchors along their property.

When Jiggs spied the tiny orange light, a synaptic impulse shot directly to his foot. He stomped the gas pedal. The truck lurched, making the trailer swerve behind him. Curly Dogs snorted a disgruntled, high-pitched roller. The horse's stamping shook Jiggs free of his panic, and he slowed slightly, never taking his eyes from the reddish glow.

At a dip in the road, he braked to a stop and grabbed a flashlight from the clutter on the seat. Dead. Bound to happen. He chucked it to the floorboard and clawed the pile, ferreting out pliers.

The door of the Ford made a *skreek* as he threw it open harder than he'd intended. By the time it had rebounded and slammed shut, he had scrambled up the low embankment to clip the top barbed wire.

The line snapped upward, catching and tearing his shirt before it coiled away in the roadside weeds. Barbs pierced his hands as he cut three more strands. He kicked at the loops tangling his feet. He yanked the wires out of the way, prongs ripping and drawing blood.

A distant growl of truck engines carried through the still air. It sounded as though they were traveling close behind each other instead of stringing apart to avoid eating dust. Help was coming. Jiggs wound a kerchief around his bloody palm. In the night sky, banners of smoke ghosted across Starvation Ridge pasture.

Bazz yelled as soon as his '68 Chevy truck stopped and he cracked the door. "Damn. This could be worse than the Crawling Stone burn six years ago." He sucked in a lungful of charred wood scent and stared at the flames climbing trunks of Ponderosa pine across the fence beyond Jiggs' property. The fire's roar traveled through the night as it exploded cedars and dropped streamers of burning cones and branches. "I got the call from the phone tree," he said, returning his attention to Jiggs. "Here. Go on. I'll fill the ditch." He grabbed a post from the rancher's truck bed and heaved it into the roadside trench.

The road filled with vehicles. Dust swirled in front of headlights. Jiggs' movements and voice slowed as he backed Curly Dogs out of the trailer. "C'mon. Time to work." The horse's nostrils flared. He tossed his head, testing the night air, and gave his opinion in several snorts.

"Yeah, that smell says run for home. 'S okay." Jiggs spoke in low assurances as the horse stamped at the conflicting messages. "Settle. Settle." He tightened the saddle cinch, talking and rubbing his friend's withers, a ritual they'd had as long as both could remember.

Jiggs barely noticed other trailers unloading saddled mounts. Figures moved in and out of headlights. Shovels and buckets clanged as they were thrown into trucks. A man's voice shouted, "Wildland firefighters are working the forest. The Rural Department couldn't get it contained. Too much understory. They're afraid it's gonna crown."

"Bound to happen," Jiggs grumbled as he led his horse in a trot, past an old man trundling a five-gallon bucket up the escarpment.

"Dad!" Nap yelled. A rafter-hipped dun followed him, the lead rope stretched taut between them as they hurried to the opening. Rocket, his blue heeler, trotted next to them. "Where do you want us to start?"

Jiggs' thoughts dived to the deep gashes across his property where the earth's tissue had torn from the Eagle Cap's uplift. It was almost enough to make him curse. He swung a leg over the Appaloosa's back. The horse stopped fidgeting except for twitching alternate ears. "We've got twenty head. They're likely in the two ravines. Stay out of the north one. It's full of brush," Jiggs shouted to Nap, knowing everyone was listening. "And get Ol' Twenty Thousand out." He wheeled his horse and took off.

"Move off the road," Bazz shouted. "The Rural Fire boys will need to get their trucks through."

"It'll be a while before they get here." Chicken Thief stood on a running board, yelling over the renewed rumble of engines. "I heard there's *buildings* burning on the other side of the fence. We're on our own over here."

A man hopped into the back of a truck, grumbling, "Those amenity owners don't live here. Don't take care of the place."

"Well now, that's old George's fault, too," said a woman in leather work boots with a bandana tied like a helmet over curly hair. She plunked down beside him. "He got too fat to take care of it and let the weeds take over. The new folks got it like he left it."

Her husband climbed onto the tailgate and motioned for her to scoot over. "You don't know what you're talkin' about. George hired the fence line cleared when he couldn't do it himself." His wife rolled her eyes and hooked her thumb toward an empty space next to Dooley Monroe, the antique/junk man. Truck tires spat gravel as they bounced off the road and up the embankment.

With a sideways grin, Chicken Thief Bob swiveled his arm toward a man built like a smackdown wrestler. "Muley! You and me. Meet at the north ravine." He folded his legs into his truck cab, his knees cradling either side of the steering wheel. The starter stuttered, then caught. He gunned the old Toyota into the field.

Bazz whipped his flashlight in circles, watching vehicles jolt over the spot in the ditch he'd filled with posts and guiding them through the fence cut. A ball-capped teenager shouted as he passed, "Who's Ol' Twenty Thousand?"

As they lurched by, Bazz gave him a serious stare. "Jiggs Woolsey's fancy-pants bull."

Headlights fanned apart, bobbing over clumps of grass and circling the rock outcroppings. One group found a few black baldies huddled in the southern draw. The cattle stupidly ogled the headlights and honking horns, their legs seemingly rooted into the soil. Men, women, and dogs jumped from trucks and hemmed in the big-eyed animals on three sides. People waved their arms in slow flapping motions. A few added herding drones, "Huhyaa. Huhyaa." The cows tightened into a clump, white faces nuzzled together, stamping, and occasionally jerking a nose to test the air.

A teenager walked up, made a looping twist in a tail, and hard-slapped a hindquarter. "Move, ya ol' rip!" The cow exploded into a run, circling behind the youth. Within a few steps, a black and gray dog cut across her exit route and matched turns to the cow's dance. "Work her, Rocket," a teen shouted. Jiggs let Curly Dogs join the chase, and the cow dashed westward, running through her beefy friends. Bumped out of their frozen stares, they trailed after her.

When cows, people, dogs, and horses walked out of the wash, their bodies cast long shadows in the light. The fire had grown. An orange wall of flames pulsed among the trees 700 yards to the east. A few white spots shimmered at ground level where the temperatures burned the hottest. Several pines, between the pasture and the fire, stood in black profile, waiting to be consumed.

Most folks had seen an out-of-control burn before, yet they paused with hypnotized stares. Shrieks turned their attention to a figure bounding across the pasture. The sepia colored light made it hard to identify the runner at first, and then smart-mouths began catcalling, "Run, Forrest, run!" "So that's how Chicken Thief steals animals."

A black bull, the size of a small locomotive, charged across the field, its head a yard away from Chicken Thief's backside. People watched as the duo disappeared into the darkness.

"Kenny, go help. That bull could hurt him," Lottie Lubach told her son as she climbed into a truck bed. The man wheeled his horse and began pulling a loop on his lariat.

"Rope Bob, not that expensive bull," Zimm shouted.

Lottie smacked her husband's arm and yelled, "Slow down, Kenny. You can't see the gopher holes."

"He knows how to ride. He's thirty-five for pete's sake," Zimm said. She frowned, watching her son race off.

A parade of cows, pursued by dogs, then followed by trucks moved away from the blaze. Behind them, in the forest, a tall pine crackled. Electric-white light shot through its needles. With a gnarring roar, the crown burst into flames. Faces turned at the sound. Many walkers stopped and watched, mesmerized by the spiral of embers funneling into the black canopy.

Jiggs and Curly Dogs were the last ones out of the south ravine. He'd ridden into its deepest crannies checking for stragglers—both cows and humans. "Keep moving," he urged in a toneless voice when he caught up to the firewatchers. The animals had broken into a trot. A rider loped ahead to keep the herd from a panicked fit. Nap whistled signals to Rocket, instructing the super mutt to run silent arcs behind strays, nipping their hocks.

People jumped onto running boards and tailgates as the trucks lumbered forward. Jiggs nudged his horse into a trot and rode ahead to catch up. "Nap! Cut the fence here. Drive 'em out on the road, then south to the Bonewash," he called and turned Curly Dogs back toward the blaze.

"Why don't we just keep 'em corralled in a corner?" Nap yelled back. "That fire probably won't make it this far." But his father was already out of earshot.

Guntis Kral squinted at the young man. "Your whole north fence line runs next to that tinder box forest." The old German's grizzled features were shadowed from the fire, but his voice growled his judgment. "You gonna wait until it starts singeing hair before you move 'em?"

The man's grown daughter gave Nap a sympathetic smile. "I hate to mend fence, too."

Nap pulled out his pliers. He opened and closed them, staring in the direction his father had ridden. That was his dad's way. *Keep moving forward.* But what about when his dad's judgment was wrong? Nap noticed the older his dad got, the more boneheaded mistakes he made. Why go barreling down a road that made twice as much work? He was always told, *This ranch will be yours someday. You'll have to make the decisions.* Yet, here he was, stuck between his father's orders and what he knew would avoid a lot of needless sweat.

He could feel their eyes casting glances at him. He heard ol' Guntis grumbling and his daughter shushing him in conspiratorial undertones. If he didn't cut the fence, one of these old geezers would do it, and how would that play out at the Two Pan Bar and Grill?

Nap dismounted, walked to the fence, and cut the first wire. Eager hands grabbed the strands and peeled them away. He led Face Punch, his horse, through and remounted. "Head 'em south," he shouted.

"There's your father's son," Guntis' raspy voice called as he rode through the gap. Nap gave him a stone-faced stare. "Buncha needless work," he muttered to himself.

"Where you goin'?" Zimm yelled.

Jiggs tore by on Curly Dogs, pointing at the dark shape of the '93 Toyota perched at the top of the north ravine.

Zimm's face froze. Burning trees had fallen across the fence. A wall of flames ate a widening swath toward the vehicle. "Hey! Hey!" he bellowed at people driving beeves onto the road. "The fire's jumped."

Trucks made U-turns and bodies climbed into the beds. Like cattle going to market, folks knocked shoulders and heads as vehicles zigzagged back across the field.

They parked away from the ravine and Chicken Thief's truck. Folks jumped out and lumbered toward the fire, burdened by shovels and five-gallon buckets stuffed with wet gunnysacks. A few people were already spaced along the fire line, their silhouettes sharp against the orange backdrop. They flailed the burning grass with wet sacks. Each wallop spewed sparks into the air, while gray ashes floated down. The fire greeted the new volunteers with flames leaping ten feet high. It devoured a stand of sagebrush and sent a black curtain of smoke to blot out the stars.

Four men headed toward Chicken Thief's Toyota. "We've got this, Jiggs." Zimm waved the rancher away. "Go look for cattle."

"You might need some extra pull," he said, eyeing the front tire hanging over the lip of the ravine.

"Go on." Muley Baker nodded. "We'll hook my one-ton to it if we can't push this rice burner out."

Jiggs turned away, and then wheeled Curly Dogs back. "Hey! Do not let anyone come in after me. I mean it. It's chucked with sagebrush." Zimm gave an acknowledging wave as horse and rider took off at a gallop.

The men took positions along the sides of the Toyota. "Hit it!" Zimm yelled. Three tires spun in the grass as they pushed. Curses flew. The truck remained anchored.

A coyote loped out of the burning woods, running within ten feet of the group, head hunkered down, eyes in sideways vigilance. "Here's one of your relatives, Chicken Thief," Muley said, looking for a rock to hurl at the rangy creature.

"How do you manage those semis full of gravel?" Zimm shook his head at Chicken Thief. "That 'yote could drive better than you. Get out. Lemme have a go at 'er."

"No. You'd steer it off in the ravine."

"Naw. Jiggs might be down there."

"Hell's bells!" A chorus of curses reached the cab as a blast of hot air sideswiped them. Muley's straw hat spun cartwheels before dropping into the void over the deep crevice. "It's pickin' up," he yelled. "Get that mother outta here!"

The blaze was working its way toward them, searing clumps of grass, sucking them into the air, and hurling glowing tendrils ahead to start new burns.

The men gave the truck an adrenalin-rushed heave. Chicken Thief stomped the accelerator to the floorboard. A long metal screech of differential versus stone came from the undercarriage. The Toyota lurched backward, shooting through the waist-high flames of the fire line.

There was a heartbeat's pause before Chicken Thief's mouth began moving like a miscued disaster movie, but no one could hear what he was saying. The grinding rasps of gears stripping and wheels spinning covered shouts of, "Get out of there!" "Leave it and run!"

Chicken Thief double-clutched and let off the gas enough to jerk forward. The tires found traction. Bodies jumped out of his way as he charged to safety. Once clear, he slid to a stop and burst out the door, running away. Folks grimaced and stared, waiting for the gas tank to explode. After a few moments, when nothing happened, they began laughing. Others imitated Chicken Thief's bugging eyes and clacking teeth as they went back to thrashing flames.

Talk stopped. Smoke stung everyone's eyes, causing tear-streaks on sooty faces. No one noticed how long they'd been digging ditches or swinging wet sacks. The crackling grass and constant suck of the fire became their background music. Sometimes a cheer arose when flames died at rock outcroppings. Cussing and yelling soon followed when drifting embers floated behind the fighters, igniting pasture yards away.

The greatest concentration of people beat flames and turned shovelfuls of sub-soil in front of the drop off into the ravine. The twenty-foot high walls of the split dropped downward in a cow-face slant. Jagged stones and loose scrabble made it too dangerous for horses or cattle to descend the walls, but they could enter through the shallow east end.

Over the years, the crack had become the wind's dustpan, filling the chasm with dead sagebrush and detritus. Broken, weathered stone slabs littered the gully floor, creating pockets and hiding places. Jiggs knew them all—even in the dark. His dad had made Pax and him spend hours in this gulch every spring, cleaning the brush that collected in chinks and crevices. The south ravine wasn't bad. It was shallow enough that spring winds blew out the debris. "Self-cleaning, like wading in the pond to get the mud off your boots," his dad would say, reminding Jiggs he'd done a chore in the most lazy way possible, and it would never be forgotten.

However, the north ravine was scut work and the boys spent most of their time squeezing into clefts to keep cool. They'd always received the biting tongue of the belt for their horseplay. Then Pax would hop to and get the job done, pounding Jiggs when he goofed around. If Jiggs fought back, and he always did, he received their dad's belt and backhand. He swore he would never make his kid clean this slit—and he hadn't.

He entered the shallow end of the ravine and rode downward. He'd done a quick count back at the fence. He was missing six heifers. This was the most likely place they'd hole up. The chasm dropped steeply through a trail the cattle had trampled in the dried brush. Bleached bushes choked cracks and side nooks, and tangled in the stirrups as Curly Dogs shouldered his way through.

Jiggs cursed himself for not cleaning this gulch since his father had died. His old man used to prepare for a night like this. Jiggs thought it was a lot of work for something that had never happened in his lifetime of memories. He could hear his dad's castigating voice, "How do you *think* you keep it from happening? Stop makin' life hard by bein' stupid. I'm thirty years older than you. I had my back broke once, and my arms twice. And on my worst day I can still beat the hell out of you. Now start listening." It had become their routine, a son's silent rebellion.

A floating ember seesawed downward, settling on a skeletal finger of tumbleweed. It died black for a second, and then glowed, birthing a wavering tongue of flame. Several more branches erupted with tiny heartbeats of orange. In an explosive *whump,* the bush ignited.

Zimm, his voice thick with smoke, rasped into the dark gully, "Jiggs! Get out of there! The fire's jumped! It's over the edge." The flames answered him with crackling and a mounting roar like wind being sucked through a turbine. "Hey! You hear me?"

Several men joined Zimm, trotting along the edge of the drop off. A calf's bawl drew their attention. In the flickering light, Zimm could see the backside of two, maybe three, animals trapped in a pocket as flames rose in the dried sage around their hooves. The animals stomped and climbed over each other. Smoke and flames eclipsed his view. The cattle bellowed in terror, then pain. Zimm turned away. The other men hollered warnings to Jiggs, stumbling, trying to foot race the fire along the ravine. They were lagging competitors. The flames leapt ahead from bush to bush.

Curly Dogs had found four heifers nosed into a crack. Jiggs worked them to the main channel, then scared them toward the entrance. He continued to ride farther into the ravine. The horse picked his way around boulders, crunching through belly-deep brush for a hundred yards. He stopped suddenly and pitched his head, rocking Jiggs backward in the saddle. The withers quivered and the horse's weight shifted to its back feet, preparing to rear. A second later shrill bellows squealed from deep within the ravine, ricocheting off the walls.

Jiggs yanked the reins, pivoting Curly Dogs and goading the horse back the way they'd come. He didn't need to check behind him. Like standing close to a freight train, the oncoming rush of flames made a sucking roar and threw yellow light before him. The horse broke into a run, jumping over boulders and jagged piles of rock. Jiggs loosed his grip and let Curly Dogs have his head. Behind them, brush piles erupted with a *whoosh.*

The Appaloosa rounded a dogleg in the gulch and stumbled headlong into the four heifers. The dimwitted calves had moved up the channel until they'd reached the bend, and then they'd stopped, thinking darkness meant safety. One heifer went down. Two slammed into each other. The last one bolted ahead—tail in the air.

Jiggs stepped on the stirrups and heaved Curly Dogs' head up. Bushes in overhead crevices exploded into white fireballs, showering them with burning embers. Clamping his knees tight, he leaned forward. The horse scrambled to gain his feet and plunged into a run. Behind them, heifers bleated, chasing after them.

In the pasture, cheers wafted from the far end of the fire line. "Keep searching the ravine!" Zimm shouted at the men who had stopped to see why people were clapping. A pumper truck had arrived. Spitting a slow spray of water, it crawled across the field, leaving curls of smoke in its wake. Bazz rode in the passenger seat like a dignitary in a parade, smiling, waving, and pointing at people.

Zimm trotted toward the pumper and hauled his bulk onto the running board. "The fire jumped. Jiggs is still in the ravine. We can't find him!"

Bazz pushed Zimm off the running board and hopped out the door. The driver slammed the brakes when he heard the door open, but both men were already sprinting across the field.

Along the line of people toeing the edge of the ravine, the words, "See him?" echoed back and forth. No one answered.

The fire had flashed through the deepest end of the fissure and rolled up the wash toward the shallow entrance. Waves of heat radiated over the burned-out chasm. Pockets of embers pulsed orange in the inky shadows.

"Get somebody down there," Bazz shouted.

"Can't. The entrance hasn't burned out yet," a voice answered. "Wait a bit."

"Like hell." Bazz plunged down the steep slope, his legs scrambling to keep up with his falling body. There was no time for swearing on the way down, but he loosed a long litany of curses once he lay at the bottom, rubbing his bruises. Bouncing rocks announced another arrival. Zimm barked each time he grabbed a boulder, braking his sliding fall. The hot stones quickly befouled his vocabulary.

"You guys okay?" someone shouted from the ridge.

"Yeah, come on down." Bazz blinked, letting his eyes adjust to the darkness. "The first step is a little tricky, but you're good after that."

Grunting, they pushed themselves up, squinting at shapes in varying hues of gray and black. "Explore the niches with your feet. Don't stick your hand in," Zimm cautioned. "In case that blaze didn't cook all the rattlers."

After several minutes, a voice floated down from the top of the wall, "Well?"

"Nobody here. We'll move up the ravine," Bazz said.

"Hey, look for my hat while you're down there."

"Is that you, Muley? Why don't you make yourself useful and bring us a light?" Bazz's voice had a sandpaper rub to it.

Zimm stared at a stinking pile of flesh. "Those calves are past doctorin'." But as he spoke, a whispered gasp came from the heap.

"He could be under the one closest to the wall. Maybe that would've protected him." Bazz used a low voice, but it carried up the gradient.

Zimm sniffed. "Smells like branding day, and I don't think the top one's even dead yet."

"Help me move it."

"Hell no." Zimm winced. "Hit her between the eyes with a rock first or feel around for a human arm or a leg."

In a quiet, halting voice Bazz asked, "You under there, Jiggs?"

Laughter and guffaws erupted at the lip of the gully. A muffled snicker turned into a falsetto echo, "You under there, Jiggs?"

"If you asses can't help, then leave," Bazz growled.

"Hey, Lewis and Clark," Muley called down. "If Jiggs is under the cow, where's his horse? Curly Dogs has more sense than both of you."

"Maybe he fell off, you idiot," Zimm grumbled.

"Well, you're down there and the horse isn't. Who's smarter?"

Bazz snagged a hot rock to fling at Muley. The profile of a horse and rider stood among the group on the lip of the ravine. "How long you been up there?" he asked.

"Not long," Jiggs said. "Curly Dogs barrel-raced boulders as the fire came down the chute. Four heifers followed us. One's blistered pretty bad. Singed off a hunk of Curly Dogs' tail. What're you two doing down there?"

"Saving your sorry hide."

Muley, his voice full of sarcasm, added, "They thought you was underneath some half-alive carcasses. They were too squeamish to make sure though." Muffled snorts followed.

"I do appreciate that, gentlemen." Jiggs ignored the banter. "You can help yourself to the barbeque."

"These animals aren't quite dead yet," Bazz said. "So you can owe us a bottle of Jack Daniels instead."

"You want Curly Dogs to pull you out of there?"

"Nope, we'll walk out, like your genius horse did," Zimm said. Curses floated out of the gulch as the men stumbled over boulders and kicked through smoldering ash piles. All but one of the spectators moved toward the pumper truck, laughing and clapping each other on the back. A woman stood listening to the irate voices rising from the ravine until the men passed the dogleg, and the night swallowed their complaints.

Jiggs dismounted next to Josie, who was bundled in heavy jeans, boots, and a long-sleeved denim jacket buttoned to the collar. She took off her broad-brimmed hat flecked with ashes, still watching the gully. Jiggs stared at her back. For some reason, talking with women felt like singing in front of people; everyone waited for the next word to come out off-key.

"Evening, Josie. I haven't had a chance to say hello tonight."

"It's nearly morning now. You've been busy."

Using up their quota of conversation, they watched the figures back-lit by the forest fire. Across the pasture, people dragged shovels and sacks as they trudged toward the helter-skelter of parked vehicles. A black line, sharp against the gray of grass, showed that 400 yards of the range, the length of the fence line, had burned.

Jiggs cleared his throat. "Is your Granddad's truck close?" She nodded. He leaned nearer. "Is his pistol still under the seat?"

On the gravel road, dogs barked and threaded between people. Cattle grazed along the ditches. Lottie yanked plastic water bottles from shrink-wrapped packages and handed them out with a concerned, "How ya doin'?" or "Ya look a little beat."

In lanterns and headlights, red faces beamed. Cheeks and chins were blackened with soot and streaked with lines of perspiration. Gray cinders covered hair and hats. Folks inspected holes in their shirts and pointed at singed sideburns. Victorious grins and laughter flitted through the crowd, though many glanced toward the forest and the battle being waged by the Wildland Firefighters. Trees were still burning, but the line of orange flames wasn't spreading.

"Jiggs shoulda got that land after George died," a man groused. "I wish he'd kick a few more realtors' butts all the way to their car."

"I don't." A woman's voice spiked with anger. "Traditional ranching's gone. Priced out of business. We need new people and their money. Those fat wallets could—"

The sound of a gunshot made people jump.

"Two heifers were burned and barely breathing," Zimm told the folks around him. At the second report, laughter and chatter stilled. "It's a mercy," a woman mumbled.

Nap rode into the crowd, his dog threading between people. "Still working, Rocket?" someone said and tossed a hunk of jerky. The blue heeler gobbled it, eyes darting to see if any more food was flying through the air. Nap made a *tsk, tsk* sound, and the dog went back to collecting strays and ambling them down the road.

"Hey, *Running* Thief Bob!" Zimm called. Voices interrupted each other, describing the lanky man legging it across the pasture with the bull breathing in his back pocket.

"That big rack of steaks wouldn't move." Chicken Thief grinned. "So I whacked his snout with my cap. He took after me like I'd insulted his manhood. Lucky for me, he can't run too far. He's pretty cranky for a guy with a harem."

Few people noticed Jiggs ride through the fence cut. He tied Curly Dogs to the trailer and ran his hands over him, checking for burns. After giving him a flake of alfalfa and a drink, Jiggs made his way through the crowd, shaking hands and offering a simple "You okay?" and "Thanks."

"You've done it for us," said a tired Dooley Monroe, his hat sprinkled with ashes.

"Anytime," was the usual reply from sooty faces.

He scanned his neighbors. Their homes ranged across thirty miles of valley and buffered the base of the mountains. The land had gifted all of them with a peculiar trait … to watch for lights. Jiggs thanked Guntis Kral's duncehead son-in-law for noticing a bright spot where it didn't belong as he enjoyed an open-air leak off his back porch. He'd called Jiggs and then started the phone tree with, "Starvation Ridge is burning. Jiggs Woolsey needs to move cattle." Jangling phones roused people out of bed for miles.

Jiggs knew their sacrifice. Shortly, they'd make long drives, change clothes, and start their morning chores. Lottie Lubach would flick on the lights of her Latte Da coffee shop at four this morning to serve cups of caffeine to folks on their way home.

"Mr. Mayor finally earned the zero-salary we pay him," Chicken Thief Bob announced, pointing toward Bazz, who was taking a pull from a beer. Chicken Thief eyed the bottle. "Kinda early, ain't it? Where'd you get that?"

"I know people," Bazz said. "As mayor, I know the timber harvester who owns that pumper truck. As his mechanic, he owed me a favor." Bazz waggled his cell phone.

Among the scattered cheers, Jiggs shook the mayor's hand with a "Thanks."

Bazz stepped closer, his voice low. "These are your neighbors. Somebody'll help with the Shiny."

"Give it a rest." Jiggs clapped Bazz on the back while waving to a truck that was leaving. "It's been a long night."

"Then you need to come to the next town meeting, and hear Jarmin's latest ploy. Though ... all that may've changed now." Bazz stared at the burning trees. "The district fire chief said this blaze started at Jarmin's. No telling what the final damage will be. Maybe it burned him out."

"Anybody hurt?" Jiggs asked. Bazz shrugged. The rancher stared, taking inventory. Smoldering trees lay over his fence. Behind the bent poles and twisted wires, deeper in the forest, rings of yellow rippled up the boles of pines. "My luck just changed." He squinted as though taking aim with a shotgun. "But I'm not sure if it's for the better."

21

Dawn

PINK SMUDGES APPEARED in the dawn over Starvation Ridge. Curly Dogs' lead slipped along the wire fence until it snugged against a post. Brushed and watered, he breakfasted on bunch grass. The horse pulled the running end of the loop and freed himself to graze in the open field.

Through the many sleepless nights of his life, Jiggs always felt an easing in his chest when daybreak finally bladed the horizon. Now, he shouldered his shovel and scanned the eastern sky, unaware of the sighing noise he made as he leaned slightly backward, stretching his spine. He'd stayed the night— what little was left of it—beating smoldering patches of grass and keeping an eye on the diminishing flames on the other side of his crushed fence. With daybreak there was enough light to see a dirty haze hanging over the charred cavity in the forest.

It was dangerous to cheer for another man's misery; it could easily turn and haunt him. But there was no doubt about it, he wanted Jarmin's land, just like Jarmin wanted his.

And *his* reasons were purer: Saving the land for the people who could use it. Keeping this from becoming a ghost town of weekend property owners. And a slice of bragging rights that accompanied being one of the biggest ranchers in the county. Unfortunately, it was going to take money that he didn't have.

Curly Dogs lifted his head and twitched his ears. The distant sound of a car floated through the morning air. Jiggs stared at the road and noticed an empty plastic water bottle in the ditch. He hated those things. He'd be picking them up for the next five miles where they'd flown out of pickup beds.

His exhaustion swelled into anger when he saw the white Escalade topping the horizon: Dr. Richard Jarmin's vehicle. He cautioned himself to offer condolences; Jarmin had suffered losses, too. He'd make a casual offer to take over this honyocker's charred acres, though he didn't have a clue where he'd get the money. Then he'd demand payment for his barbequed cattle.

The Escalade pulled to a stop next to the empty bottle. Dust flumed forward. A petite woman in pressed jeans and embroidered vest got out. She waved in front of her face, trying to clear the air.

"Hi. I wasn't sure whether this road would go through." She walked toward him. "I wanted to see how far it had burned this way."

Jiggs frowned, glancing behind her, looking for someone else to get out of the car.

"Are you okay?" she asked.

"Morning." He gave a quick nod. "Jiggs Woolsey." He extended his hand, then pulled it back, holding up soot-smudged fingers.

"Oh." She gave a half-hearted wave of her manicured fingertips. "I'm Samantha Jarmin. My husband and I own *that*." She flung her hand toward the section of carbonized trees, "It's a mess over there. I can't get near it without getting black. Some of those firefighters stayed all night, watching the fire. Can you imagine?"

Jiggs discarded the first comments that came to mind. He gave her a nod. "It's a tragedy. How'd it start?" As the sun edged above the horizon, shadows of burnt snags and pointed, limbless trees inched across his pasture.

"Well," Samantha Jarmin bit a crimson thumbnail, "I don't see how it could be, but the firefighters said it was from our campfire—two days ago. The kids and I came for a visit. We had a marshmallow roast down by the new stables. The fire burned to ash, but ... well, a firefighter said the coals burned into a tree root. It cooked underground until the burn traveled close enough to the surface to ignite pine needles. Anyway, they plowed up the paddocks. Smoke rolled out of the dirt. It's still smoking."

"Yeah, they can smolder underground for a long time. That's why I stayed—"

"Fortunately, the horses weren't here, but we lost our new stables and several work sheds. The firemen said we built too close to the trees. Too bad the house didn't burn, too. Nothing was close enough to ignite it."

Jiggs blinked, trying to keep his voice neutral, "You don't like the place?"

"It's a 1940's nightmare. It creaks and groans and blows a fuse every time I use the hair dryer. I wish it had burned, so insurance could cover a new one."

" 'Scuse me for asking, ma'am, but if you hate it, why're you here?"

"My horses. And the only way Richard will let me have them is if I stable them here. I only come to ride. They're my salvation. You understand how a horse carries more than the weight of the rider." She eyed Curly Dogs.

"You might be happier over by Joseph. Closer to your husband's work."

"Probably." She stared for a long while. With a tired sigh, her voice barely rose above a whisper. "He may make me sell them. Richard had quite a fit when he heard the new stable burned down."

"I bet," Jiggs grunted. "Well, it can always be rebuilt."

"I think if he allows reconstruction, it'll be at Devil's Thumb. That's why we're not remodeling the house."

"Never heard of it," Jiggs said. "Is that the name of his elk resort?"

"No. He gave up on that, you know. Too many permits. Too many animals. He's not an animal person. His new vision is a vacation community. Summer homes. Wine shops. Bistros. Gas station. A swimming pool for the residents."

"There?" Jiggs pointed at the vintage ranch house.

"Oh, no. Some land up by the mountains will be available soon. This place isn't scenic enough, and now it's really ugly. They took a chainsaw to almost every tree, and that's why we bought the property. To live in the forest, you know?" She frowned at him and cocked her head.

"No, ma'am, I don't know. I don't get why city people move to the country then try to turn it into the place they left. It's like the 'snowbirds' who move to Arizona and put in lawns with sprinklers. Here, in fire country, you can't have bonfires under trees, trees next to buildings, and buildings surrounded by shrubs." He took a step back, his arms at his sides, fingers curling tight.

"Well, now I know." She leaned forward slightly, scanning his face. "Did I say something wrong? We just met, but it feels like ... something else is going on here."

Curly Dogs walked down the embankment toward them, the second time in the last ten hours the horse had saved Jiggs. "It's been a long night, ma'am." He patted the Appaloosa's neck and led him to the trailer. The horse stepped inside like a passenger boarding an overdue bus.

"I apologize. I think we've gotten off to a bad start. And I could really use your help." Mrs. Jarmin raised her voice so

Jiggs could hear as he slid bolts and secured the trailer door. "You seem good with animals. I'm looking for what's known as a 'ranch butler.'" Jiggs arched an eyebrow at her. "It's more than a foreman. It's a manager who'll take care of the place. Tend the livestock. Keep things in order and looking nice for us and our guests. This fire wouldn't have happened if we'd had someone walking down to the barns every day. We had a man but, obviously, he didn't work out very well." She stared at the burnt trees. "Richard says lots of people need work around here. Would you be interested or know of anyone?"

Jiggs stared at her, as if she'd reared up and offered to mud wrestle. If she'd been a man, he'd know exactly how to lead off. He blinked, searching for courteous words. "Sorry, ma'am." He picked up the empty plastic bottle, got in his truck, and rolled down the window. She gave him a quizzical frown as he cranked the engine. He wanted to simply drive off. That's what he did when his kid said stupid things. Leave, and let Nap think about it for a while. He'd wise up— eventually. But she wasn't a kid.

Jiggs poked his arm out the window, resting it on the door. "Seems you aren't too happy with your ranch. You interested in selling?"

"I am ..." She tucked a blonde lock of hair behind her ear. "But Richard isn't. He feels there's potential for development around here. I've threatened to dust off my realtor's license if he doesn't dump his present land man ..." She quickly put her hand over her mouth. "Oh no. You're not related to him, are you?"

Jiggs shook his head. "Nobody in my family sells parcels. We only buy them."

"Oh, thank heavens." She rolled her eyes, adding a nervous laugh. "And here I offered you a job when you're looking for an investment. I keep saying the wrong thing. I'm so sorry. Well, if you're looking for a good venture deal, ask Richard. He's already got several investors lined up for Devil's Thumb."

"Now exactly where is this project located?"

"Somewhere near the mountains." She swirled her hand. "Richard and that weird realtor are hush hush about it. Fine by me. I'm busy with my horses. If you're interested, he said he'd be explaining the first stage, The Leadership Center, at some local town meeting. That's about as much as I know."

"I'll look forward to hearing all about it, ma'am. And you know ... you might have a hard time finding a sitter for your property. Most everything around here, big and little, is a working spread. Most folks do their own grind." He pointed to trees lying over his broken wires. "For instance, that can be your butler's first job. Because out here, when you burn some- one else's property, *you* get to fix it. Good luck finding a manservant, ma'am."

He gave her a nod and lifted a hand as he drove away. Ob- viously his luck *had* changed. He needed money and he'd just received a job offer—to be a ranch nanny. Too bad the Boss of the Universe had such a mocking sense of humor.

Within fifty feet, he pounded the steering wheel at his tongue-tied hurry. He'd been so stunned about Devil's Thumb and butlering her barn, he'd forgotten to demand payment for his baked cattle.

He glanced in the one-ton's side mirror. Samantha Jarmin was waving her hand in front of her face as she walked to her Escalade. He set his jaw and stared down the road. He was headed toward the sunrise and a new day—but the wrong direction to get home. "Keep moving forward," he mumbled. He wasn't turning around now.

22

End of The West

"AND THEN WE'LL have a Fourbucks Coffee Shop and a Yak In The Box Drive Thru. How am I supposed to compete against that?" Lottie Lubach randomly shook her fist, punctuating her words. She'd been wildly gesticulating the entire time she'd spoken at the Two Pan town meeting. With a scrunched up face, she'd pooh-poohed Jarmin's statistics, pointing at the empty wall where his Power Point graphs were no longer displayed. Disgust curled her mouth. "And this—" With an open palm, she smacked a thick poster board revealing the blueprint for the new Leadership building. The metal tripod scooted backward a foot.

Her husband stood, spinning one hand for her to *Come here*, and the other hand pointing *Sit down* next to him. "Lottie, I ran the grain mill for thirty years, and I understand how this works," he said. "We'll have a bigger tax base because more people will visit."

"Shut up, Zimm." Her head of graying curls shook as she whirled to face him; an angry bottomlessness in her eyes made him jerk. "If you want to run things, go back to work at the mill. I've got the floor right now, and I'm going to talk without you correcting me." Her stance made her seem formidable. A tiny woman whose stocky legs had been climbing over problems all of her life.

Eyes widened. Tension skittered through the room, skipping Millie Capper who drawled, "It's hot in here. I make a motion we end this meeting. Whit would second if he was awake."

"You're out of order, Millie." Bazz banged his gavel twice. "Let's cut out these cross discussions. Zimm or anybody else, if you've got questions or comments, you direct them to me." He banged his gavel again. Lottie launched into why the Leadership Center was a threat to the human race.

Jiggs got up and left. He needed a break. The discussion was pitting families against each other. He shot Jarmin an accusing look as he passed him sitting in the back of the room with his lackey realtor, Max Buddy. They'd made a impressive presentation flashing numbers and pie charts, which had folks nodding, squinting, and some scratching their heads.

Dr. Dick had proposed to start the revitalization of downtown by constructing a new building on Main Street. A destination training center for business people. That sounded all right to most folks. Then, after the high-powered workshops, participants would enjoy the wonders of the Eagle Caps. Tourism. Money. Jobs. Win-win for everyone. He'd hung a custom-printed banner across the front of the room: *Capitalize Our Community For Competitive Advantage*. The catchy slogan had also appeared on every colorful Power Point slide and glossy handout.

Jiggs sat on the Opera House's new concrete steps, feeling righteously riled. The sun had dropped behind the mountains, painting the twilight sky with purple streaks, leaving two silver stars overhead. He'd intended to catch a few ranchers and talk with them about leasing the Shiny, but the letter he'd gotten this morning ended that plan. So he came to listen. To hear what the future would look like. It made him sick to his stomach.

He'd tried standing in the way of progress, and it had broadsided him. It was painful to learn that moving on was as certain as the gold mines playing out, the stagecoach's final run, and the timber mills closing. But he still needed to speak up. He might be out of the battle now, but that didn't mean he had to stay quiet while Jarmin snapped the reins and ran willy-nilly over everyone. Jiggs took a deep breath, got up, and walked back through the door.

"Lottie," Bazz interrupted, watching Jiggs stride up the aisle like a knight on his way to save a damsel, "are you in the vicinity of a point?" Cold, banked fires behind her eyes made him mutter, "Sorry."

Jarmin stood up. "If I may?"

"Not yet," Bazz said. "Everyone gets a chance to speak before you get a second round. Jiggs, I don't need you throwing gasoline on this fire right now."

The rancher ignored him. He took off his hat. "Have you had a chance to say what you wanted, Lottie?" The short woman stepped away, holding her palm out to present the spot where she'd stood. As she left, she bumped the tripod and blueprint. They clattered to the floor. She daggered Zimm with a glare, then crossed the room and sat away from him.

Jiggs was unnerved by all the eyes looking at him. He'd held many community conversations at the Bar and Grill, but he hadn't felt their eyes boring into him. Folks stared as they resettled themselves, trying to find comfort on the metal folding chairs. Jarmin's yap had gone on too long. Captivated by the cat and dog fight between Lottie and Zimm, people had stayed, but now they squirmed. Likely the only reason they were ignoring their aching backsides was the hope of seeing fireworks between him and Jarmin. Maybe even collecting on their bets.

From the back corner, Chicken Thief Bob nodded with an *I've-got-your-back* look. Josie and Nap gave him a thumbs up.

He would act. Not react. Did so many people always come to these meetings?

"I'm not a speaker." Jiggs picked up the fallen tripod and set the blueprint in place so the blank side faced the audience. "But I think we should thank the doctor for being concerned about this community." He hung his hat on top of the tripod. Folks glanced at each other. "We could sure use more jobs—*if they were good jobs.*"

"If you haven't had a job in a while," Max Buddy called from the back of the room, "any job is a good job." Bazz rapped the gavel.

"Spoken like a realtor who hasn't made a sale in a while," Jiggs said with a smile. Folks laughed, and he quickly picked up his topic before Buddy started yammering his sales record. "Anyone remember the sheep bridges here?" A number of hands went up.

"There're pictures of it in the bar if Junior hasn't changed *that.*" More people laughed. "It was before my time, but my dad told me sheep used to be a big industry in Two Pan. The city built special bridges over streams and creeks to move them around to various pastures. In case you didn't know, woolies won't walk through the water like a cow. If they tip over or get soaked, they sink like a rock. At one time, this place had thousands and thousands of sheep. Photographs show big shearing parties on Main Street. Their wool filled long lines of train cars—which, by the way, don't run through here anymore either. Only a few families keep sheep now, and that's just for 4-H and FFA projects. The point is—things change. And all of you know I hate change—but it's inevitable."

"You finally figured that out?" Max Buddy called out.

Jiggs continued, "The main problem I see with this plan," he waved toward the banner, "is that it repeats the same mistakes of our past." Their eyes studied him. He could see their questions: Was he a guy who had a better plan? Or was he going off half-cocked again?

"You'd know about mistakes," the realtor called out. Several people turned and looked at him. Jarmin glanced at Buddy and shook his head.

Muley Baker turned around, his beefy arm hanging over the back of his chair. "Shut up, or *I'm* gonna hit you in the face." Bazz rapped the gavel, but didn't say anything.

"I've surely made enough blunders to be an expert on stubborn." Jiggs nodded. "That's why I can speak with authority that this plan won't work. It's not honest. It doesn't bring our community together. In fact, it's just the opposite.

"When we counted on one business for our economy, we shriveled and almost blew away. So when the gold mines played out—so did the town. When timber sales dropped, the mill closed, and more folks went under. Cotton became king ... sheep farms were abandoned. With each event, this place died a little more. Sitting here tonight are mostly the survivors. We're what's left of the generations that came before us." Jiggs took aim at the doctor. "So I'll tell you a truth you can put weight on: relying on outsiders for our income won't save us."

Jarmin's hands lay in his lap, balled into tight fists. "Still stubborn," he said to his realtor loud enough for everyone to hear. "Still without a clue about what creates prosperity."

"These folks know my history. And I know theirs. It's true; we're more acquainted with poverty hollow than the gates of prosperity. There's hardly a person in the room who hasn't spent a sleepless night worrying about paying bills or leaving something for their kids. I've felt that darkness on my back. I still feel it. It invades my dreams. My nightmares."

Restless shifting on hard chairs had stopped.

The realtor opened his mouth, but Jarmin waved him off. After several quiet seconds the doctor said, "That's a sad way you've chosen to live, Mr. Woolsey. You can have better. We all can have better." Jarmin shook his head as though confused how anyone could make such poor choices.

Folks glanced at each other. Jiggs wished that Jarmin would look at the faces around him. These were people who needed the truth, not a sales pitch. But the doctor and realtor were whispering with each other. He wished it hadn't come to this, but there was no backing down now.

"Is this an example of the leadership you're proposing? If someone opposes your ideas, you outspend them? You become the biggest corporation in town, and everyone bows in your direction because they're afraid to offend you. Then you can do whatever you please?"

"That's nonsense." Jarmin scowled.

"Then tell them the truth. Tell them about Devil's Thumb."

"I—" Jarmin froze.

"Mrs. Jarmin was kind enough to share her husband's vision with me the other day, after burning off part of my property." Jiggs walked back and forth across the front of the room, catching the eyes of his neighbors. "This Leadership project is Stage I. It ends in a vacation community with its own stores, coffee shop, gas station, and pool for the housing plats. It's not about supporting this town, it's about selling property for a new one—down the road."

"That was just brainstorming. Idle speculation," Jarmin said, overly loud.

Jiggs tapped the back of the poster holding the blueprint. "Is this speculation, too? Is it true? Will there be more than one or two leadership workshops a year? Or is it nothing more than an excuse to build cabins and sell lots?"

Jarmin stared, his anger visible. As if he couldn't understand how his four-color brochures and audio-assisted slides had gone from a presentation to a debate.

Max Buddy gave a derisive snort. "You're taking up our time to sputter your own prejudices, Woolsey. It's understandable that you don't trust others, given your history of violence first and asking questions later."

"Can you guarantee there'll be a leadership workshop once or twice a month for the next few years? That there'll be a steady flow of folks coming through here, or will the workshops peter out in a few months, leaving you with nothing to do, but sell land and build another town around here?"

"I can't—"

"You're not accountable to me," Jiggs interrupted. "You're promising them." He fanned his hands toward both sides of the room. "Can you explain your plans? All of them. Or will you dodge this question like you have the others?"

The audience stared and murmured. Jarmin clasped both hands in his lap, staring around the room, like a teacher waiting for the class to be quiet before he spoke. "As you aptly pointed out earlier, the economy affects us. I can't predict if budgets will get cut. But I can assure you, I have enough commitments for two workshops already. It won't make money at first, but I'll finance the venture because I believe in it. These are business leaders. We should be proud of their association with this town. They'll support it, once invested here."

"Your financial logic is astounding," Jiggs said coldly. He saw Bazz look down and smile at that. "You've got forty people who would come to town for two days. How much would they spend here, and how much at that compound you hope to build?"

A flush of red worked its way up Jarmin's neck and angular chin. "I believe we've bothered with this line of argument long enough. Why should anyone take economic advice from someone known to barely hang onto the projects he jumps into?"

The familiar heat swelled through Jiggs' chest. Chicken Thief stood, rapidly shaking his head as the room grew silent. Jiggs ran his hand through his hair as he looked down. Thank heavens for Bazz and his fifth-grade teacher. Act, not react.

He smiled at Jarmin and waved at Chicken Thief to sit down. "It's good that you're getting to know the background of folks in the community, me in particular. Let me help you learn more.

"Instead of constructing a building we don't need," Jiggs smacked the blueprint poster, making it scoot back like Lottie had. "Why not invest in this community? The elementary school could desperately use new windows and desks. You could hold your workshops in those classrooms." Jiggs held up a hand, cutting Jarmin off as he tried to speak. "And if it's during the school year, you could rent this place. Why not make another donation to the Opera House? It needs repairs, too.

"And, you could use local places to cater meals. That goes without saying. So how about using teachers or high schoolers, looking for summer and after-school work, to serve, and clean up? You could even buy welcome sacks for all your participants. There's plenty of fine bakers and craftsmen here who'd sell items for those bags.

"In other words," Jiggs held him with a stare, "Two Pan's economic plan should involve more than your realtor. I'm suggesting you take the money you were going to spend on a building, and seed it among more people."

"You still haven't solved the biggest problem." Jarmin's voice had a strained patience, as though he were explaining physics to a stump. "Where will attendees and their families stay?"

Chicken Thief rose halfway, saying, "We hosted 2,000 cyclists, when Bicycle Oregon pedaled through here."

"I hardly think the caliber of executives who will attend the Leadership Center will want to sleep on the ground in tents—or sit in child-size desks, for that matter." A verbal eye-roll tainted his voice. "To make this a respected destination program, it must have distinction."

"Ye gods and little fishes." Millie threw both hands in the air. "Next thing you know, we'll outlaw Hermes because we can't have ass crap in the street."

Jiggs held up a hand, waiting for the laughter and voices to fade away. "If you'd think about something other than trying to sell off part of this county, Mr. Jarmin, you'd find Minam has a motel. It's twenty miles away, but right on the river. It's only a summer business, serving rafters and kayakers, but you could work a deal for other dates. Again, you'd be helping the community instead of lining your own wallet. But if that's your intent, why not host participants at your house? You could charge them rent. Just don't have bonfires at your night meetings."

Jarmin's eyes narrowed. His voice sharpened. "Your ignorance hurts this city. No place can prosper with a man whose idea of traffic control is to tie a carnival toy to the street." Max Buddy's puffy hair waggled as he nodded vigorously.

"It got you to slow down." Jiggs shrugged. "If you're really training leaders, have them do community work. Pull nonnative weeds for the Nature Conservancy. Heck, I'd let them come work on the ranch for a real-life 'dude' experience."

"Bold words from someone who's teetering at the edge of losing his land." Jarmin spoke the words with a malignant calmness, his eyes daring Jiggs to deny it.

The room quieted. The rancher lifted his hat from the tripod, wondering how that snake got his information. Judging from the silence in the hall, Jarmin had released something spooky into the room, his words clutching not only Jiggs' stomach, but others' too. It was a clever turn of the conversation. Something his dad would have done. But his father would've used it to scare sense into him. Jarmin threw it like a spear.

He couldn't manage a smile. The seriousness in his face served just as well. "That's old news, Jarmin. Folks around here have been hearing that for years. Ox Woolsey would say it to anybody. Between you and me ... I wish I wasn't needed here. I'd like to forget this mess and get back to only raising cattle. But I can't until you're honest and tell us what your real intentions are. Whether you know it or not, the Bible truth is—None of us can hold back time. The best we can do is herd it. And that's what we're doing."

Jiggs put on his hat as he walked down the aisle. "Because after all the angling is done, we here in Two Pan need to make sure we can live with whatever you change. It's our families who'll be here *long* after you've made your money and moved on."

He walked out the double doors. The room was silent for several seconds, and then the buzz of small talk arose from the crowd. Jiggs kept walking to the sound of Bazz pounding his gavel. He'd considered staying, seeing the meeting through, but his patience had topped out. People would bandy more words back and forth. The chairs would get harder. Nothing would be solved.

Jiggs walked up and down Main until he didn't feel like hitting anything. Each time he'd passed the Two Pan Project, he'd glanced at the photos in the window. He knew most of the events that had caused the wrinkles and visible scars captured on his neighbors' faces.

Spooner waved him inside. The streets were empty and Jiggs was sure that the artist, he, and the hound lounging belly up on the sidewalk were the only ones not at the meeting. He grabbed the rheumy-eyed old mutt, and dragged it inside. "I'm not much for posing, but this old stray has earned citizen status. If you take his picture, then I'll go along, too." Spooner obliged.

Having fulfilled his citizenly duties of attending a meeting and having his picture taken, Jiggs camped out on Bazz's porch swing. The deep veranda and wide front steps of the former cathouse had once been advertising space for the ladies to lure passersby. Now it hosted the old dog.

Dusk had fallen. Jiggs sat in the swing, drinking a beer and watching folks leave the meeting. Some went over to have their pictures taken, too. A few chatted next to their trucks. He couldn't tell how the rest of the conflab had gone. Lottie and Zimm drove off together. He figured the conversation inside their vehicle was making the windows shake.

"What're you doing here?" Bazz strolled across the cobblestone sidewalk to his front door.

"*Su casa es mi casa.*" Jiggs held up a bottle.

"You should be at the meeting, collecting pats on the back. You're a hero. Both the school and the Opera House are getting sizeable donations." The swing groaned as he dropped onto the seat beside Jiggs and tossed his notebook to the decking. "I believe they'd elect you mayor."

"I thought Jarmin wanted the job."

"He couldn't get a position as Hermes poop-scooper right now. You won."

"But I lost the war." Jiggs shook his head, holding up an envelope.

Bazz took it, inspecting the front and back. "It's too dark to read. What is it?"

"A demand letter from the bank. I missed another payment. I have fifteen days to make it all up, along with late fees, or I go into default. Then the entire loan will be due. I sold hay and got enough for one payment, but McGinty wouldn't accept it. Won't let me trail a month behind. Wants both payments.

Right now. He's the agent for other banks participating in the loan, and says he has to protect their interests. I've never been late before, and all he can say to me is, 'Sorry. We're no charity.'"

"Why didn't you say something at the meeting? Your neighbors will help you."

"I called a couple of guys this morning after I got this letter. Their pockets aren't as deep as I thought. Nobody can let go of money right now with the drought and depressed market."

"You think McGinty told Jarmin?"

"Could be." Jiggs shrugged. "Or maybe his idiot realtor heard I'm trying to sell Ol' Twenty-thousand and he figured it out."

"I have a little savings I didn't put in the bar. Not much, but you can have it."

Jiggs waved him away. "No. I don't want to end up owing everyone in town." He stared at the ground. "Funny, but I thought my dad didn't know squat when I was younger. He was a flint-hard slave driver, working me because he thought the only way I'd learn something was through suffering. It seems Dad may have been smarter than I thought."

"They usually are."

"I can't find a local guy who has the funds, so ... for the first time in my life," Jiggs said, "I'm going to take a piece of Dad's advice: *When you find yourself in a hole—stop digging.* I'm not going any deeper."

They sat without talking, the porch swing keeping rhythm to the thoughts they didn't want to speak. Jiggs finally broke the silence. "I knew I'd lost the battle to Jarmin, but I couldn't leave the fight without squeezing the truth about Devil's Thumb out of him."

"Fifteen days until the end of the West," Bazz said.

"Or fifteen days to figure out how to start over." Jiggs drained the last of his beer.

23

Big Headedness

JIGGS SAT ON his patio, drinking coffee and watching the sun nudge the eastern sky. He'd dreaded the threat of a demand letter. Now that it had arrived, an inner calm had settled over him. For weeks he'd felt like a boulder bouncing down a cliff face. Now he'd crashed onto the canyon floor. There was no farther to drop.

Until Morris Archer rapped on his back door.

The owner of the funeral home had stopped by Jiggs' house on his way to work to hand over a packet. As the undertaker explained his mission, Jiggs felt a menacing heaviness latch onto his shoulder, its talons driving into the back of his neck.

"You're kidding me?" The rancher's face was a wreck of anger and confusion as he poured Mr. Archer a cup of coffee, then waved toward a chair on the patio. "That's the stupidest thing I've heard. There're at least ten people I know of buried on Shiny Creek. And probably even more graves from when the Indians and miners ranged through those hills."

The undertaker's narrow face softened and his eyes stalled in sympathy. He was skilled in finishing his sentences, even when the listener eddied with other thoughts. "Perhaps you remember I explained this earlier, when your dad passed on. Burying someone on your land is entirely up to you, but it devalues the property."

"No I don't remember. Why should I? I was mucked up most of the time, trying to sort out the mess he'd left in the ranch accounts. Why does this matter now? Most of the remains on Shiny Creek don't even exist anymore. Only a few coffin nails—if that," Jiggs said.

"That's probably true. But laws have changed since the time those folks were buried. These papers," the funeral director tapped the large brown envelope, "provide the latitude and longitude of Hop Hopkins' grave, as determined by GPS. It's noted on the death certificate and must be recorded on the deed. You also need to fence it and do the same for the other known gravesites. You should do that for your dad, too."

The funeral director agreed to stay for breakfast. And no matter how many ways Jiggs reframed his inquiries, the answer was as unchanging as granite: his land had devalued below the price he'd paid for it.

When Mr. Archer rolled down the driveway an hour later, Jiggs supported himself against the doorframe, watching him leave. A fog of thoughts jammed his head. He leaned back, looking up at the sky, trying to rub away the headache throbbing upward from the nape of his neck.

That's when he noticed the cloud.

He squinted and assayed the little puffball on the horizon. This one appeared different. It hadn't come rolling over the mountain with its gray friends, making noise, kicking up dust, and then fading like a bully whose threat was called. The dinky cotton-white ball hovered as though it were waiting for something.

Dull with rumination, the rancher went about his morning chores, filling the stock tanks and checking the cloud. Maybe it was growing. Hard to tell. No use declaring it and jinxing it from happening. Clouds were fickle. Crap. All of life was fickle.

He was pulling a rotten wall off of one of the feeding shelters when his hammer punched through the plywood. He yanked the tool back out, ripping a jagged hole. The old wood was as fragile as his dreams. He'd tried to prove he was a great rancher. The attempt had crumbled and sieved into particles.

He hit the decomposing wood. It split from top to bottom. He swung again and again, gritting his teeth, blows coming faster.

Not even Dr. Dick could use a property so riddled and devalued by graves. He'd berated the surgeon for collecting farms, but he'd done the same thing—collected acres to prove ... what exactly?

Wood flayed into long, thin splinters. Shredded chunks flew through the air. He was a man of the land—like Hop Hopkins and four generations of Woolseys. Big deal!

The pounding thuds echoed across the field. His knuckles left skin and blood on the wood's ragged edges as he punched through the wall. For years he'd felt he'd let down his brother and disappointed his dad. He'd been trying to please dead men. He was a fool.

He started in on the 2X4s. The rafters shook from his battering. A support stud broke loose, and swung down. He didn't stop. He beat the beams until only the raw truth was left. He'd dreamed of making the Rocking W bigger than his father had. Well, he'd gotten his wish. Now, he was going under, trying to make payments on something valuable only to him.

With both hands on the hammer, he swung, knocking away the last ragged, plate-sized piece of plywood. It cartwheeled through the cow lot, kicking up dust as it bounced, ending with a *plop* in the soft dirt.

His chest heaved. He took in raggedy gulps of air. His bloody hand, heavy with the hammer, lowered in front of him.

Easing his grip, he stared at the tool. Whole and unblemished. It looked the same as it had thirty-seven years ago when his dad had shoved it at him, telling him to put his cow out of her misery. *Do what you have to do.*

No more could he blame Pax's death for his half-thought-out acts. And his dad wasn't around to resent anymore. All he had left was himself to shoulder the fact—he was his own fool. He jerked as though a tether had caught, stopping his freefall, knocking the claws out of his spine. A body-limp relief washed over him.

The laugh started deep in his belly and rumbled from his mouth. He was a big deal. A big-acre rancher. He'd achieved his dream. Unfortunately his asset had lost much of its worth. If there were ever a trick to humble big headedness, this was it. Dying was a body's natural process, but putting a callused, bone-worked corpse into the soil was not an organic act. It devalued the land. Maybe God did have a sense of humor—an ironic one at that.

It seemed strangely peaceful after his emotional tornado. His black-rumped herds grazed in front of the Eagle Caps. Ox's idiot old milk cow, Harriet, had her nose to the ground, eye-balling a squirrel next to her. He laughed, then inhaled the morning air hinting of sage and second chances. The truth felt cleansing. He smiled. He figured he was cracking up.

With a renewing exhalation, he moved debris out of the way. After securing the support studs, he grabbed a new piece of plywood from the truck. *Keep moving forward*, he reminded himself. With a bandana around his knuckles and a double heft of the hammer, he struck nails squarely like a man who has found rightness in the world.

He was almost finished with his second shed when his stomach reminded him it was noon. Mopping a kerchief across his forehead, he surveyed the southern horizon. Sometime in the last two hours, the little cloud had grown a limb, a pudgy arm protruding from its side. But it had no color. White clouds didn't rain.

He tossed the hammer next to the shed. A transparent balloon of dust puffed into the air. Lunch in town sounded better than the ingredients of the bologna sandwich waiting in his fridge.

As he motored to the Bar and Grill with an elbow poked out the window, an unexplained feeling of composure bloomed inside of him. He felt empty of worry, as though he were watching someone else's trials instead of his own. Maybe he should pound the wood off a shed every morning. "Whaddya want—grilled cheese or fried chicken?" he asked his stomach.

It preferred a burger with sweet onions, but that wouldn't justify a trip to town. He had plenty of ground sirloin in his freezer.

This was becoming a good day. The light slanted golden-white to the ground, not overbearing. Earlier, when he'd taken a break under the scrub oak, a mountain breeze had filtered through his cotton shirt, turning sweat to goose bumps. He'd leaned against the shade tree, watching his cattle graze and smack their backs with their tails; even the birds weren't too dry to sing to each other. And now, there was hope on the horizon. Not only had the little cloud sprouted another arm on the north side, it had grown taller.

He parked the one-ton in front of the Bar and Grill. Down the street, sunburned kids sat on the bench outside of Grubb's Mercantile, swilling pop and tossing a ball for the rheumy-eyed mutt. Frank Hopkins and someone dressed too well for Two Pan sat at the big spool table in Hop's front yard. They waved, between bites of their food, and continued talking.

A hyena bark of laughter shot down the street. The dog stared toward the noise, drool threading from its mouth as it gummed the ball. Jiggs walked that direction.

He hadn't planned to eat at the cramped, canoe-studded hut. He didn't even know what the Latte Da served on Tuesdays, but when he saw the red, flowery tablecloths in front of the shack, he decided he'd eat crust-free sandwiches and drink tea out of china cups, if need be, to enjoy the outdoor company. It seemed most of the town was there. Camp chairs and upside-down buckets circled picnic tables. Folks sat on tailgates and tack boxes.

"Did I miss an announcement?" Jiggs looked at the faces.

"Hermes came around town this morning with a sign reading, *Forgive 'N' Forget at Latte Da. Fifteen percent discount.*" Muley Baker pointed his paper-wrapped meat pie toward Lottie.

Several people waited behind a Ford Taurus in the drive-thru, so Jiggs got in line. He caught Bazz and Junior's eyes as they sat at a crowded table. Bazz hoisted his chin, then his meat pie at him, his mouth too full to speak.

"I suppose you wanna eat, too?" Zimm groused as he walked by with a pitcher of blackberry lemonade. "You'll have to hold your spit. I'm on my way to Grubb's to get supplies. We ran out." He set the lemonade in front of the mayor, and left.

When Jiggs reached the window, he gave Lottie a thankful smile. "I didn't get a chance to tell you I appreciated your support at the meeting."

"I've got twenty dollars on you. Together, we'll beat Dr. Dick one way or another."

Jiggs winced. What was she going to say when he defaulted on the loan and Jarmin snapped it up for his Devil's Thumb project anyway?

"I was so mad at that meeting. I said some ugly things to folks." She leaned forward and whispered, "But I meant most of them. Anyway ... it's a great excuse to have a make-up party."

"Is Zimm still in the doghouse?"

"Always." She waggled her head. "Others must've wanted to patch things up, too. They started showing up like carpenter ants. At first, one or two, and now they're everywhere. Zimm tried to call you. We're out of turkey tarts—that was today's special. If you can wait, he just went to get sandwich fixin's."

Jiggs warred with himself. He had two more sheds to fix, but missing something called a turkey tart had to be a sign of good luck.

"Here's a cup." Lottie made the decision for him. "Have cold lemonade while you wait."

He pulled out his wallet, but Lottie waved his money away. "Let's see how the sandwich turns out. You may be eating bologna."

Jiggs slapped neighbors on the back and answered questions about last night's meeting as he made his way to a table.

"You can have my spot," Junior called as he struggled to hike his leg over the crowded picnic bench. "If Miz Belle Chere can stand your malarkey."

The seventy-year-old woman next to him whipped her head toward the conversation, spanking Junior in the face with the coon tail on her cowboy hat as she turned. "What the deuce! You left the bar unattended?" She grabbed his heel and shoved it over the top of the bench. "The place is probably full of fifth-graders with their mouths under the taps."

Junior stumbled several steps. "I'm leaving now to kick the juvies out."

"Don't help me." Jiggs warned as he climbed into the vacated space. "I'll live longer. And not that you honestly care about schoolchildren, but Misty is probably watching the Bar and Grill."

"Damn!" A wry smile crossed the woman's suntanned face. "I'd hoped to steal a beer from an abandoned saloon."

"Miz Belle," Bazz leaned around Jiggs, "if it rains today, you come down to the bar. I'll buy the first round, provided you dance in the street while you drink it."

"In the rain? With you?"

"She only dances after she's shot somebody or run over their dog." Jiggs threw her a dark look. "You kill anything today, Mabel?"

"If I point a weapon, you'll be the first to know, *Tool*." She drew out the last word, giving him a cool stare as her fingers mimed a pistol and her thumb cocked, priming the bullet.

Kenny Lubach stood back, tapping her shoulder with a single finger. "Your truck's clean, Miz Belle." She turned to look at him, her coon tail brushing Jiggs' nose as it lashed past. Clamping a hand on Jiggs' shoulder, she pushed him into the bench as she climbed over the seat.

As soon as she handed Kenny a ten, he began his sideshow barking again, "A clean truck! Sure way to make it rain. Git'cher clean truck here." Several more vehicles pulled in line.

The impromptu carwash for the Two Pan Band had started after a drum banger and a clarinet player volunteered to get wet. By the time Jiggs received a fat ham sandwich, they'd made fifty dollars. "Fundraiser" is what folks nodded and told each other, but everyone knew they were buying a lottery ticket for rain. They couldn't say it or the cloud might stop its mitosis. Already, it had divided and piled layers on top of itself.

When Jiggs tried to pay, Zimm informed him someone had taken care of lunch. He felt sheepish. Maybe word was filtering out that he could use help. He hoped they didn't know about the demand letter yet. Bazz and Josie had suggested lending him money. He'd declined without letting them know he needed way more than they could offer.

He looked around, trying to see who to thank for lunch, but most people were watching the teens squirt water into the crowd whenever someone yelled, "You missed a spot." He tipped his hat to whomever might be watching and strolled toward his truck.

Shouts and screams rocked him to a stop. Old Man Tower's '53 Buick idled in the street. The driver's gimpy, outstretched arm signaled that he may be turning into the Latte Da or he may have a cramp.

Knowing that he drove by memory and in slow-blinking moments of sight, Jiggs waved and ran toward the car. Folks scattered from their chairs to find shelter behind the building or down the street in case the old fossil decided to take a shortcut through the patch of grass. Tower squinted at the commotion, and then pulled across a lane—without looking—rolling into the Latte Da driveway.

Jiggs loped alongside the car, then stuck his head through the driver's window, shouting into the old man's ear, "Whoa! Whoa, Mr. Tower."

The old coot stomped on the brakes—twice. Once, because the head sticking through the window scared him, and the second time to stop and see what the head was saying. Jiggs bucked backward with the second abrupt halt, landing in the gravel. There seemed to be a collective sigh as people peeked out from barriers and hiding places.

"You can't park in the drive, Mr. Tower," Jason Markum yelled, taking Jiggs' place. "We're having a carwash today. There are vehicles in this lot."

Watery eyes, clouded with cataracts, stared straight ahead as though trying to confirm his report.

"Did you hear, Mr. Tower?" the teenager asked over the stuttering motor. "This lot's full."

The old man gave a grunt and twisted his neck, bound with age, to look around. His head, ringed with yellowing hair on transparent skin, didn't turn far. His thick glasses made his pupils look like BB's, which probably explained why only parts of his craggy face were shaved—the parts he could feel.

Jiggs shouted past Jason, "You want us to move your vehicle for you?"

The codger leaned back, tilting his chin, inspecting the teen's face. "Hell no!" He blasted the boy with cottage cheese breath. "I can still park a car!" Grinding the gears, he drove straight at the truck being washed.

Taylor Kruger should have been helping with vacation Bible school, but she hoped volunteering at the spontaneous car wash would ease any punishment her parents might dole out when they discovered her sin of omission.

Belle Chere yanked the girl to the side. Grabbing the hose, the old woman angled a blast of water through Tower's open window, yelling, "Treat him like one of your show cows!" He stopped immediately.

Jiggs smiled as he walked to his truck. It would've been entertaining to stay and listen to Belle Chere cuss and convince Tower he deserved a good soaking, but he'd been here too long already. This was what he'd hoped to shelter from Jarmin.

The clouds had mushroomed, forming a barrier across the southeastern sky. They slowly expanded and drifted as the rancher drove the snaky road home. He kept the window down; the wind whipped papers off the seat and shuffled them to the floor. He shouldn't feel this good. He was more lighthearted than he'd been in weeks.

He stuck his nose closer to the window and sucked in air. No smell of rain yet, but it was a satisfying day already. A free sandwich, support from neighbors, entertainment and ... he told himself not to think about the possibility of putting up late hay. There had been clouds before. Teasers. This one might not leave anything behind either. He stared at the gray patches blooming on the underside of the billows and drove a little faster. Now he was sure of it. This cloud was alive.

At home, the air felt energized. He pounded nails into the sheds with urgency. Finish before it rains. It had been a long time since he'd had that sort of deadline. *Two years of drought, a hundred days without any type of moisture*, the weather woman had said. The wind announced itself by shaking the scrub oak for applause and making the pines sigh. It carried the essence of mountain skies and pushed the smell of dirt and dying grass closer to the ground.

Two dust devils corkscrewed across the dirt, shrinking when they hit patches of weeds, then erupting into funnels on bare ground. Jiggs snatched open his truck door as he chucked his hammer in the back. The tool knocked over the old coffee can, and nails tap-danced across the truck bed. He chided himself as he backed up to the hay barn. Slow down. You've seen rain before.

Hopping out, he used his arm to quickly sweep nails back into the can before bucking bales into the back. Grass had been spotty at Shiny Creek this year. He wasn't keeping many head there, but they were his prime breeding cows—and the bull. Ol' Twenty Thousand reminded him of Santa Claus. Big, seldom agitated, and always giving gifts. When he was servicing the girls, he tended to lose weight, so Jiggs gave him extra rations and checked on him daily. The docile bull usually stood at the gate, waiting for him.

The clouds had billowed into dark layers with yellow-green bellies. Jiggs' rear tires spun out as he drove down the gravel road. He wished he hadn't gone to town for lunch; he could use an extra hour to finish chores. But if it rained, the grass would green in no time—no more hauling alfalfa until this winter.

Something niggled him about that last thought. He shook the idea until the problem fell out. A nail might have rolled into a corner and could be working its way into one of the bales right now. It was catastrophic for any animal, but the way his luck ran, it would be the bull that ate it.

A serrated thread of light etched the sky. A voice shouted in his head in the same cadence that TV preachers used to announce a prayed-up miracle, *It's going to rain. Bound to happen!*

The cattle were waiting for him. Part of the herd milled about the feeders. He could tell he was running late because seven Angus, including Ol' Twenty Thousand, looked over the gate like puppies peering out of a cardboard box.

Inspect the bales. You aren't going to melt. He slammed the pickup door knowing he had to check or he'd spend half the night imagining a crime-scene video of a nail piercing a pink, juicy lining, ripping its way through the bull's gut.

A deep-throated rumble of thunder greeted him and made him hurry. Be sure. He stood at the back of the truck, lifting bales. Use your fingers. It'll mean sleep and peace of mind later. A fat splat of water hit the tailgate.

The rancher grinned. Blocky, black heads, broad muzzles, and doe-like eyes stared at him. He should get a picture of this sometime. The best of his herd hung over the tilted "W" welded to the gate. One of the cows bawled a hurry-up message.

The scent of fresh rain vaporized. The hair on Jiggs' arms lifted. A second later, a blue-white light stabbed fingers through the sky and slammed the rancher's body to the ground. Sparks flew from the gate. White, arcing death shot along the row of cattle. Each one crumpled to the earth after the last one, like stooges in a vaudeville show.

Jiggs lay immobile in the dirt. His muscles didn't work. His voice foundered in a guttural rasp. He could only blink. An explosion of thunder ripped his eardrums. Beyond the gate, a few downed cattle clawed the air with their hooves, trying to stand. The ones that still had strong heartbeats ran, terror rolling in their eyes. Water rushed through the gash in the sky. Niagara Falls poured on the parched land.

24

No Man's Land

JIGGS' MENTAL COGS were welded together. His command center puzzled *What happened?* His muscles froze, unable to operate. Shortly, instructions rang through his brain like alarm bells, *Get up! Stand up*! He struggled to prop himself onto an elbow.

Rain pierced the twisting smoke rising from the cattle. He stared. If he had only driven through the gate. If he hadn't knocked over the nail can. If ...

*I've told you before...*his dad's voice fuzzed his mind like a tinny radio announcement from the family archives. He mentally flicked the switch, shutting off the transmission, but the words, *It's over,* sprang from behind his eyeballs, imprinting his view.

No more! He tried to yell. Only gurgles sounded from his throat.

Rivulets poured down his face, yet he couldn't feel the chill of the water. He couldn't pry his eyes from the black pile of hair and hooves. Working his jaws, he was finally able to close his mouth. He could wiggle a foot. Fingers and arms tingled as nerves began to respond.

After long moments of testing his body, he used the bumper to pull himself up and stagger to the gate. The pins and hinges had melted, forming a flux trail down the support post. Metal splatters solidified in the charred grass.

Forcing his knees to bend, he clambered over the gate. The Rocking W insignia hung skew-jawed from the bars. His legs gave way, and he fell onto the warm cushion of beeves.

Scrabbling over the bulky chest of the bull, Jiggs stabbed his fingers into the neck, looking for a pulse. He grabbed the bull's lower jowl to clear the mouth. Charcoaled flesh peeled into his hand. The jaw muscles offered no resistance. Pulling the tongue flat, he held the raw throat and stuck his nose into the bull's nostrils. The rain beat away any pulse or breath he might've felt. He flicked the black eyeball bulging from the head. Flicked it again. Again. Water washed over the staring orb.

He shook his head, trying to clear his thoughts. CPR. Maybe CPR. With futile hope, he jerked at the tangle of legs and torsos. His hands slipped off a bloody knob of flesh and gristle. The hoof had blown off. Several legs ended in bloody stumps of cartilage.

He wedged himself between two cows. Using his legs, he tried to heave the bull's 2,000 pound mass so he could get to the chest, but it was jammed between the other bodies. He stopped pushing when he felt ribs breaking beneath his boots. The black carcasses lay like boulders deposited by ancient floods.

Jiggs lay back, arms spread wide: his head pillowed by one hulky body, his feet arching over another. A crucified man. The torrent lashed his face. Chilly fingers of rain ran under his chin, dripping off the back of his neck. The body of the bull felt warm under his fingers as he stroked the carcass. His mind floated without thought. He turned his head and lay with his ear on the massive barrel of ribs. There was no heartbeat, only the clapping hands of the rain as a tendril of steam curled from Twenty Thousand's body.

How he got in the truck, he didn't know. Water was pooled on the seat around him and dripped from his elbows. The storm beat at the glass, demanding entry.

Jiggs rubbed a small circle in the foggy windshield. He stared at the backbone of his breeding program lying dead behind a gate welded shut by lightning.

That seemed like a pretty clear message. He'd thought the penance for vanity was monthly payments on overpriced land. Apparently, it was eviction.

He could try to contest the decision, but former experiences had taught him not to go to war with God. He'd tried before. God always won.

Grudgingly, Jiggs was aware that every catastrophe was burdened with some annoying life lesson. He was an unwilling student. He didn't ask to be enrolled in any self-improvement program. As a matter of fact, he'd told God as much after Katie had died. Obviously, he hadn't been expelled or released. He kept receiving lessons over and over until he learned them. That was the devious way it worked. As long as he was alive, there were lessons to grasp. He wished he could learn more easily instead of requiring the Almighty to beat it into his brain in a fisticuff experience. For a loving deity, He sure was stubborn.

Jiggs' shoulders sagged another inch. Any foggy remnants he'd secreted of getting out of his predicament and still being a big-time cattle king had burnt away. This exclamation point of lightning had emphasized what he needed to do. He wouldn't wait for the bank to take the land. It was up to him to find a buyer for his devalued property. Maybe he could get enough to pay off a big chunk of the loan. He'd find someone as soon as possible. He scrubbed his hands over his face as he admitted ... whoever possible.

The rain rapped the one-ton, then slowed, stroking the cab. It whispered to Jiggs to rest. He fought the urge, grasping at ideas darting at the edges of his mind. Maybe he'd get a cell phone. He'd definitely have to keep Charlie the Mobile Slaughter King on speed dial. Right now he needed to call the vet. Vogel's was the nearest phone—four miles.

He pulled a hunting knife out of the glovebox, tossing the leather sheath on the seat. With a groan, he made the stiff-legged climb back over the fence. One more time he listened for heartbeats. The great chests were silent. Only the lightning's entry and exit points had charred flesh. He doubted that the meat could be saved, but if there was even a remote chance, then the carcasses had to be bled out.

Jiggs straddled one of the cows. Grabbing the ears, he yanked her head off the ground and slashed the knife along the crusty, black throat. A crimson stream splattered on the ground. With quick jerks, he slit the necks of the other cows.

The rain had diminished to a mist, but another bank of black clouds was rolling his way. Jiggs stared at Ol' Twenty Thousand. It seemed wrong to kill such a magnificent animal again. Electrocution was enough of an indignity. He hesitated with the knife at the bull's cauterized neck. Could he trust his lightning-fried thoughts? The massive head was heavy in his arms as he watched mist bead on Twenty Thousand's genetically orchestrated face. Even the eye muscle was a positive prediction of retail beef yield. The animal had been a factory that churned out walking steaks and roasts.

It would be a worse brickbat to let him go to waste. Winched onto the flatbed and dumped at the bone yard in the farthest corner of Starvation Ridge, Twenty Thousand would become coyote bait. Nap and his friends would see how many they could shoot, not even making a dent in the hordes that reveled through the canyons. With a quick jerk, Jiggs slit the throat. Without watching the red ancestry drain away, he walked a few paces to wipe the blade on bunch grass. If it was harvestable, he'd donate the meat. It would be the most expensive hamburger the Daughters of Two Pan ever used for the Chili Feed.

He paused on the top rung of the fence, looking back. A few feet closer, and he would have been dead, too. With numbing clarity, Jiggs felt stupid for trying to make the Rocking W bigger and better than his father or brother could have. He'd wagered everything to be able to put his brand on the gate. Now he'd finally achieved his insignificant place in the scheme of things. He was a temporary fixture. The land he'd been so proud to save from urban developers neither cared for nor answered to any man.

A fine mist laid a silvery blanket over the animals. Stems of charred grass glistened with red droplets. Jiggs watched the pools of blood diffuse into the soil.

The thirsty land drank.

25

Running With Snakes

A CROW SEEMED TO be screeching in Jiggs' left ear. His right brain interpreted the jarring noise as a phone. He blinked at the bedside clock. The burnt-out segments of the LED created a display of E:30. He'd overslept. The rancher had dropped into the slumber of the dead last night. Had he really stood under a pop-up tent and watched the skinning and gutting of the heart of his livelihood? Like coyotes slinking around prey from all sides, grim images came back to him. He stared at the jangling receiver. Early news was never good.

Maybe the sheriff had Bazz in the hoosegow after last night's dance-in-the-street rain party. He probably needed bail. Jiggs hadn't been there, but he imagined they looked like drowned cats, staggering around, pouring beer on each other—some of it may have actually hit their mouths.

"Uh-yeah," he grunted into the receiver.

"Dad. I've got bad news!"

Jiggs sat up, fully awake. Images of blood, glass, and crumpled metal flickered through his mind. "You all right?"

"I'm okay. But I'm at Shiny Creek. The gate's knocked down. Twenty Thousand is missing with some of the cows.

Instead of thievin' them to sell at auction, it looks like they butchered and hauled them out during the storm when nobody would be driving by. Bring Curly Dogs so—"

"You drove out to check on the cows this morning?"

"Did you hear me? How much did you drink last night? You were still snoring when I left."

Jiggs interpreted the clock: 6:30. He swung his feet to the floor and rubbed the back of his head. "I didn't party. The bull and six cows got hit by lightning. They're hanging in the meat locker right now."

Nap was silent. Anger raced along the telephone line before his words. "When the hell were you gonna tell me? When am I going to be part of this ranch?"

Jiggs couldn't answer. He'd once said the same words to his father. His old man had to die before Jiggs could make any decisions. He knew exactly how the heir to the throne felt when the king lived to be a thousand. "Nap," he shook his head at his own jackassery. He could hear his son's desire to hang up. "You're right. I'm sorry. Thanks for checking on the cows this morning. That's ... exactly right. You're ... a good man. How about coming home for breakfast? I've got a business proposition that needs your opinion."

Jiggs wasn't the type to ignore what he passed every day. He noticed changes in the scenery on each trip into town. The rain had washed summer dust from the air, leaving a crisp scent in the breeze. His neighbor had rotated his cows onto a new pasture. They weren't gaining weight any faster than his. Spirit Swamp, a small bog that usually dried to paper algae in the summer, now glistened and promised shape-twisted fogs for the next few mornings. The ol' hawk circled the thermals over the graveyard. In the mornings the raptor worked the open fields. Now in the heat of the day, it had moved to God's Hollow, looking for reverent mice.

Jiggs parked his one-ton in front of the Hopkins' place on Main Street. Hop's old truck was parked under a tree, collecting maple leaves in the bed and grime on the windshield. A pumpkin-colored Mazda pickup sat in the driveway. Energy efficient. That was a good idea. Gas prices were really climbing. Maybe a Toyota Taco would be good to use to run up and down these roads.

He stared at Hop's '70 Ford. Years without wax had faded the black paint to primer gray; the bumper was scratched and askew. Weeds clustered around the tires. A shiny strip of chrome still clung to a fender—the only telltale sign this truck had carried its owner with status to auctions and feed stores. Life had moved on. The trappings of a former life sat rusting, no longer used.

Jiggs waited through several rounds of door-knocking at the small cottage behind Hop's house. Frank answered, rubbing his eyes and yawning an apology. "Midnight to five seems to be my best hours to study. Habit, I guess." He shrugged.

"Nap and I had meeting this morning. I need to discuss something with you."

"Sure." Frank pointed toward the spool table under the shade tree, and Jiggs followed him.

"Good thing you caught me. I'll be leaving for a while," Frank said as he sat down, "to finish my Master's. The funny thing is that I'm coming back."

Frank explained he'd found a business partner who wanted to retire. The mentor would teach him the technical tricks if he would deal with the clients. "With the Internet and living in the hinterlands, I won't have to see many of them in person." He had a thoughtful smile. "I worked all my life to escape this place. Now I've decided to stay, at least for a while. Wouldn't Dad lipfart that idea?"

Jiggs pushed his straw hat back at an angle, and rested his elbows on his knees. "Is your partner one of Dr. Dick's cronies?" Frank made a face and shook his head. "Good. That's good. I don't think it matters where you live, your life will come find you."

They sat for a moment in silence, Jiggs waiting for the younger man to add something, Frank nodding, as though not knowing what else to say. Bazz provided a distraction by crossing the street, carrying a white sack.

"Am I interrupting a global summit meeting here?" He set the bag on the table.

"Not if you brought food," Jiggs said.

"I brought tuna sandwiches. I figure you'd seen enough beef after last night." He hooked a thumb toward the Bar and Grill in answer to the question on the rancher's face. "Nap dropped in for lunch. He told us about the lightning."

Frank nodded his thanks and opened the bag. "What happened?"

Glancing at Bazz, Jiggs pointed to an empty chair. He recounted his story. He usually wasn't "full of alphabet soup"—his description of wordy people—but he included the nails, the what-if's, and sitting among the cattle, his hands on their ribs, feeling the heat leave their bodies.

"And that's why," Jiggs looked at Frank, "I want to let you know Nap and I need to sell Shiny Creek. We're hurting for time to rebuild the herd and generate some income. The market's down, and we've sold most of the hay we've baled. I know it's been a bad spring and summer for everybody, but another year like this, and it'd be impossible to even keep what was passed on to us. We've looked at this every which way. I'm truly sorry. The Shiny is a privilege to own."

Frank had stopped eating, listening carefully to Jiggs' story. He began rewrapping a triangular half of sandwich. "You know, since you and I buried Dad out there," he gave the rancher a somber look, "and I've been free of the ranch, I don't mind it so much." He mitered a corner and snugged it tight. "Actually, I've been out there a few times ... exploring. Going back to some of the places I remember as a kid." He paused for several heartbeats. "It was a comfort and a relief to know you were taking care of it."

Jiggs took off his hat and scraped his fingers through his hair as he stared at the ground.

Frank sat, expressionless. "It seemed like the right ending for Dad's life work. He sure rested easier knowing you had it."

"I'm sorry as all get out, Frank. I've wrestled with it for a while now. I've drained all my resources. I thought we could hobble along until next spring's calf crop ... but now ... I don't know where to go to keep this whole project afloat." Jiggs stared at the ground, avoiding Frank's gaze. "Maybe you'd buy it back, now that you're staying? I could take it off your hands later when I get my feet under me again."

Hop's son shook his head. An unbalanced awkwardness tipped back and forth between them. After a moment, Frank asked, "What happens now?"

"I'll look for another buyer," Jiggs said. "Someone who'll take care of it. Worst case scenario—the bank will take it back. I used the land as collateral for the loan."

"You'll be out your payments and whatever you put down," Bazz said. "And you know, if you default, First National will sell it to Jarmin as soon as they get clear title."

"Actually, I don't think he can use Shiny Creek. He'll eventually get his hands on something though. I finally realized I can't stop the flood of city refugees who're tired of being piled on top of each other and run out here to squat on an open space. They complain about deer in the road and how the coyotes and starlight keep them awake. They zip around and build houses until they've run over all the animals and brighted out the stars. Then they'll move, leaving the place to the coyotes again."

"That's basically accurate," Frank said as he rubbed the sleep seeds out his eyes. "Rural development cycles grow and ebb every ten years—barring disasters such as food shortage, global flooding, or nuclear war."

"You sound like that Department of Transportation engineer that charged us for building speed bumps." Bazz looked at Jiggs with smirk. "Say again why you're staying?"

Frank thought a moment, his fingers checking the tightness of a bolt head in the table. "I suppose it's a less complicated life. I breathe easier since I've buried most of my pain."

Bazz stared at him. "Now I know what will make Junior enjoy the restaurant more. I just hope I'm dead before he buries me."

Jiggs wadded his wrapper and dropped it into the bag. "I'll try to find someone who'll take care of it the way Hop did. I thought I'd head out to Arvie Norcross' place after chores this evening. See if he's interested. That okay with you?"

Frank nodded his head a fraction. The rancher acknowledged the communication with an equally small raising and lowering of his chin. The young engineer arose, holding up his sandwich. "Thanks again."

"I'll keep you posted on what's happening," Jiggs said, but Frank was already walking away. "Funny duck," the rancher said quietly, watching the young man disappear inside and close the door.

"He's just more comfortable with his books than he is with people," Bazz said.

"It's a shame how ol' Hop spent a lifetime building up that ranch, and he wants no part of it." Jiggs still stared at the closed door.

"Or else they have their own ideas how it should be run." Bazz stared at the Two Pan Bar and Grill.

Sunlight filtered through maple leaves, dappling the two men with shadows. They mulled the thoughts of their respective worlds for a while. "Can you let me know how it goes with Arvie?" Bazz finally said, still gazing at the bar. "I've got an idea."

"You interested in becoming a rancher, now?"

"Just let me know how it goes."

Arvie Norcross didn't want another thousand acres. His kids wouldn't help him with it. His twenty-nine-year-old boy preferred to work in a body shop customizing cars, and his daughter had married a nimrod who lacked the intelligence to know which end of a shovel to hold onto.

Jiggs jounced home in his one-ton along deserted back roads. He'd figured Arvie would turn him down. Shiny Creek was twenty-two miles from the Norcross ranch, but a rocky hogback split most of their acres. He thought the old Swede might be interested in grazing property. Arvie would've been perfect. He could be trusted to take care of the land, and then sell it back after Jiggs' wallet fattened up.

A truck sat in the middle of the road ahead of him with its hood up. He pulled behind it and got out, wondering why some woman tourist was so far out on the back roads. The clean, red Dodge sported beadlocks, chrome rims, running boards, mesh tailgate, and a bumper sticker: *I've got estrogen and I've got a gun.*

A face leaned out from the front end as he approached. Jiggs pulled up, surprised, and then exchanged hot-eyed stares with the man at the engine. "Got a new rig?" he asked.

Dr. Richard Jarmin went back to jiggling wires as though one of them would magically make his engine start. "It was time. My work puts a lot of miles on a vehicle."

"I can imagine," Jiggs said. "This the way you take to work? Kinda remote."

Jarmin's stare said it wasn't any of this bone farmer's business. "I was looking for a shortcut from Joseph to Two Pan. No one has been by since it stalled out."

"Yeah, a mountain range is a real shortcut killer." Jiggs narrowed his eyes as Dr. Dick popped and reconnected spark plug wires. He could sense the physician's awkward discomfort. Jiggs suspected he'd be equally unsettled if the situation were reversed, and the plastic surgeon watched him stitch up a calf. The realization gave him a bit of empathy, and when Dr. Dick glanced at him, Jiggs pulled his mouth into a maybe-give-it-a-shot expression. The physician got in the cab and cranked the engine. It whined without catching.

"Could you give me a jump?" Jarmin got out of the truck; his grimace and hostile tone implied he hated asking.

"Your battery's fine." Jiggs leaned against the fender, watching the doctor. "You can hear the engine turning over. Better shut your door. You're parked smack in the middle. You don't want it knocked off again."

Jarmin slammed the door, giving the rancher a disgusted glance. "What does it matter? We're at the edge of nowhere. And this really isn't my forte." His eyes were set in a stony glare, signaling there was a limit to the noise he'd take from a manure spreader like Jiggs.

"Something's wrong with your fuel system," Jiggs said. "Or a sensor. You'll need a computer to tell." He nodded, his face not quite expressing his fake sympathy.

As they turned their attention back to the engine compartment, Jiggs cursed this fated opportunity to sell the Shiny. Providence had brought them together, but he still couldn't stand the guy. Had Jarmin been a bull, a city-farmer would have bought him—if he wanted something showy. But if he needed something that actually produced, he'd dump him at the dog food factory and keep looking.

Jiggs' devilish spirit had his good nature in a headlock, sniggering and burnishing knuckles over its righteous skull. The rancher took a breath, willing his virtue to find some grit and break free. Guilt jumped in to help, striping him with reprimands. *After Pax died, you swore you'd never leave another person stranded.* He sighed and walked toward his truck. "I'll give you a ride. Put her in neutral. We'll push her off the road."

"It's fine. No one is around for miles."

"You want a ride or not?" Jiggs gave him a pointed look.

"All right. All right."

When they'd finished moving the truck, the physician opened Jiggs' passenger door and stared at the pliers, papers, and a coil of rusty wire on the seat.

"Push that stuff onto the floor. Except that. Hold the bottle upright and keep the cap on tight. That's screw worm dope. You probably don't have parasites in your line of work." A slight smile edged Jiggs' mouth. "You try calling for help?"

"No service out here." Dr. Jarmin crammed the dropper bottle in the cup holder among pencil stubs and vicious looking staples. "I deal with blood and lesions every day. It'll take more than worm medicine to yank my chain."

Jiggs nodded, accepting the challenge. "Your satellite assistance didn't work either?"

"I haven't activated it yet." The doctor furtively wiped his hand against the door.

Jiggs patted the threadbare seats. "Yep. Me neither."

They drove several miles in silence, watching the dusk transform sagebrush and cattle into formless shapes. Jiggs figured if they didn't small talk, he could damper the irritation spitting inside of him.

"So why did you stop?" the doctor asked.

Jiggs glanced sideways, his eyebrows in a knot. The city boy wouldn't let well enough alone. At some point, he'd talk his way around to Shiny Creek. "Couldn't get by," he mumbled.

"There's obviously no love lost between us, and you're not the type who minds driving in ditches to prove a point, so why did you stop?"

What kind of bottom-feeder was this guy? If a doctor didn't understand helping others, how could he explain it to him? Jiggs cocked his head and let a mile roll by before he spoke. "You know who Chief Joseph was?" Jarmin gave him a stare that implied he wasn't stupid. Jiggs felt it and continued. "He was here before all of us *white* necks. The chief rescued a settler lady and her baby who'd slipped into a flooding river. He rode right into the whitewater, snatched them up, clutching one on each knee so the horse had room to swim. Smart. Honorable.

"We paid him back by driving him off his land and chasing his people around the country. Warriors—protecting their home, just like we do today—are buried throughout these hills. Most folks say all of this land is sacred." The rancher glanced at Jarmin's face. He looked bored.

"Anyway ..." Jiggs' voice flattened with failing, "even way back then, Chief Joseph lived The Way."

Silence filled the cab. "All right." The doctor finally said, sounding as though he'd like to kick himself. "I'll play along. What way is that?"

"If someone needs help, you stop and give it—even to your enemy." Jiggs fixed Dr. Dick with a stare. "There're all manners of hurt out here: snakes, scorpions, dehydration, rustlers, gunkheads that blast down the roads too fast."

"So you're saying someone would have blown by and picked me up, ultimately?" Jarmin smiled.

"I mean, we help each other." Jiggs squinted at the man. "Don't doctors have a code they live by?"

"The Hippocratic oath? It's been changed and modernized. 'The health of my patient will be my first consideration. I consecrate my life to the service of humanity.' There's more, lots more." Jarmin waved. "Many schools don't even administer it anymore."

"Seems a shame. Does that oath extend to land, as well?"

From the doctor's loud exhalation, it was clear he'd had enough insinuation from the local good ol' boy. "I'm not quite sure why I rankle you so much, *Mr. Woolsey*. You seem to think I'm some sort of environmental anarchist. I don't intend to plow the soil and create a dust bowl, or introduce non-native plants into the ecosystem. All that I want is to live here, to enjoy this country, and to share it with my friends ... the same as you."

"No. That's not the same as me, *Dr. Jarmin*. What rankles me is leaving a truck in the middle of the road, and then some poor sap who's been sweating and loading cattle all evening comes along, pulling a trailer, and can't get by. So he has to back his cart, full of livestock, half a mile down a gravel road, in the dark, to find a place to turn around, just because some self-serving, plastic cowboy is afraid of getting his wheels dirty. As dry as it is, it could be a water pumper or a fire truck that needs to get by."

"Sorry, I hadn't thought of—"

"Well, sure. What's a fire to you?" Jiggs' decibels clicked up a notch. "It just rankles guys like you. Hayseeds, like me, take it too hard. We blow it all out of proportion when we see our fields, cattle, or buildings that we put up with our own hands, go up in smoke.

"I suppose it's no big deal. We've all got plenty of cattle. They're just hobbies for us anyway. Most of us go to the office like you to make our money. When you see the local grunts out clearing the fence line and cutting trees, it's just for beautification purposes. We aren't worried about cooking livestock or the cost of fencing and feed. No one considers it a tragedy to burn your neighbor out."

"I'm sorry, Mr. Wool—"

"Look around you ... at this land you say you enjoy so much. We don't get a lot of moisture here. Even in a good year, most of this area is ready to spontaneously combust. So it more than galls me when it's not treated seriously."

"I'm sorry, sir," Jarmin said too loudly.

Jiggs glanced at him. In the dim light from the dashboard, he didn't look sorry. He probably practiced that voice to tell patients their nose jobs weren't quite perfect.

The doctor cleared his throat. "If you're saying the compensation I gave you for your losses wasn't enough ..."

"I'm talking about something different. When my place was burning, there were probably forty people out there—"

"You're a man rich in friends," Jarmin interrupted.

"No. When you live here, you go when your neighbor calls. You drop what you're doing and come running because you know he wouldn't ask if he didn't need help. Actually, he doesn't even have to call. People see smoke or lights on the horizon, they show up. Or if you notice someone's cow or horse loose, you stop and drive it back through the fence and find the owner. You take care of it like it was your own livestock.

"We misfits and hardscrabble are bound by the one thing we have in common. This is where we beat our bodies into an early grave to coax a living out of the soil. This isn't our vacation home. We tend the land so we can *eat*. We work hard to keep it producing, so our kids can have the same chance we had to survive. It's our *life*."

"I *am* sorry."

Jiggs flinched. *That voice again.* Jiggs had used that same semi-sympathetic tone when he'd apologized for his high school adventures—like turning hogs loose to root around on Minam's football field.

The doctor's timbre sounded smooth and polished. "I didn't intend to belittle your livelihood. I thought perhaps we could work out some of the differences between us like reasonable men. We're neighbors. I'd like to pull my weight in the community. It's a bit hard being an outsider."

"No. No, it's not." Jiggs felt his better nature reminding him: *Never miss a good chance to shut up*. Instead, he invited his inner hooligan to cut loose. "Other outsiders have bought into this area. They tried to fit in, not turn it into condos."

Jarmin shook his head. "Are you referring to our competition for Shiny Creek?"

And there it was. Jiggs drove a little faster. He knew the peckerhead would eventually goad him about buying the devalued property so he could make a cheap offer to buy it. Well, Ox Woolsey had taught him how to horse trade better than that. "No. I'm speaking of you fitting in, instead of blasting through town like it was a freeway and lying to folks about your plans—"

"I only—"

"*and* lining your pockets. That's a big one there."

"Are you finished?" Jarmin was using his overly patient voice.

"Nope, but I'll give you a turn, 'cause I'm a decent guy."

The physician stared in front of him, his fingers tapping his knees. "All right. I'll speak plainly." He shifted, turning slightly toward the rancher. "I hear Shiny Creek is for sale."

Jiggs had known that once Nap gabbed the storm losses at the Bar and Grill, it would spread like hawkweed. He glanced at the man. The doctor didn't even have the decency to hide the possum grin on his face.

"According to my realtor," Jarmin continued, "you've had quite a setback from a lightning strike. It killed your expensive bull and breeder cows. Now you might be willing to sell the place."

"You see, that's why you don't fit in. Most anything human would at least express condolences. You're like a coyote. Sneaking around the edges, waiting to nip a hunk when anyone stumbles."

The doctor's eyebrows rose at the insult. A slight smile flickered across his face. He cranked his window lower and rested his elbow on the door. "Many cultures revere the coyote for his cleverness, buuuuuuut—" Thumping over the washboard ripples in the road at high speed made his voice yodel and his teeth chatter. He took another breath. His features changed to a heavyhearted face. "But ... you are quite right, Mr. Woolsey. It's terrible to lose part of your business. I wish you no misfortune. I only related what I heard as rumor and wanted to see if there's anything I can do to ... help?" He let the end of the sentence fade in an open question rather than a statement.

Jiggs stared at his headlights and drove in silence. He'd figured the man would goose him about his missed payments. But he hadn't. The rear wheels bucked sideways as they flew over another washboard. He was traveling too fast, but the sooner this trip ended, the better. If he were going to do business with this lunkhead, he needed to get it over with quick.

The road-rattle filled the truck as Jarmin spoke again. "I.I.I.I ... apologize if I've offended you ... may I call you 'Jiggs?'" He didn't wait for an answer, but continued, his voice plaintive. "I know you're a self-made man and a well-respected rancher in these parts. I simply thought if you had soured on the idea of owning Shiny Creek, maybe I could buy part of it. Perhaps work out an acceptable split? You keep the fields and pastures for your cattle. I could take the rough, unusable mountain area off your hands."

Jiggs let out a guffaw. Jarmin's realtor must not know there was a problem—or hadn't told him. This would be the perfect opportunity to sell Jarmin devalued, unusable land. He grinned at the doctor.

"I don't see the joke," Jarmin said.

Jiggs' conscience flogged him again. One side of his mouth sneered at the thought of letting go of such a satisfying stunt. Surely it wasn't wrong to scam someone who so thoroughly deserved it? His beneficent voice kept punching him repeatedly: *Do the right thing. These situations have a way of turning and squaring you in the stones.*

Jiggs let out a huff of air. "Crap." He cocked his head toward Jarmin. "Lemme tell you something. Your big-haired little realtor isn't doing his job. Since we're putting it all on the table ... this whole thing started over a hundred years ago with a quirky pilgrim who decided to tame a little patch of these hills. The next heir shifted the homestead to an even bigger parcel, and so it goes right up until present. You with me?" Jiggs glanced at his passenger.

Jarmin gave a single nod, staring into the dark countryside.

"Good," Jiggs continued. "This land attracts unpredictable people. It seems these ranchers, and whoever worked for them, picked out the best site on their property to bury themselves. They sure weren't German. An old German will build his house in a swamp, so he can farm every inch of arable land. But these folks pegged the best view, like they were going to stare at it for eternity, and sunk their coffins there. The rest of the family simply cleared off another patch and moved. And so it went. At least five generations of family, friends, and strangers are buried all over those pastures and mountains you covet so much." Jiggs chuckled. "It's a regular memorial for pioneers out there. You can't build over them. State doesn't allow it."

"So?" Jarmin's voice had a hint of rebel in it. "We'll exhume them to that little cemetery outside of Two Pan."

Jiggs snorted a laugh. "I'd enjoy hornswoggling you, but I don't believe this place was intended to be a vacation mall, and that's the brilliant part. It all started years ago and ends at this very moment. You *can't* dig up the bodies."

Jarmin put on a faint derisive grin. "Well, it may surprise you, but the deceased can be moved."

"Yeah, you're right. It's possible." Jiggs gave him a sad smile. "But the state of Oregon considers someone's final resting place sacred. Especially pioneer or Native Americans' graves. I have to locate all the burial sites and fence them. Livestock, animals, and people can't trample them. They're holy ground. Protected by an arm's length of laws and regulations."

"Oh, we'll find a way. I know people—"

"They're scattered all over the best places, and I doubt even you can move them. Not even with your high-powered legal connections. You need written consent from the original families to disturb them. Some of them, we don't even know who they were, and Frank Hopkins won't give permission for any of his family. So there. I've done my duty," Jiggs informed both his conscience as well as Jarmin. "You can't say no one told you."

They drove in silence, the doctor flicking skeptical glances at the rancher. Dusk had passed into moonless evening. The stars winked above the black spread of sage-broken hills. After several miles Jarmin breached the silence, his voice low. "Even if what you say is true, I usually get my way. I find that people, including lawmakers and government officials, are interested in my projects, especially when it benefits them. And there is enough opportunity here to benefit everyone. Including you. How about it? It would help you out of your predicament."

"Sheep guts! What're you saying? What about your own code? The service of humanity and doing no harm? Does that fly out the window if you don't get your way?"

"I find a means to make them both work together." Jarmin nodded with a practiced smile.

"Well, good luck." Jiggs grabbed the crown of his hat and re-settled it tighter on his head as though he were expecting a bumpy ride. "I've learned the hard way, when the Almighty closes a door and you try to prise it open—then you're begging disaster."

Gravel flew as Jiggs sped up. He felt the doctor studying him, and ignored the audit. Why should he help a slopsucker like Jarmin? He'd rather suffer the public humiliation of a repo and let the bank take the land than sell out to this crawler. His conscience smugly agreed.

"So you think I'm tempting God?" the doctor interrupted his thoughts. "I'm curious about your beliefs, Mr. Woolsey. Do you believe your god will bail you out of every crisis, or do you think he expects you to be self-reliant? I mean ... what do you do when the answer to your prayer is that something important to you ... dies?"

Sound faded away as Jarmin's words slammed into his guts. He felt stunned for a half a second. Then he stood on the brakes.

Jarmin was thrown forward, his head inches from the windshield. He braced himself as the truck skidded sideways across the gravel. The rear tire dropped into the bar ditch. The truck came to a stop, dust fluming around them.

"Get out." The words vibrated like growl.

"I merely asked—" Jarmin's voice notched higher.

Jiggs threw open the driver-side door. It rebounded on its hinges. He shouldered it aside, bolting out and rounding the truck in a few strides. He jerked the passenger door open, grabbed a shirtful of Jarmin, and hauled him out of the truck. His roar broke through the night like a twister touching down. "You will not bring my wife's death into your schemes!"

"Oh, no. I meant your bull. No. Not your wife," Jarmin's words ran together, his voice squeaky as he moved backward, waving away such a morbid suggestion. "Good lord, no. I meant your future is hanging by a thread. Cowboys are about to go the way of steamboat captains. You're running out of options. I was merely asking how you felt about your god frying your expensive bull."

Jiggs cocked a fist, his muscles tightened like pulled springs.

Jarmin gave a strange, high-pitched squawk as he turned his back, ducking and wrapping both arms around his head to cover his face.

Jiggs stared. The man hadn't even tried to defend himself. "Hey!" He gave Jarmin's shoulder a hard shove. The doc twisted, turning farther away. Jiggs considered punching him in the back of the head. That'd make him uncover his precious face. "Hey!" He shoved the other shoulder.

Jarmin sprang forward in a run. He clipped the back of the truck, stumbling two steps, sliding on his hands and face through the gravel and ditch weeds. Quickly, he tucked into a ball, reminding Jiggs of the grade school duck-and-covers they'd been forced to practice under their desks during tornado drills.

Under the red hue of the tail lights, the doctor had turned into a pill bug, a human mound rolling in on himself when poked. Jiggs had never fought any creature so ...

Several heartbeats passed. His fists slowly lowered to his sides. He took a step back to keep from hovering. Sometimes a fellow needed space to collect himself. He gave Jarmin a moment to push his nerve over the top of his fears.

Jiggs glanced at his truck. He didn't remember turning it off, but it sat silent, the headlights tunneling white beams through the night. No coyotes howled. No distant planes trailed through the quiet. Nothing disturbed the empty miles, except Jarmin's nervous breaths. Jiggs waited. The form before him didn't move. Not even to peek out between arms or fingers like the small kid in the alley fight Jiggs had refereed.

"I almost feel sorry for you." With a single shake of his head, he walked to his passenger door, slammed it, and passed around the front of the truck to get behind the wheel.

At the sound of the second door shutting, Jarmin looked under his arm. When the engine started, he slowly began unwrapping himself.

Gravel and dirt sprayed from the tires. His hands flew up, covering his face again. The Ford gunned out of the ditch.

"Watch for rattlers, you rat bastard," Jiggs yelled, leaving Richard Jarmin in a cloud of dust, sitting in the dirt and darkness.

26

Still Awake

JIGGS LAY IN bed searching for regret. He didn't have any. Well, perhaps a small one. Punching Jarmin would've been satisfying—but only for a moment. He couldn't beat him—at least not the way his dad had taught him to fight. Today's brawls were done with attorneys and moneyed men. Tomorrow he'd call a land man who'd look nationwide for a decent buyer. His dad would've disagreed. The old man would've unreeled the doctor and knocked his teeth down his throat. "It's not the Wild West anymore," he mumbled with the relief of a man who had not become Ox Woolsey. "Rest in peace, Dad." He slept deeply through the night.

The next morning he cleaned out the garage as he waited for a call from a land broker he'd contacted. When the phone rang, he spooked, then cursed himself for being skittish.

"Jiggs?" His insurance agent, Elmer Scott, talked continuously, even though every third or eighth sentence was the only thing that carried any meaning. His nasally voice wittered on, "I've got good news and bad news. Which do you want first?"

"Just dump it all on me." Jiggs rolled his eyes, his patience frayed. *Jeep 'n' Eagles, why did people speak in idiotic code like that?*

"Well, I scanned the policy looking for leaks. You're covered for falling aircraft, riots, attacks by wild dogs, floods and ..." Elmer paused like he was introducing a Vegas stripper, "lightning!"

"I *know* that," Jiggs growled. If Uncle Elmer hadn't been Katie's relative, he would've ousted him for an insurance agent who could deliver news without causing apoplexy or thoughts of murder. "You said I probably invalidated the policy when I slit the cattle's throats and bled 'em out. You said the bean counters could be picky about that sort of thing. Did I?"

"What? Oh. I'll read it to you. Lemme find my glasses ..." Papers shuffled in the background. "Say, did you hear about, Belle Chere? She shot at some guy trying to steal a cow ..."

Jiggs listened for a moment, pacing back and forth in the garage. "Elmer! Just tell me about my claim."

"Oh. The legal beagles are fine. The adjustor has the vet's statement. The claim was approved. See, I told you, you wouldn't regret extra coverage. I told Belle Chere if she's going to shoot at folks, she needs an umbrella policy like—"

"What's the bad news?" Jiggs' voice rose, scaring two crows out of the maple tree next to the garage.

"No need to shout. I can hear you fine. Yep, this might be bad news: it'll be a week to ten days before you can get your check."

"I'll have my banker give you a call. Try not to give him too much information, Elmer. Please. Just tell him the check's in the mail." Jiggs hung up, wondering if he should go ahead and have flowers sent to the hospital for the stroke McGinty would have trying to get clear information out of Elmer Scott.

A grin spread from ear to ear. Ox Woolsey had never taken out insurance. But then ... ranching was experience and guess back then. They bought good-looking animals with decent records, and the breeding schedules were pencil notations on calendars. Sometimes the progeny was a crapshoot.

Now days, a specifically engineered bull like Ol' Twenty-thousand was delivered in a biosecure trailer. All of the Rockin' W's records and schedules were maintained with computer software, and the cattle wore their information in chips in their ear tags.

Ox Woolsey would have resurrected and keeled over again if he'd known how much the insurance had cost. Jiggs shook both fists in front of him. Finally! He'd done something right.

The phone rang.

Jiggs stared at it, hoping it wasn't Uncle Elmer with more news. Relief washed over him upon hearing Bazz's *Hello* when he answered. "Hey, pard," Jiggs said, "I just got some good news—"

"That's great. Bring three T-Bones and come out to Shiny Creek tonight to talk business." The mayor hung up as if it were a drug deal and the phones were tapped.

Jiggs scowled at the receiver in his hand. Everything coming out of the phone was in code today. He hadn't had a chance to brag about his foresight and wisdom. Not even Nap was around to help him visit their skinflint banker. The little moneybags could feed those default papers to Hermes. He and Nap had agreed if the insurance money came through, they'd use it for loan payments until they could find a buyer.

As Jiggs walked out the door, the phone rang. He kept walking. He wasn't deciphering any more code today.

When he arrived at Shiny Creek that evening, Bazz's truck was already there with a note flapping under the windshield wiper, *Bring steaks. Follow flagging tape. South fence.*

No wonder Bazz had been so mysterious; he must be trying to cajole Junior into buying the land. As the seller, Jiggs would provide a steak dinner. This was going to be a train wreck full of California cusswords.

A tail of pink plastic tape hung from a bush. He slipped through the barbwire fence and hiked up an old deer trail through brush and pine trees. It was a heart-pounding trudge, but his footfalls were quiet and light. He wasn't lugging the pack of worries he'd freighted for months.

After a mile, the trail widened beside a sheer dropoff, fanning outward in a vista of the valley below. Light green rectangles of pasture muddied into rangeland and dissolved into distant hills, turning lavender-gray as they faded to the horizon. He hadn't jerked cattle through this rough, steep terrain due to the risk of turning a hoof or missing a cow. It seemed a pathetic worry now that seven beeves had died looking over the gate.

Bazz and Junior knew nothing about caring for a place this size. He'd have to help them. Nap would pitch in, too. But if they could take it long enough for Nap and him to get straightened out, then the deal would work. They'd have to watch Junior. He'd probably sell out to a nuclear dumpsite if it netted him enough money to retire to Hawaii. Junior and Jarmin seemed a skosh alike.

Twilight crumbled and muddled the colors of the valley. He picked up a stone, glancing at the scars and marks on the back of his hand. At some point he'd stopped noticing them or remembering which slip of the knife or barbwire fence had created them. And that's the way he'd carry Pax, Katie, and his dad now. Marks on his life. They made him who he was.

Changing himself was like breaking a horse. He kept landing back on the ground, poking his body to see which parts were broken, then cursing himself for falling off.

He winged the rock off the cliff. He'd be okay if he kept climbing back on. Time and life did their own sculpting and pushing. Without watching the stone fall, he turned and headed up the trail.

"Welcome!" Bazz shouted when he broke into a small clearing beside a creek. "You know Ennis O'Day here." Jiggs looked around for Junior, but only the three of them stood there. He shook hands with the short, red-bearded man.

The Irishman nodded toward the mayor. "This gump and I go way back."

"Then I'm sorry for you," Jiggs said as he held up the steaks.

"Great. I'll put them on. There's Bud in the cooler." Bazz pointed.

"You carried domestic crap up that hill?"

"The mule may have helped." Bazz shrugged. "I heard you gave Jarmin a ride last night." He grinned at Jiggs' raised eyebrows. "Chicken Thief picked him up."

"Too bad. I'd hoped he'd gotten lost and headed toward Canada."

"Chicken Thief said he didn't look so good and was carping about you and the 'damnable gravel' which was chewing up his Italian-leather shoes. He set the doc out about a mile from his house. Told him The Way wasn't a taxi service." Bazz laughed and then became distracted, correcting Ennis' distance between the grill and the glowing coals.

Jiggs gave the Irishman's base camp the once over. A weathered supply box was the only indication of permanence. Bazz took a hammer from it and pounded nails into three wooden camp chairs, threatening them if they didn't stand upright. A stone ring corralled a small two-log fire.

To the north, a few tree branches had been trimmed, creating a natural picture frame of Two Pan and the country beyond. He watched the valley discolor behind the cloak of the mountains until an uncomfortable feeling of staring eyes chivied his thoughts. When he turned to find the source, Bazz and Ennis started poking the steaks.

"All right." Jiggs gave the pair a frown as he walked toward them. "You two look like dogs that killed a sheep and are waiting for the yelling."

"Would you like something with stronger backbone than the beer?" Ennis asked.

Jiggs shook his head. "Why am I really here?"

The red-bearded man flexed his shoulders and ducked his head as though preparing for a heavy load. "That'd be my doing." Ennis held out a small leather pouch. "I suppose I should have been tellin' ya, but I been workin' on other projects, and it wasn't at the top of my thoughts. There's no excuse for it. But there it is."

"Is this what I think it is?" Jiggs hefted it in his hand.

"Placer gold." The miner pointed toward the creek.

Jiggs squeezed the sack. The solid *scrunch* called him back to the addictive dreams of his youth when he was going to get rich. He had hunched over a sieve box until his guts were in a permanent kink, and he'd learned that gold was a frustrating mistress. Always promising a prize in the next pan. Always whispering of the things he desired if he'd give up everything and search for her.

"Bazz explained the fix you're in," Ennis said. "That's rightfully yours. I figured I've taken about twelve hundred dollars since you bought the land."

Bazz held the grill with a pair of pliers as he turned the steaks. "When I talked to Ennis last night, he told me what he had in mind. I said to give you half his poke since he designed the equipment and did all the work. He insisted you have it all."

"We thought you should come out here to see what you owned, or rather what you didn't know you owned." Ennis pointed to the pouch. "I'll let you run my equipment. I don't spend a lot of time at it anymore. I'm getting old and lazy, and my consulting work pays more than I need. You might make enough to take a bite out of your payments. Maybe you'd even find a nugget instead of this dandruff—though I never have."

Jiggs looked at the Irishman uncertainly, one eyebrow rising higher than the other. In the last few minutes the guy who stayed on his land had gone from drifter to consultant. "Who are you, and how'd you rope up with this *gump*?"

"Bazz is incorrigible, but smart. We share several patents." The dusk and beard hid the smaller man's face, but his eyes betrayed amusement at admitting something positive about the mayor. "He takes messages for me and helps with manufacturers and design problems."

Jiggs squinted with disbelief at Bazz, shaking his head.

"There are still secrets to be discovered in Two Pan." Bazz smiled. "And gold."

Jiggs bounced the pouch in his hand, shaking his head. "Everybody knows there are sprinkles of gold around here. I did a bit of prospecting when I was sixteen. Dad gave me a summer to get it out of my system. I was gonna get rich, become one of those bindlestiffs ordering everyone else to do the sweat work while I sat on the veranda, drinking sweet tea. After a month bent like a staple, sluicing and picking, I gladly went back to chasing cows and getting kicked." He pushed the bag into the Ennis' hand. "Thanks. I know for a fact most of what's sifted out is mica, pyrite, and quartz. You had to work like the devil to get that. Keep it. Consider it trade for the jobs you do around here. And even then, you're getting the crap-covered end of the stick."

"It's true, the veins only show color if you've got a good imagination. But if you worked it hard and constant, maybe there's two hundred a week after fees and refining if the prices remain high. Using my equipment would make it a mite easier."

Jiggs smiled and waved him off. "I'm a rancher."

"Hop never wanted the gold, either," Ennis said. "I think he was glad to have someone living on the land, fixing things, and checking on the cattle. When it starts getting cold—I go to the Caymans." He cocked his head toward the mayor. "As he said, I have a number of clients in my consulting work. But maybe you'd consider taking the gold for the purpose of redemption." The Irishman smoothed the hair around his mouth, but the beard fluffed back out like the bristles of a brush. "I was full of cheap liquor and big dreams when I was young—"

"Still are," Bazz mumbled.

Ennis cast him a foul stare and continued, "My dad was from the old country, and I promised him I'd get my education. Somehow, in between working for pennies and looking for fights, I got a paper that said I knew something about civil engineering. That's how I met this grease monkey." Bazz accepted the compliment by raising his blue enameled cup.

"We worked at the same intellectual hellhole for about ten years. Bazz had settled down by then—wife, family, the usual mooching-sort of neighbors. It took me a mite longer. Actually the process was accelerated when the gal got pregnant, but I thought I could do the right thing. We married. I acquired a next-door neighbor who used my yard for his dog's latrine. I wasn't a family guy.

"When I was a lad, my old man would rather belt me than look at me. I decided to save my son from the same doom by not lookin' at him. When the kid came, I left rather than torture their lives with my criticizing. That was twenty-four years ago."

"You've been coming and going out here for twenty-four years?" Jiggs gave him a disbelieving stare.

" 'Bout eleven. I rolled around the world the first thirteen years. There are always jobs for men who have nothing to do but work. I checked in with family at regular times. I sent money, whatever they needed ... except myself," he replied to Jiggs' cold stare. "I finally ran myself to a ragged stop. Hop invited me to use his woods; he and my dad had survived Korea together. I'd hoped there was something here for me.

"And it wasn't the gold." Ennis returned Jiggs' icy look. "It was the pitiable creature I'd become. I'd abandoned my family, and damned any hope I had for self-respect. I was a man in need of healin' or killin'. I saw the Eagle Caps—spread out to eternity. I figured they'd be decidin' what I deserved—death or life."

Jiggs sat down. "Well, you're still alive. You healed?"

Ennis' eyes drilled the rancher. "You ever been sick and numb inside?"

Jiggs considered the hunks of time he'd lost, grieving over Katie and feeling guilt over Pax. Forgiving himself was like awakening from a long sleep, one that he'd never known he'd fallen into. When he looked up from the burning logs, Ennis still waited for an answer. He cleared his throat. "I've known the darkness."

"Then you know it's not one of those take-a-pill or just-believe-it kind of fixes."

Jiggs nodded, returning his gaze to the fire. Bazz pulled the steaks onto chipped enamel plates and added foil-wrapped potatoes before he handed them around. The men globbed butter and sour cream from the beer cooler onto spuds.

"I was lucky if I sluiced even ten dollars a day." Ennis studied the palm of his hand as though a ledger were recorded in the calluses. "But I'm a civil engineer by trade, so I invented a better way to harvest it." He popped the top on a beer as they settled into chairs. "Then Hop told me some California mechanic had bought the bar. I figured I needed to move again. The place was becoming polluted with sissy gear grinders—then I found out who it was." Again, Bazz saluted with his speckled cup.

Ennis opened his pocketknife, wiped the blade on his heavy denim pants, inspected it, then cut several hunks from his T-bone and laid the knife in the middle of the table. "The mountain almost beat me to death—she's a harsh teacher—but I started to hope. I've spent the last eleven years trying to make it up to my family. They'd gone on without me and had lives of their own."

A somber quietness settled on the clearing. Darkness blurred the surrounding forest. Without getting up, Bazz chucked a piece of wood onto the fire. Sparks popped upward, trailing red streamers, then bounced on the ground and lay glowing.

Jiggs glanced at the Irishman whenever he reached for the communal knife. Only a coward abandoned his family. *Or someone too angry to pick up his drunk brother.* Who would slink off and hide in the woods? *Is that any different than hiding your mistake from a whole community?* He tried to hate O'Day, but couldn't work up the gumption. The man was trying to find his way back to peace. They both were on the same journey.

"Ben," Ennis whispered and tossed a piece of fat toward the woods. A wolf-size dog rushed from the shadows, gobbled it, and then lay his head on his paws, pricking his ears at the sound of a coyote's howl.

"They're talking tonight," Bazz said as an eerie yodel, followed by a choir of yips, rose from the east.

"Pups. Listen to the funny attempts to mimic their parents'. Lots of 'em. All announcing changes," Jigg said. Bazz gave him a questioning look.

"My brother, Pax, and I refused to shoot pups." Jiggs stared into the blackness pinpointing where the sound was coming from. "But when they got older, we spent a myriad of starry nights like this, picking off adult coyotes. County paid five dollars for each scalp. Officials punched a hole in the ears so they couldn't be counted again. It was one of the few worthwhile county programs so, of course, they stopped paying."

"How many did you get?" Ennis asked.

Jiggs shrugged. "Money didn't matter. We still shot coyotes. We did it because we found our missing dog's red fur in the field. Because Mom couldn't keep a cat. Because they chewed up my first show cow and calf. I got pretty good at imitating their calls. But usually, I couldn't get the pack to come within range of our twenty-twos. Excitement squeezed my throat. I couldn't hear the difference, but the 'yotes could. They're clever. They know when there's a change. They'd stop answering. Sometimes a couple showed up afterward, a few feet away, like ghost-hounds checking us out. Scared the crap outta us."

Jiggs reached out to pat the dog. It leaned away from his hand. He continued his story in a low voice as though he were talking only to the dog. "Now, Pax used a different technique. He could bend his voice into a wounded jackrabbit or an injured bird, trying to lure them. I'd show you, but you might eat me."

"He might," Ennis agreed.

As Jiggs stood, he pointed his three-tined fork at the mayor. "I thought I was going to sell you and Junior this land tonight. Now I see you were just angling for stories and a free T-Bone. For that ... I'm drinking all the beer."

Ennis waved the thought away. "We need something with more combustibility than hops or fermented grapes. You'd think you were still in California, Bazz." He stumped to the beat-up camp box and pulled out a bottle of whiskey. "As I said, you're here because of redemption. I'm trying to make my life right. It's your stream. Your gold."

The Irishman filled his cup half full, pushed the hammer, nails, and plates aside, and set the bottle on the table. Using his fingers, he tweezed his steak bone from his plate, and tossed it to the dog. Jiggs shook his scraps into the fire. "Sorry, Ennis. If I didn't work for it, I don't claim it—unless it's beer. And why don't you move into the ranch house whenever you get tired of being out here. It could use a mousetrapper."

"I might take you up on that," the short man said. "Now that Frank's my partner, I'll be around more. He'll be the front man so I can continue my invisible life without junk mail and unsolicited phone calls."

Jiggs and Bazz exchanged "ah-ha" looks.

"I hope he enjoys your 2:00 in the morning visits. I won't miss them," Bazz said.

"Am I the only one in the county who doesn't know about you?" Jiggs squinted at them.

"Can you keep something to yourself?" Bazz asked.

"You have no idea how many secrets I drag around."

"Only four people know about Ennis, here. You, me, Frank ... and Andy Grubb. The mercantile's business would probably collapse if Ennis didn't haunt around as the ghost of Two Pan."

"*You're* the dentist's spirit?"

"No. He's real." The Irishman bugged his eyes. "Creepy things happen there. One night I stopped to get my supplies and a stock boy was havin' a party. Before I could scare them out, something crashed in the upper room. I checked it out, and I can tell you, there was something in there. I hightailed it out right after the boys." Ennis shivered his arms, dispersing the willies. "But Bazz, I'll still knock at your door if you leave a light on. Nothin' changes."

"I'll tell you about change." Bazz held out chocolate bars. "Junior's still yammering to convert the bar. Upgrade the food. Foo-foo the décor. It's like firefights and grenades when we talk. He wants to remove the Bonehead Hall of Fame. How will folks remember us?"

"Why do you want anyone to remember you?" The Irishman wore an amused squint.

Bazz and Jiggs looked at each other, then at the fire as though an answer would appear in the flames. "I'd like to think

I've done something of value," the mayor said. "If we're so easily forgotten, what's the purpose of this whole adventure?"

The question hung in the air while the men gave it brain time. Jiggs finally spoke, staring at the dancing sparks over the top of the flames. "When Dad rode the Starvation fence line, Pax and I would camp with him. Ox would light his pipe—that's all we could see of his face as he said, 'A hunnerd, maybe two hunnerd years ago, somebody sat where your little butts are right now. They stared at the very same stars we're looking at.' Then he'd go on about how the past was covered by today's dust. The bones, the blood, the gold, the lives—all covered over. He'd say, 'If you listen real close, boys, you'll hear the earth give a tired sigh and the coyote sing of change.'"

Jiggs shook his head. "I figured Dad made up lies because the howling pack on Starvation Ridge scared the bejeebers out of us kids. No Bonehead Hall of Fame could memorialize those times."

"You know," Bazz said, "it seems you've guarded that property faithfully, and it's paid you back with wildfire, bad neighbors, and barbequed cattle. Maybe you should get rid of Starvation and keep Shiny Creek instead."

"Can't." Jiggs scanned the sky, his hand blocking the firelight. "I buried Dad on it."

"Good grief. Why are there even cemeteries in East Oregon?" Bazz rolled his eyes. "What if we all buried our relatives in our backyards?"

"When did you start swimming around the edge of the pond instead of the middle?" Ennis squinted at the mayor. "I plan on being buried right here." The Irishman tilted his chair back and scratched his dog's head. "I came here tonight to lend you my equipment, Jiggs, and clear my debt, but maybe you'd consider selling Shiny Creek to me?" He gave the rancher a measured look. "I would've made Hop the offer when he was alive, but you beat me to it. I'll pay whatever you gave Hop. You could still pasture your cattle on it."

"It's not worth what I paid Hop for it. There're too many bodies in it."

"Perfect. That's what I'll be usin' it for—my grave."

Jiggs rubbed his chin, looking for answers in the bearded man's face. The Irishman would take care of it. He'd already proven he was a good manager. He wouldn't let Jarmin or anyone else develop or mine it.

"You plan on staying here much longer?" Jiggs asked.

Ennis had worked a rock out of the ground with the heel of his boot. He picked it up, inspected it, and then flung it into the forest. "This is home base now. I told Hop I'd finish what he started and watch out for his son."

"You might have Jarmin pestering you," Jiggs said.

"Good luck to him working through my attorney and blind corporations. He wouldn't be the first person to pursue and burden me."

"He might not even find out the land has changed hands. That way, if you're willing to sell it back to me, he can't interfere."

Ennis shook his wooly head. "That'll be a problem."

"Why?"

"An old Greek, Hippocrates, said the human soul keeps on growing right up to the last breath. I know for a fact that once we get on the downslope of being grown, we start looking for peace. When Frank gets to that time, I figure he'll want to take back the family homestead. If I sell the land—he gets the first chance to buy."

A slow smile crept across Jiggs' face. "I figure that's about right. What about your family?"

"My wife forgave me before she passed on, though little I deserved it. My son ... he's a dwarf ... a little person. He's made a fine life for himself. A few months ago, he came all the way to

Two Pan just to tell me to go to hell." Ennis' eyes glistened in the firelight. "I don't think I've ever seen a man stand as tall as my son at that moment."

Stillness settled around them. Finally Bazz scanned the town below, naming whose lights were still on. Jiggs got up and walked to the edge of the campfire's shadows, gazing at the same view.

The offer seemed like a good deal. He was looking for a buyer, so why was it hard to dislodge himself and let the property go? Nap would approve, but he was just a kid, what did he know? Jiggs snorted. Ox had said the same thing about him—even after his fortieth birthday.

And that was another notion that was hard to ungrip. His dad had been hard, but he hadn't been all rock and whang leather. He'd taught him how to knap arrowheads and helped him fix up his first truck—even though he'd preached it'd be a gas guzzler. Each time the old fellow had visited Katie in the hospital, he'd brought bouquets of wildflowers and pungent weeds, saying the "outdoors" would hang in her room.

It wasn't so much that Ox had been hardhearted, but that he'd partnered with fear. Afraid life would run out before he'd transferred all the wisdom a pigheaded son needed to know. Fearful that slip ups were a threat to what he'd built. Mistakes came with scalding lectures. There was no room to try and fail. And that's why Jiggs was a fool—a jackrabbit—he jumped and took risks.

Behind him, Ennis and Bazz were in a heated discussion about a blue light glowing in Two Pan. One swore it was Miz Cliva's lawnmower shed, the other chided that the old woman wouldn't be outdoors at midnight unless she was making hooch.

Jiggs scanned for the moonshine light and then looked for his holdings. Black hills blanked out his land. *Holdings.* A surge pulsed under his breastbone. If he were gut-honest, this whole disaster was not just about saving the community or making payments on his guilt for his brother.

He'd pillared his childhood wish with every harsh word his dad had used to judge him. Nights in bed as a youth, he'd nursed the idea, seeing his ranch spreading in every direction, and his dad eating crow for an apology.

Strange how childhood ideas imprinted a lifetime. Now, he could keep moving forward. Nap would approve. So what was snagging his decision? Jiggs stared at the hammer lying on the table. Maybe selling or keeping the Shiny had nothing to do with proving himself to his father.

Maybe it was about what he'd do with rest of his life—now that he had nothing to prove.

He spent a long moment letting the thought take root. He didn't hear Bazz and Ennis still arguing about the blue light. His mind was flying with plans.

When he interrupted the men, he held out his hand to the Irishman. "You bought yourself a big burial plot." They grinned and clapped each other's shoulders. Whiskey-filled cups saluted the exchange.

"I'll have the papers drawn up and drop by your ranch on Friday night for the signatures," Ennis said.

"Nope. Not next Friday." Jiggs shook his head. "I've got a date with Josie."

A coyote chose the moment to sing a single lament. The men exchanged wordless glances, smiles growing on their faces.

A miner, a rancher, and a mayor sit in a fireside meeting. In comfortable camaraderie, they debate the reasons folks cling to this forgotten end of the earth. Their words distill into laughter and the simple hope of a good night's sleep.

With their business transacted, philosophies shared, and problems resolved, their conversation dwindles into syllables.

Then ... finally ... silence.

Overhead, a starry canopy encloses them in its dome.

––––––––––––

One hundred miles or perhaps a continent away you may be standing at the store reading this rather than some rag on celebrities' pets. It would be even better if you're lazing on a couch at home or a lakeside cabin. Lord help you if you're trying to rest in a chair at the airport—waiting.

Wherever you are doesn't matter.

Day or night.

Stubborn, creative, eccentric, or perhaps ... just a little sleepless. You're not alone.

Someone in Two Pan is awake.

There's always a light shining in Two Pan.

***

Jottings

This book was too long in the making. And heart-hard to finish.

The kernel of the idea began as simple, one-page stories. Mom suffered a debilitating stroke. It was hard for her to hang onto long plots, and I couldn't find many short tales that were funny. With hope. And truth—the kind you find in forehead-rubbing real life situations.

So I spun simple yarns about people just trying to get along. Flawed people like those we knew and those who loved us (and some who didn't).

I can still see her lopsided smile as we populated the town of Two Pan. I wanted her to have the secret comfort of knowing there were people going through troubles like she was, folks dealing with the pain of different kinds of change. I wanted to let her know during late nights when fear and what-ifs pushed in, she wasn't alone. There were others on the earth whose lights were on during the dark hours.

When she passed, I liked to imagine her gaining the full range of both arms and legs and galloping toward the heavenly gates, waving and shouting, "My days of dealing with change are done!"

The characters quietly lived in the bottom drawer for seven years. And as Miz Cliva once said, "Grief takes as long as it takes." So finally, I cut bits from the original tales and stitched them into this story. I don't think the whole saga will ever be done because our lives keep changing. And I doubt that Mom, who is making quilts and brewing beer for the eternal mansions, will ever know that I wrote this piece of it.

But it's because of her and life's bramble of troubles that it exists—with all the hope, humor, waving arms and galloping legs I could give it. Thanks, Mom.

***

Acknowledgements

A big thanks to the following. The development, design, and editing of this book would not be possible without the team of: Ken K., Greg F.; Pat Lichen; Pat Johnson, Linda Appel, Orice Klaas, and Mary Jean Rivera.

For those technical details: Rancher/Storyteller/Muleherder: J. Kooch; Ranch Fires: N. & M. McGinnis; Donkey Mentors: M. & J. Madzier; General bull/cow/and horse quirks: Wallowa County Extension; Intermountain Livestock; and the Oregon Angus Association.

And a big thanks to the good-natured residents of my favorite eastern Oregon town. May all your changes be heartwarming ones.

More humorous stories about change can be found at:
Before Morning Breaks
www.barbfroman.wordpress.com
or
www.barbarakayfroman.com

Sneak Peek: Book Three

Women and Thieves of Two Pan

ON TWO PAN'S Main Street, a single blue light glowed through the night. Yesterday, Spooner Hunter had screwed the specialty bulb into the socket along with his hopes. He believed the light would draw the curious and they would stare, and then participate in his Two Pan Project: a collection of as-you-are photographs of each citizen in the area. So far, folks had been slow to jump in front of the camera.

A late-hatched pine beetle circled the bulb. The neon-blue glow cast an eerie pall over the twenty-five photos posted behind the plate glass: The good ol' boy, Chicken Thief Bob, was frozen in a pose, forever pointing a wave and a grin at the camera. Mayor Bazz Hinton veed his fingers in a Nixon impression. Old Millie Capper wore a puckered smile and untied tennis shoes; for some reason, she was holding up a fork. Some people smiled; others simply looked at the camera. Jiggs Woolsey was the last picture in the long row. His cowboy hat was pushed back on his head. He squatted next to a loose-skinned dog; both of them looked like they were waiting for ice cream.

Tonight, below the pictures, on the blue-lit sidewalk, lay the rangy, homeless mutt. He had taken to sleeping there. The photographs were his company, especially the picture of his cowboy friend. He raised his head, his snout dipping and rising, nosing the air. He stared through the darkness at a noise.

Though the fleabag couldn't tell colors, he clearly saw the small light moving down the street. Behind it was a human. The man stopped to shine the red beam into Grubb's Mercantile window, his face close to the glass, watching it move across the dark interior.

After a moment, the footsteps turned and kept coming. The boots toed out, and the heels never brushed the concrete, each step remaining on the balls of the feet. Even with such a strange tread, there was a hitch in stride, as though the hip had to muscle the right leg forward. *Bob-push. Bob-push.* The musky smell of unwashed man traveled up the street. The light beam hesitated; it shone down the alley, jumping wall to wall between buildings for several heartbeats, and then it moved onward.

The dog put his head on his paws. His eyes followed the light. The footsteps passed. Stopped. The street was silent.

The steps came back. *Bob-push. Bob-push.* The red beam doodled on the sidewalk beneath the blue light, making a purple circle dance on the concrete.

The hound looked away, staring into the darkness like a kid pretending he doesn't notice a neighborhood bully. The man-smell was memorable—one of the kicking rowdies, breathing through his mouth with a low grunt each time he moved. The dog's rheumy eyes flitted sideways, watching, but not staring.

The red light dotted the pictures above him. It stalled on one photograph. For a long moment there was no sound. The sharp scent of anger and alcohol rolled off the man in ever-increasing waves. The dog pushed to his feet, his head low.

Koooouuuggghhhh. The draining sound came from deep within the man's gullet. A loud, wet blast of phlegm flew from his mouth, splatting hard against the window.

The dog took a couple of steps away, his tail hugging his belly, his long claws making *scritch-scritch* noises on the sidewalk. The man looked down. He grunted and quick-stomped, aiming for a paw. The mutt was old and skinny, but lately he'd been gifted with enough hotdogs that he could skitter backward fast enough to avoid the boot. The misstep made the man stumble, shuffling forward, catching himself against the glass, his hand smearing his own spit.

"Dammit to hell!" A few more fiery words, grumbled into the night as the man rubbed his hand on his pants, careful to avoid his unfaithful leg.

A deep furrow appeared between the hound's shoulder blades as he sunk his head lower, trying to be still and small and invisible. The man palmed his hip as he aimed his stare at a photo. "Just you wait. This is all on you." He turned and limped away, the red beam bobbing in front of him.

The dog watched until the sound and light disappeared. He gazed up at the photographs, then at the sidewalk. He couldn't sleep there now. The man had marked the area. A poisonous stink. He padded to the side of the building, away from the brown drool scented with tobacco, hatred, and hooch. Away from the ooze smeared across the window over two photographs: his cowboy friend and a woman. A woman wearing a coon-tailed cowboy hat and a go-to-hell smile.

***

Thanks for visiting the folks of Two Pan.

Ebooks and Paperbacks are available through major on-line retailers ... or ... support your local bookstore and ask to order The Two Pan Series.

Book 1: Mornings in Two Pan
Book 2: The Lights of Two Pan

Thanks for reading!

www.ingramcontent.com/pod-product-compliance
Lightning Source LLC
Chambersburg PA
CBHW030530270626
47155CB00024B/2659